Family Reunions

Family
Reunions

Connie Monk

PIATKUS

First published in Great Britain in 1996 by
Judy Piatkus (Publishers) Ltd of
5 Windmill Street, London W1

**The moral right of the author
has been asserted**

*A catalogue record for this book is available
from the British Library*

ISBN 0–74–99–0350–3

Set in 11/12pt Times Monotype
Typeset by Datix International Ltd, Bungay, Suffolk
Printed and bound in Great Britain by
Biddles Ltd, Guildford and King's Lynn

Chapter 1

Teddy Carlyle put his case on to the back seat, then, relishing the assurance of freedom, laid his bleeper by its side. Today there would be no more calls. He switched on the ignition, thinking with satisfaction of the changes that time had brought to his practice.

More than thirty years ago, his period as hospital houseman behind him, he had moved south to Hampshire where he'd taken over a country general practice. In a rural area bordering the New Forest his rounds had been scattered, his working days long and his nights often disrupted. Thank God for the new scheme of things that had brought with it the Medical Centre! Now there were four doctors and a full-time nurse. Night duties were on a rota basis and only rarely involved him, the senior doctor. That was one of the advantages of the passage of time he told himself silently, and today, on his sixtieth birthday, with a light heart. He was as excited as a child going to his first party. He pushed a cassette into the player and settled to enjoy his homeward drive. The undulating open commonland stretched far into the distance ahead of him, the gentle hills purple with heather. A party of riders were following a well-worn track, ignored by ponies busy nibbling the gorse. To his left was a forest enclosure, oak, beech, chestnut, trees so different from the firs planted for their timber today. A forester had set his pigs to forage for acorns on the grassy perimiter; customs and traditions here were as ancient as time. As if all that weren't perfection enough, a curlew flew high overhead.

Seldom a day went by when he didn't drive along the forest roads, but today his perception was heightened. He indulged in letting his mind wander where it would. Down the thirty or so years he'd served the community here? No, further . . . uninvited the image came into his mind of the day he and Claudia had been married. How proud he'd been as she'd come towards him up the aisle on her father's arm, petite, elfin-like, carrying a bouquet of summer flowers: sweet peas,

pinks, rosebuds. Funny how he could remember his pride, could remember the scent of the flowers she'd carried and the way her dress
had shimmered in the rays of the sun beaming through a high
window, yet it was like looking back at two different people. Was that
what the passage of years did to you? Made you grow together so
that you hardly saw each other or noticed nature's gradual changes?
He glanced into the driver's mirror, not to check the empty road
behind but consciously to look at the man he'd become and compare
him with the bridegroom of thirty-five years ago. He'd kept his hair,
it was still as thick, albeit a dull grey with white at the temples; he'd
kept his figure too, and to prove it he sat straighter in his seat. Another glance in the mirror showed his thin face, lined and yet not
careworn. He bared his teeth, still his own; he was a couple short at
the back but there was no evidence of it. Recently the optician had
prescribed him glasses for driving. He turned away from the mirror
and the sight of the dark tortoiseshell rims.

And what about Claudia? He could recall her low clear voice as she
made her vows, he could picture her huge dark eyes fixed on him as
she spoke; he could conjure up the memory as vividly as if it had
been a film he'd watched only hours before. Then into his mind came
the image of the Claudia of today: still girlishly slim, still with that
same energy and vigour for life. So where was the difference? When
had the childlike trust in the future been taken over by a need to fill
her days, rush here, dash there. A sudden urge to redecorate could
bring him home to find her balanced on a plank between two pairs of
steps painting the ceiling; or an unseasonally warm day in March
might send her into the garden to reshape the herbaceous border or
tempt her to the nursery to buy a frame to build an arch where the
clematis could climb. From one day to the next he never knew what
she might dream up. A quick frown puckered his brow, but only for a
second; he wouldn't let himself listen to the silent voice that told him
she ought to be content instead of chasing one hare-brained idea
after another.

Today the family were all coming home. The last movement of
Beethoven's First Symphony filled the car. Teddy turned up the
volume and added his lusty and slightly off-key baritone to the
joyous sound, his fingers beating time on the steering wheel.

Under the railway bridge that spanned the narrow forest road were
five ponies, taking shelter from the afternoon sun. Teddy slowed
down, blew his horn as he edged gradually forward. The ponies surveyed him with interest, jostling against the side of the car, one
standing in front of the bonnet. His thoughts were back in place, he
was a happy man, content with his lot, his family by now well on the

2

way, travelling home to share the celebrations. If the innocent and untried bride and groom had no connection with today, that must be because the years between had been satisfying and successful.

Slowly he inched his way forward until the ponies lost interest in the game and wandered out into the sunshine giving him a clear road. The car reverberated with Beethoven's final chords, Teddy 'pom-de-pommed' his contribution, a smile on his face – lines, spectacles, greying hair, all these things forgotten as he sped homewards, delighting in the thought of those other three cars all setting out from different places, all converging on Avonford and 'Russets.'

As Claudia turned into the driveway, Gwen Pomfrey appeared from the path at the side of the house. For more than twenty years she had worked at Russets three mornings a week, 'doing for the doctor' as she put it to her acquaintances in The Bell where she imbibed her nightly single glass of stout. Gwen wasn't a woman given to excesses. Time and familiarity had done nothing to alter her dour countenance.

'You're late going home, Gwen,' Claudia called cheerfully as she drew up outside the garage.

'Doctor got bleeped. He asked me to wait, listen in case any of them phoned. Broken down on the way or anything. Never know what trouble they might run into on the roads.' Gwen Pomfrey's voice was as expressionless as her face.

'That was good of you.' Claudia ignored her gloomy prophecy. 'Did he say how long he expected to be?'

'He'll be back as quick as he can, you may be sure of that, Mrs C. Seeing I'm here, I might as well give you a hand in with all that shopping. Looks like you've got enough to feed a regiment.' Still there was no lift in her tone, nor yet a smile.

'Bless you, Gwen. I only went to pick up a few last-minute things after I'd had my hair done, I want to have plenty in the house. Thank goodness someone else is taking care of this evening. Imagine, Gwen, I don't have to raise a finger. The caterers are due at five o'clock. These things are just to be sure I shan't run out of anything tomorrow. I do hope they'll all be able to stay on. Although James is bound to have to be home by Sunday morning. Even with this load, you can be sure there'll be something I've forgotten! I've got out of the habit of feeding the five thousand. If you can take those two bags, I can manage the box. I'll leave the crate of bottles, one of the boys will bring that in, whichever one gets here first.'

Gwen ignored her instructions and picked up the heavy box. 'Best I take this big one, can't have you putting your back out or some such

3

nonsense before the party. A good job I hung on when the doctor got called away, there was a call from your James's wife.'

'From Jennifer? Nothing wrong is there?'

'I wrote the number down. She wants you to ring. Seemed quite put out when I said you wouldn't be back for an hour or so. She didn't say where she was, but it wasn't her own number. The rectory is 246186, I remember that one. But the code was the same. I did say to her, "We thought you'd be half way here by now". "I've been delayed," that's as much as she said. Well, none of my business I suppose she thought. You'll see the number on the pad on the dresser. I'll put these groceries away for you while you have a word with her, I'm in no panic. And today, well it's not an ordinary day, I'm glad enough to give a bit of my spare time.'

'You're a dear, Gwen.' There was a smile in Claudia's voice – a smile at dear, dour Gwen who didn't imagine it was obvious she hoped to stay until she'd been told whatever it was that Jennifer had considered wasn't her business. On her own Claudia would have gone into the drawing room to make the call, sat in comfort to talk to her daughter-in-law. Instead she used the kitchen extension to dial the unfamiliar number.

'Hello?'

She could tell from the one word that Jennifer was agitated.

'It's me. You said to phone when I got home. Where are you? Is something wrong?'

Gwen Pomfrey had never taken to James's wife, this afternoon's conversation had done nothing to make her change her mind and seeing the anxious look on Claudia's face reinforced her opinion. She took a long time to sort the shopping and put it away, all the while straining her ears. But for all her effort she had to make what she could from a one sided conversation.

'Not coming! You mean, none of you? What's happened?' . . . 'No. No, of course I can see how you feel. You say the others had come on ahead. Doesn't James know you won't be following?' . . . 'No, they haven't arrived yet. But surely, if there were any trouble your friend would have heard – any real trouble I mean – an accident?' . . . 'Can't you try and boost her with some reasonable reason why he's so late. Maybe he broke down miles from anywhere last night?' . . . 'Yes, I suppose he would have. You know best what you must do. I'll get James to ring you when he and the children arrive. If her husband suddenly turns up you could get here even now. Teddy will be so disappointed if we're not all here' . . . This time Jennifer's answer was longer, Gwen turned her head but even the tone of voice eluded her. 'I see. I'll give Teddy your love and explain to him.'

4

'What was the trouble then, Mrs C?' Gwen couldn't run the risk of not being told.

'Jennifer is with a friend. It seems her husband was due home from a business trip to Scotland last night. He didn't come. She rang the hotel and they said he'd checked out yesterday morning.'

'Has she spoken to the police?'

'I didn't get the impression it was an accident Paula – that's her name – imagined. He had identity, the police would have reported it. He has a car phone too. Jenny implied there is some sort of problem between them. She can't leave her friend alone, Teddy will understand.'

Gwen sniffed. 'Glad I never got myself caught up. Free to be my own boss, and thankful for it. He travels fastest who travels alone, isn't that what they say?' She nodded sagely, she whose travelling, apart from her nightly walk to The Bell, went no further than the one and half miles from just inside the forest boundary to Russets, just outside it, and once a fortnight by bus to Christchurch to do her shopping. 'Hark! There's a car drawing in. The doctor home, I dare say.'

But Gwen dared say wrong.

'We're here!' In the front garden car doors were slamming, but already Melinda had run ahead and was charging through the back door.

'Melly! You're the first.' Noise and excitement seemed to switch a light on in Claudia. She hugged her youngest, stood back to look at her, then hugged her again. In appearance they were nothing alike. A tall, handsome young woman, Melinda's genes came from Teddy, the same light brown hair, light blue eyes fringed with dark lashes, and the same cleft in her chin. But from her mother she had inherited an urgency to live every moment to its fullest, to look and really to see, to take in the scent of the garden or the appetizing smell of dinner and relish it, to listen to the cries of nature and really hear. There were no half measures about Melly.

'Mum, we've brought someone with us. That's OK isn't it? I knew it would be.'

'Someone who?'

'Oh, you'll love him. Adrian Crighton. He's an artist – not my sort of thing, portraits mostly.'

'You're going to need the old nursery room, Mrs C.' Gwen's melancholy face came unusually near to breaking into a smile. Instead of going home there was work for her to do. Already she was taking off the scarf she tied around her head for her cycle ride.

5

'Gwen, you're an angel!' Melly, always blind and deaf to Gwen's defensive reserve, hugged her.

'Poor Gwen, you'll never get home at this rate,' Claudia laughed, seeing Gwen's intention to stay. 'I'll come up with you. We'll do it together.'

Normally there was nothing Gwen liked better than doing things together. But today wasn't normal.

'You stay and see Trevor and this friend of Melly's in, I'll do what's needed upstairs. Anyway, I'm not having you untidying that nice new hair-do messing about in the airing cupboard getting bedding.'

Plodding up the stairs she felt hers was an important role in the family celebrations. Poor Gwen Pomfrey, as a child her thin wispy tresses had earned her the nickname 'nine hairs' amongst her class-mates; grown-up and working on the buses during the war she'd been left out of the laughing gossip amongst the other young conduc-tresses and never once had she awakened any male interest – not so much as a whistle or a catcall. Large-boned, long melancholy face with a criss-cross of purple veins, long bluey red nose, tall angular body, powerful hands, flat feet in size eight shoes, physically there was little to commend her. But she was loyal to those she loved – and she loved Claudia and so it followed that Dr Teddy Carlyle and their family fell within the same bracket.

'Where's the birthday boy? Surely he's not taking calls, not on the day he becomes entitled to his Senior Citizen's Railcard!'

'Apparently he got called out just after lunch. But he'd arranged that from three o'clock onwards he'd be un-get-at-able so that will be his last. What made you bring a friend? You *know* you always can, he's very welcome. But I hadn't expected it, not on your father's birthday.'

'It's a long story. He'd arranged to move into a flat, to share it with someone. But he changed his mind – he had good reason. He has something else in the pipeline, but in the meantime he's been staying with us. I insisted he came. I told him there was always bags of room – and if you've got full house he won't be a bit fussy, he can always doss on the sofa or something. Mum, I'll go and give Gwen a hand with his bed, she'll like that.' And she was gone.

Claudia had faith in her premonitions, and what she heard filled her with gloom. Today of all days the last guest Teddy would want at the feast was some drop-out with nowhere to live and who wasn't fussy where he dossed.

'Hello Mother,' Trevor Woodward appeared at the back door. 'Is there an order for parking or is it first in, last out?'

'It has to be. Teddy will stay outside until all you others are parked, so that he can be off in the morning.' She raised her face to kiss her tall, thin son-in-law. It never ceased to surprise her that Melly should have fallen in love with anyone so unlikely. From the day she started art college she had never been without a boyfriend, she was the sort of girl who, as the aura of romance faded from a relationship turned a 'boyfriend' into a 'friend'. Then, at nearly twenty-four and with her first exhibition behind her, she had met Trevor, a science teacher in the State comprehensive system. No-one could call Trevor handsome, nor even manly. As for personality, it seemed to Claudia that he was devoid of it, but loyalty to Melly prevented her admitting to it. There was no doubt that he worshipped at the pedestal on which he held Melinda. Could that be what she wanted? To Claudia it seemed an ill-balanced partnership. But perhaps she was wrong. Simply because there was so much of herself in Melly, that didn't mean that the girl must look for the same qualities in a man as she would herself. And anyway, she told herself now as all these thoughts rushed to collide, arousing memories of her own then immediately replacing them with a truth that had nothing to do with the expectations of the soul-shaking experience of falling in love: what happens to those dreams of romance when day-to-day living takes over? They were no more than the roots, but roots had to be strong to grow a healthy plant. Like the party game they used to play, one word led to another . . . roots . . . tree . . . family tree . . . branches . . . children . . . grandchildren . . . She gave Trevor a quick and vigorous hug, at the same time being carried along with the word game . . . birthday . . . anniversary . . . sentiment.

'Mother, let me introduce Adrian, Adrian Crighton. Adrian this is Melly's mother, Mrs Carlyle.'

Relief . . . pleasure . . . surprise . . . interest . . .

The man who took her hand couldn't have been less like the drop-out she'd imagined. Wearing jeans and a Guernsey sweater, with his dark curly hair and neatly trimmed beard he would have looked more in place on the quay in nearby Lymington than in an artist's studio.

'I wish they'd phoned you first, Mrs Carlyle.' He spoke with that unmistakable tone of the English public school. 'Melly insisted that you thrived on the unexpected.'

'I do.' And at that moment, so she did. 'And of course I'm glad they brought you with them.'

Another car was heard pulling in. Doors slammed, young voices talked at once. James and the children had arrived. Claudia felt guilty that she couldn't mind more that Jennifer wasn't coming.

There are plenty of men of the cloth who only wear their dog collar 'on duty'. The Reverend James Carlyle wasn't one of them. This early September day was warmer than midsummer, but he looked perfectly comfortable in his dark suit, black vest and stiff white clerical collar. The children, Barry at eleven and Patsy at nearly ten, were very much of today's youth in jeans, T-shirts and track shoes.

'Mum got sidetracked,' Barry said as he pecked Claudia's cheek, 'gone off do-gooding.'

'Wouldn't call that do-gooding,' Patsy had a pout in her voice. 'Hello Gran. We've got a huge parcel for Grandad. Where is he?'

'Out on call. He'll not be long. James!' She felt herself taken into her son's bearlike hug and forgot all else. Not to anyone would she admit the special place in her heart he held. 'Jenny feels she can't leave her friend. She wants you to phone her. The number's on—'

'I know the number.' His voice was tight, she could sense his anger. 'James, don't make her feel badly about Teddy's party. He'll understand.'

Patsy's glower followed him as he went out through to the drawing room.

'I hate Mrs Stonehouse. Mum's always running round there to her. Poor Paula, she calls her. Pushy Paula, that's what she is.'

'Mum doesn't see through her, that's the trouble.' Barry spoke in his mother's defence.

'Well, I hate her anyway. Mum always used to be at home when we came in from school unless it was Mothers' Union or the Young Wives or something.'

Trevor nodded understandingly.

'It must happen sometimes though for a clergy wife.' They liked him, he never spoke down to them. 'People must bring her their problems, she automatically has a sort of welfare role to play in the parish.'

'Sssh – Dad's coming.' Patsy had more than her share of tact. 'Where's Aunt Melly? Can I go and find her?'

Jennifer's non-appearance was glossed over. Luggage was brought in from the cars, there was much tramping up and down stairs as they took over their rooms, and Claudia was relieved to see that, like Trevor, Adrian Crighton carried in a hanger with his dinner suit on it. Part of the fun of tonight's party was that it was to be an excuse to dress.

Teddy arrived home to be followed almost immediately by their second son, Harvey. From early childhood when he'd sat on a book on the piano stool and practised his first exercises, it had been obvious to his teacher that Harvey was no ordinary pupil. He'd read music far more readily than he'd learnt to read the written word. The local teacher had soon suggested he should be put into better hands than her own and for the next few years Claudia had driven him to Christchurch twice a week for lessons. At fourteen, with his sights firmly fixed on a professional playing career, he'd been accepted at a music school. From school to college, from one music competition to another, Harvey had climbed the ladder until now his reputation was international. About eighteen months ago he had married Erica, a pretty American he'd met on tour in her country. She had been swept off her feet by his attention, and by the fact that, with him, she lived in the aura of his success. Teddy and Claudia had delighted in the match, the couple seemed perfectly suited, Harvey had never been happier and Erica openly adored him.

The Carlyles were home.

The hum of conversation from the drawing room grew louder, interspersed with the occasional hoot of laughter.

'These are the expressions that elude one,' Adrian said as Claudia came to join him on the padded window seat. 'I painted Melly, you know. We talked while I worked, she smiled, she laughed – but not like this. You can feel the – the joy, you can hear it, it's there to see.'

'Just Melly?'

'No. Every one of them. It's as if they light a lamp in each other. Your family. How proud you must be. You shouldn't be wasting time with me, a stranger.'

'You think my lamp is burning low?' she laughed.

He didn't attempt to conceal his admiration as he looked at her.

'I think your lamp gives both light and warmth.'

She felt as uncomfortably gauche as an awkward teenager. It was as if his eyes undressed her and yet at the same time made her feel ridiculously young and desirable. Unfamiliar excitement stirred, to be immediately stamped on. Perhaps she was being cowardly to turn away from him, but in that second of panic she was frightened that if she let herself read his expression she would see that he was pandering to the vanity of a woman old enough to be his mother. Thankfully she let her eyes meet Teddy's; she was safe again, her feet back on the ground and her confidence restored.

'It was a good party,' Teddy said, hours later as he reached to switch off the bedside light. 'You looked very pretty. I was watching you, thinking how pretty you looked.'

'I thought we all looked rather splendid, family, friends, everyone. We ought to find an excuse to dress up more often. I'd forgotten how distinguished you were.'

9

He pulled her closer.

'I wasn't the only one giving you admiring glances,' he said content-edly. 'That artist chap had his eye on you every time I looked at him. You know what he asked me? He said would I have any objection if he asked you to sit for him.'

She giggled, that earlier excitement back again but, lying so close to Teddy, none of the embarrassment.

'Draped or undraped?'

But Teddy wasn't listening.

'Do you think he's trying to find favour because of Melly?'

Claudia frowned, not following his reasoning.

'What's Melly got to do with it? He's her friend, hers and Trevor's. Why should he want to curry favour with us?'

'It was just a niggling feeling I had.'

'That he has designs on Melly?' She laughed, not taking him seriously.

'That she is leading him on. I was watching her—'

'Rubbish! Melly's a natural flirt, she can't help herself and it means nothing at all.'

Silence. He eased her a little closer, ready to change the subject.

'I was thinking about us this afternoon. It's been good, all of it, hasn't it.'

'Been?' And again that teasing laugh. 'You don't intend to let elegibility to that Railcard tip you over the hill I hope?'

'What do you think?' His caressing hand spoke volumes.

'I think it's been a lovely day so far, but the best is yet to come.'

He thought so too.

In the room that had been his as long as he could remember, James lay awake in the double bed. He felt unsettled and restless, his brief and distant conversation with Jennifer made sleep impossible. He tried to tell himself that he could understand her decision not to leave Paula alone; to walk away from trouble and unhappiness was the coward's way. His initial anger had been because he was disappointed, he'd looked forward to all of them being here together, he'd imagined that once away from home these last weeks wouldn't be important. Then a voice he couldn't deny reminded him that it was no new thing for Stanley Stonehouse to stay away from home. No sooner was that thought formed in his mind than it was chased out by another, one he felt was unworthy and yet he couldn't ignore: Paula probably hadn't been expecting Stanley home, when she'd phoned Jenny, frightened that something had happened to him, begging her to come, she'd probably not been expecting him. Paula and Stanley Stonehouse's marriage was going over a rocky passage, but how could Jenny smooth it for them? She was an outsider, all she could give was prejudiced interference.

Jenny and Paula had been friends from the time the Stonehouses had taken The Old Foundry, it's one-time barns converted to an artificially attractive dwelling with plenty of room for a study where Stanley wrote detective stories – each one a bestseller – and a studio for Paula to indulge her hobby of wood carving. If James were honest – and in the silent night there was nowhere for him to escape the truth – he had been uneasy about the relationship from the start although he couldn't have said exactly what it was that bothered him. Jenny never needed to be idle, she'd thrived on work. Bringing up two young children, more often than not keeping his own diary up-to-date, looking after a rectory built in the days when it was taken for granted staff would be employed, teaching every other week in the Sunday School, organizing the local social events that revolved around the church, using friendly tact amongst the St Luke's Ladies, as the village helpers called themselves, to make sure they all provided the right dishes for the Patronal Lunch and the Harvest Supper, arranging the Sunday School outing, the flower rota . . . the list was endless. She still did all these things, but the willingness had gone. They were an intrusion on time she wanted for other things. She used to make sure she was home when the school bus delivered the children; now sometimes she was there, sometimes he was there himself, or sometimes they found the key on the hook in the shed. And whatever he said, Jenny wouldn't listen to him. Her answer was always the same: Paula was unhappy, how could he ask her to neglect a friend who needed her?

When first Jenny had hinted that all wasn't well between the Stonehouses, he had called on them. This wouldn't be the first floundering relationship he had helped steer back on course. He had come without criticism, but with a deep thankfulness for his security in his own marriage and an even deeper thankfulness for the strength he found in his faith. In today's busy world he could understand how easy it was to lose sight of the thing that mattered most. At The Old Foundry his seeds of healing had fallen on stony ground. Stanley had been cordial, had offered him whisky and general cheery conversation, and told him with a twinkle that took the sting out of the words that he 'had no truck with god-peddlers'. Paula had been less friendly, less outspoken, but had left him with a sense of failure. Was that when he had first sensed danger in Jenny's friendship with her?

How often he'd tried to be an intermediary amongst his parishioners, tried to help families face grief, tried to mend broken trust, to give courage and hope. Perhaps Jenny could succeed where he failed.

11

Could that be what frightened him? Ah, but he did what he did in God's name; interference, friendship, support, under whatever guise it came, Jenny might help Paula Stonehouse over a bad moment, but the root of the trouble would be there to grow again. Only in God could she find that 'Peace of mind that passeth all understanding', yet when he'd tried to reach out to her she had been cold and deaf to him.

James turned on to his back, staring at the dark ceiling. He thought of his parents, the stability of his own childhood bright in his memory. But no-one's life can be without problems, they must have had theirs too. Yet nothing had cast a shadow on the home. Barry and Patsy had the right to a happy home. Was he 'god-peddling' to his flock and failing those nearest to him? Confused and humbled he threw back the duvet and got out of bed, going to the window as if the reassuring sight of the moonlit garden would banish his self-doubt. But his mind was filled with other pictures: himself offering guidance to the Stonehouses, himself walking through the village as he did every day of his life, visiting the sick, gathering in the stray lambs, laying hands on the dying, God's emissary, above reproach. Because his mission was to do God's work, had he stumbled into the deepest pit of all, believing himself better than the next man, believing his words were God's words? In front of the window, he dropped to his knees.

'Forgive me. Help me. I've been blaming her, I didn't look for faults in myself. We were happy, now even the children can sense it's wrong. Dear God, bring her back to us, make her want us.' He lowered his head on to the crook of his arm on the windowsill, he felt himself to be in a black abyss, hearing his silent plea and hating himself for what he hadn't the strength to pray: 'Not my will, but Thine'. But he couldn't say it. He even bargained: make things like they used to be and he'd never again fall into the trap of self-righteousness.

How long he knelt he had no idea. Prayer, the deep healing prayer he sought, eluded him. Give her back to me, give me another chance.

The first light was painting the eastern sky when he crept almost silently down the stairs. Not quite silently enough though. Claudia had slept fitfully, enjoying lying in the warm, comfortable bed, re-living the evening, looking forward to the day. James's door was next to theirs, she heard it open, she listened as he crept past their room. The bathroom was the other way, he must be going downstairs. A shadow darkened her daydreams. Listening hard she heard the sound of a tap being turned on. He must be making a drink. Alone down there . . . worried probably that this Paula person was giving Jenny a hard time . . . Inch by inch she moved to the edge of the bed, pushing

12

the duvet closer around Teddy before she lowered her feet to the ground.

Down the stairs she crept, pulling on her dressing gown as she went.

'Mum!' No more than a whisper. 'I didn't want to wake anyone.'

'I was awake,' she mouthed back as she closed the heavy door. 'I often wake early, it's nice to have someone to talk to, Teddy sleeps like a log till seven o'clock.' She unhooked a mug from the dresser. 'You look a bit after-the-night-beforeish, did you have too much party? There's some super stuff I got from the chemist, it's called—'

'Mum . . .'

At the sound of his voice she forgot the mug and somehow found herself at his side.

'Jamie, Jamie love, what is it?'

Sitting at the kitchen table he turned towards her, the shock of seeing his contorted face making jelly of her arms and legs. He felt himself cradled to her, the last of his control went as he buried his face hard against her. He tried to speak, opened his mouth but couldn't form the words, the sounds he made tore at her heart.

The seconds ticked by, gradually he grew quieter.

'Is it Jenny?' she prompted.

'No. Yes. It's me. I thought we were fine, I thought I was—' and again his voice broke, 'was a hell of a good chap, what I did must be right, to argue with me would be like arguing with God—' He hadn't cried since childhood, now he felt torn to shreds and couldn't stop trembling.

Claudia dropped to her knees by his side, looking up at him.

'That's not true, Jamie. I've never known you self-righteous, you've tried always to act as you believed He wants. Whatever else goes wrong, hold on to that.'

'I was blind. For me everything was good, I thought it was the same for her. I never doubted. That's what's hurt her, you see. I took it for granted that she found the same reward in it all as I did. Reward? Do we do what we do for reward? I don't mean money, I mean satisfaction – but satisfaction can turn to smug self-gratification.'

'That it never was,' she defended him hotly. 'Not with you, Jamie.'

'Then why couldn't I see it wasn't enough for her?'

Claudia stood up, concentrating on making their tea. Probably neither of them would drink it, but she needed action.

'Living in the shadow of a man's career isn't easy. I did it for years when we used to have the surgery here.'

13

'You? But that was different, that was the just the way we lived, the way the practice was run. I never thought . . .'

'No, I don't expect you did. Nor Teddy either. I was the one to answer the phone, if someone wanted him urgently I was the one to phone around and try and contact him on his rounds, I was the one to open up the surgery on time and to keep his appointment book. The back-up team, the dog's-body.'

Despite himself, James smiled.

'You? Dog's-body?'

'It's often what I felt like, Jamie, and so does Jennifer I'm sure. To start off with it's good to see you're needed, needed by someone you love. You think of the two of you as a team. But it's not true. You – or in our case, Teddy – are the ones who matter. The things we wives have to do can never make us a team. But they are things that have to be done. So we carry on. Gradually the novelty wears thin, youth starts to slip away, a spark of hope in us dies. Tiny things magnify, we see slights where I'm sure none are intended, our self-esteem gets ground down.'

He started to drink his tea.

'I'm sorry about all that, Mum, about making such a fool of myself.' His voice was his own again.

'Does us good sometimes to blow our cork. And if that's what Jenny has done, if that's what's worrying you, it's probably done her good too. You've had more than twelve years together, happy years for both of you despite your blind spot about the way we women feel,' she calculated the teasing note in her voice would help him back on course. 'Give her time to get up, then ring her, why don't you?'

'I will. Mum. I'm glad we talked. Fancy you feeling like that about the surgery.' He looked at her as if he was seeing her afresh.

'It's too early to be up. We'd better creep back upstairs for an hour or two.' She dropped a kiss on his head. 'You're a good chap Jamie my love, just be honest with her, tell her the things a woman likes to be told. And remember to let her see you appreciate the hundred and one things she does.'

'Thanks Mum.'

Stealthily they crept back to their rooms. As she got into bed Teddy, half disturbed, turned over and reached to put his arm across her, then sank back into sleep. Her mind was racing, she wished it were time to get up. Poor darling James, men can be so blind. And Jenny, at everyone's beck and call, how she must sometimes long to escape it all, tell the Mothers' Union to take a running jump and the St Luke's Ladies to organize their own beanfeasts.

14

In his own room James took off his dressing gown and started to get into bed. Then, as he had been taught as a child, he knelt at the side, his chin on his clasped hands. The anguish was gone, the way was open for him again, 'the peace which passeth all understanding' was within his reach.

The house started to come to life by about seven o'clock. Teddy and Claudia's luxury was an *en suite* bathroom, a one-time small bedroom next to their own. Their day began in its normal way, he showering and shaving while she bathed. These were always some of her favourite moments, odd snippets of local news, nothing worthy of the name 'conversation' but friendly and intimate.

While they had time and space, the rest of the household had to jostle for place in the family bathroom.

As Claudia came down the stairs James appeared in the doorway of the drawing room. His night had left its mark on him.

'I rang home. She wasn't there.' His voice was flat.

'She couldn't leave Paula, you mean? Why don't you try her there?'

'It's on Answerphone. Sorry there's no-one at home to take your call. Please leave name and number.'

'It's still early. Most likely no one's up yet. Did you leave a message?'

'At the Stonehouse place? Of course I didn't.'

Claudia considered he was being unnecessarily dramatic, but she swallowed her words and didn't tell him so.

At breakfast he was quiet, he played with a slice of toast and drank half a cup of black coffee. His silence cast a blight on the others gathered around the table, but only Claudia knew the reason for it. The family supposed, as she had originally, that he was suffering the effects of too much party.

At the Medical Centre the duty doctor was in the surgery for emergencies. Teddy headed out towards Bransgore for the first of his visits. This morning he only had four to make and meant to get home by mid-morning.

Long before that, though, James had gone.

Watching him reverse out of the gate she kept a smile firmly in place, she waved to the children, called 'Love to Jenny' just as if the dawn confessions had never been. Only at the last second did she run round the car to the open window by James's side.

'Keep in touch.' She might have said it any time he'd gone back from a visit, but the way James reached his hand to feel it taken in her firm grip, told her he understood.

15

'I will Mum. Love to Dad. And – thanks.'

From the back seat the children were leaning forward, shouting goodbyes. The car moved off.

James pinned all the blame for the widening rift between Jenny and himself solely on her friendship with Paula Stonehouse. If Claudia could have believed that, her heart wouldn't have been so heavy. No outside friendship could come have come between them unless the gap had already been there waiting for it.

She couldn't forget the look on his face that morning. Her secret weighed heavy. But secret it had to be. A warning voice told her that this was a situation she couldn't talk about to Teddy. He would never understand Jenny's frustration; he wouldn't try to understand.

Chapter 2

By good fortune Teddy's birthday had fallen on a Friday, leading the way to the family all being free to stay on for the weekend. After the four calls he had to make he planned to be home in time to suggest he and Harvey – and Erica too was his grudging mental rider even though he found his pretty American daughter-in-law a delight – would go down to Lymington and take the boat out.

'You're nice and early, darling,' Claudia greeted him.

'That was my intention this morning. Where's everyone?'

'James and the children have gone. He said to give you his love and say he wished he could have waited. But he was worried, Teddy, anxious that Jenny was having a hard time with her friend.' The lie slipped out so easily. 'In any case he would have gone soon after lunch, he had to be back to say Evensong sometime this evening. Last night old Canon Metcalf came across, but he couldn't manage this evening.'

'No one's ever there except on a Sunday, he has the church to himself. I fail to see what difference it makes if he goes through the motions or not. As for Jennifer, she managed to cast a blight on the visit for all three of them. Anyway,' he turned his mind in a cheerier direction, 'where's Harvey? I hurried through the calls, I thought we'd take the boat out for a few hours.'

'Oh, Teddy, what a shame. I give you two guesses where they are – although you'll get it in one.'

'You mean they've already gone? I wish they'd waited until I got home.' He tried to cover up his disappointment by adding, 'Erica's had no experience, he and I are used to each other.'

Sometimes Teddy persuaded Claudia on to the water with him, but she wasn't a useful crewman, nor yet a good sailor. It was Harvey who gravitated to the sea, even in a single day at home he had to find time to drive the few miles to Lymington. Sailing made no call to

James, but Harvey couldn't think of a time when he hadn't loved to crew for his father. Their first 'proper' sail, as he'd thought of it at the time, had been across to the Isle of Wight; even though they'd only been ashore an hour he'd insisted on their sending a picture postcard of Yarmouth home to prove how far they'd travelled. Round the island, to the Channel Islands, to the Isles of Scilly, to Brittany, whenever Teddy had been able to find a locum during school holidays the two of them had gone adventuring.

Now Harvey and Erica would be somewhere out there on the Solent, Teddy was left at home. He watched the other three in the garden, Melinda and Adrian lying facing each other on the grass in the sunshine, absorbed in whatever it was they were talking about. He could tell from her animated expression that she was enjoying herself. Trevor, on the seat under the sycamore tree, was concentrating on the newspaper and paying them no attention. Teddy scowled, he didn't like what he saw.

'Melly is too interested in Adrian Crighton. I could see it last night. If I were Trevor I'd put my foot down.'

'Ho, ho,' Claudia teased, coming to his side to see what he was looking at. 'And a fat lot of good putting his foot down would do – or your's either. If Melly were falling for the dashing Adrian a carping husband would only push her along that bit faster. But she's not. Is she?'

'Ah! So now you're beginning to wonder too.'

'Nonsense. If she were, she wouldn't have brought him down to stay here. We know her too well, we'd see too much. But who could blame her? Trevor really is a doze. Here you are anxiously watching *his* wife and another man, and what is *he* doing? *The Times* crossword. Why did she do it, Teddy, why did she want to tie her life to anyone so – so—'

'There's nothing wrong with Trevor.' Teddy moved slightly away from her, only inches but the movement spoke volumes.

'I didn't say there was anything wrong with him, I just worry that he's wrong for Melly.'

'I wonder he has the chap staying in their house. While he's at school all day you can't make me believe he doesn't think about those two at home, up there in the attic she calls her studio, daubing at the canvas. She's an attractive girl, he's asking for trouble pushing them together.'

'If trouble comes that easily, then it'll find its way whatever he does. But he's putty in Melly's hands, he always has been. If she offered hospitality to the devil himself Trevor would open the door and welcome him in. I can't think how she stands it! I've just never understood.'

18

Uneasy about Melinda, disappointed that Harvey hadn't thought to wait for him, Teddy had to find a reason that he felt so at odds with them all. And Jennifer was tailormade for his purposes. He had never taken to her, not like he had to Erica. Of course he'd never let his feelings show, not for the world would he risk hurting James. But physically he found her unappealing, he couldn't imagine how James could have found the desire to want her in his bed. Intellectually they probably had a good deal in common, but hang it all, there was more to marriage than intellect. Once, many years ago, he'd read something that had stayed with him: that marriage was like a country, full of variety, mountain peaks, deep ravines, busy towns and tranquil pastures, but of all these the capital city was the double bed; the richness of the country depended on the success of that capital city. He thought of that now, his frown deepening as he pictured James and Jenny. A purposeful young woman even thirteen years ago when first she'd been brought to Russets. Not fat so much as thick set, chunky, uncomely to use a good oldfashioned expression, the sort who made an expensive suit look as though she had picked it up at Oxfam. She wore her hair short; she wore her skirts long; despite her short neck she wore her collars high, despite her short legs she wore her heels low. He'd been disappointed in James's choice of a wife, he wanted his sons to have a marriage as full as his own – but Jennifer gave him the impression she considered sex solely a necessary function of procreation.

'You say James went because he was anxious about Jennifer? I can't think what's got into that woman. You don't disappoint your husband and children because some clinging friend has a row with her husband, and I imagine that's what's behind all this. Would you have behaved like it? Of course you wouldn't. The children seemed quite unsettled, did you notice the anxious way little Patsy watched James? She could sense he was bothered. It's not right.' He glared irritably at Claudia as if the whole thing were her responsibility. 'She had no business disrupting their plans at the last minute. Did she have the decency to explain herself to you? To apologize? This friend of hers – I'll tell you something else too, I'd expected she must at least be a member of the church, I'd assumed that's why Jennifer had become involved. But she's not. She has nothing to do with it. I asked Barry. Utterly selfish of Jennifer.'

Claudia knew how much he wished he were sailing with Harvey and Erica, Jenny and her failings were no more than a butt for his disappointment. But Teddy touched her on a raw nerve when he implied that it might be excusable for Jenny to carry her wifely duty to this extreme, but not to look outside it. Loyalty to her own sex and

19

to so much that she could understand in Jenny's life wouldn't allow her to ignore his outburst.

'You can hardly expect all her friends to come from James's flock, especially the St Luke's Ladies! She's an intelligent woman, she has a right to a life beyond St Luke's flagging congregation. It may be *his* life, but she's his wife not a substitute curate.'

'She has a family – and duties. Did James talk to you about it?'

'Not really,' she lied, sure that he didn't believe her. 'Teddy love, do go and get the others in. Perhaps we could drive down to Lymington and be there to meet Harvey when they come back in. What do you say?'

His expression lifted. Jennifer became less important.

It turned out to be an afternoon after his own heart. They arrived just as Harvey and Erica were coming back down Quay Hill from the pub where they'd had their lunch. As Teddy had said, she wasn't an experienced crewman, they'd spent the morning only just offshore rather than taking the boat out into the open water. Now Teddy was here, Melinda too and, just as Claudia had imagined when she first saw him, Adrian turned out to be an experienced and keen sailor.

Everyone piled aboard, motored into the open water, then unfurled the sails. Teddy had put his errant daughter-in-law out of his mind.

'I've had a talk with Adrian Crighton,' Teddy said as he sat in bed watching Claudia massaging cream into her face.

'Teddy! Whatever have you said? Heavens, you might even put ideas into his head that weren't there! You know what Melly is, she just likes to feel she's attractive. It doesn't mean anything.'

'Calm down,' he laughed. 'Not about Melly. About your portrait.'

'Oh Teddy, you didn't remind him?' She was horrified. 'When he suggested it, it was probably just the champagne talking. They're going back to town tomorrow, that'll be the last we shall hear of it – or of him probably.'

'That's what put the idea into my head. I told you, I don't want him at the house with them. I had to think of some way of preventing it. It's not as though he has a regular job of work to go to. Perhaps you're right and to Melly it doesn't mean anything, but the man's human and she's an attractive young woman. Apart from that, the more I thought of having your portrait painted, the more I liked the idea.' When he smiled at her like that he still had the power to make her his slave. 'He'll have to go back with them tomorrow to collect his things, but he's agreed to drive down here again on Monday.'

'I feel dreadful. I wish you hadn't reminded him of what he'd said! Perhaps he didn't really mean it. All the lovely models he must see, he couldn't possibly want to paint *me*.'

'You can still look very pretty. I thought so last night, I told you so.'

'Thanks a bundle,' by which she meant 'Thanks for nothing'.

'I've no idea whether he was serious in his suggestion, for all I know he might have forgotten the whole idea. So I told him I wanted to commission him to make a portrait of you. By the time the portrait's done this flat he's taking will be ready for him to move into.'

She leant forward, her face close to the mirror. Initially the idea of sitting for her portrait had been exciting; when she'd heard that Adrian had suggested it she had felt attractive, she'd imagined herself with the delicate complexion of youth, her neck smooth, her eyes bright. If only she could wave a magic wand . . . In any case, until Teddy spoke to him Adrian had probably forgotten all about it. She felt humiliated.

'Never mind all that cream,' Teddy laughed affectionately, 'Crighton's artistic licence will do more for you than expensive potions.'

'You might have asked me what I felt before you spoke to him.' She didn't try and hide the pout in her voice. 'It's going to take a lot of sitting around. You know I hate sitting around. And why should he want to be stuck down here? His friends are in London, his interests are in London—'

'How the woman does nag! Come to bed, you look fine as you are without any more of that rubbish.' He held back the duvet and, as she got into bed, drew her towards him so that when he peered at her his face was only inches from hers. 'My funny girl!' With his arm still around her they lay down and he reached to switch off the lamp. 'You know, I think I nipped it in the bud before it happened. He didn't make excuses to stay on with Melly. But I could see *she* was disappointed. You must have been worried too, Claudia, you must have noticed the way her eyes follow him. Proximity and opportunity could only have led to trouble.'

'If he's such easy prey, I wonder you invite him here.'

'How do you mean? Oh, I see,' he chortled, rubbing his chin against her cheek and removing most of her expensive rejuvenator, 'you're thinking of trying your hand at cradle-snatching?' Contentedly he wriggled closer to her. 'It's been a nice day. A pity they can't get here together more often. I wish Jennifer hadn't messed it up for James.'

'She was probably home when he got back.' And silently into the darkness: 'Please, please, help poor darling James, I'll never forget seeing him cry like that. Help him to be strong. Make her love him like he needs.'

'You know what I was thinking just now?' Teddy said companionably. 'Crighton ought to have moved in with James, we shouldn't have had to worry about him wanting to entice Jennifer to be unfaithful.'

'That's a rotten thing to say. James adores Jenny. To poke fun at her is like poking fun at him.'

'I don't poke fun. The truth is I'm too angry to poke fun. At breakfast I thought the boy looked quite ill. The children say she's always out. She can't make the excuse that she's bored, she has plenty to do in the parish.'

'Melly has her painting, I wish Jenny had something of her own.'

'Jennifer has the family, she has a home – and I give her her due, she does him credit in the way she looks after that great house – she has a position in the village.'

'Before they married she was doing well in a career of her own, it must have meant a lot to her. A good degree, work she loved—'

'Work she hid behind if you ask me. Researching the roots of English language! Are you telling me she was better off then than having a proper life of her own, a husband, children? Damned lucky that a fellow like James looked at her. Older than he is, no-one could call her God's gift—'

Claudia rankled under what she heard as male arrogance but the memory of James's unhappiness was too vivid for her to argue, it haunted her.

'She sings like an angel' was her only comment.

For a long moment Teddy didn't speak; he was ashamed of the venom in his outburst. Then he gripped Claudia's hand tightly in his.

'Please God she's singing tonight,' he whispered.

Claudia felt the hot sting of unshed tears.

'Metaphorically?' She needed to tease, it was the only way she could answer.

But Teddy wasn't in a teasing mood.

'We've always been lucky, haven't we, you and me?'

Yes, they had, of course they had. In that moment there were only the good times. She drew their linked hands to press his against her mouth, nightly beauty treatment forgotten.

Having her portrait painted didn't turn out a bit as she'd expected. She had thought that she would have to sit in the chosen position frightened to speak or move, wearing the most glamorous garment her wardrobe could produce. Not a bit of it. Instead, her hours with

Adrian were spent enjoying themselves as if he were visiting for a holiday.

They drove into the New Forest, parked the car and walked, picking up the first chestnuts to fall, occasionally finding them already formed enough to munch as they went; they went to Mudeford and were rowed across the narrow strip of water to Hengistbury Head where they strode along the clifftop to Christchurch; in the ancient Priory church they sat silently and listened to the organist taking choir practice. They spent a morning in Lymington where they jostled amongst the market-day crowds in the High Street, then bought the makings of a picnic lunch to eat aboard Teddy's *Sea Urchin*, rocking gently at its mooring at the far end of the quay. They ate pub lunches and cream teas. It ought to have been an ill-balanced relationship, he an up-and-coming young artist, she with sons older than he was himself. But that wasn't as she'd expected either. Often she'd turn to say something to him and find he was more than looking at her, he seemed to be looking into her. Of course, she reminded herself, it was so that he could remember when he was working on his canvas in the playroom. But having someone hanging on her every word, noting each movement she made, apparently delighting in what he heard and saw, was a new and heady experience. Long ago it had been like that with Teddy, for him and for her too, both of them had known and rejoiced in it as they'd hurtled into love. Now they no longer needed that sort of conscious awareness, time had moulded them so comfortably together that it could have no part in their lives. But she enjoyed it for all that, even though she didn't openly acknowledge it.

Occasionally, like the day they sat on a pile of hewn trees in a forest clearing eating apples and drinking cider from plastic mugs, he made sketches. But that was as near as he came to turning their outings into work sessions. Most of his drawings were done from memory, with each one he came a little closer to seeing in his mind the image he would create.

Gwen Pomfrey said nothing – and missed nothing. If the young fellow had seemed down on his luck, fretful about something, then she could have understood why Mrs C spent so much time with him. Painting her picture, that's what she'd been told. But you don't paint a picture while you're out gadding around the countryside. On his easel the canvas was blank. If you asked her, he was wasting his own time and the doctor's money. Not that it was her business, she added out of habit.

For nearly a fortnight the golden days that carried summer to autumn lasted and Adrian's pile of sketches grew. He knew every angle of Claudia's face, he knew every curve of her body. There had been plenty of women in his life, beautiful women, professional models; there had been others he'd been commissioned to paint, lady mayors, a headmistress, a senior nurse, society beauties, high-ranking service personnel with medals to prove it. Claudia Carlyle was in a sphere of her own. Twice his age, but years had nothing to do with it; her face had lost the blank smoothness of youth; happiness, pain, love, disappintment, excitement, all these things had left their mark. He sensed a depth of understanding in her, and a depth of passion too; to his artist's eye these things added to the beauty she must have had as a young woman.

The moment came when he knew he was ready to start painting, he must capture her spirit, it was in his power to reproduce her features but more than that, to transfer to his canvas the spirit that was Claudia. He shut himself away in the nursery and started to work, using his sketches and using his memory.

Claudia's days seemed strangely empty. Not prepared to acknowledge how his interest and open admiration had sparked some dormant excitement, instead she told herself she missed their outings, the easy, soul-searching discussions. They'd aired their views sometimes with knowledge, sometimes in ignorance, they'd talked about everything, from books, to architecture, to fox-hunting, to euthanasia, to marriage and divorce, to badger-baiting, drugs, homosexuality, free love; sometimes they'd agreed, sometimes they hadn't. When their views differed, each was given a new window to the other's mind, it added zest and sparkle. But Claudia didn't analyse any of this, she just knew that once Adrian shut away to work life was suddenly dull.

'You'll miss Adrian when the picture's done and he goes,' Teddy observed idly. The evening meal over, their young visitor had returned upstairs to paint. 'He's fitted in like one of the family.'

His tone of complacency irritated her, she didn't ask herself why it should.

'Yes, of course I shall miss him. I could know someone for years and not feel as close as I do to him. We've got on remarkably well. We've both enjoyed these weeks.'

'And was I right, getting him away from Melly?'

She was angry, hurt that it was Melly he jealously guarded. But Adrian was younger than her own sons, she was frightened that Teddy might suspect the way her thoughts had turned and laugh at her.

'Melly?' she answered him, 'I'd forgotten all about your wild ideas. He's not a bit interested in Melly – except as a friend. He admires her work.'

24

'How's the portrait going?'

'I've not seen it. He's working from his sketches still. In a day or two I shall sit for him.' No mention now of hating to sit still. 'Where shall we hang it?'

Teddy laughed. 'Let's wait and see what it looks like. The place of honour over the mantelpiece in here if it's good, otherwise up in the attic!'

On 1 October Adrian was due to move into his flat. On his last evening at Russets he called them up to the one-time nursery to see the finished work. In the final days Claudia had sat for two sessions, so this wasn't her first viewing. But to Teddy the portrait came as a shock: in it he saw Claudia today and Claudia as he'd first fallen in love with her. The face on the canvas looked at him, the dark eyes were full of love, full of hope and anticipation, yet they were ready to shine with sudden laughter.

'Good God!'

'You don't like it?' Adrian was clutching at straws in the wind in the sudden hope that he could take the portrait back to London with him.

'It's uncanny, it's so real. It *is* Claudia.' Artistic licence had smoothed away ageing lines, just as Teddy had told her it would, and yet it hadn't given her back her youth, it was the face of a woman who understood life.

Adrian turned from Claudia on canvas to Claudia in the flesh. Each day he'd spent with her he'd fallen further under her spell. There she stood gazing at the work into which he had put every fibre of his being, her hand loosely in Teddy's. He turned away, making a show of cleaning his brushes, anything rather than let them see how he felt. His Adam's apple was too big for his throat, his hands felt clumsy. There was no sense in it but there was no escaping it either, the thought of making love to her obsessed him.

Thank God tomorrow he was going back to London. He would put these weeks behind him, forget the way she haunted him.

But next morning his good resolutions were fading.

'I wonder if you'd let me take the canvas back to town with me. I'd like to be allowed to choose the frame. How would you feel about that? Or have you a firm idea of what you want?'

He spoke to Teddy, yet Claudia sensed that the suggestion was aimed at her.

'I'm sure you'd have a much better eye than we would,' Teddy answered. 'The only thing against that is that I've no idea when Mellie might come down again – I imagine you were thinking of handing it over to *her*?' Only Claudia knew the way his mind was working, and Adrian's reply soon laid his fears to rest.

25

'No, I'd thought that I might drive down with it. I'd like to see you were satified with the end-product.'

'We'll look forward to that.' Teddy glanced at his wristwatch and stood up from the table. A minute later, a light kiss on Claudia's forehead, a handshake and assurance that they'd look forward to seeing Adrian again in a week or so, and he was gone.

'I may come again, Claudia? You've not said anything,' Adrian prompted as they heard the front door slam.

'You're always welcome,' she forced a note of bonhomie into her reply, 'Teddy was saying only the other evening, you're like one of the family.'

It was a mistake to look at him so directly as she answered. His expression was hard to fathom, the only thing that was certain was that it mocked her words, it held nothing filial.

During the next five days Claudia was determined to fill her time: one day was spent in Bournemouth where, despite it being only the beginning of October, she gave her expedition a purpose by choosing Christmas presents for James, Jenny and the children; another was spent in Lymington where she gave an end-of-season clean to the cabin of the *Sea Urchin*; another was in sorting out the woodshed and stacking the first winter delivery of logs. The autumn stretched ahead, this year the thought of greys and misty days was duller than ever it had been in the past.

Then on the sixth morning after Adrian had left, just as she was busy lifting the dahlia tubers and burying them in sand so that they could winter in the potting shed, she was disturbed by the sound of a car turning into the drive.

'One picture, framed and ready to be admired,' he wound down the window and called to her as he switched off the engine.

'Adrian!' She made no attempt to hide her pleasure.

'I drove down early. I wanted us to go over to Buckler's Hard for lunch. You will, won't you Claudia? The garden will still be here tomorrow – and Teddy ought to be O.C. portrait hanging don't you think, so that can wait until this evening.'

'I'll just scrub my hands and get ready. Go and make yourself a cup of coffee or something while you wait, I'll not be two shakes.'

Her delight was so obvious, it would have carried him with it under any circumstances. He'd gone back to London determined to put her out of his mind, but that wasn't possible. It was like placing a meal in front of a hungry beggar, then taking it away after the first taste. His pulses quickened at her eagerness.

'I'll hurry,' she told him.

'I won't bother with coffee. Leave your tools, I'll see to them when I've taken the picture inside.' He didn't attempt to take the wrapping off it, she didn't suggest that he should. That could wait for this evening and Teddy.

She hurried. Less than five minutes later he reversed the car out of the drive.

As he drove he reached for her hand and brushed it with his lips.

'I've missed you,' he told her. His light tone belied the grip of his fingers.

'Me too. I'd got used to having you around.'

'One of the family?' And she knew now that he was teasing her.

The days since he'd left had been filled with action and empty of meaning. Suddenly she was gloriously happy. She felt young, she felt free, she felt alive.

That evening he and Teddy hung the portrait. To Teddy it was a reminder of 'his Claudia', the woman he'd fallen in love with long ago, the woman of today, the only woman he would ever love and who had become part of himself. To Claudia it was a reminder of the man who'd seen into her soul and reignited a flame that through the years had given way to warm and constant embers.

'I hope that you won't stop coming to see us just because the portrait is finished,' Teddy said to him.

And what better invitation could there be? Down the motorway it was a quick drive, quick enough that he could come even as he had that day, to take Claudia out for lunch at one of the many pubs in the forest where the trees were a riot of autumn glory, or for a few hours walking in the open grassland.

More than once while Claudia was picking up chestnuts or stretching to pull down a bough for a prickly cluster just out of reach, she would see Adrian had his sketch pad out. The knowledge filled her with exhilaration, she felt vital, alive.

'I think you're unjust.' Jennifer faced James squarely. In a checked woollen skirt almost to her ankles and an unbecoming yellow acrylic jumper that had been washed until it was baggy and shapeless, her chunky figure was a confirmation of Teddy's opinion. But she was oblivious to her appearance. 'Yesterday I spent all the afternoon with the Mothers' Union, all the evening arranging the lunches for your Christmas Market, this morning—'

'Not my Christmas Market, Jenny. *Ours*, the village's. You've always enjoyed it. If Paula's unhappy and lonely, why don't you try and involve her, help her to make friends.'

'Don't try and sidetrack me, James. Just give me space, can't you? And she's not lonely and unhappy, she's happier than I've known her. This trip is important to her. Her wood carvings are beautiful, I'm sure she'll do well and get orders too.'

'I don't see what she's doing it for. She can't need to earn money, Sydney Stonehouse must be a wealthy man.'

'You expect she should make her life revolve around him. She isn't involved in what he does, you know that. Anyway it's not for the money. I would have expected you to understand it's not just earning money that makes one work. Was it for money that you went into the Church?'

'That's a different thing entirely. If Paula wants a mission, why doesn't she put her energies into trying to save her marriage.'

'It's hopeless, how can I talk to you!'

For years Paula had made wood carvings, in the beginning simple shapes, gradually progressing until now her forest animals were exquisite. She was showing them in an exhibition in Exeter. In James's opinion it was ridiculous, at a season of fogs and dark evenings, to travel two hundred miles simply to have the satisfaction of seeing her work on display. If it had been in Oxford, Northampton or even Henley-on-Thames, somewhere within easy driving distance each day he could have understood her, although even then he wouldn't have been happy about Jenny's decision to go with her.

'You're right I don't understand. What's more important, getting orders for something she does as a hobby, or trying to find their way back to what their marriage used to be?' The Stonehouses? He and Jenny? Couldn't she understand what it was he was trying to say to her?

'The orders. Her woodcarving is her way of finding expression. I don't know what sort of relationship they had in the beginning, she's never talked about it to me. But I do know that they live like two strangers, their lives separate.' She felt her face grow hot with embarrassment. In self-defence she glowered. 'She finds him repulsive.' Her bald statement met with silence, in the silence the words seemed to fill the room.

If they'd been discussing someone they'd both been trying to help, if her tone had been confidential, then the statement 'She finds him repulsive' might have bound them together, it would have represented a shared mission. But he felt it was aimed at him, it put her in Paula's camp and made him an outsider.

Desperate to draw the conversation back to a manageable level,

Jenny rushed on: 'Surely even by your standards it's not a sin to look for personal achievement. She has a wonderful gift, I told you her work is exquisite. I would have expected you to believe that if one has a God-given talent it is a duty to use it.'

'But you, Jenny? Where is the God-given talent in helping her carry her boxes, put up her stand, write down her orders?'

She ignored his comment.

'I shall be gone three days, that's all. There's plenty of food in the freezer so you won't have to bring your do-gooders in to look after things.'

They were in James's study. Now he took shelter behind his desk, busying himself tidying a sheaf of papers and hiding his hurt from her.

'You didn't answer what I said,' he pressed. 'What personal achievement will you get out of helping Paula transport her handicraft to Exeter, letting yourself be used as a general dog's-body?' At the expression he thought of his mother and the September morning at the rectory. He daren't let himself look at Jenny.

'A change from being yours and the parish's.'

'That's not fair. Jenny, where have I gone wrong? What is it you want?'

'I just want a chance to be myself. I work hard in this house, I'm cook, scullery maid, general skivvy, receptionist. Six days shalt thou labour, well I do my six days, then on Sunday for a treat I take Sunday School. What do I want? I want space.'

'Have you hated it so much?'

Jenny ran her strong hands through her short hair. She'd said too much. More than anything she wished she could burst into tears, sob out her frustrations and disappointments. She envied the women who could cry. But she couldn't. Her misery was a physical pain, like a football being pumped up in her chest, straining her muscles, choking her. Her strong hands were sweaty, her teeth ached as she clamped them hard together.

The shrill bell of the telephone shattered the silence. She hurried to the hall to answer it.

'Brightley Rectory . . . Yes, Mrs Handley, I'll tell him, of course he'll understand. I'll give him your apologies . . . Yes, I'll tell him that too. I hope you find your daughter better . . . Train? Aren't you driving? . . . I see. How are you getting to the station? Can we help?' She was surprised to hear herself make the offer, speaking out of habit. 'Of course it's no trouble . . . one or the other of us will collect you at ten to four.'

Back in the study she found James standing by the window, he

29

must have moved nearer the door to listen. The tension was lifted, for once she was grateful to the claims of the parish. Her voice was her own again, the air had been let out of the football that had threatened to burst.

'Mrs Handley. Her apologies, she won't be at the PCC meeting, her daughter is in bed with 'flu, she has to go and look after the children. Oh, and she's down to read the lesson at the eight o'clock on Sunday but she won't be back. I said we'd take her to the station this afternoon.'

'Jenny,' he moved to put his hands on her shoulders, 'Jenny, I heard you talking to her. This is your world. Here, the people, our people.' Then, with less certainty, 'Me.'

'I couldn't let her go on the bus and I doubt she's got money to burn on taxis.'

'Say something, Jenny. Not about Mrs Handley – about us – about all this.'

'No more, James. Let it rest. I'll be away three days, is that such a lot to ask?'

He mustn't let her see how frightened he was. She was his rock and his strength, he loved her, he was no good without her.

'Don't worry about Mrs Handley,' he said.' I shall be that way, I'll take her to the train. Ten to four you said didn't you?'

'Good. I've got a lot to do if I'm leaving in the morning. I'll let you have a telephone number when Paula arranges the hotel.'

'Three nights in the sort of hotel the Stonehouses are used—'

'She doesn't want me to pay anything, she's quite adamant. I suppose my hotel expenses are a sort of fee for helping her.'

'I can't let Paula Stonehouse pay your hotel. I'll find the money.'

'That's just stupid pride. If I'm there to help, then I'm earning my board, I don't need you to pay. Anyway money doesn't mean anything to them, not like it has to to us.'

He glanced at his watch and started to gather up his vestments. It was his morning for sick visiting, home eucharists. There were few people in Brightley he didn't know, some regularly attended St Luke's, some donned their best for occasions such as weddings, christenings and funerals, and some, of course, belonged to other denominations. Naturally James knew his congregation best, but it was seldom he was given less than courtesy on his parish visits to non-attenders. Old Mrs Bedlow was one of those. Nearly ninety-four, hers had been the sort of independent spirit that had never let him persuade her into his church, although she'd always enjoyed his visits and had been keen for him to stay and talk about anything – except religion. He'd grown very fond of the stubborn old lady. But now her days were numbered, and about three weeks ago he'd had a telephone call from her. If he was passing her way, she wouldn't mind having a word.

He'd called the next day, finding her propped up in bed.

'I've had time to think,' she'd told him as she nodded towards the bedside chair indicating she wanted him to sit. 'You've been a good friend to me, never pestered me with Holy Jo talk. But, well, you never know,' her watery old eyes had twinkled as she teased him, 'I've got nothing to lose have I? The bread and wine – I've been thinking – but don't you get talking over what I say with my daughter and all of them downstairs, it's just between you and me. Do you reckon I've left it too late?'

James had smiled at her, touched by her need for reassurance.

'It can never be too late.'

'And tell you the truth, I like you coming to see me. If when you come you bring your pots and things you use with you, well I think I shall like that too. You're a good young fella, never shot me down for taking so long to give in.'

James had great respect for her. One Ada Bedlow was worth a pewful of those who'd never wavered.

She was his first call when he set out from the rectory and, just as she always did, she managed to soothe his own problems. It was as he got back into the car to drive on to Dick Townley, a one-time church warden with a broken hip, that he thought of a way to avoid letting Jenny be beholden to Paula Stonehouse and at the same time avoid a hotel bill he couldn't afford.

'It's all arranged,' he couldn't keep the note of triumph out of his voice as he came into the rectory kitchen, savouring the welcoming smell of homemade soup. 'I've spoken to Mum on the phone and she's fixing it in Moorleigh. The key's with the next-door neighbour, so she's getting the heating put on tonight and the electric blankets put in the beds ready tomorrow.'

'The cottage! I never thought of it.' She put his plate of soup in front of him as he sat down. Then, almost shyly, let her hand touch his shoulder. 'Thank you, James. How far is it from Exeter?'

'I'm not exactly sure, I'd say eight or ten miles.'

'I really am glad. I know Paula has bags of money, but I'd like to be the one to provide something. I'll ring your mother this afternoon. I want to thank her.'

'You do that.' James was suddenly happy.

'Lucky for James he spoke to you, not to me.' Teddy's voice was

31

unsmiling. 'Damn stupid nonsense. If Jenny is so brainy that she's wasting herself doing the things other clergy wives do, as you seem to believe, then what in God's name is she thinking of trailing about with some craft stall. She's tough as a man, I'll give you that, so I assume she's there as humper.'

'Would you have had me refuse James?'

He ignored the question. He'd bought Applegarth, a terraced cottage on the green at Moorleigh in south Devon, the year before Melly had been born. At that time it had had oil lamps, Calor gas for cooking. Situated between Dartmoor and the sea it had been their holiday home as the children grew up; it was full of happy memories. Over the years and as Teddy could afford they'd improved it until now it was comfortable, well equipped – but, unlike the days when the children were young, it was seldom used. Recently Teddy had talked of selling it.

'This time of year, I'd have thought she'd have had enough to do in Brightley. If she can't be bothered with the parish and the things she ought to be doing as James's wife, then what about the children's end-of-term things at school? When I phoned the other evening she was out. She's besotted with that woman!' He glowered at Claudia as if she were responsible.

'When she spoke to me this afternoon, she was simply grateful for the cottage. She said that Paula had insisted on paying the hotel bills, James had insisted he wouldn't let her, and this way she – Jenny – was thankful to feel she was doing her share. Does that sound as if she's being taken over by Paula Stonehouse? You talk nonsense. Next you'll be telling me they're a pair of lesbians!'

Teddy took a larger-than-sip of his neat whisky.

'This is James's wife,' he growled, 'it's not some stranger we're talking about.'

They'd been talking *at* each other. Now, unprepared, they found themselves looking directly at each other. There was nowhere to hide. They were frightened, powerless to help.

'She can't be. Teddy, she can't be. They've been married for years. They have two children.' She chewed her bottom lip, out of her depth, helpless. 'Tomorrow we'll phone the rectory, talk to James. I don't mean ask him anything, but just talk to him after she's gone. Of course it's nothing like that, she's a good wife, a good mother.'

'A good girlfriend to the right woman . . .'

'Stop it. She's James's wife.'

Teddy picked up the *Times*, Claudia pretended to read her library book.

'Sometimes I wonder why anyone has children,' he said after a moment. 'They grow up, go their own ways. You'd think our worries with them would be over. At least Harvey and Erica don't give us any problems.'

'I don't see that the others do.' He *must* be wrong. He's just angry, wanting to be spiteful. But it's James that matters. My darling James . . . please, make him happy, make things right for him.

Unaware of her thoughts Teddy went back to what he'd said.

'You're always telling me that Melly is married to a drip. Now all this business with Jenny.' While Claudia wouldn't admit to worries, Teddy exaggerated them.

'Melly doesn't see him as a drip,' Claudia answered him. 'And as for Jenny, that was a wicked thing you said about her. She's probably frightened to see a lifetime ahead of her moulding herself into what James wants. I suppose that's what you think she ought to do. It'll do her good to have a break from them and I was glad to say she could use the cottage.'

'Humph!' Hardly more than a grunt.

Staring at her open book Claudia couldn't concentrate on the words, her half formed thoughts were chaotic. Her glance wandered to the portrait hanging over the mantelpiece and she felt a surge of longing for the freedom of those autumn days. Yet even then she'd known that things weren't right for James, the nagging worry could never quite lift. She'd tried to make herself believe that his unhappiness had been a temporary hiccup, but each time she'd spoken to any of them on the phone the cloud had grown darker. Sometimes James would be bright – too bright; that was almost worse than when he'd been quiet. But she mustn't let him think she criticized Jenny, she mustn't condemn. No matter how her heart ached for James, she must keep her fears hidden. The only way she could help them was to be natural, normal. This afternoon when she'd talked to Jenny she'd understood her need to get away. But, this afternoon she hadn't even considered what Teddy had suggested.

Chapter 3

The buzz of the bell warned Adrian that someone was coming up to his flat on the top floor of the Georgian house. There was no security door, the only warning that visitors were on the way was if, as in this case, they pressed his bell as they entered the building.

'Blast!'

Here he was, in his own studio, painting for his own pleasure, yet like a thief fearing he'd be caught red-handed he took the canvas from the easel and mindful of its wet paint, propped it carefully facing the wall. Then he replaced it with an almost finished commissioned portrait and was ready for when the knock came on his apartment door.

'Melly! A nice surprise. Come in.'

'Can I? I'm not disturbing you? You're working, I ought to have phoned you.'

'This is much more pleasant. Anyway I'm not working.'

The smudge of paint on his hand was fresh, so she knew he was lying – she suspected on both counts. She felt he was on his guard.

Melly had a natural magnetism, she took it for granted that the opposite sex were attracted to her, just as she took it for granted that she was the one to decide just how far friendship should go. Adrian was like no other, she had no illusions about him but he had more physical appeal than any man she knew. At one time she had had an affair with him, and then she'd met Trevor – 'dull, boring Trevor' as Claudia thought him. As with all her boyfriends, Adrian had slipped into the bracket of 'friend' but, even so, she resented the suspicion that he didn't want her here.

'We haven't seen you for weeks.' She mustn't let it show that she felt rebuffed. 'Mum said you've been to Russets—'

'Well, of course. I brought the portrait back, they asked me to arrange the framing. When it was finally ready I took it down and helped hang it.'

'I know. They love it. But she said you've been since then—'

'I was working in the vicinity.'

Melly laughed.

'Lucky for Mum! She was chuffed as anything. Told me all about your visits, that you've taken her out to lunch and so forth. That's kind of you Adrian.'

He was beginning to relax.

'It's nothing of the sort,' he laughed. 'Your mother is delightful company.'

'Oh, I know that. But we others – James and Harvey and me – we don't make the time to go down as often as we ought. It's not that we don't want to, don't get me wrong, but we're all busy, every weekend there seems to be something. And that brings me to my reason for coming – I'll tell you in a minute. I was saying about Mum, though. She does love going out. Not like Dad, except for getting away in the boat, he's happiest at home. Anyway, I didn't come to talk about the parents, I came to tell you I'm arranging a "laptop lunch" this coming Sunday. I know it's short notice, but we only thought of it yesterday evening. On Saturday Harvey's playing at the Festival Hall, then he and Erica are spending the weekend with us. We've known that for ages, but we suddenly decided it called for a party. One or two friends of Trevor's, one or two of mine – and that includes you. You will come, Adrian? Please.' How could he refuse those wide, blue eyes? 'I want to show you off.'

'With Harvey Carlyle there, no one's going to notice a mere painter.'

'There's nothing "mere" about your work and well you know it. Instead of fishing for compliments, why don't you let me see what you've been doing?'

His mind leapt ahead of her to his studio, mentally checking it was clear to take her in. But, once there, their usual easy comradship that stemmed from a shared craft took over. It was when he was called away to answer the telephone that she was left alone. To her it was the most natural thing to look through the used canvasses he had stacked about the room. Kneeling on the floor she took them up, first one, then another, her admiration for him growing.

Thinking along these lines she picked up the next canvas, her brow pulled into a puzzled frown. These weren't draft sketches, these were finished works – works done for his own pleasure. Her mother's face looked back at her from the canvas, the pale shoulders appearing like a wraithe from the mist. Almost silently she replaced it, then looked

35

further through the pile. An alsatian dog, a toothless peasant . . . unable to believe what she saw she stared at the next. She felt a shock that was physical, her brain was paralysed, not wanting to accept what she saw. There was no doubt it was her mother, completely naked, standing raised on her toes, her arms stretched high towards a hanging cluster of prickly fruit from a chestnut tree. The forest was unmistakably familiar, her mother like an ageless woodland nymph.

Melly hardly glanced at the other canvasses, she knelt up and crawled to the next pile, sifting them through. There she was again! This time her pale body was visible through a thin black veil, her expression was provocative.

He was coming back. He mustn't know she'd seen them!

By the time he came into the room she was in front of the easel, her head on one side as she gave every impression of deep concentration. Her play-acting didn't go beyond that; she needed to get away. '. . . only a quick call . . . stayed longer than I meant . . . see you Sunday.' She heard herself saying these things, she felt her face smile.

Driving home she let her mind go back to what she had seen, she had no power to stop it wandering even further and facing the things she didn't know. The forest scene must have been memory, but what about the figure? Had her mother posed for him? Was it possible that during those autumn weeks when he'd lived at Russets he had flattered her into having a brief affair with him? Brief? He still went there, often her mother mentioned that he'd been. Thinking back, she could imagine a note of boastfulness in Claudia's voice as she related where they'd been and what they'd done. It was disgusting, humiliating! Stupid woman! Anyway, if Adrian was especially anyone's friend, it was *hers*, Melly's. It was ridiculous, he was younger than James and Harvey, he was handsome, attractive to his own generation, whatever would he waste his time flattering Mum for? No, they couldn't have . . . Could they? Melinda thought of the home she'd always taken for granted, the easy bond between her parents; she thought of her father and was shaken by blind rage at the suggestion that her mother could deceive him.

Adrian had promised to come to the lunch party, but she wished now that she hadn't invited him. Just to look at him would remind her.

Ahead of her someone stopped suddenly, instinct made her jam her foot on the brake and for a moment pull her thoughts back to the crowded road. But not for long. If you hurt Dad, I'll never forgive you, Mum, never be able to love you, never want even to see you. But even her anger couldn't ease the pain. She'd had friends whose parents had been unfaithful – but this wasn't other people's parents, it

36

was her own, hers and James's and Harvey's. Stupid woman, what's the matter with you? Frightened of not being young any more? Anyway, it's disgusting! Mum, taking all her clothes off, and looking so – liberated, so encouraging. Did she take them off as if she were behind the curtain in the doctor's surgery, folding them neatly on a chair, or did she try to titillate him, fancy herself a striptease artiste? It's revolting! I don't want to think about it. But I can't think of anything else. What's he going to do with the paintings? He can't be planning to put them in an exhibition. I wonder if Mum's seen them yet, if he took them with him when he went there? If only I could talk to Trevor about it. But I can't because, if they are having an affair behind Dad's back, to Adrian it would be a passing fancy, but Mum wouldn't see it like that. That's why I can't talk to Trevor about it, it would be like betraying Dad; all of us knowing, talking about it, and him not even suspecting. He's the only one who could make her see what a fool she's making of herself chasing after someone half her age. Is it kinder to tell him or leave him blissfully ignorant?

That evening she tried to act normally, but Trevor was always sensitive to her mood.

'You're not worrying about Sunday, Melly? What are we going to give them to eat? Can I do any of it?'

'Give them a glass or two of something to dull their palates, then it'll be fine. No, of course I'm not worrying. I went to see Adrian this afternoon, by the way. He's promised to come.'

Adrian. Was that what had upset her? Trevor knew there had been a time when she'd thought herself in love with the handsome artist.

'That's good.' He answered evenly as he stacked away the school papers he'd been checking, poured them each a glass of red wine then turned on the television for the nine o'clock news. Something was bothering Melly, he was sure of it; perhaps she'd hit a bad patch with her work. He put his arm around her shoulder and drew her closer.

The newscaster chattered on, seeming to smack his lips on the series of disasters he was able to put on their evening menu: unrest in the Middle East; a hurricane in America; nearer home the body of a missing woman found murdered; an elderly pensioner left mugged and dying in her bungalow, a cashbox forced open and her life savings gone; a coach crash on the motorway with two killed; and a police swoop on a house found to contain a haul of cannabis.

Trevor switched it off and refilled their glasses. When he started *The Times* crossword she leant forward determined to make herself concentrate and push away the images that forced themselves on to her. What were they doing this evening at Russets? It was cowardly of her to wish it, but she wished with all her heart she'd not gone to see

Adrian, not looked at his hateful pictures, not asked him here on Sunday.

'I'm going to have a bath,' she said. Then, making an effort, 'It's not as though I make any useful suggestions. You'll finish it quicker without me.'

But when she'd gone he put the crossword to one side. Something was worrying her, he'd expected that pouring over the puzzle together she'd tell him. He imagined her with Adrian in his studio, he felt inadequate and every bit as dull as Claudia thought him. Standing up, automatically he folded the newspaper then put it in the cupboard on top of the growing pile that he took once every few weeks to the salvage bin for recycling, his mind all the while on Melly. He expected to find her still in the bath, she loved to lie a long time in the deep, warm water; the aroma of the bath oil was enticing. But the bathroom was already in darkness.

Melly had retreated to the bath hoping it would restore her, take away this empty, dull ache. She was ashamed for her mother, that she could be making such a fool of herself. To Adrian women were easy prey, he'd had numerous affairs since she and Trevor had married. But none of them had hurt like this. Is it because she's deceiving Dad? No, it's worse even that that. She's not caring about any of us. Perhaps she's always been the same, has had men before! It put a stain on all her memories, on things she was entitled to be able to take for granted.

The warm scented water caressed her, she longed for it to wash away her wretchedness. Instead, she shied away from the sensuous smoothness of her skin. Sitting upright she rubbed herself vigorously with the loofah then let the water go. In her present mood she didn't want the flimsy nightdress, instead she borrowed a pair of Trevor's pyjamas. They were too big but the feeling of them was a comfort; they were his, she felt enveloped in his love, a love she was certain of. And that brought her full circle, a thousand pictures crowded her mind, all the happy years at home . . . in that moment she believed she hated her mother.

She could hear Trevor moving about, he must be coming to bed early too. Quickly she lay down and pulled the duvet high around her shoulders.

'I was coming to talk to you in the bath. You were quick.'

'I didn't like it very much.'

A few minutes later when he joined her in bed, she had already switched off the light.

'What's all this?' Drawing her close he discovered the all-enveloping pyjamas.

'I was cold.'

'You won't be. I promise you won't be.'

That night was the first time she had ever pretended. Just as a little while before she had longed to sink herself into the warm water, so now she yearned for his loving. He would drive away the devils that haunted her. Greedily and without preamble she pulled him to her, this way she could blot out every other thought. But it was no use. Her mind was flooded with images of Adrian and her mother . . . Trevor and her . . . Adrian and Mum . . . stop . . . stop . . . Desperately she wanted to lose herself in these moments, but her body felt numb. So she whipped up a frenzy, she acted a part, and when she knew the moment was right for him too, she faked so convincingly that he had no idea.

Afterwards, when he was contentedly asleep, she lay on her back, wide awake, staring at the darkness. I'm a grown woman, I love my work, I love Trevor, this is my home. Yet whatever I am is because of the past, home, Mum, Dad, the boys, even poor old Gwen Pomfrey. If I hadn't been alone in the studio today I wouldn't have suspected – so could there have been other men? Like a pageant, her years passed before her, a cloud of suspicion and doubt hanging above them.

I'm a grown woman, again she told herself. This is my world, here with Trevor. She wriggled close to him, thankful he was asleep yet at the same time needing his reassurance. When, still in his sleep, he turned towards her and pulled her close, in her mind she poured out all her misery to him. Perhaps it was the warmth that soothed her, or perhaps it was the culmination of a day filled with emotion. Within minutes Melly was asleep.

That was on the Thursday, the same day that James had spoken to Claudia about Jenny and Paula using the cottage.

If the pageant of their years was alive in Melly's mind, perhaps it was some form of telepathy that triggered Claudia's memories. Long summer holidays in Moorleigh with the children, Teddy coming to join them as often, and for as long, as he could get a locum to look after his single-handed practice. When he hadn't been there, James had made himself man of the family, proud of his two years seniority over Harvey. She could see him so clearly lugging the picnic basket from the boot of the car when they reached their favourite spot on the moor, posing for his photo holding up a two-and-a-half-pound bass he'd caught, cleaning all their shoes before a trip to the theatre in Torquay. The other two were there too in her memories, but to-night especially it was recollections of that young and trusting James that tore at her heart.

By her side Teddy's breathing was deep, he must believe he was fooling her that he was asleep. There was so much she wanted to say to him, but she could say none of it. 'Poor darling James' would be confirmation that she knew things weren't as they ought to be, as they used to be, for James and Jenny; 'A few days' break will do her good' would set their minds on exactly what the two days' break might entail; 'To even suggest what you did about her is wicked. Just because she isn't pretty and girlie, you have never liked her.' There's more than a grain of truth in that, she told herself, perhaps all men are the same. Erica can do no wrong, but then if a woman looks like Erica and takes pleasure in making the best of herself, then of course she can do no wrong.

She moved an inch or so closer to him, if he'd done the same they might have been able to reach across the barrier that divided them.

His back towards her, his eyes wide open, Teddy hid his unease behind a pretence of sleep just as recently he'd hidden it behind his anger at Jennifer. Not that I haven't meant every word I've said, he told himself silently, she's betraying James and the children. Dear God how must he feel tonight, knowing that tomorrow she'll be sharing the cottage with her girlfriend? That's what she is, it all falls into place. But to take her there, to behave like that in *my* cottage! The place will be full of memories, doesn't she care that it's the home where she and James and the children have holidayed together? And Claudia upholds the bitch, plays into her hand! She's awake, I know she is. I want to hold her, to be deep inside her, to know we're together in this. She wouldn't try to stop me, and afterwards I'd sleep. Sleep and escape – escape what? We haven't quarrelled, for all her championing of Jennifer I know her heart's with James. But there's no unity. No, that's not true, it can't be true, Claudia and I have always had unity. So what's gone wrong? She's on the defensive, I can feel she's guarded. One move and I could be on top of her, that's where I want to be. She wouldn't push me away, but she would feel used. What's happened to us? How can that cursed wife of James's drive us apart like this?

Worry, tension, anger, emotions that filled him with physical energy until minutes later he made that one move. Wordlessly he forced himself on her, wordlessly she received him. She felt no warmth of love, only his desperate need for physical relief, quick, rough and demanding.

So soon he was blissfully exhausted. He'd told himself he couldn't do it to her, she'd feel used. Wrong. In truth she felt untouched.

'Let's get to sleep,' he murmured, his back once again to her and already three quarters there himself. 'It's late. I have a busy day ahead tomorrow.'

'Bully for you!' Claudia's childishly rude answer sprang from her lips of its own volition.

She felt isolated, lonelier than she could ever remember. Jennifer had a duty to James, isn't that what Teddy had said? A duty to be used like that? And be grateful? For Teddy and her, sex had always been an expression of love, sometimes gentle, sometimes passionate, sometimes a lusty romp, but always it had held them close in unity and love. Perhaps that was because life had always been easy, until now they'd never had to stand by helplessly and watch someone they loved suffer. So what was she saying? That she and Teddy couldn't withstand life's knocks, that they pulled in opposite directions? Determinedly she closed her mind to him; she was frightened to let herself think of James. Easier to retreat into memories of Adrian, willingly she let herself sink into that half sleeping and half waking state where dreams merge with memories. In a symbolic gesture she hunched the duvet around her shoulders, turning her back on Teddy.

Paula stood back to admire their handiwork. The stall looked as attractive as any, more attractive than many. Her white, even teeth clamping her bottom lip she looked as excited as a child. The West Country Craft Show was open to the trade on Saturday, and to the public on Sunday. Now, on the Friday evening, she was ready for the crowds!

'I think that's it. We're ready for battle to commence.' She smiled at Jenny, indeed she smiled at the world at the beginning of this weekend she'd worked towards for months.

'I hope you won't get more orders than you can cope with. You're single-handed.' Jennifer, too, envisaged the impact of Paula's intricate and delicate carving.

'There's only one Picasso, only one Henry Moore.' Paula laughed, recognizing she was over estimating her abilities and revelling in hearing herself do it.

'Let's put the shrouds on, then we'll stop and get some fish and chips for supper and take to the cottage.' Already Jennifer was covering the stall, stowing away the locked cases of spare stock. She liked to think they were working as a team at the Craft Show: Paula had the talent, but on days like this one had been, her own practical contribution was just as necessary.

She looked forward to getting to the cottage. Mrs Freeman from next door had promised to see it was warm, the beds aired and two

41

pints of milk in the fridge. As for the rest, it was the practical Jenny who had packed a box of groceries.

They took the Plymouth road out of Exeter. She'd stayed at the cottage several times, but always in the summer and always with James and the children. For a brief moment she wished she'd resisted James's suggestion that she and Paula should go to Moorleigh. In the unfamiliar surroundings of a hotel in Exeter she wouldn't have been haunted by memories, nudged by her conscience that this afternoon had been the Nativity play at school. She had wondered as she cut up an old sheet for Patsy's costume and a faded curtain for Barry's whether they had been given the roles of Mary and Joseph on merit or because they were the children of the rectory. Mrs Humphreys, the head teacher, came under the bracket she mentally called 'high days Christian'; probably she was expecting her act wouldn't go unnoticed, it couldn't do any harm to keep on the right side of the rector, it might even get her a seat nearer the front in heaven. On the other hand, the proud mother in Jenny argued, they had been the right choice, they'd learnt their words perfectly and wouldn't let the side down by mumbling. James would have been there to see them. Conscience, guilt, both of those were whispering 'You should have been there with him, when they looked at the rows of parents in those horrid little chairs, they ought to have seen both of you.' Yet this afternoon she'd been so busy working with Paula, half past two had passed and she hadn't given a thought to the start of the performance.

'Turn left here, Paula.' Approaching the crossroads she woke from her reverie.

'Are you sure? The sign said Moorleigh to the right.'

'We have to get the fish and chips, remember? There's a super shop just down the hill as you go into Deremouth. You're not fussy about the smell in the car? Some people won't have it.'

'I shall love it,' Paula laughed. 'If it lingers, it will remind me of this evening. Free of everyone and everything. If it weren't so cold, we could be really abandoned and eat it from the paper in the car. Is this the shop? You stay in the car, I'll get them.'

Jenny's mood was lifted. She felt ridiculously young and carefree. No-one could make any demands on her, the telephone wouldn't ring in the middle of a meal, she wouldn't be expected to take down details of the hymns for a funeral or arrange when James would be free to talk to a young couple about to get married. What if it were her job to talk to them? What would she say, how could she prepare them? She wouldn't think about it, not tonight, not this weekend. It was a relief to see Paula coming back with a well wrapped package.

Then a three-point turn in the empty road and they headed back towards Moorleigh.

Claudia and the children had often come down during the Christmas school holidays. It had been easier to get a locum then than in the summer so usually Teddy had come too. Walking on Dartmoor had been the attraction, the moor in winter, wild and empty, then home to the snug warmth of the cottage. Snug warmth in a house left unoccupied all day only came from central heating and that had been high on the list of priorities.

The heating had been on since Claudia spoke to Mrs Freeman the previous day, so this evening warmth met them as they went through the front door. This was better than any hotel, or so thought Paula. Jenny was less at ease, too many ghosts were waiting for her. But she was determined that nothing would spoil this weekend, she felt it was symbolic, it was her way of proving to herself that she was still her own person, she had a life outside the demands of the village and the family.

How companionable it was, pulling the small table near the electric fire (an unnecessary extra), uncorking a bottle of wine, then settling down to demolish fried plaice and a huge pile of chips. At home she never bought chips, for one thing they were too expensive and for another she considered them an unhealthy diet. But this evening she relished them for that very reason. To hell with being careful and sensible! Across the small table she smiled at her friend.

'We're like a pair of old maids, all we need is a cat curled up in front of the fire.'

'Men!' Paula scoffed, 'Who needs them? Not us.'

'Let's talk about tomorrow. Are you putting a limit on the orders you can take? Tomorrow will be trade people, they probably won't want one of this and one of that, especially when they see what you do.'

'I think I'm going to have to play it by ear. Don't take any orders without referring to me first, at least that way I can give a delivery date I feel I can keep. You know Jenny, this is a wonderful opportunity for getting orders, but what we really need is a place of our own, a base and an outlet to the public.'

'But there couldn't be any scope in Brightley.' Jenny had no intention of letting them get carried away making plans for the impossible.

'Bugger Brightley. Maybe in Oxford, there are always tourists there, masses of Americans. And we could advertise in the weekend papers sometimes if things were slow. I could get lots of press coverage when we opened the shop, Sydney's name is useful.'

'You mean Sydney would be prepared to be involved?' Jenny was

43

surprised and, although she wasn't certain why, she was disappointed that Paula was prepared to use him when it suited her.

'I could probably persuade him to do something, even to organize a publicity stunt of him making it an official opening, but we wouldn't need him once we were launched. As well we wouldn't, he's much too busy being interested in his own affairs.' Paula refilled their glasses. 'Don't let's talk about husbands, homes, not this evening.' She raised her glass, her blue eyes smiling over the rim. 'To us, to the miracle that brought me to Brightley, to the months that have brought us to this.'

Jenny sipped her drink, then added a toast of her own:

'To the success of the weekend and to the future.' Then another afterthought: 'I give you Picasso ... Henry Moore ... Paula Stonehouse.'

She was glad she'd come, she hadn't any regrets. So why did she have to keep telling herself so? It was nearly nine o'clock when she decided to ring home.

'Leave them, Jenny. You sound like some fussy old hen. They'll be enjoying their freedom just as much as you are.'

But Jenny liked to make her own decisions. She dialled the familiar number.

'Brightley Rectory,' Barry's voice answered her in his best telephone manner. She could imagine him standing in the hall, pencil and pad ready to write down the message. For James must be out or he would have answered the call himself.

'It's me. Mum.'

'Cor, that's good. Hey, Patsy, it's Mum. Is it all right there Mum? When are you coming home?'

'It's fine. I'm at the cottage.'

'Lucky thing! Wish we were.'

She wished they were too, she felt quite weak with wishing it.

'How was the play? I was thinking about you.' Surely it was better to lie than tell them she'd not given anything at Brightley a thought all afternoon?

'That was OK. Dad came. He seemed to like it. Not many fathers, mostly it was mums. Hey, Patsy, don't you want to speak to Mum?'

Patsy was less effusive, there was a coolness in her greeting. She was angry that her mother had preferred to go off with Pushy Paula instead of coming to school.

'Hello.'

'I wanted to know about the play. Did you remember your words, Patsy?'

'Yes, 'course I did. Aren't you going to tell us it's time we were in

44

bed? Isn't that why you phoned, to make sure we weren't doing anything wrong?'

'I just wanted to speak to you.' Jenny knew Patsy wanted to hurt her, for a second she was tempted to blunder on with explanations that would have been far beyond the child's years. But she pulled herself together and put the familiar spirit in her voice. 'Now you come to mention it, why aren't you both in bed? I take it your father isn't there?'

'It's Friday. Have you forgotten he's out on Fridays? He's not back from choir practice yet.'

'Patsy, when he comes in, tell him I phoned, tell him I'm glad he thought about us using the cottage. Mrs Freeman had been in and got it ready. Now I'll really make you jealous – we've just had shop fish and chips for supper.'

'I expect that was nice.' She spoke with the cool composure of an offended adult.

'Patsy . . .'

'Yes?'

'Nothing really. You're sure everything's all right?'

'Course it is. After school me and Barry and Daddy sorted out our jobs. He wrote a list and pinned it to the reminder board.' With a childlike giggle of delight she couldn't repress, she bragged: 'You know what he put at the top of the page? He put "Rota for the A Team". That's us. The A Team.' Standing close by, Barry frowned at her. It was beastly of her to talk to Mum like that, as if they were shutting her out. He nudged his young sister with his elbow to make sure his glare was noticed. 'Ouch, stop thumping me Barry.'

'Well done.' Jenny didn't let them think she'd heard. 'It's lovely to know I needn't worry.'

'I told you, we are absolutely fine.'

'I'll be home by the time you get in from school on Monday.'

'Yes. You said.'

'Give Daddy my love. Tell him I'm OK.'

She heard a skirmish as Barry took the receiver.

''Bye Mum. I'll tell Dad. See you Monday.'

It was Barry's eager voice that brought home close. Tomorrow she'd find something nice in Exeter to take back to them. Needing to keep herself busy she stacked the supper plates on to a tray.

'While you rinse those things I'll go and run a bath,' Paula told her. 'Messing about in that hall makes one feel so soiled.'

A minute later, the bath tap turned full on, she was back downstairs carrying a silk nightie and matching negligée.

45

'You didn't tell me there was no radiator in the bathroom. I'm going to undress down here by the fire.'

'OK. I'll be out of your way, I'm in the kitchen.'

Already Paula's shirt was off and she was stepping out of her jeans. Jenny picked up the tray and turned away. She felt uncomfortably aware of her friend's scantily clad body, wearing only the briefest of pants and bra. Rattling the crockery, letting the water gush into the sink, she made a parade of the few dishes. When she peeped back into the sitting room Paula had gone, her clothes strewn where she'd shed them.

Jenny looked down at her own chunky figure, in self-mockery she picked up the bra and held it in front of her. Flopping into an armchair she still held the garment, so feminine, provocative . . . Her imagination was running riot. Supposing she'd been glamorous and sexy, the sort of woman who could wear these little nonsenses, would that have made a difference to the way things were? She threw the bra to land on the rug with the rest of the things and with disgust let her hands explore her thick waist and rounded stomach. Into her mind sprang a picture of herself in the lacy garments – if such things were made in her size! came the scathing rider. What was the matter with her? First she complained that she wanted a life of her own, a chance to use her own skills, her own brain; and yet as soon as she got away she was dreaming of awakening some latent passion in James. Was that the root of the trouble? If she could drive him wild with desire for her, would she accept without complaint being used by the parish as a doormat?

'You're a long time clearing up,' came a call from Paula.

'Nearly done.'

'Good. The water's piping hot.'

'It's a big tank. I'll have mine as soon as you've done. But no hurry.'

The interchange hadn't broken her train of thought. She went back to the question. Jenny's honesty never let her duck the truth. And the truth was that she could never be glamorous, hers had never been the sort of body that could turn a man's mind to sex. It was easier to look as though she weren't interested, hide behind shapeless clothes, jeans and huge sloppy jumpers, skirts that fitted where they touched and didn't touch anywhere. Was James ashamed of her? He certainly couldn't be proud. In the beginning, to make up to him for her failings she'd thrown herself into the parish work, taken on more than she need. Yet it was *his* world, it wasn't hers and never could be. So resentment had crept in . . . strengthened and grown . . . grown and strengthened.

46

'Jenny, aren't you finished?'

'Yes, I'll bring your things and put them in your room, shall I?'

'Here a minute.'

The prudish streak in Jenny was uncomfortable at being summoned into the bathroom. But she mustn't let Paula suspect that's how she reacted, Paula was uninhibited, a woman of today's world; not like her, full of hang-ups from a narrow childhood with elderly parents in academic surroundings.

The steam filled room smelt of expensive bath oils.

'Have you forgotten something?' Jenny asked from the half open doorway.

'I'm lonely in here all by myself. Come and talk to me. Sit on the edge of the bath.' She raised one leg as she lay on her back, surveyed it critically, then slowly lowered it.

Self-consciously, Jenny perched on the rim.

'Come up this end, then you can do my back for me,' Paula passed her the soap. 'I was never much good at school, but I loved the intimacy. Bathtime was always fun. Did you board?'

'No. I'm not much good at – well – intimate sorts of things.'

'But Jenny darling, intimate only means familiar. Do you sit on the bath and talk to your James?'

'In our house bathing is jump in, a quick wash and jump out. The bathroom's huge and like an icebox. Even the perfume in here is relaxing.'

'Ummmm.' It was almost a purr. 'That's lovely on my back. Now my shoulders.'

'You can reach those.' Jenny pushed the soap at her and dried her hands.

'School, I was talking about school. It wasn't any great shakes if you judge it on A Levels, university places and so forth, but it taught me a lot else – wood carving to name but one. An odd sort of place, there were only about twenty-five boarders, some as young as seven, some right up to eighteen. In my class there were three of us. Intimate, familiar, whatever name you give it it's the same. We knew everything there was to know about each other as we grew up. Examined each step towards adolescence with far more interest than we had for algebra or history. I didn't grow up thinking there were parts of me that had nothing to do with living.' She gave herself a final rinse. 'That's me done. Pass me that towel can you.'

It would have been natural for Jenny to avert her eyes as she passed it. But she felt flattered and excited that Paula had called her in, had shown that she thought of them as intimates. How pretty she was

47

with her red-gold hair pinned on top of her hair and tied round with a white band, her figure so pale and slender. Hardly realising what she did Jenny wrapped the towel around her as she stepped from the bath.

'Don't let the water go.' Reared on economy, Jenny couldn't see that glorious bath oil wasted while the water was still hot. 'I'll hop in quickly.'

Paula glanced at her, surprised and pleased. Jenny's next words showed her she'd misconstrued the invitation for her to stay, their positions reversed while she sat on the rim of the bath.

'You go on down into the warm – dry by the fire. I'll only be two shakes.'

'OK. See you downstairs in a few minutes.'

Instinct told Paula that Jenny hadn't come to the stage when she could take her clothes off with an audience. So, humming contentedly, the towel secured around her and her nightie and negligée on her arm, she went back to the fireside.

One bottle of wine finished and a new one opened, they talked more freely than ever they had. Jenny's cheeks were exceptionally red, probably from a combination of wine and warmth. Or it could have had to do with Paula's uninhibited disclosures of her disappointment in married life with Sydney.

'We've come to a sort of mutual arrangement, at least most of the time. I see the home is run efficiently, if he brings friends home for weekends, or invites people useful to his career, then I never let him down.'

It was impossible to imagine that any man could be less than proud to present her as his wife, she was beautiful, she could be the perfect hostess. Listening to her, knowing herself to be one of those chosen to be her 'intimate', Jenny even felt herself to be more attractive. Small wonder if her face became flushed. She'd had plenty of women acquaintances in the parish, but never a friend until Paula had come to Brightley. Claudia, her mother-in-law, was the nearest she had come to finding a friend, but there were some things you could talk about to a mother-in-law and some you couldn't. Not that she was doing much of the talking. To start with she'd wished Paula wouldn't disclose the intimate details of her marriage so openly, no-one had ever said things like that to her before.

'Jenny, you've listened, you've understood,' Paula dropped so gracefully to her knees on the hearthrug. 'I know why you've understood. Because you and I deep down are the same.'

'Well, of course we are. We've been friends from the start.'

'More than that. More than you even realize. Jenny, my dear innocent Jenny, I love you, I want us to be together.'

Jenny's heart was pounding, she could feel it in her chest, she could feel the pulse in her neck. What was Paula suggesting?

'We've drunk too much wine.' She snatched at the first excuse that came into her head, instinctively pulling the tie belt of her candlewick dressing gown tighter around her thick waist. She wanted to make it easy for Paula's words to be glossed over and forgotten. 'Let's leave these glasses for morning and get to bed. We ought to be away by half past eight.'

'Jenny, you're lonely and miserable,'

'You imagine things.' Jenny stood up, she wanted the evening over before it was spoilt beyond redemption.

'I don't. I can read you, I know you haven't found what it is you're looking for.' Paula got to her feet. 'You wash his socks, iron his shirts, oh yes and I expect you roll over when he has a mind for it. Is that the sum total of life? It needn't be. When did you last have an evening like this? We're kindred spirits. Yet you hold yourself away from me. Let me in, Jenny, I want to know everything, all that you are.'

Jenny was out of her depth. All she wanted was to get away to her solitary bedroom. She was unprepared for Paula suddenly dropping to her knees, the warmth of her hand as it touched her leg. And Paula was unprepared for the sudden movement that knocked her off-balance, leaving her sprawled across the hearthrug.

'Get up.' Jenny's strong hands half lifted her as she got to her feet.

Paula was trembling and not far from tears.

'I shouldn't have done that – didn't mean to – please Jenny, say it's all right.'

'Forget it. It's the excitement of the Show, that and too much wine. Let's go to bed.' There was nothing in Jenny's capable voice to hint how unnerved she felt. She switched off the fire, went to the kitchen to lock the back door, anything to keep moving, to give them time to regain an outer composure.

One behind the other they went up the narrow stairway.

The evening had been all Paula had hoped for, until she'd moved too fast. Every instinct in her told her that they had been on the same wavelength, she'd even seen confirmation of it in Jenny's invitation that they come to the cottage.

'Take the electric blanket out of your bed before you get in, it's the oldfashioned sort, you mustn't lie on it. Sleep well.' Jenny's prim tone made it impossible for Paula to do anything but turn away into her own room.

*

49

Surprisingly once in a warm bed Jenny was asleep in minutes.

It was still quite dark when she turned over in her sleep, even the presence of a warm body close by her didn't immediately wake her, it was normal for her not to sleep alone. What wasn't normal was the gentle caressing of soft, warm hands. She moaned softly without waking, moving closer to the probing warmth.

'Don't send me away. Let me stay, let me be close to you.'

'What . . .? Who . . .?' Her wits were coming back to her.

Paula's only answer was to move her hands away, Jenny might have imagined her touch. The dark room was full of silence.

'Go back to your own room,' Jenny said at last, uncertain how much had been real and how much she'd dreamt. She spoke quietly, almost as if by keeping her voice low she could hold away from what she didn't want to know.

'Let me stay. Jenny, I can read you, you can't pretend to me that you don't need the sort of love we could find together. How can a man ever understand? Not like we can. Let me stay. You want to love me, Jenny. I know you do. You want me to love you.'

The caress of her hand spoke even more clearly than her words. Jenny jerked away and clambered out of bed.

'You're mad! What the hell game do you think you're playing.' No longer did she keep her voice down.

'It's not a game.' Paula was crying, kneeling up in bed now, her hands reaching out towards Jenny. 'Hold me. I love you. It could be wonderful, better than you know. Let me show you.'

'Get out of my room.' This time she shouted. Did Paula guess that she was whipping up her anger to crush a yearning she didn't try to understand? 'I believe you came here meaning this to happen!'

'Of course I did. So did you. Don't pretend, Jenny. Oh we could be so complete, yes, Jenny, yes, yes, yes.' There was a threat of hysteria in Paula's crying now as she got off the bed and tried to shake Jenny's solid form.

Unprepared for the sudden movement as Paula pushed her, she tottered to fall back across the pillows. She was so much bigger, so much stronger, yet in that second Paula was in control. Marriage to James hadn't prepared her for this. Shock seemed to paralyse her, but only for seconds. Paula had said that together they could be complete. Her body was alive with repressed longing, but her mind was sickened.

With a violent movement – all the more violent because she was frightened by her own response – she threw Paula away from her. There was a crash as the bedside chair was knocked over.

'I told you to get out! I meant it! And in the morning I want you gone.'

'You're a hypocrite,' Paula yelled, 'that's what you are. You think you can make me believe you get all you want from that Holy Jo of a husband. Easy enough to get a couple of children, but how often has he ever loved you till you've ached with loving? Never!'

'Shut up and get out.'

'It's true. You know it's true.'

'The only thing that's true is that you make me feel soiled, degraded. If that's how your intimates behave, then thank God I'm a loner.' She'd been so proud of her friendship. What a gullible fool she was.

Without another word Paula left her. She lay where she'd fallen, drained of all strength. From the next room she could hear sounds of departure, doors being slammed shut, first the wardrobe, then the bedroom and finally the front door. Then she click of high heels on the brick path, the wooden gate left swinging to rattle, the engine starting. Paula had gone.

'. . . loved you till you ached with loving.' Alone Jenny had nowhere to hide from the truth.

Chapter 4

It was second nature to Jenny to be methodical, automatically she went through the cottage checking each room to see it was left tidy. She emptied the kettle, tipped away the remains of the milk, made sure the electric plugs were all pulled out of their sockets and the curtains drawn evenly. Then, satisfied, she hung her bag from her shoulder and picked up her holdall.

Saturday morning, not yet ten o'clock, her weekend of liberated freedom was over before it had begun. She was going home. But first she had to return the key to old Mrs Freeman in the neighbouring cottage. The door was opened almost as she touched the knocker.

'I happened to be by the window,' Mrs Freeman explained needlessly. 'What's this, then? Luggage? You're not off already? I must have misunderstood young Claudia,' she was an octogenarian plus five, thirty years ahead of 'young Claudia', 'I took you to be here all over the weekend.'

'No, just the one night. It was lovely and warm for us, thank you so much for switching everything on.'

'Where's your friend gone? I thought I heard the car go off before first light. Isn't she coming back to collect you?'

'No.' Jenny knew Bertha Freeman well enough to realize some sort of a tale would be necessary. It was surprisingly easy to pluck one out of the air. 'She had to rush off early to collect some more things she'll need in Exeter. Once the Show is on it's easier for her to stay in the city. I only came down to help her set up her stand yesterday – and you know I never miss a chance of coming to Applegarth. That's why I'm returning the key.'

'Not calling back for you? So how are you managing? It's a longish step to the crossroad for a bus.'

'I know, I'm looking forward to it. In fact I thought I'd go on right into Deremouth and get the train from there. The exercise won't do me any harm.'

Life was quiet in Moorleigh, old Mrs Freeman had to make the most of any snippet of interest she could muster. And it was her opinion that the two women had had a bit of a ding-dong before this friend had cleared off so early. It might have been too early for her to have seen much, but she could have sworn she'd heard raised voices.

'I'd have thought that with a motor car she could have slipped back and got you, leaving you to walk all that way with your bag.'

Jenny could tell Bertha Freeman wasn't entirely satisfied with the tale she'd been told.

'I can't arrive in Moorleigh in the dark, leave again in the dark, and all by car,' she laughed. 'Moorleigh is a place for walking – you know what my lot are! I'd be ashamed to show my face at home and tell them I haven't so much as crossed Picton Heath. So that's where I'm off, then on down into Deremouth. I can get the train there and change in Exeter.'

'You're a beggar for punishment! I don't know where you get your energy. When I was a girl there was no other way to get down into town. But today's living makes us soft.' She wasn't ready to admit that age had anything to do with it! 'You give my love to that James of yours. Always was a favourite of mine, such a solemn little lad he was when first they started coming here. And your little ones, tell them old Bertha Freeman doesn't forget them. Bet a pound to a penny they can't remember me. Can they?'

'Yes, of course they can.' Could they? Jenny had no idea, but it came naturally to tell the old lady what she wanted to hear. 'They often talk about you.'

She could feel Mrs Freeman's scrutiny. She wasn't a woman to be fooled easily. Even so, her next remark came as a shock.

'You're a good woman Jennifer. I'm not asking for your confidences – none of my business and you can tell me so to my face – but just you bear in mind that there isn't a single life that runs its course smoothly. James all right is he?' Clearly an invitation for Jenny to unburden herself.

'He's fine. Very busy. Brightley is a scattered parish, he's had to take in two outlying churches. As far as services go, it only means that he alternates where he takes Evensong on Sundays, but it gives him a lot of extra visiting.'

'My George worked for the baker here in Moorleigh. Harold Arkwright was master baker in those days. You wouldn't remember George, he's been gone this thirty years. If he had extra hours to do at holiday times and the like, and it meant we didn't have time to get

53

out for a bit of enjoyment, he and I we would have a right good go at old Baker Arkwright – behind his back and out of his hearing, mind you. But we felt the better for it. Not so easy for you and your James when he's extra burdened, he can't come home to you and have a good cuss about *his* Boss.' Then, her eyes bright with mischief, 'If we're to believe all we're told it wouldn't do his chances much good, with a Boss like he's got he even has to watch how he's thinking. So he has to be humble and snatch at all the work that's put his way in the hope of getting another soul in his net.'

Jenny's spontaneous laugh was the first for so long. But it was short lived. There was more truth behind the words than she cared to admit. She was tired of playing second fiddle. And at the thought an image sprang into her mind of the community as an orchestra, his God the conductor on His dais, James the leader of the orchestra, the one who gave the note as the others tuned up, the one who played the melody. *His* melody, but it was God who set the tempo, God who with a wave of His hand could suppress one section to silence and raise another in a mighty crescendo. And as for her, whoever heard a second fiddle? Better to play a triangle, perhaps only strike one clear tone, but at least it would be heard, it would be solo.

'A pity you can't stay a day or two, Jennifer child, you look as though you need a rest.'

'I look a sight, that's nearer the truth.' The words escaped her, she could feel the corners of her mouth twitching out of control.

'That you most certainly do *not*. You look the same as the day your James brought you to meet me. Proud as a peacock he was. Just a mite tired, that's the only difference. Look at us, all this time on the doorstep, anyone would think it was summer instead of Christmas only just round the corner. Why don't you come in for ten minutes before you set off on your walk.'

'I'd love to, Mrs Freeman, but I'm not going to. I want to be in Exeter by lunch time. You've got the key back haven't you?'

'In my pinny pocket. I'll hang it straight back on its hook. Now you come back soon, bring the children. Tell James from me, doesn't matter how good a Boss he has, he's not going to turn himself into a saint by working every hour of the day. Anyway,' she chuckled, 'who'd want to be tied to a saint? Not me, that's for sure. That's one thing I never did have to worry about, my George was always ready for a bit of fun.'

Jenny leant forward and kissed the wrinkled cheek, surprising herself by the action. What was the magic formula that, widowed for three decades, yet the old lady could still look back and be warmed by her memories?

Another minute and, bag slung on one shoulder, holdall on the other, she was striding away from the cluster of houses around Moorleigh Green, Bertha Freeman standing on a footstool by the front window to get a better view of her retreating figure. A sight, she'd said she looked a sight! How could a woman with a good, honest face like that ever look a sight? She must mean because she wasn't all prettied up-to-the-minute like her friend who'd gone off this morning; too dark to see her, but she could tell by the click-click of her high heels she was a very different kettle of fish from James's Jenny. Broad across the beam to be wearing trousers, but a healthy looking body of a woman. Ah, you knew where you were with Jennifer Carlyle, what you saw was the real thing, no fol-di-rols. Gone out of sight now. Could have sworn young Claudia said they'd be here all weekend. You don't listen properly, Bertha Freeman, that's your trouble, you're getting old and silly. Or was there something they didn't tell you?

Once away from the village Jenny slackened her pace. She'd made up her mind to go home, but home was hours away, hours that were solitary and precious. She must think. She must use her time in trying to untangle her emotions, look at each strand.

Last night was one she wanted to forget. But not yet. First she had to look at it squarely. It had happened, so it couldn't be ignored. To run away from it would leave it for ever as a scar. So much of her friendship with Paula had been good. Or had it? For her it had, she had luxuriated in the warm companionship of a real friend. She had felt herself enriched by it. And all the time, perhaps all the weeks leading up to the weekend, had she and Paula been moving towards different goals? She shied from the memory of waking to the touch of Paul's warm hand. And yet she must think of it, she must even carry her thoughts forward picturing what so easily might have been ahead of them. Only then could she throw out the whole incident, discard the real with the imagined.

She couldn't go home and not be able to tell them she'd walked on Picton Heath, she'd said. Yet here she was, marching along the narrow road that cut through the heathland to cross the main Plymouth to Exeter road, and she was seeing none of it. Instead she was back in the cottage, hearing the sound of Paula's crying, remembering her words, '. . . could be complete', '. . . loved till you ached with loving . . .'

When had things first started to go wrong between James and her? In the dark bedroom she had made herself face the situation squarely, not lay blame so much as trace the road back, find where they had gone off course. So back she traversed, not ducking what she didn't want to see. The first coldness, the first need to rebuff each other, had come at about the same time that she'd grown discontented with sharing James with the parish. But hadn't she always shared him? Go back further, back to the happy times . . . be honest. The parish had always made the same demands on him, he wasn't a man who could give less than his best. So was the fault all hers? Start from the other end, start from the beginning of their marriage. Just the two of them – but there had always been the parish. She hadn't minded, she had wanted to help him, share his work, share his people; only it hadn't worked like that, her place had been to serve not to share. So soon she'd been pregnant, their future had been secure and perfect. By the time Barry started to walk she'd been expecting Patsy. She had her babies with the ease of any peasant woman, and while they'd been small and dependent her life had been full. Then they'd started school, first Barry then Patsy. With no small 'helper' the upkeep of that huge uncomfortable house had become a thankless chore. No, be fair, be honest: the house was no bigger, no colder, than it had been in the beginning. It wasn't the house you came to hate – yes, hate, say it again, hate, hate, hate – it was the parish. You cooked meals, occasionally we were all together to eat them, but the parishioners always had to come first. Someone was in trouble, someone had been taken to hospital, someone's husband had beaten her up, someone's daughter was 'in trouble' and someone else's had run away from her husband: whatever the call on James, he was there. He had time for everyone else. Everyone but me?

On she strode, the heath behind her now as she crossed the main road and started down the long hill towards Deremouth.

If she'd been a member of his congregation (oh, but she was, that too was part of her duties, she thought bitterly), if she'd been a *voluntary* member of his congretation he would have made time for her. So why didn't he hear her cry for help? Why didn't he care that she was bored. Mentally she tripped on the word. Bored? That's what she told him, that's what she'd made herself believe. But today was Truth Day. To let herself be bored was a sin against her intelligence, but it was easier to sink into boredom than to face up to the root of her misery. He accepted her as his secretary,. housekeeper, cook, methodical in what she did, methodical and uncaring; he was polite, cool, apologetic when he was unpunctual – but then so he would be to a secretary, housekeeper, cook.

What were they doing to the children? She remembered her happiness when they were small, her thankfulness that they would have a home where there was laughter, love. That's what all children deserved. Didn't they? Look back to your own childhood, where was the laughter there? Was there love? There must have been, a sort of dried up affection, respect. Was that why I grew up like I did, full of inhibitions? Perhaps my parents were satisfied with what they had, perhaps that's all there ever is once the first excitement is gone.

Hardly realizing how far she'd walked, Jenny found herself in Deremouth. At the railway station she bought a ticket to Oxford. Brightley had no railway, the last part of her journey would be by bus. There was a London train due in five minutes, stopping at Reading. She'd change there for the Oxford train. Already it was lunch time, she couldn't possibly get home until evening. Imagine their surprise . . . she could picture Barry's smile, the thought of it gave her spirit its first jolt upwards. She was less certain about Patsy – and James? Of course he'd be glad to see her home sooner than he'd expected, she was the oiler of wheels, the smoother of paths.

The train was almost full, most people seemed to be secure in seats previously booked. After walking through three compartments she found an empty seat. A young man sitting opposite her went off to buy himself some food and came back with two rounds of pallid sandwiches and a tin of beer. The triangular slices of bread, two of their edges soft pale brown crust, had little to commend them but Jenny needed the comfort of eating so she lurched through two swaying compartments and joined the queue in the buffet car. The return journey gave her only one free hand to grab the seats as she made her unsteady progress, in the other she clutched a polystyrene container into which were crammed a double round of cheese and tomato sandwich, an apple, a bar of chocolate and a large coffee (or was it tea?). There was still an hour and forty minutes to kill before they were due at Reading, after her morning of self-analysis her mind was too numb to think.

At last she bundled out on to the crowded platform, jostled by those pushing to get in while there were still vacant seats. She checked the timetable on the wall to find the platform and time for the next train to Oxford. In an hour there was one heading north, Oxford its first stop. That was what she'd anticipated, it would get her there in time for a bus to Brightley. But suddenly and quite positively she saw what she meant to do. The slow train, a Sprinter, was due out in forty minutes. It stopped at every station and halt, it wouldn't arrive in Oxford until long after the other one; but that didn't matter, by then she wouldn't be on it. Goring and Streatley. Often she and James had come that way when they'd been going down to Russets, but that wasn't why she wanted to go there. Her memories of the district went back much further.

In the buffet on Reading Station she sipped a black coffee and dug her teeth into a spiced currant bun. That there were only five currants went unnoticed. Jenny felt a strange tug of excitement. She knew just how it would be as she emerged from the station at Goring, left and immediately left again over the railway, she could picture it clearly. On along the road to where the bridge spanned the Thames, dividing the twin villages of Goring and Streatly. She'd been seventeen when she'd gone to spend the long summer holiday with the Sheldrakes. Her parents had had the address given to them by their doctor. At the time she hadn't wanted to accompany her mother. Although she was still at school she was no longer a child, she resented having her arrangements made for her. She'd wanted to spend her spare time with 'Second Chance', a voluntary organization to help the illiterate. That was something worth doing. To fritter the summer holiday away with nothing to do but roam the lanes appalled her. But her father had insisted it was her duty to do something for her mother for a change. When Mrs Sheldrake had written suggesting she should bring her bike the prospect had brightened. Always a loner, her mother had been over forty and her father nearly fifty when she was born, both academics who needed no child in their lives. They had never been unkind to her, but even in her early years Jennifer – for they never shortened her name – had taken it for granted that she should make herself as inconspicuous as possible. She'd never been allowed to bring a friend home, nor to join in outside activities that they considered unsuitable. There had been no television in the house, the radio had been strictly for news bulletins, discussions or the occasional opera or symphony concert. Not unnaturally the circle of schoolfriends had closed leaving her on the outside. A psychologist would have understood why the plump little hand was so often in the biscuit tin, and why as she grew bigger a bike ride on her own had more purpose to it if there was a packet of food in her saddle bag to be eaten in some isolated country spot. When they'd stayed with the Sheldrakes her mother had been recovering from surgery, the doctor had suggested a long rest in the country. Mrs Sheldrake was a qualified nurse, no longer working officially, but with three spare bedrooms in the family home she was always glad to take semi-invalid guests.

Jenny remembered the background of the visit, but it wasn't that that drew her back today, a day when she was taking stock of her life.

Claudia always wrote her cards in the kitchen, spreading them in sets on the table, chosing the right one for each person. To do them on the dining table, or sitting at the bureau in the drawing room, wouldn't have been the same thing at all. There was a changelessness about the Aga-warmed room, with its old-fashioned dresser and scrubbed wooden table that suited the occasion. It was a task she looked forward to, never ceasing to get from it the same undefined flutter of childlike excitement that she still felt when the Christmas tree was erected on Avonford village centre. Even to Teddy she had never confided the importance, almost solemnity, of the Monday afternoon before the last guaranteed posting date each year. Card writing was *her* job, Teddy might make a suggestion – don't forget so-and-so has changed his address, or we ought to add this person or that to the list – but it had always been Claudia who chose the cards and wrote them. Some of them needed letters to be enclosed, but those she had written in readiness so nothing got in the way of her steady progress down the long list.

This year she found it hard to concentrate, she even found herself putting the card for the practice's junior partner and his wife into the envelope addressed to Trevor's parents. The trouble was Jenny. Claudia laid down her pen and gave rein to her thoughts, elbows on the table and her chin resting on her clenched hands. If only she could have talked to Teddy, told him how worried she'd been all the weekend, willing the telephone to ring yet dreading that it might. The morning after the birthday party James had entrusted her with a confidence she would never break, not even to Teddy – perhaps especially not to Teddy who was so full of venom towards Jenny. So she must hide her anxiety, act a cheerfulness she didn't feel.

What luck that it had been his Saturday morning for the surgery, and what even greater luck that he'd remembered a job needing his attention on the *Sea Urchin* on Sunday morning, always finding his own special solace amongst the boats on the quay.

The loud tick of the kitchen clock was the only sound as Claudia let her mind drift to mid-morning on Saturday, the shrill bell of the telephone. When she answered it, it was to hear the unmistakable voice of Bertha Freeman.

'I thought you'd like to have a quick word from me, to let you know Jennifer has gone off safe and well this morning. Silly me, you know what I took you to say? I expected she and her friend were going to be here until Monday.'

Claudia's mind had never worked faster. Don't sound surprised! Don't let dear nosy old Mrs Freeman guess at the surge of thankfulness! So Jenny hadn't stayed, she'd gone home to James and the children.

'I expect it was all our chattering, Mrs Freeman. I ought to have made it clearer. I probably said I *wished* they could stay until Monday, I think every woman deserves a break from family once in a way. How was she? Of course there's not a hope of their getting down for Christmas, but I expect James will bring them for a night or so before school starts again.'

'How was she, you say. I'll not make a secret of it, I was worried about the girl. She looked well enough, don't misunderstand me, a mite tired but well enough. There was something about her though. Edgy, that's how she seemed. No troubles with the little ones are there?'

'No, they're fine, and James too. I expect she was worried, leaving them to look after themselves. She promised to give me a ring this evening when she gets home.' She amazed herself how she could lie so convincingly. 'Now tell me, are you going to your daughter for Christmas the same as usual?'

The subject had been turned, Mrs Freeman seemed satisfied with the explanations.

When Teddy came home from surgery what was it stopped her mentioning the call? Surely nothing would please him more than knowing the pull of home had been too great for Jenny to resist. Yet lately it had been easier to avoid talking about her at all. Up until his birthday, to Claudia and without any real malice, he'd openly voiced his opinion of James's choice of a wife. Yet, over these last weeks, he'd not mentioned her; a call to Brightley, or even talking to James or the children, always gave him a closed-in expression that warned her off the subject. So on Saturday when he'd arrived home with the suggestion that they should have a pub lunch at Burley then drive on to Lymington or Christchurch for oddments for the Christmas tree, she'd snatched at the offer of normality and, basking in the relief of Mrs Freeman's call, had willingly and thankfully put James and Jennifer out of her mind.

Although she had told Mrs Freeman that Jenny had promised to phone on Saturday evening, she'd said it to give substance to her story, not really expecting a call. So when she hadn't heard, she hadn't been bothered, instead she'd enjoyed imagining the excitement at the Rectory.

Sunday and, breakfast eaten, Teddy was away. If he was surprised she hadn't suggested going to the boat with him he didn't say so, she suspected he was looking for solitude. He'd come home in a much lighter frame of mind, *Sea Urchin* never failed to lift his mood. Add to that the news she would have for him, and the outlook was brighter than it had been for weeks. Morning service – and the

Sunday School timed to coincide with it – at Brightley started at half past ten. By a quarter past twelve she could wait no longer. She wanted to speak to them, not to ask questions, but just to hear the relief in James's voice. She'd pretend to be surprised when he told her that Jenny was home.

'Brightley Rectory, Barry Carlyle speaking.' Bless him, he tried so hard to sound grown up.

'It's me, darling. Gran. I just phoned to see how you're all getting on with Mummy away.' Wait for it, listen for the change in his voice.

'You shouldn't worry, Gran, we're doing pretty well. Do you want to speak to Dad?' It didn't make sense. Did it mean Jenny and this wretched Paula had moved out of the cottage just to go to a hotel? But why? I was so sure she must have gone home. What about those prayers I said, she thought accusingly, asking for Jenny and James to need each other? And James, darling James, he must have prayed. If You didn't listen to me, surely You would to him.

'Is he back from church?' she answered Barry cheerfully.

'Yes, he's just here now. Dad, it's Gran.'

'Mum? Nice of you to be anxious about us. But you mustn't be. We're fine, honestly.'

'Have you got a proper lunch?'

'Can you imagine Jenny leaving us without food? She cooked enough for a siege, the fridge is bulging.'

'James. . . .' Her one word asked a thousand questions. She knew in the pause that followed that for both of them those nighttime moments in the kitchen here at Russetts bridged the miles.

'Mum, she'll be home tomorrow. It's been good for us—'

'And for her, James.' Please God, for her too.

'Yes.' Only a slight pause then, and she was sure for the benefit of the listening children, 'I wish she could see what a good team we are, she'd be proud. Patsy's standing here, she wants to tell you herself.'

'Hello Granny. Dad and Barry and me, we had a – what was it Dad, you know, when we all sat down and you wrote the list?' A prompt from James. 'We had a Cabinet Meeting. That bit's my job, the cabinet and things. You see Dad wrote on a big piece of paper and put it on Mum's reminder board so we can't forget our jobs. Cabinets come under my things, all the dusting and vacuuming are for me. Barry takes Henry for his walks and feeds the cats and the rabbits and sees to the rubbish and shakes the rugs that don't get vacuumed. Oh and he washes up too and I dry. Dad lights the fire, and all the important things. So we are managing 'stremely well.'

'Mummy will be really proud.'

Always the actress, Patsy gave a sign of weariness.

'I'll give you back to Dad.'

'James . . .' And again there was no way she could speak the half understood fear she couldn't escape. 'Have you spoken to Jenny? How's the Show going?'

'She phoned on Friday evening, told the youngsters everything was fine at the cottage – including shop fish and chips which made them feel really hard done by. I didn't speak to her, I wasn't home from choir practice. I tried last night but there was no reply, they must have gone out to eat.'

'Well, wouldn't you?' She laughed. 'They must have been stuck in the hall all day long and fish and chips two nights running – even shop ones – would be a bit much.'

'I'll try again this evening.'

'I expect you'll find the same thing, don't you? They won't be making their own meals. Never mind, love, it'll soon be tomorrow and she'll be home.'

When Teddy had come home to lunch she had kept the same cheery pitch in her voice as she reported her conversation, even managing to make him laugh as she mimicked Patsy's account of the Cabinet Meeting.

Now, reliving her own weekend she saw it, just as these days she saw everything concerning James and his family, against a background that would stay with her as long as she lived: his dear face suddenly unfamiliar as it had contorted in helpless misery, the rasping sobs he couldn't hold back.

'When she gets home,' she begged silently, 'make them see beyond whatever it is that's gone wrong, make things right again.' But even as she asked it, another voice tempted her astray with a reminder that her prayers had been ignored once, what was the use of trying again? Perhaps it was superstition that made her deaf to it, fear that it would count against today's plea. She told herself that when prayers weren't answered straight away, then the only thing to do was to trust, keep faith, never to give any quarter to doubt. Oh, but it was so hard. 'If it were *me* I could bear it, I'd at least have some sort of control. But here I am, miles away from them all. Teddy is so warped about Jenny. What would he say if I told him all I know? Imagine how he'd look if I told him about how miserable James had been that morning – his mouth would be tight, his eyes full of hate. No, I must never do that. When it's all behind them – and please, please let it soon be behind them – Teddy would never forget. He'd say James would be better off without her. Just because he's never taken to her himself, he thinks there can be no right on her side for anything. He's bigoted, takes it for granted that what *he* thinks must be right. If she were a Page 3

62

model he'd have been thrilled for James. The trouble is Teddy sees her as the eternal Martha, he has never understood how James could have wanted her. But today she'll be home, she'll have a good reason for their moving on from the cottage, everything will be explained and I needn't feel I'm the keeper of some guilty secret.' And then, taking no chances: 'Please, I don't know how you'll do it, but please make James happy.'

She took up her pen and made a huge effort to concentrate on her list.

From the station, Jenny set off towards the inn where she meant to book a room. It was more than more than nineteen years since she'd first come to know the village, she couldn't expect it to have remained unaltered. Some buildings untouched by time, some shops with different names over the frontage and plying a different trade, today it seemed that her years were telescoped. Dusk was early, in not much more than a week it would be the shortest day, but with her room booked she wasn't ready to stay indoors. Instead she walked the short way on to stop and gaze from the river bridge. A summertime mecca for visitors, but on this drear December teatime she stood alone, her elbows on the parapet as she gazed.

Her planned weekend in Exeter and Moorleigh had been a means of escape. Not from the endless chores, certainly not from the children, not even from James in those rare moments when they saw each other except as part of his infernal parish. In Brightley she'd been swept along on the current. It wasn't that she was desperate for a career of her own; if she were seen as 'James' wife', that would be fine. But she wasn't. She was the unspoken support of the parish priest. His challenge was to nurture the souls of his flock and in so doing to serve his Boss – her mouth twitched into something like a smile as she remembered old Mrs Freeman. Her position was less clear. That was the trouble, she had no challenge of her own. Or had she? Was hers to accept what she found unacceptable? It wasn't the St Luke's Ladies she resented, nor yet the way they fawned around James, even though she found them irritating: how grown women could wrangle amongst themselves about who made the sausage rolls and who made the mince pies for the Christmas Coffee morning, or who decorated the font and who decorated the pulpit for the Patronal Festival, she could never understand. But those things she could ride. It was the others of the parish, those who might occasionally put in an appearance in church and yet took James for granted, expected him always to be there for them as their right. These were the people she was supposed to subjugate herself to, always to be smiling and friendly, an example of Christian living. Damn them, damn each and every one of them. James bore them no resentment, he tried with endless patience to guide them into his fold. He didn't seem to notice that they only turned to him when they needed something, a sort of 'God belongs to everyone' mentality, which meant that if they thought James wasn't always waiting to receive them with open arms then they saw it as a rejection from on high.

At home on his desk he had a huge pile of Christmas cards, each bearing details of all the services in St Luke's. Next week, when the children had broken up, it would fall to Barry, Patsy and her to hand deliver each one of them. And how many would come to church? Some at midnight on Christmas Eve, straight from their parties and ready to sing lustily; a few extra would join the regulars on Christmas morning, but most of them would say 'Who does he think has time on Christmas Day, what with the turkey to cook, all the excitement of opening the presents, and Aunt Flo to be collected . . .?' If they were short of cards, James's might be put on show to make up the numbers, otherwise it would go straight in the bin.

If James could have suddenly materialized by her side on Streatley Bridge at that moment, Jenny would have held nothing back. She ached with love for him that he could be used so casually. Then her natural spirit got the upper hand. Just because he was prepared to be kicked and come back for more, was that any reason why he should expect her to be fool enough to put up with it? Did he ever consider how she hated trailing up and down garden paths pushing his unwanted cards through letter boxes? Or was he no different from all those others, did he take it for granted she found joy in service?

A swan rose up as if to fly, flapped furiously then relaxed back on to the water to glide gracefully with the stream. Jenny watched, seeing it as a symbol. The lovely bird gave the appearance of being carried by the motion of the water. But it wasn't true. Look at those webbed feet. Dignified, proud, the swan chose its own course as it swam with the current.

With a sigh, she turned away and retraced her steps to the inn where she was staying. Tomorrow she'd climb Streatley Hill. Again time telescoped. Later she would take the lid of that other box of memories, it was important that she did.

The cards written and all seventy six envelopes stamped Claudia put on her sheepskin coat, tied her head in a scarf to save her hair being blown too wildly, then walked into the village to the post box. That's how it happened that she wasn't at home to answer the telephone.

That evening she and Teddy were going to Beeches Lodge to

dinner with Donald and Cynthia Howard-Peters. It was an annual event, black tie, long dress, and unfailingly a spirit of festivity. Known in the village simply as 'the Brigadier', Donald had retired from a career in the army. Cynthia organized with the precision of a Mess party and with such efficiency that the whole event appeared effortless.

'Turn around, let me look at you,' Teddy's tone set Claudia's evening off to a good start. Obligingly, and enjoying his patent admiration, she turned slowly round to show herself off in her new moss green dress. 'You look like a wood nymph,' he told her as he held her wrap to put around her shoulders. 'Claudia – I'm sorry. I've been venting my spite on you. We musn't let it come between us. Say something Claudia.'

'I guess I've been ratty too. She'll be home this evening. Things will be better. Tonight let's forget everything but enjoying ourselves.'

She had no feeling of guilt that she should turn her back on her niggling worries. She was determined this evening would be good, she would concentrate on enjoying herself with Teddy and forget everything – and into this bracket there was no escaping the carefree Claudia who'd walked with Adrian in the autumn glory of the forest, who'd secretly picnicked with him on *Sea Urchin*, who'd gloried in his glances of admiration and felt young and liberated and in whom hope sprang to the surface each time a car slowed down outside or turned into the drive. While the Howard-Peters' party was living up to its usual standard Jenny would be arriving home. The next few hours were their own, hers and Teddy's. With her wrap folded around her she turned and wound her arms around his neck.

'Steady,' he warned, pulling away from her but smiling all the while, clearly liking what she did. 'I don't want all that rubbish from your face over my jacket.'

'There's a way to speak to a girl!' she teased. 'Shan't offer again.'

'Yes please.' He kissed her forehead. 'Let's come home early, shall we?'

'It'll be the first time ever if we do. Ready?' The evening was getting off to a wonderful start. 'I love Don and Cynthia's parties, the dining table laden with silver and cut glass, everything so grand.'

'You make it sound very pompous,' he laughed.

'Oh, no, it's – it's utterly unpompous. It's always a really fun evening. It's what we need, Teddy. Some fun.'

For a second he lost his smile, but not for long. How could he resist her when she looked at him like that. Was it fun their lives had been lacking lately? He wasn't sure what the reason, but something had changed, he had sensed that Claudia had been guarded with him.

65

Forget it, for this evening forget it. If what they were in need of was fun, then this evening they'd find it. And the prickles would be gone.

Already it was frosty, he went on out to clear the winscreen while she took the opportunity to switch off the Answerphone. Tonight was going to be there own, and she wasn't having it spoilt by patients who still sometimes phoned him at home instead of ringing the surgery for the doctor on call. Then they were off. As he pulled away from the house the phone started to ring. But it was too late, neither of them heard it.

The party lived up to expectations. Sixteen sat down to dinner, a dinner provided by caterers and served on a table with all the leaves extending it to its fullest length. Then, on the marble floor of the square hall, they danced. Foxtrots and waltzes gradually gave way, via a tango and a rhumba to what they called 'today's tribal dancing.' In fact, by that time they got as much pleasure from it as a bunch of twenty year olds.

It was one o'clock when Teddy and Claudia drove the short distance through the village home.

The promise of the evening had held, it was still with them as he unzipped her dress and carefully took off his dinner suit and hang it up. Usually they were in bed long before this. But tonight sleep was miles away, they had been stimulated by the party. Four nights ago his lovemaking had been one stage short of rape; tonight the memory of it was erased.

'I know you and Dad are always up early, Mum, and I wanted to speak to you before the children came down.'

Still struggling into her dressing gown as she picked up the phone, all last nights happiness evaporated as she recognized his voice.

'James! What is it? What's happened?'

'I've a Diocesan meeting this afternoon that I must be back for, but Mum may I bring the children down to you, just for a few days. They broke up yesterday you see.'

'Of course you may. But James, isn't Jenny there? What's happened? Is she ill?'

'It'll only be a few days. She's coming back Mum, but – just this time of year and holidays too – Mum there's no-one else I can ask.'

'James, you don't need to ask. We'll love to have them down here. I'll expect you for lunch.'

'I shan't be able to stay that long, I have to be back by half past two.'

Teddy had appeared at the head of the stairs, his brow furrowed, not understanding; and from the look of him, ready to condemn.

'I'll be glad to have them, they can help me get ready for Christmas.' She forced her voice to sound bright, partly for James's sake and partly because she knew Teddy was waiting for evidence that he'd been right in his opinion of Jenny. Poor little scraps, though, they ought to be at home decorating their own house, putting up their own tree. 'No, wait. James, hang on! I've a better idea. I'll drive up to Brightley for a couple of days. Your father will understand and Gwen will see to things here. You just stay put, I'll be there by midday.'

When she put the receiver down she knew the moment had come, she couldn't hide from the truth any longer.

'Well?' One word, but interpreted it meant 'Didn't I tell you so?'

'Just for a day or two Teddy. The children have broken up – and Jenny isn't there. You know how busy James is just before Christmas, extra visiting, carol concerts, things he's expected to do. And how can he if he's worried about the children?'

'Bloody woman! What's she done, run off with her girlfriend?'

'I don't know. Oh Teddy, our poor darling James.' She looked at him helplessly, she'd never wanted his comfort more and he'd never been less able to give it.

'So it falls to us. You have to rush off, I have to be left down here, just so that she can – can—' He turned back into their bedroom pushing the door closed with a firm click.

In the kitchen Claudia filled the kettle and switched it on. Her hands shook, she felt empty, hopeless. Please don't let it be like Teddy thinks, make there be some really good reason why she couldn't get home. Don't let her have stopped loving him. And the children – what sort of a woman could walk out on her children. Not Jenny, surely not Jenny. Please make her think again, help them all to be a proper family again, please—

Her silent words mocked her. What was the use of asking? If help was wanted then it had to be up to her to give it in the only way she could.

Chapter 5

The children were watching from the front window. As soon as Claudia turned into the gate the waving began. At home she'd tried to keep an open mind, be ready to defend Jenny against Teddy's attacks, but seeing those two eager faces she was shaken with rage.

'We were watching for you, Gran,' Barry shouted unnecessarily as they opened the front door. 'Dad's gone over to the vestry to collect something he needs for a meeting he has to go to. But we're here.'

'This is a real treat,' Claudia hugged them, 'I thought I'd have to wait until after Christmas to see you.'

'I'm going to get your bag, that's my job.' Barry took control.

'And I've got the table ready for lunch. You see that's one of my jobs. I have lots of things I have to do.' Patsy shrugged her shoulders, palms uppermost and a look of resignation on her podgy face. ''Cos I'm the girl I suppose.'

'What about your poor Mum, she does all your jobs.'

'Silly,' the little girl, so like her mother, laughed. 'That's cos she's Mum.'

A lasagne, home made before Jenny's departure, had been taken from the freezer and thawed out ready for the oven. The children looked on with relief while Claudia took the reins from them.

'If your father's out this afternoon, that means it's just us. Let's take Henry for a walk. On the way back we could stop at Mr Oswald's and look at the trees, see if we could chose a nice one for him to deliver.'

'You'll come with us? You mean you'll let us get it today?' The shadow of the last few days had hung heavy over Barry, now it was suddenly lifted, Gran looked cheerful as anything. Unable to contain his relief he danced in front of Patsy, his clenched fists striking at her and stopping within inches. 'Cor! Hear that, Sprog? We're going to get the tree!'

'Don't call me *Sprog*. Dad said you weren't to.' Instinct to champion her father vied with anxiety that he'd leave his shopping too late. 'He's promised that if Mum isn't soon back he'll stop at Mr Oswald's when he's passing. But, Gran, we go every day to look at the trees and each time another nice one has gone, that's the problem. Can we truly get it this afternoon?'

'I think we'd better if they're selling like that. With these high ceilings you'll want a large one. We'll have to get Mr Oswald to deliver it, we won't be able to carry it.'

'Perhaps he'll bring it right away . . . or tomorrow . . .'

It took so little to give them back their sense of security. Another minute or two and they were planning 'when Mum's home and we decorate it'. Fear and uncertainty had gone.

So engrossed were they in hunting in the cupboard under the stairs to find the box of baubles they'd be needing, that they didn't hear James come in.

'Mum, you're here! You don't know how grateful I am.'

'Silly, of course I'm here. The children are sorting their decorations,' which really meant 'the children are out of earshot'. 'I didn't ask you anything when you rang. Has the Show not finished?'

'Paula Stonehouse is back. I called there this morning. She was very offhand, said Jenny had walked out on her. I don't know what happened, she wasn't very forthcoming.'

'And Jenny? She's gone from the cottage, James.'

'Jenny's in Streatley.'

'Whatever's she doing in Streatley?'

'She and her mother spent the summer there once, long before I met her. She went to see the family they stayed with. She tried to get in touch with you yesterday, phoned all the evening to talk to you and ask you to look after Barry and Patsy for a few days. Then, very late last night – Mum I was crazy with worry, midnight and she hadn't come home, didn't know whether to ring the police or whether I'd be stirring up a hornet's nest. I was still up, listening for the car, when she phoned. Said she must have time – space, she actually said. Said she'd been trying to talk to you and would I get you to look after the children.'

'It's all right, James. You don't have to worry about Barry and Patsy, you know you don't. But Jenny – I'm out of my depth. Does she need help James? Psychiatric help, I mean?'

'No!' he rasped. 'What a thing to suggest!'

'No normal woman walks away from her children. Space be damned! It's nearly Christmas, she ought to be ashamed of herself.'

'Please, Mum, don't. I can't listen to you talking like that about

69

her. Jenny would never neglect the children. I told you, she'd been trying to contact you. She wasn't walking away from them. She knew she could depend on you and Dad having them for a bit. Mum, it's not Barry and Patsy, they're no problem. I just want Jenny to come home.'

Claudia bit back her retort. James had anxiety enough without her making things harder for him.

'In the meantime, while you're at your dreary meeting this afternoon you can think of the children and me, we're going to chose the best Christmas tree in Mr Oswald's shop.'

'You're a saint.'

'Nearer the truth, I'm a sucker for Christmas. I did our cards yesterday and got them off and if Jenny hasn't got back by about Friday I'll take Barry and Patsy home with me for a few days. They can help decorate Russets. Anyway I don't want your father to have the weekend by himself.'

'Gwen will look after things at home, will she? Dad'll be all right?'

'He's not a halfwit to be looked after.' She wished she didn't feel so edgy, so resentful.

'I didn't mean it like that.'

He looked at a loss, her mind jumped back to when he and Harvey had been little, probably about seven and five. James had invited a friend to play – and within half an hour Harvey had taken over 'whatever-his-name-was', she couldn't remember, the two of them playing ping-pong. James had waited patiently for them to finish so that it would be his turn for a game, but their hoots of laughter had firmly excluded him. He'd come down from the playroom looking pale and miserable. A tummy ache had been his excuse at seven years old. At thirty-four there was no such easy escape from the rejection he was scared to contemplate.

'Collect up the children and I'll dish up.' She changed the subject, her cheerful smile pulled back into place.

They neither of them have any conception, she told herself as she tossed the salad in its dressing. Jenny needs space, James takes it for granted that I can drop everything at a moment's notice. Well, of course I can, of course I do, willingly. But do any of them think for a moment that I'm anything other than 'Mum' or 'Gran', someone they can depend on? It's not words of gratitude I want. But why is it that they can't appreciate that they aren't the only ones with lives to live? Mum's not busy, Mum will come . . . Mum hasn't any ties . . . Mum doesn't need a life of her own! Mum . . . Gran . . . and that's what I am, that's what they make me. But I'm *me*, a woman with a mind and

70

soul of my own, a woman who still has dreams and expectations. They'd laugh at that, they'd think I'm too old to matter. They make me feel old, as old as time. But I'm not, I'm the same now as I always was, always will be.

Her thoughts took a new turn, her mouth relaxed, even her eyes got the message and smiled. Nothing could rob her of the memories and dreams she kept locked safely in a secret compartment of her mind. The knowledge that they were there helped her accept today's situation. Two weeks to Christmas, the Mum and Gran in her reasoned, I've our own preparations to make, but does anyone think about that? They take it for granted I'll have the house decorated, presents on the tree, masses of food, all the catering organized. None of them think, not even Teddy. No, that's not fair, Teddy has always known I've liked doing it. So what am I moaning about? 'Jenny tried to phone you, she knew you'd look after the children,' came the echo of James's words. Of course she could be relied on, of course she wanted to know they needed her. Having worked through to that point another truth hit her: they want to be able to use me, they love me, I think both of them do and I know James does, but they want to keep me on the outside of whatever is wrong between them. They don't even consider that their unhappiness involves Teddy and me too. They hug it to themselves, don't consider for a second the effect it has on our lives.

'Come on, you lot,' she called along the corridor, shouting to make herself heard above the excitement of discovering tinsel, fairy lights and baubles. 'We want to get lunch cleared away so that we can go tree hunting.'

'Coming Gran.' The cardboard boxes were abandoned in the passage.

'Can I have a large piece please Gran. I'm really 'stremely hungry.' For all her self-importance in getting the table ready, meals hadn't been the same for Patsy since her mother had been away. Her eyes shone with greedy anticipation as she took her plate. Soon Mum would be home, but until then it was jolly good having Gran smiling and being cheerful.

'Mum, there's one thing I'd be really grateful if you could do. Jenny and the children always do it, but time's getting on, I can't wait until she gets home.'

All three spoke at once.

'Of course, dear, what's that?' Claudia agreed innocently.

But the children needed no telling.

'Not the cards?' In horror from Patsy, the thought dampening her relish in the large helping of lasagne.

71

And 'Oh, Dad, they're Mum's job. With her not here do they really have to be done?'

'Of course they have to be done. She isn't here to take them round, but they have to be delivered just the same. I want you to go with your granny, make sure you don't miss anywhere, you know all the tucked away places.'

'I'm at a loss.' Claudia suspected this was one of the jobs that had gone into the making of the straw to break Jenny's back. 'What has to be done that they know all about and I don't.'

'My parish Christmas cards.'

'Whyever don't you give them out in church?'

'Hardly likely to reach the village that way. I send to every house, not just to the regular congregation. There are always some who come simply because it's Christmas, they want to know times and so forth.'

'If they were that interested they'd soon find out. But of course I'll do them. It'll be fun, kids, you can show me the village properly, I'm sure there's a lot I've never seen.'

After he'd gone out, while Barry was washing up and Patsy drying the dishes, Claudia unpacked her bag then looked in to James's study. On the desk, done up in batches with elastic bands, were the cards. Hundreds of them! She picked one up and read it. A homily from James, simply written; she felt the sting of tears as she read. Darling James, he was a truly good man. But sometimes the good can be so hard to live up to. Could she honestly blame Jenny for feeling used, trapped?

On the Sunday Jenny tramped out of the village, up the hill to the golf course and beyond, along half remembered lanes. She'd almost not packed her stout walking shoes, thinking she'd have no opportunity to use them. But on that Sunday they came into their own, well worn and comfortable. To walk all day would have been Henry's idea of heaven, it seemed strange not to have him furaging for sticks to bring for her to throw. Soon though she forgot him, purposely she tried to empty her mind of everything: James, the children, the Sunday School having to manage without her, their personal Christmas cards still waiting to be written, the mammoth pile of parish cards waiting to be delivered. Don't think at all, just walk, listen to the silence. If only she could clear all the angry frustration, that surely would be the way to see ahead. But to make her mind a blank was impossible, the harder the tried the more the memories crowded in on her.

Not for a moment did she consider not going home, but before

72

then, in silence and solitude, she had to marshal her thoughts, decide dispassionately exactly what she had to make James understand.

Stopping by a five-bar gate she stared unseeingly across the winter ploughed fields.

Lots of women have to subordinate themselves to their husband's career, they take a pride in playing a back-up role. So why can't I? Am I jealous that he loves his God more than he loves me? No, no it mustn't be that. Is it all those wretched 'hangers-on', the St Luke's Ladies with their brass cleaning rota and their everlasting squabbling over the flowers and who does what for the bazaar? No, I don't believe it's even them, although they drive me potty. Perhaps that's coming nearer the truth: they *must* drive James potty too, but he only sees the good in them while I let myself get screwed up and angry. I don't hate any of them individually, yet collectively I'm threatened by them. But it's more than that, it's the others, those who do damned all for him and yet he drops me like a hot coal if one of them beckons.

With an audible sigh she turned back to the road and continued to walk. What if she found there was another woman in his life. Someone like Paula – no, not like Paula! Don't think about that, not yet. Shut the lid of Pandora's box quickly, if you start thinking of Paula you will lose your strands of reasoning. But supposing you found that James was seeing another woman, someone pretty, the sort men found attractive instead of a lump like you, wouldn't that be worse?

Another break in the steady tread, this time to sit on a five-bar gate and let her imagination run riot. Suppose you dieted, bought new clothes, smartened yourself up – oh, but damn it, all the clothes couldn't make me the sort of woman men would want to go to bed with. She laughed mirthlessly, a loud guffaw that on a more weepy type could have turned into the relief of tears. I don't want *men*, I just want James and me to be like we once were. But perhaps all men like to think their wives are admired. Is he ashamed of me? I couldn't blame him if he were.

'I'm fat.' She said it aloud, demeaned and humiliated to hear the words spoken even here in the empty countryside. Instead of being sorry for myself, I ought to be sorry for him. He must want more from his marriage than he's getting, just like I do. He probably looks on me as the cross he has to bear: secretary, housekeeper, cook, a frumpy wife to walk the dog and discipline the children. When did we last make love? Weeks ago. Nights pass, weeks pass, and all the time we're getting further apart. If he touches me in bed I half expect him to apologize. Am I so awful? Or is this what happens to marriage?

73

Help me to see clearly, help me to accept and not to fight. But what's the good of asking You, You couldn't be on my side. I'm the one who is wrong, I must be. James is good, he lives like we are supposed to live, caring for other people, never putting himself first. Nice old Mrs Freeman knew what she was talking about when she said she couldn't be doing with living with a saint!

At the inn where she was staying Jenny had asked for a packet of sandwiches. Sitting on the gate she worked her way through them, then none too daintily climbed down ready to continue walking. Perhaps soon she'd find a pub, a pile of sandwiches needed something to help them along.

And so Sunday passed. She came no nearer to seeing the light at the end of her tunnel, but facing her disappointments was a way of finding acceptance. If this was the best she could expect, then she must stop looking for the impossible. It was as she lay in bed on the Sunday night that she thought again about Mrs Freeman and her George who'd liked a bit of fun, and she knew that somewhere she and James had lost something precious.

Next day was Monday, the day she had to go home. But not yet. She wasn't ready yet. Once she got back she'd be swamped, like a chameleon she'd take on the mantle each one expected. She'd be Mum to the children, cleaner to the house, walking companion to the dog, messenger to the parish . . . and to James? No, she'd give herself a few hours more, at the same time as she'd got off the stopping train on Saturday, so she'd get back on on Monday. Two stolen days, completely her own.

So as soon as she'd finished breakfast, despite it being a grey, dank morning, she set off again. Yesterday she had examined her present plight; today she would make herself climb the hill, Streatley Hill, just as she had so many times during that long summer holiday. She'd go to that same place where it had happened, she'd make herself remember.

The climb seemed steeper than it had nineteen years ago, before she reached the top her legs felt as though they were made of jelly. Each breath was an effort, she panted audibly as she struggled upwards, only determination prevented her turning back as her pace got gradually slower. She didn't hear a movement behind her and was startled by a retriever leaping up in friendly greeting.

'Bruce! Down boy!'

It was a relief to stop walking, so out of breath that even now she was gasping as she turned to see who was calling the dog.

'Surely . . .?' The man hesitated, looking at her in dawning recognition. 'Can it be? I don't believe it!'

74

Jenny's face flooded with colour. Ken Sheldrake! It was as if he'd been conjured up by her thoughts. And worse, it was as if he must know, here of all places, where those thoughts had been. She hadn't seen him for more than half a lifetime. From a shy, plump seventeen-year-old she'd turned into what she was today. In that moment of coming face to face with him she had no more self-assurance now than she'd had then.

'Jennifer Webster! See, I even remember your name.' He grinned at her, holding out his hand. A tall, weathered man, not handsome if looks come from features alone, but seeming to be brimming with good health and good humour.

'Jennifer Carlyle now,' she told him, hoping her marital status would turn his thoughts from the girl she'd been. 'It's been a long time – you were at university, I was still at school. How are you Ken? And your mother?'

'My mother died nearly two years ago. Me, I'm much as ever, half a lifetime older and very little wiser.' He was so completely at ease, so patently pleased to see her.

She laughed, her embarrassment slipping away.

'What brings you to Streatley?'

Surely the truthful answer must be blazoned all over her!

'Impulse,' she lied. 'We live at Brightley, my husband is rector of the parish church. I was going home from Devon and the Oxford train stopped here.'

'Jennifer? A woman of impulse?'

He was teasing. She turned away, memories swamping her. Had he forgotten? Perhaps he had, it couldn't have been as important to him as it had to her.

'No, I'm not a woman of impulse. But I'm not expected home until this evening. I was running two days early and when the train stopped here I decided that before the rush of Christmas I'd give myself a solitary break.'

'And along comes Ken to spoil your plans. It's twelve o'clock. Where were you thinking of eating lunch? When I've given Bruce a run on the hill I was going to drive to my favourite watering hole. Come with me, Jennifer, let me buy you lunch. We'll catch up on what the years have done for us.'

While Bruce wasted energy rushing up the hill after his ball, then chasing it as it rolled back down, Jenny found it remarkably natural to be here with Ken, answering his questions about James and the children. What an enviable quartet they sounded, she was proud of the picture she painted.

'And you? What do you do? Are you married? Have you a family too?'

75

'Sometimes I believe I'm a bachelor gay, sometimes I think I'm missing out on the best things in life. From which you'll gather I've never married. As for what I do, I take it at the rectory you don't read crime fiction?'

'You mean you write? I'm sorry, ought I to have known?'

'I'll forgive you. I can't imagine the Jennifer Webster I remember being a fan of my Inspector Durrant. He earns me a very respectable crust and leaves me time to believe I'm a free man. Hence, here I am walking the dog on a Monday morning while most people are chained to their desks.'

'Inspector Durrant? Don't they have plays on television about him? But I've never seen your name.'

'By the time they get to the screen I'd hardly recognize them myself. "Based on the book by Kenneth Sheldrake" appears in very small letters, somewhere down by the tea lady.'

'You're right, I don't read crime. But I shall break the habit and get acquainted with your inspector, even if only so that I can boast that I know the author.'

It was fun to be with Ken again. Her original confusion had melted away. But what was the matter with her that she could find him so easy to talk to, easy to laugh with? She wanted to believe it was because she'd left that shy, gauche seventeen-year-old far behind. Happily married, mother of two, that's the impression she'd meant to convey and his unquestioning acceptance lifted her out of the wretchedness that she'd not been able to find her own way though.

It was like living a dream, she thought as she watched him ordering their meal at the bar. Not that she'd ever consciously dreamt of being with him, in fact she'd not thought of him at all for years. What an unworldly seventeen-year-old she'd been, no wonder she'd fancied herself in love with the first man she'd talked to! Man? She'd seen him as suave and experienced beyond her wildest dreams.

She'd never had any illusions about her appearance, plump and dowdy; except for size, her summer dresses might have been cut from the same patterns as those she'd worn when she was twelve. She'd longed for affection, she'd been more than ready to rush into romance. And Ken, on vacation from university, could he really have enjoyed being with her? At the time she hadn't questioned, it had all been part of that glorious summer.

'Gingerbeer shandy.' He put it down in front of her. 'I hope you haven't acquired more sophisticated tastes with the years, I didn't ask you.'

'I haven't drunk it for ages, but I know I shall still like it.'

'Happy memories.' He raised his glass. 'They were happy, Jenny? All of them?'

'You mean, did I have any regrets?' She frowned, looking for the truth. 'No. I think I was glad it had happened. Reassured in an odd sort of way. If I had regrets at all it was later, when I met James.'

'You wished you'd been a virgin for him?'

Colour flooded her face. She made an enormous effort to sound casual, as if that long-ago evening on Streatley Hill hadn't been the most momentous one in her young life.

'I don't expect many brides are. Anyway, Ken, it's all far back and forgotten.'

And until today so it had been. Their friendship had been natural, both of them young and on holiday. When it had moved to the hand holding, even the kissing stage, she had gloried in imagining that this was what love was all about. And yet her heart hadn't really been touched, she knew that afterwards. A grassy patch on the summit of the hill, the last evening of her holiday, and she had followed desires she hadn't even understood. She hadn't been ignorant, but she had been totally unprepared for her own passion. Over the weeks with him there had been times when she'd forgotten she was plain and clumsy, she'd felt happy and carefree. On that evening she had believed her body to be beautiful, she had gloried in sensations that were new. As his passion mounted, so had her yearning to satisfy it. He wanted her, her heart had cried, she was a woman, this was real life, wonderful and awesome.

The next day she and her mother had returned home. She had gone back to school for her final years. He hadn't written to her, she hadn't expected him to; their magical few weeks had culminated in that last evening, there was no way they could have followed that. She'd known that the gauche, uncertain girl she'd been had gone for ever; she was proud of what she'd experienced. She'd not seen Ken from then until now, nineteen years later. How strange it was that she could feel so comfortable with him.

They sat a long time over lunch, then he drove her back to what he called his bachelor pad. A small thatched cottage on the edge of a coppice and only about half a mile from his old family home. There was just one living room with his desk and typewriter at one end, bookshelves, two easy chairs, a gateleg table, a trolley with bottles and glasses. It was a lived-in, welcoming room, warmed by central heating even though the log fire had burnt almost to nothing while he'd been out.

He showed her the kitchen and, while he rekindled the fire, she made their coffee. Catching sight of herself in a mirror on the back

77

of the kitchen door she smiled at the reflection. 'I'm fat' she'd told herself only yesterday. And so she was but, as she carried the tray into the living room and Ken Sheldrake looked up from where he knelt trying to coax the flickering flames, she felt a quickening of excitement.

She knew she wouldn't catch that teatime train to Oxford. Even before Ken suggested that he should drive her back to where she was staying and then take her out to dinner, at the back of her mind was the certainty that she would spend another night at the inn. With something like triumph she thought of the days leading up to Christmas, James's crowded engagement book as his parishioners claimed his presence as their right. Today the children broke up from school. At that thought she had a stab of unease.

Her afternoon call to Russets brought no reply – how was she to guess that Claudia was only along the road posting her cards? The same thing happened in the evening; three times she tried, little knowing that Claudia and Teddy were enjoying a carefree dinner party.

Her guilt that by now James must be expecting her only added to her enjoyment of the evening. It was after midnight when she saw Ken off from the inn and went to the pay phone in the foyer. This time it was James she spoke to, explaining briefly that she'd broken her journey in Streatley to see the Sheldrakes and wouldn't be coming for a few more days. 'I really do need to stay, but James take the children to Russets if you're busy, your mother will love to have them. I'll slip down and collect them when I get back or at any rate by the end of the week.'

She wasn't planning as far ahead as that, in fact she wasn't planning anything. She was living by the hour. Her depression had lifted, she was excited and yet she had no reason to be. Just as she'd stolen her few days of isolated freedom, so now she was stealing – what? When had she last felt like this, alive, vital? Late though it was, she ran a bath, revelling in the scented bath oil from the sachet left for her use. For a while she lay there, a smile playing with the corners of her mouth. She wasn't remembering any particular moment of her unexpected day so much as indulging in the unfamiliar feeling of knowing her presence had mattered.

Once out of the bath she draped a large towel around her and padded on her wide, bare feet through to her bedroom and the long mirror. Dropping the towel she gazed at herself. 'I'm fat,' this time she whispered it, moving the flats of her hands across the mound of her stomach then taking a hand mirror and turning so that she could

78

scrutinize the backview, her wide rounded buttocks. Consciously she made herself stand with her feet together, not her natural stance. Normally she planted them apart, more easily to accommodate her fat thighs. Then turning back she viewed the thick waist, heavy matronly bosom. For so long she'd hidden from herself, from bath to nightdress without going near a mirror.

Yet this evening her overweight body didn't repel her. She didn't ask herself why.

'I had a good journey, no hold-ups anywhere,' Claudia told Teddy. 'We've ordered the tree, sorted out the decorations and even delivered some of James's parish cards.'

'How is he?' Then, without waiting for an answer: 'Claudia, what the hell's happening? What does she imagine she's playing at?'

'It's not for us to say, Teddy.' She kept her voice bright, she couldn't be sure how much the children could hear even though they were supposed to be in bed.

'It may not be expected for us to voice our opinions, if that's what you mean, but for Christ's sake Claudia they can't expect us not to have any! You just tell me what's more selfish than for a woman to go gallivanting off just as her children break up. And you want me not to speak my mind for fear of upsetting the silly bitch.'

'Teddy, don't.'

'As far as I'm concerned I wash my hands of her. She expects you to drop everything to suit her convenience. You know my feelings.'

Upstairs she heard the creak of Barry's door, she knew he was trying to piece together what was being said.

Out of context, acting a part, she forced a spark of excitement into her tone as she told Teddy, 'We had a really exciting afternoon. We chose the biggest tree in the shop. It's being delivered tomorrow. I wouldn't mind betting the thought of it is keeping the children awake, it must be tall enough to touch the ceiling.' Surely that would give him a hint that she had to watch what she said.

'When's she coming back?'

'I think it's hard for her to be sure. You see she went to see an old friend in Streatley, someone her mother used to know. It seems there's some sort of problem, the old lady can't be left.'

'Humph. That's a cock and bull story if ever there was one. How often has she ever put herself out to visit this old friend who suddenly depends on her?'

'We wouldn't know, would we, darling? We're not here. Anyway, Jenny will be home in a day or so, but if she hasn't come by Friday I'm bringing Barry and Patsy down to Russets. She'll drive down and fetch them when she gets back. I don't want to leave you alone for the weekend.'

'I shan't be alone. That's one of the reasons I rang.' Teddy's voice altered, brightened. 'I'd just got in this evening when Melly called. She said she'd been trying to get you earlier, couldn't understand how it was you were out all day. They're both free now that Trevor has broken up and Melly wants to come earlier than they'd arranged. I said nothing could be better.' His tone was warm with affection, Claudia knew he was looking back, nostalgic for years that had gone. 'You know how she always loved the carols round the tree in the village. That's on the 19th, so she'll be here for that instead of waiting until the 22nd.'

'But the 19th is Friday!'

'I know it's Friday. You ought to be home when she gets here, Claudia. When Jennifer contacts the rectory, tell her you have to be come away by Thursday. We have our own lives to live. It's great about Melly, isn't it.'

'Yes, lovely. Leave a note for Gwen, about Melly and about the children, ask her to see the rooms are ready. Don't forget, will you.'

His ruffled feathers seemed smoother.

'You didn't answer me when I asked about James,' he prompted her. But the edge had gone out of his voice.

'He's fine. Very busy. Avonford doesn't see much of our Reverend Clarke, but James never has a minute to himself.'

'Old Clarke has lost his youthful enthusiasm.' But he wasn't criticizing, the ageing cleric seemed to him to be perfectly adequate for Avonford's needs.

'Youthful enthusiasm? Is that what James's is? He's been here a long time, I don't see any sign of it wearing thin. It's gone nine o'clock and he's still out. We were having dinner when one of his sidesmen phoned him in an awful state, his daughter's husband had walked out after a row. James didn't even stop to finish his meal.'

'He's a fine one to give advice! How is he really, Claudia, underneath the veneer?'

She paused as if that would put Barry off the scent, then answered with just one word.

'Frightened.'

'I knew I was right. There's more to it than they want us to know. If she deigns to come back while you're there, it's up to you to talk to her, make her see sense.'

'None of it's up to me, nor to you either.'

The door opened a few inches further, she heard it squeak.

'Get Gwen to see to the rooms, Teddy, there's a good chap. And I'll see you in a few days.'

By the time James arrived home she had let Henry out for his last run, banked up the Aga, locked the back door and gone to bed. Tonight when she smoothed her magic potions on her skin she hardly glanced in the mirror, she felt tired, without hope. Teddy wasn't being fair, not to her, not to James, not to Jenny. A happy person doesn't fall out of step with life; and that's what Jenny had done.

Pulling the covers high around her shoulders she closed her eyes as if that would shut out her helpless worry. Then another truth presented itself, one there was no escaping: it was easy to fall out of step with life, over these last weeks it had happened to her and it had happened to Teddy. Out of step with life and with each other: she, telling him half truths; he, sweeping her into the realms of the guilty because she was a woman and because she tried to defend Jenny. What was it Gwen Pomfrey had said? He travels fastest who travels alone. No-one to grieve for, no-one to rejoice for, to worry about, to care about or to pray for. Was that what she wanted? Bring her back to James, please put them back on the track again. Why should the children have to suffer, or Teddy get bitter and spiteful, or me . . .? Me? I just want everything to be like we used to believe it was.

That day there had been no word from Jenny, neither was there the next. That was Wednesday, a day Claudia and the children had spent largely in delivering Christmas cards. Most of them were for Brightley, but there were two other piles for the outlying hamlets taken under James's wing. By the time daylight started to fade it was raining steadily, all three of them were cold and wet. But the last card had been pushed through the last letterbox.

'I just hope all our efforts bring you a few customers,' Claudia teased James at dinnertime.

'Mum hates the cards,' Barry put in. 'She'll be dead chuffed to know they're done.'

'Gran, if she isn't home by the morning, will you do the tree with us?' Patsy was getting worried. The day after tomorrow they had to go Russets and the rectory didn't look even a bit like Christmas yet. Dad had hauled the tree in and put it in its tub, but just a tree, dark green and gloomy with no lights was almost worse than knowing it was in the garden waiting.

'No, not with Gran!' Then Barry flushed at his quick outburst. 'It's just that Mum always does it, she'd be hurt if we'd gone on without her. Wouldn't she Dad?' His father's confirmation would take away some of his embarrassment at the way he'd shouted about Gran.

'Yes, Barry's right. We'll wait for your mother. We mustn't go ahead with Christmas things without her.'

Claudia felt herself bristle, but no-one would have guessed from the smile she gave Barry.

'If you come home with me on Friday, you'll be more than busy doing ours.'

'Perhaps we won't need to, Gran. There's still tomorrow. She might phone up this evening to say she can come home tomorrow.'

But the day passed with no word from her.

He didn't come to Goring and Streatley Station to see her off, she didn't want him to. They'd said goodbye last night when he'd brought her back to the inn.

There was no buffet car in the Sprinter, but this morning Jenny didn't need the solace of food. On the way to the station she'd bought a newspaper, she read the main headlines, she read the main news item, and at the end she had no idea what it had been about. She gave up all pretence and closed her eyes.

Supposing the culmination of their summer nineteen years ago had been different, would she have behaved as she had last night? When they'd gone back to his cottage they'd both known where they were heading, she'd been eager, impatient. There had been no hiding herself away, ashamed of her heavy body. Just like he had that first time, he had made her feel beautiful. He didn't live the life of a celibate, he must have had plenty of women, attractive, slim, glamorous. Yet as his eyes had devoured her, she had known she was desirable.

'I'm hefty, overweight,' she reminded herself silently as the train rocked and swayed over the points. But this morning she smiled at the thought. Perhaps Ken Sheldrake had a predilection for oversize women! She had rejoiced in her figure, her well covered bones, her soft flesh, her wide thighs. In that hour she had known herself to be the perfect epitome of womanhood.

Imagine if she were honest and told James why she hadn't come home on Monday, confessed . . . Confessed? But what sin could there have been? She felt no shame, surprise perhaps and triumph too that she had found her way to exalting in her own sexuality. What she had done had given her a new pride in herself. If only that hour could have been shared with James. She loved James so dearly, she admired him even though she couldn't live up to his principles. Last night she had stretched her imagination to the full, pretending that it had he who brought her such ecstasy. Ken was good company, a friend, nothing more. Was it just because he had been her first – first and only except for James – that she gave her body to him so willingly? If only it could be like that with James, if only . . .

'We shall shortly be arriving at Oxford,' the steward's loud voice put an end to her dreaming, 'Oxford will be the next station stop.'

Ignoring the expense in a most un-Jennylike way, she took a taxi to Brightley. As they drove into the village, through the December midday gloom she could see the lights shining through the stained-glass windows of the church.

'Put me down by the church, will you.' Her heart was pounding. There wouldn't be a service at this time on a Thursday, James must be in there on his own. She pushed the money into the driver's hand, over-generous in her tip, then slinging her bag on her shoulder almost ran up the path to the west door.

Heads turned as she went in. The St Luke's Ladies were in full voice, aided and abetted by one or two regular choir members who no longer worked. She recognized immediately what they were practising for, every other year she had been one of their number. It was an annual event for them to join the full church choir for their visit to the hospital. In each ward they sang a few carols, James brought the message of Christmas.

> 'O little town of Bethlehem,
> How still we see thee lie,'

they carolled. She gripped her bottom lip between her teeth, humility, thankfulness, hope, shame, all these things were part of the emotion that gripped her, battled for the upper hand against the sense of vigour and well-being that still lingered from last night. The organist hadn't seen anyone come in, he played on, frowning at the slight hesitation on the part of the singers.

> 'Above thy deep and dreamless sleep
> The silent stars go by.'

From his seat in the choirstalls James saw her standing at the back of the church. The singing went on uninterrupted as he walked through the small assembly and down the aisle.

'I'm back. I got a taxi from Oxford.' How silly it sounded, when her heart was full of a thousand things. The St Luke's Ladies increased their volume as if that way the organist wouldn't suspect that their attention was elsewhere.

'Thank God,' James whispered, taking her in his arms mindless of the audience, 'thank God'. He held her away and looked at her searchingly. 'I've been so frightened.' Words that had never been spoken before.

Jenny clung to him. Relief flooded through her, and triumph too that here in the church, in front of all the local busybodies, he was thinking only of her. She rejoiced in the certainty that before evening the village would have heard of their reunion even though she'd been away less than a week.

'It's going to be different, James. We'll sort things out. This is all that matters – you and me.'

But even as she said it she knew it could never be the whole truth.

'Leave your bag, come and join the others. The third verse has always been your solo.' His arm around her shoulder he turned her towards the chancel. 'Listening to them, Jenny, it was your voice I heard, yours I prayed to hear.'

'I'm home, but not as deep in as that. Buck up and get rid of them. I'll go on indoors and get our lunch. Tomorrow I'll drive down and fetch the children back.'

'Back? But they're here. Mum came up here instead. I'm glad she didn't take them away from the village, the carollers do the first roads this evening,' he nodded towards the Ladies as he spoke. 'You know some of them take their children. This year ours are old enough, but I didn't like to ask Mum. Now you're home it's all right.'

'And you?'

'Widow visiting.'

'Oh, James!' Even though they spoke in whispers she couldn't keep the exasperation out of her voice.

'It's a hard time of year for them, especially those who haven't been alone long. And evenings must be hardest of all. That's why I try and do it then. But you always go out with the singers, they need your voice. I'll tell them shall I?'

'If the kids are keen, I suppose so.'

She shouldered her bag and turned to the door. Outside the churchyard smelled of rotting leaves and burnt out bonfire, the clouds hung low, the air felt damp. She was home, already she had been caught up in the current.

Chapter 6

'So, tell me again,' Teddy prompted as Claudia poured his after-dinner coffee. 'I say, this is more like it. I haven't enjoyed my evenings on my own. When I hadn't heard anything I thought I'd have another today. Gwen's been writing me notes, telling me how long my dinner has to be in the micro before I can eat it.' He didn't take sugar in his coffee, he probably didn't even realize he was stirring it as he sat and gazed at her. 'Seeing the light on when I came towards the house . . . you've no idea how good it is to have you home.' A long speech for Teddy.

'And to be home. I don't know what I expected, it seemed like tempting fate even to talk about it. I feel ten years younger. It's such a relief – seeing the look on James's face, and Jenny's too, made me ashamed of having doubted.'

'I still don't understand. They were supposed to be in Exeter for the weekend, what was she doing in Streatley?'

'You know as much as I do about why she walked out of the Show. When James called on the Paula woman, apparently she was very off-hand, it seems she and Jenny had a bust-up of some sort.'

'But why break her journey in Streatley? Damn it, she was only an hour from home.'

'Impulse, that's what she called it.'

'Humph.' Clearly Teddy didn't think Jenny a woman to be ruled by impulse.

'Once she was back, I was anxious to get on the road so I only saw her for the few minutes it took to have lunch. Naturally, Barry and Patsy had masses to tell her, they deserved her attention. But I gather she called to see this friend of her mother's, someone they'd stayed with for a whole summer holiday when she was still at school and her mother had just come out of hospital. She found the old lady all alone and not well. You know all this already. I told you that's what she'd said when she phoned James.'

'So you did. But I didn't take it in, to be honest I thought it was a blind so that she could stay longer with her girl friend.'

A week ago a remark like that would have made Claudia tight-lipped, hiding her own misgivings behind anger at Teddy. This evening she could laugh.

'Now you can eat humble pie. She managed to contact the son and he arrived this morning to take over.'

'Well, let's hope she means to settle down now and put her family first. I suppose neither of you told her how her little escapade had messed up other people's lives – James's, yours, mine, her children's—'

'Henry's, the rabbits', the Sunday School children's . . .' She was teasing him and this time he smiled, reaching to take her hand.

'Good to have you back. Sorry I was niggly on the phone, just that I missed you.'

She came round the table to where he was sitting.

'"Make me a lap, I'm needing a squeeze."' It was an expression familiar from long ago, originating from when James was a toddler and taken on board in turn by the other two once they'd cottoned on to its infallibility. 'Make me a lap, I'm needing a squeeze' or, coming into their bedroom at first light, 'Make me some room, I'm needing a squeeze.' There was laughter in Claudia's voice, and love too.

Teddy made a lap.

The evening was their own. Together they cleared the dishes, she filled him in with the doings of James and the children, they looked through the Christmas cards that had so far been received while she did a mental check that none of the senders had been forgotten. Tomorrow Melly would be here, they'd buy a tree, go out collecting holly, sing carols round the village Christmas tree, decorate the house, wrap up last-minute presents . . . But that was tomorrow; this evening they had only themselves, it was an oasis of peace.

With her shoes off, Claudia was curled on to the settee, leaning against Teddy's shoulder. The television was on, the news washing over them only half listened to.

'Let's put this off and go to bed,' he rubbed his chin against her hair, the familiar shampoo smell adding the finishing touch to his contentment.

'Um, let's.' She stretched luxuriantly, then turned to him with a teasing twinkle. 'It's been quite a day, a long drive, I expect I'm ready for sleep.'

'Your day isn't over yet. If I were a quarter the man I feel I am at

86

this moment you wouldn't be asleep for hours. Be grateful I'm all talk!'

'Talk or action, I'm grateful.'

He wasn't all talk.

'Thank God I was wrong about Jenny,' he murmured half an hour or so later. She noticed that tonight it was 'Jenny' not 'Jennifer' in that cold manner he so often kept for her. 'If the youngsters do as well as we have, Claudia, they'll be all right.' He turned her so that she fitted into his lap for sleep.

From Melly and Trevor's arrival right through to the middle of January Russets hummed with family living and, amidst the bustle of activity, it went unnoticed that Melly kept a suspicious eye and ear on her mother. Claudia was so normal, clearly enjoying all the noise and action just as much as she always did, that although the question remained unanswered at the back of Melly's mind, she began to believe Adrian's inspiration had sprung from his imagination.

It wasn't until New Year's Eve that his name was mentioned.

'Where did Adrian go for Christmas?' Claudia asked her as Melly put the finishing touches to the preparations for a buffet supper. 'He was here for our last party, remember?'

'Half the village was here for our last party. I hope those who are coming this evening aren't anticipating a repetition, that was Dad's special night. We can't compete with the spread the caterers put on. Do you reckon the salmon mousse is going to tip out to look anything like a fish?'

'Of course it will. I think we've done rather splendidly Melly – and hasn't it been fun?'

So different in appearance, but so alike in their hunger for excitement, the two of them surveyed their efforts spread out to cover the old-fashioned kitchen table and overspilling on to the dresser.

At that moment Teddy came in to fetch a corkscrew. It was time to start uncorking.

'My word! But I didn't realize my girls had such talent!'

'Mum is the whizz kid – but look Dad, this wondrous pavlova is mine. Not a flaw in it anywhere. Don't you think it earns me an A plus?'

'It earns you a quick G and T before you go up to dress.'

But his expression told her that she deserved an A plus simply for being Melly.

'I was asking her about Adrian, Teddy. I didn't think to ask him about Christmas when he came in last – Teddy didn't see him, Melly, he collected me and took me out to lunch, arrived from out of the blue.' Immediately Melly's guard was up, but Claudia didn't notice. 'I wish I'd thought. Thanks,' she took the second glass from Teddy, 'just the boost we were ready for. You didn't tell me, Melly. Has he friends he stays with?'

Why was Melly looking at her so strangely?

'Adrian is never short of friends. I suppose he's doing whatever it is he always does.'

It wasn't like her to sound so off-hand. Claudia frowned.

'I wish I'd thought to ask him, I just forgot Christmas was almost on us. Have you seen him lately? No-one should see the New Year in on their own.'

'Yes, Mum, I see him sometimes. I was in his studio quite recently. His work is really outstanding, he must have sketched a good deal in the forest. But you must know that, Mum. He must have done most of his sketching when he was here with you.'

'Occasionally. He based the portrait on casual sketches.'

Melly laughed – so what made Claudia so sure there was no mirth in the sound?

'There was nothing of a casual sketch in the paintings I saw. You could almost feel the cool depth of the autumn woods. Fantastic how he captures the atmosphere.'

'I didn't think of Adrian as a landscape painter,' Teddy said.

'Oh, there's always a figure. But figures are two a penny, it's the colours of the leaves, just changing for autumn, the beams of light – you should see what he does, Dad.'

'He's certainly very talented,' Teddy said. 'I hope he hasn't been alone. Christmas always seems a lonely time for those without family.'

'I wish we'd asked him,' Claudia said again. But was it the complete truth? When he came to Russets, it was to see *her*. What if all the family was here, what if Melly were monopolizing him and looking at her like she had just now?

'Adrian won't be short of friends. You don't need to take him under your maternal wing, Mum.'

She watched for Claudia's reaction, assuming from the tightening of her lips that the jibe had struck home. And just as she scrutinized her mother so, unnoticed, did Teddy scrutinize his daughter. All three of them followed their own thoughts.

It was a little later, as he watched Claudia carefully applying mascara, the finishing touch to her preparations for the evening, that Teddy referred to Adrian.

'I was really worried about Melly, you know, when they came for my birthday.'

'I told you you had no need to be. When Adrian stayed down here I promise you he wasn't pining for Melly. I know his parents split up years ago, he told me that. He never mentioned any other family while he was staying here – nor when he's been down since. Christmas is for families, not for riotous parties.'

'Like Melly says, he's probably not looking to be taken under someone's maternal wing. I'm still sure she looked for a bit of dalliance with him, a good job we lifted him out of temptation's way. She seems to have got over him now, but I thought this evening watching her, any man must find her attractive.'

'I'll tell you what we'll do. Just after midnight we'll ring him, wish him a Happy New Year. If he's not there then he'll never know, but if he is he'll be glad to be remembered.'

'You're a funny girl,' he laid his hand on her shoulder lightly, 'but I like you.'

'That's a blessing,' she laughed. 'Come on, Let's go down. I bet Erica looks a million dollars.'

As they spread out round the room, arms crossed, hands clasped, and sang the time honoured 'Auld Lang Syne', Teddy's glance went to the portrait. Claudia, as lovely as she'd been when first she'd bewitched him – in a way, a Claudia he'd almost forgotten as the years had moulded them close – yet it was still the Claudia of today, a woman who had experienced life. Someone meeting her for the first time, comparing the portrait with the reality might take a quick glance and think the artist had been intent on flattering. But Teddy saw in it the hope and trust of the girl he'd married; the love that had been woven into the pattern of their lives, as certain as the first flowers of spring or the falling leaves of autumn, unfailing and taken for granted.

The last notes of the song died away, kisses, handshakes, blessings and good wishes were still being exchanged when Erica flung wide the front door to let in the New Year and Claudia dialled Adrian's number.

She listened as she counted the number of times the bell rang. Ten . . . eleven . . .

'Are you calling James, Mum? Can I speak when you finish, just wish him a Happy New Year.'

'No, James goes to the church and Jenny doesn't wait up. I wouldn't call them.' She replaced the receiver at the fifteenth ring. 'Adrian. But he can't be home.'

Teddy came into the hall, presumably for the same purpose.

'No reply?' he asked. 'Then you needn't feel badly about forgetting. He must have had plans.'

He didn't understand Melly's expression as she looked at her mother. Anger? Jealousy? Even dislike – except that that was ridiculous. Even so it stirred the dying embers of his original unease.

'I told you not to fuss, Mum. Adrian is a very popular young man, he isn't looking for a mother figure.'

Teddy frowned at the way she said it.

'One doesn't have to be a mother figure, or a father figure either, to care about ones friends.'

Melly hesitated, then looking at him earnestly she said, 'I know that and you know that, Dad. But he isn't used to family life – you know what I mean? – older people wanting to see younger ones are OK. He might interpret it differently. Most women run after Adrian, even those who are young and gorgeous, he has the pick of the best. It would be humiliating if he put the wrong interpretation on Mum fussing over him. He's younger than her own sons.'

Teddy laughed. 'So? Surely that means she can be concerned without any ulterior motive. It's one of the few advantages about getting older.' He linked an arm through each of them and turned back to the drawing room. 'It sounds as if folk are making a move, we'd better go back to the others.'

Twice a year the baby grand was tuned. The tuner had come during December in readiness for Harvey's stay, and now for two or three hours each day the house was filled with the sound of his playing.

'Shall I annoy you if I listen?' Jenny asked him. 'Can you forget I'm here?'

'If you promise you'll go when you've had enough. Sometimes I sound very repetitive, you may not even notice any improvement.'

'You mean you take a phrase and perfect it?'

'As best I can,' he smiled. There was a charming humility about Harvey.

'I'll be quiet and you put me out of your mind.'

But he didn't. In fact instead of working on the Honegger piano concertino he was adding to his repertoire he played Liszt and Chopin.

Jenny didn't so much listen as absorb the message of the music as she let her mind wander where it would. Since those few stolen days, lost to the family but so important to her, she had withstood the claims of the parish. James had accepted, yet she found herself always on her guard in case old habits tripped her. Her first evening home, for the sake of the children, she had joined the carol singers, but instead of taking Sunday School she had gone walking with Henry. She had phoned the greengrocer and asked for sixty oranges to be left in the church porch, then she'd walked across to the vestry with a reel of florists' ribbon, two boxes of cocktail sticks, four packets of fruit jelly sweets, half a pound of raisins and a note for Mrs Sanders, St Luke's Lady No. One, saying that she had things to do and wouldn't be working with the team assembling Christingles this year. This year? Any year! Shutting the vestry door firmly behind her she had walked home with a firm tread and a new freedom. On Christmas Eve she had let the children stay up and had taken them to Midnight Mass, they could never be too young to know the awesome wonder of the still, winter night; but the next morning she had stayed at home and cooked the dinner like nearly every other woman in the village. Yet even now, all these days later, she couldn't be comfortable with herself that she could treat James like it, she hated to see the puzzled, hurt way he sometimes looked at her. If there was to be a way forward for them, though, this must be it. She wanted a husband, father for her children, not a saint who expected them to be grateful for their chance to serve a community, half of whom didn't give a fig for him and his beliefs.

Now they were into a new year, a fresh beginning. She'd told Miss Harper, the assistant Sunday School teacher, that she was giving up. If they wanted to continue then they must find another helper.

She ought to be rejoicing, surely this was the 'space' she needed. Yet she was left with a feeling of failure, even loss; not for the community, there wasn't one amongst them she had been able to look on as a friend. They saw her as an appendage to James, some sort of unpaid assistant who washed all the tablecloths after the Harvest Supper, helped clean the brass, took their messages, traipsed round the village putting the *St Luke's News* through their doors each month. So it wasn't friendship that left the void, it was simply that her parish work had been a point where her life and James's had touched.

She realized now that the piano was quiet, Harvey was watching her.

'Does it disturb you having me here? It must do. I'll go.' Clumsily she heaved herself to her feet from the low chair.

'I like you being here. My practising drives poor Erica mad.'

'I can understand that.' Then, realizing her bad choice of words, she felt herself colour. 'I don't mean it the way you think. But Erica and I have a lot in common.'

'How's that?' He'd never seen two women less alike. There stood Jenny, embarrassed by her gaffe, her feet apart and firmly planted, her clothes shapeless, her hair as devoid of style as everything else about her. How could she be likened in the remotest way to Erica, slim and graceful, her clothes and manner bearing the hallmark of her own country? Jenny was practical, serious-minded, a 'good woman'; Erica was greedy for excitement, she thrived on their being fêted.

'We're not women who see their husbands go off to work somewhere else. I mean, you spend hours at home practising and James is in and out during the day, home's a sort of base where his study is.'

'That sounds good to me. You must like him being around the place better than if he went off from breakfast time until evening surely?'

'I don't know that that's true.' She looked at him so seriously, he turned on the piano stool to give her his full attention. 'If he came home at six o'clock each day we'd know that at least for the hours that were left he belonged to *us*. You with your music, him with his God, you with your practising, him with his running around hoping to find a soul to save, it boils down to the same thing. Both of you are fulfilled by what you do. Erica and I are expected to find that enough for us. Perhaps she does. She's newer at the game than I am.'

'It's not like that. Not for either of us, James or me. Of course you come first to him, and when I work it's for her as well as for myself.'

'Good. Anyway, I shouldn't have said what I did. It's none of my business.'

He could see she was embarrassed, it was a rare thing for her to let her tongue run away with her. Not knowing what to do with her hands, she tucked her blouse tighter into her skirt, keeping her eyes averted from him. Before he could stamp on the thought, he wondered what James's flock made of her, and hard on the heels of that his mind shot down the track so often travelled by Teddy and he marvelled that James could ever have fallen in love with her.

'That's what families are for, Jenny, to point out what we sometimes can't see for ourselves.'

'Don't say anything to James. Promise me, Harvey. And for heaven's sake never suggest to him that his family should come before his work. Seven days a week, twenty-four hours a day, waking and sleeping, that's the obedience his Boss expects.'

'Boss?'

She forced a laugh.

'Remember Mrs Freemen, down at Moorleigh. She and her George often used to have a grumble together about his boss, she told me; she said she couldn't be doing with a Boss you couldn't even hide your thoughts from.'

'I can just hear her saying it,' Harvey smiled. They were on safer ground with Mrs Freeman than with James's devotion to duty.

'Now I'm going to leave you in peace, Harvey. I don't expect I shall meet the others, but I think I'll have a stomp for a while.'

Avoiding the village she went up the lane to cross the cattle grid and into the open forest, grass, patches of gorse, and to the right a steep incline to a thin clump of trees. She started to climb.

How was it that she could say those things to Harvey and yet not to James? Coming towards the top of the slope she sat on the stump of a hewn tree, leaning forward and resting her arms on her wide-apart knees in the inelegant way she found comfortable. If she said to James what she had to Harvey, he would imagine she was trying to pull him away from his Duty. To him Duty and God were synonymous. So was that what she wanted? No, she loved him as he was, she loved him for what he was. Was it a mortal sin to want to express that love with the whole of their beings? She'd come home with such hope, in her 'lost' few days her eyes had been opened to what their marriage had lacked.

Neither of them ever found it easy to express emotion, but James's relief at her return had broken down his reserve. 'I've been so frightened,' he'd told her in the church, then later that same evening, 'I prayed, I tried to trust – and yet I was frightened. What sort of a faith is that?' . . . 'I don't know what I'd do if I lost you.' Joy and thankfulness had overwhelmed her. This was only the beginning, she'd told herself, soon the full expression would burst on them.

As memories flooded back she closed her eyes tightly as if that way it were possible to escape from what had followed. Lovemaking at the rectory had always been a behind-closed-bedroom-door, lights-out, affair. Perhaps it had to be in every household where there were children, but she knew that even if they were alone in the house nothing would ever change the pattern. That night she'd believed that once in their room she could lead the way. In the bathroom she'd got ready for bed. Perfume was something she'd never possessed, so she'd smoothed talcum powder into her skin then, despite it being December, put a summerweight polyester housecoat over her nakedness.

A pyjamaed James was already in bed. As she came in he'd pushed the covers back as a sign of welcome, at the same time turning out the light.

A slight intake of breath had been the only sign that he'd noticed she wasn't wearing the customary tentlike nightgown.

Only the evening before, she had closed her eyes, fantasizing that it was James who drove her into a frenzy of longing, who raised her to heights of joy she'd never known.

The December afternoon was closing in on her, she ought to start walking back. Anything was better than reliving those next short moments, moments of hope, desire, and so quickly moments of disappointment that left her frustrated and angry, counting his deep and peaceful breathing as an insomniac might count sheep. Finally she must have slept, for when she woke it was to find James already up although it hadn't started to get light. No sound from downstairs, so she'd got out of bed to see where he was, even though in her heart she'd already known. The curtains were undrawn, the moonless dark was broken by a shaft of light from the church.

Conscious of her naked body she'd felt humiliated, no wonder she'd decided to get up and dressed, put the night behind her.

She'd been in the kitchen, the table ready for breakfast, when James had come through the back door.

'You were out early,' she'd greeted him.

'You're early yourself. Good, you're making tea.'

'Was something wrong in the church?' She'd known that wasn't what had taken him there, she'd had to turn the knife in her wound and hear his answer.

It wasn't quite what she'd imagined, but the meaning was the same.

'Nothing is wrong. Nothing.' She remembered his gentle kiss on her forehead. 'If you knew how fervently I'd asked, you'd know I needed to go there, to say thank You.' There was never anything sanctimonious in the way he talked of his faith, he simply spoke the truth about the guiding force in his life. 'Jenny, afterwards I just sat there, I tried not to think of anything, just to – to feel the peace. I didn't work things out for myself, yet gradually I knew what was expected of me. Dearest Jenny, I have no right to let the parish use you, if you want to pull out from the things you have let yourself get involved with, then I must understand. Space, that's what you said you wanted. It was as if a voice told me, that's what I had to see you were given. That way you will find your way back, not just to me, thank God it wasn't space from me you wanted, but to the whole of our life here.'

'You mean you aren't going to make it difficult? I'll do the magazines *willingly*, I quite like walking around by myself doing those. It's the people. I get swamped by things that I find so pointless. All the fussing with flowers, the stupid arguments amongst the women as if it matters a damn who does what. That's what I can't stand. If I weren't married to you no-one would dream of asking me, I wouldn't push a flower in a pot from one year to the next. They know I'm useless yet no-one has the guts to tell me so in case they upset you – and that might earn them a black mark up yonder.'

94

He had laughed; her irritations had seemed not to matter.

'Jenny, the children are up, I can hear them. Before they come down,' he'd rested his hands on her shoulders, 'last night, it was like it used to be. Darling, it was . . . it was . . . knowing it wasn't me you wanted to run from, having you again . . . I don't know how to say it, yet I must . . . it was . . . a benediction.'

How she envied him, she thought as she marched steadily back to Russets, him and his God. While he was taking all he wanted, cramming it into two or three moments, and reaching a goal of holy bliss, what had she been she left with? If the words formed themselves into a question, it was one she had no intention of answering. To dig would be dangerous.

Harvey had no engagements until the end of January, when he was starting a month's tour on the Continent. He and Erica were in no hurry to go back to their flat on the outskirts of Manchester, and took little persuading to stay on at Russets until then.

'Paris, Berlin, Salzberg, Vienna and Prague. Cosseted and waited on in hotels. What a life!' Claudia passed the itinerary back to Erica as she spoke.

'One concert hall is about the same as another. Some of Harvey's friends yak on about acoustics, pretending they understand about the variation of sounds. Baloney! That's what I say it is, a sort of affectation to make sure we ignoramuses respect their esotericism. Harvey knows what I think. Maybe he does understand these things and knows what he's talking about, but he never plays clever clogs about it.'

Claudia laughed. What a darling Erica was, she thought, always with the confidence to speak her mind, and speaking it in phrases that often sounded extraordinarily out of keeping with her American background. Perhaps I enjoy her so much because she is so pretty. I know it's not fair, but it's a pleasure to watch her. Even this morning in jeans and trainers, a shirt of Harvey's, her silky mane pulled tightly off her face and fastened in a pony tail, there was an air of sophistication about Erica. How different they were, all three girls: this was the way Melly so often dressed, but on her the end result was casual, it shouted that she was in her 'play clothes', ready for anything; Jenny? Claudia's thoughts ran away with her before she could stop them. If ever a woman was unsuited to jeans it was Jenny, but she wore them just the same – they were hardwearing and practical, they suited her character even if they did nothing for her figure – the top part of her body shrouded in some sort of a shapeless blouse and the whole giving the impression that clothes were simply a means of hiding

95

behind. There was no criticism in Claudia's picture of her daughter-in-law, only a tinge of affectionate sympathy. But back to Erica. How was it she managed to look as though she were modelling in some teenage magazine? Her make-up was immaculate, accentuating her dark eyes and yet giving the impression that her looks came entirely from nature.

'Maybe they can hear something the rest of us are deaf to,' Claudia answered lightly. 'As long as Harvey doesn't get high and mighty, that's the important thing.'

'Harvey's OK. It's just the rest of the bunch.'

'But he's a soloist, he's not attached to one particular orchestra.'

'On tour he will be. The same orchestra, I guess mostly it'll be the same programme. Oh, it will be all right, I'm just being a grouch. A day or two in a new city is always interesting. I like to see fresh shops – but I'm not into museums and art galleries, all the tourist things. I do go to them, not like lots of people do, studying catalogues, making notes, lapping up everything the guide tells them. To please Harvey I take some pictures. I think he gets a kick out of thinking I'm doing the tourist bit while he's working.'

'But I thought you loved it!'

'First time around, especially when we were newly married. His friends *saw* me then. By now I'm just a bit of his luggage as far as they are concerned.' She looked at Claudia helplessly. 'I'm not wanting to be one of them. I just can't seem to work up excitement about learning my way around on the Metro, all that sort of thing. You'd think a strange city would be thrilling, but when you're on your own it's often dead boring.' Seeing Claudia's concern she realized she'd said more than she'd intended. 'You won't tell Harvey what I said, will you. Nor Teddy or anyone. Trouble is, Claudia, it's easy to say too much to you.'

'Of course I wouldn't repeat what you've said. I promise.' It was easy to promise, she couldn't bear to destroy Teddy's faith in the happy couple. And they were a happy couple, nothing could alter the fundamental thing. Erica was wise, she didn't pretend.

'Harvey never seems to be disappointed, but the fact is I'm just not into his kind of music. Don't look like that, Claudia, I wouldn't have talked about it if I'd imagined you'd worry. I don't love his music, but I do love Harvey.'

Claudia put her arm around the girl's slender shoulder and hugged her.

'I'm glad you told me. I ought not to have needed telling. As for worrying, you are much too right for each other for me to do that.' But, despite her smile, despite the positive tone of voice, the seed of worry was planted. No matter how frail and weak a seed it might be, it would always be there whether it took root and flourished straight away or lay dormant waiting for each opportunity to take a firmer hold.

'It's not Harvey's fault I get bored. You would too, Claudia. Music, all the time it's music. I might as well not be there when he gets with the orchestra.'

'But he likes you going on tour with him, if you didn't go, Erica, he'd be lost.'

'Of course I shall go. If I didn't go on his tour then I'd have to go off somewhere else. I'm surely not staying in that flat and waiting till he gets home. Anyway I want to go with him, even though I know that most of the time I shall be by myself, one town after another, one hotel after another. The only thing that's the same is the music!'

'The same? They vary the programme surely?' Claudia had always been sure that life was all roses for Harvey and Erica. She was seeing it from a different angle and felt herself in sympathy with the pretty and pampered young American girl.

'Don't listen to me, Claudia. Of course the programme varies.' Then with a laugh rather like a naughty child pushing her luck to see how far she could go. 'I expect it's just me who can't tell the difference.'

As pleased as a child being offered an unexpected treat, Erica heard that she and Harvey were travelling on their own, meeting the orchestra in Paris. Claudia drove them to Heathrow and, watching them disappear through the barrier, she forgot even that small seed of worry. They looked like any happy young couple going off on holiday, jeans and anoraks, hand luggage slung on their shoulders. They turned to give her one quick wave, then they were lost in the crowd and she was alone.

She'd told Teddy that possibly she'd drive on into town; he'd suggested she ought to arrange to meet Melly. But in that moment, standing alone in a crowd, Claudia knew just what she meant to do.

She mounted the stairs and went to the door marked 'No. 6', then pressed the bell before a second thought had time to get in her way. The buzz of the bell rent the silence of the building. Supposing he was busy, supposing he had someone else with him, supposing he wasn't pleased to see her, supposing he wasn't at home – and in a moment of panic she clung to the hope that he was away. She could put a note through his door, a friendly note saying she had been nearby and—

The door opened. They were face to face, his pleasure chasing away her fears.

'I took Harvey and Erica to Heathrow. I was going into town – then I thought . . .'

She didn't get around to saying what she thought. He drew her into the room, holding her hands in his he kissed her forehead, then releasing her he unbottoned her coat and slipped it from her shoulders.

'Do you believe in the power of thought? I spoke to Melly yesterday, she told me you were coming to Heathrow. I asked her what plane they were getting, I made up my mind I'd go there and find you. She didn't know.'

But Melly knew perfectly well! Claudia remembered Harvey's exact words when she'd phoned to wish him well on his tour. He'd told her, 'Mum is driving us to Heathrow. We aim to get there at nine-thirty for check-in, so it'll mean an early start.'

'Power of thought?' she queried.

'I willed you to come here. See,' his smile was as guileless as a schoolboy's, 'I've even tidied up ready for you.'

Her spirits soared. Mum, Gran, family matriarch, she slipped out of the role as easily as she did out of the hip-length suede coat she found comfortable for driving. Under it she wore tawny brown trousers and jumper, and knotted loosely at her neck a multi-shaded scarf of greens and browns.

'A forest nymph, just as I've been seeing you.'

He could say these things with no affectation, she wished she had the assurance to accept his words gracefully.

'I wanted to come here. I wanted to see where you live, where you work. You're sure I'm not disturbing you?'

'I'm sure you *are* disturbing me, disturbing me in a wonderful way.'

She pretended not to understand, it was easier to talk about his work.

'Your studio is here at the flat? Melly was telling us she'd seen some of your work since you stayed in the New Forest, the forest in autumn. That's when we were there together. Did you make your sketches then?'

'I carried the picture in my eye.' He seemed to be weighing up how much to say, then he made his decision. 'Come with me, Claudia. It was our forest, you were part of that glorious autumn. Come with me, I would like to show you.'

There were many more paintings of her than the three Melly had found. It was the others he showed her first. Dressed in jeans and sweater, her hair blown in the wind as she stood aboard a sailing ship.

She was glad it wasn't *Sea Urchin*, just as she was glad none were against a background of home. She felt like Alice finding herself in a world beyond the rabbit warren. When he passed her a canvas and she saw her body pale and mysterious through a black veil she felt a thrill of excitement, but she hadn't the courage to meet his gaze.

'How can you paint what you don't know?' She asked it as if it were a technical question, she mustn't let him guess she had no more control of the situation than Alice had in her Wonderland.

'But I do know. I have watched every movement. Say it's because I have spent years painting the human form if that makes you easier; the truth is more complicated. In you, Claudia, there is everything. Still beautiful, but not the beauty of an untried girl; your body has known love, you have borne children, nothing has changed your lithe grace.' He picked up a canvas that stood facing the wall and passed it to her. 'You remember this day?' The final picture, the forest scene, like a dryad she was poised reaching high to the overhanging branch of the chestnut tree. She recalled the smell of the autumn leaves, the first tints of golden glory, she remembered the feel of the green, prickly chestnut cases, the sound of their walking through dead leaves – this year's leaves, last year's, the rotted carpet of time past. She remembered the heady certainty that he saw her as an attractive woman, and her answering thrill in the realization that she was more that 'Mum', 'Gran', 'the doctor's wife', she was still *herself*, a woman with a zest for life.

'But how could you paint it like this? Yes, of course I remember it. I remember it all.'

He rested the canvas on the easel, took the one she was still holding from her and rested it against the wall, then his hands on her shoulders compelled her to look directly at him.

'You see how I've used my weeks here. Living on memory, living on imagination.'

The whole scene was unreal, she wanted to end it yet at the same time she wanted to hear him say more. Out of her depth, yet exhilarated by the floundering strokes that were keeping her afloat.

'Teddy says my portrait is nothing short of a miracle,' she clung to a life raft, 'he says it's a mixture of me as I used to be and me as I've become.'

'That's because I see the fundamental "you". Many people have sat for me, not one of them has given me the satisfaction, joy, fulfilment, that you did. You have a wonderful face, you are a truly beautiful woman—'

'A day out and remarks like that as a bonus, what more can a woman ask!' She felt her cheeks blaze with embarrassment as she said the first words that came into her head, the life raft slipping out of her grasp.

'Claudia, you are joking, I am serious. Look at you now, discomforted by what I tell you and yet excited, telling yourself that I am teasing and yet wanting to believe. Am I right? So much of the young Claudia, the Claudia that was, is still there and will be there as long as you live. Never let anything destroy it.'

His mouth was inches from hers, it drew her like a magnet. The water was deep, she stopped floundering, stopped fighting as she sunk, to be taken into the arms of a life saver.

She had borne three children, two of them older than he was himself, yet in that hour time had no meaning, neither minutes nor years, she knew herself to be desirable, a woman whose passion had no limit. Like a young giant he carried her to lie on his bed; gently, with something akin to reverence he took each garment off her. She was stone-cold sober, she knew exactly where she was heading, yet she had no will to pull back. It was as if the Claudia of her familiar life was an on-looker on this other woman, Adrian's forest nymph.

When at last their passions were spent, the sudden silence hurtled her back to reality. A strange bedroom, Adrian like a young god in his nakedness, and her . . . Claudia Carlyle . . . breathless from making love.

She tried to close her mind to the echo of Melly's words, but how could she now that she realized what pictures she had been talking about. Plenty of women friends of his own age . . . he wasn't looking for a mother image . . . and 'you should see the picture of the forest, Dad . . .' Could Adrian have shown them to her? But even that was pushed to the back of her mind by the enormity of what she'd done.

She rolled away from him and put her feet to the ground.

'No. Don't go. Stay. Wait.' He pulled her backwards and leant across her.

'Let me go! I must be mad! This isn't *me!*'

He didn't try to stop her as she struggled from the bed and grabbed her clothes from the floor.

'No? Darling Claudia, it may not be the *you* who runs an efficient home, worries about her family, loves her husband – and you do all those things – but this is you every bit as much.'

She was frightened to listen. She'd been happy with her life; until he'd come along and ignited a dormant spark she'd been content. Now what? It was her own fault, she ought to have driven straight home from Heathrow. Oughtn't she?

By now he was on his feet too, only inches from her. When he put his arms around her and pulled her to him reality stood between them in the form of her bundle of garments.

'I'm going home. I shouldn't have come.'

Silently they began to pull on their clothes, the romantic adventure already changed into a cold winter's midday in an untidy bedroom, the rumpled duvet a mocking reminder that she'd broken faith with everything that mattered.

'I'll make coffee,' he said. 'And there's food. I told you, I hoped you'd come, I got food ready.'

'How can I stay and eat lunch, just as if – as if – oh, you'd never understand. You don't owe loyalty to people you love. I expect you feel fine, you meant this to happen.'

'I wanted it to happen.' He sounded so calm, his voice quiet. If he'd argue it would have been easier. 'For months I've wanted you, imagined you.'

'Well, now you know.' Like a child who couldn't find a smart reply she glowered at him.

'Now we both know. Listen, Claudia, I haven't taken anything that was anyone else's; all those times we enjoyed being together, in the forest, in country pubs, on the boat, did you tell yourself you shouldn't have been happy with me because you owed all that you are to the family.'

'That was different. You wouldn't understand! I'd never slept with anyone but Teddy . . .' For a moment she was afraid she was going to cry, she wished she hadn't put it into words. Today had been a milestone. 'I'm going home. Don't talk any more. Just let me go.'

'Home you go, Mrs Carlyle, back to the bosom of your family. But they'll never touch the nerve in you that lusts after freedom and adventure. That belongs to me – to us.' His mouth was hard against hers.

'No.' Pulling away she grabbed her coat. 'You don't know the meaning of loyalty, you can flit from bed to bed –' She'd been speaking wildly, now the words dried up and, dragging her coat on as she went, she left him.

Chapter 7

'House'll seem quiet as the tomb, Mrs C. Shan't know ourselves,' Gwen Pomfrey observed dolefully when she arrived the next morning. 'More than a month, it's been, since there was only you and the doctor. Even peeling the 'tatoes won't take but two minutes.'

'We shall get used to it.'

'Shall have to, we're not given a choice. But I don't mind telling you,' as if it needed saying! 'my favourite times are when we've got the whole lot of them here, when you have me in to give a hand a bit extra. Place fair buzzes then, that it does.'

But as Gwen said, they were given no choice but to get used to it. Teddy welcomed the return to their old routine. He enjoyed the family coming home, but after a busy and sometimes harrowing day, he looked forward to evening, a quiet meal shared just with Claudia, half-heartedly listening to television or reading the paper in the winter, perhaps mowing the grass or just sitting in the stillness of evening in the summer dusk, Claudia by his side, a glass of wine in his hand. Then there was the pleasure of having their friends for an informal dinner, convivial conversation, comfortable companionship.

Claudia liked those things too, she reminded herself just how much she always had enjoyed them, as if that way she would erase where that lust for adventure had carried her. There was no word from Adrian, no unexpected visit. And she was glad, she kept telling herself so . . . Yet, each time the phone rang or a car drew up outside . . .

It was late February, a morning aiming to fool them into believing spring had arrived. It wouldn't last, of course, it was trying to trick keen and gullible gardeners into giving the lawn it's first cut of the season only to find that by tomorrow the shorn blades of grass would be white with frost. Claudia wasn't to be fooled, but even so as she watched Teddy drive away she was aware of a need to be active. It wasn't one of Gwen's days, but with a house as tidy and shining as

Russets there was nothing to use her energy on there. When she turned her hand to house cleaning she liked a real muddle to sort out, there was nothing satisfying about dusting already shining surfaces or vacuuming a clean carpet.

My trouble is I never really stick at anything, she admitted honestly to herself – to admit it to anyone but herself would have been quite another thing. That's what Teddy thinks, that's why he gets uptight sometimes when I dive off into some new scheme. He's right, I know he's right. There was the pottery . . . her disappointment had faded long ago, now she could smile at the recollection of her few misshapen pots; there was jewellery-making . . . oh, but that just wasn't my scene at all; what about the time you went to car maintenance classes? Or ages ago when Melly first started school, remember the canoeing? Now what, though? It's no good gardening. I could go to Bournemouth or Southampton, but a day at the shops has nothing to show for it except things I can do without.

She was still undecided when the phone rang. It was Sally Downs, a friend from the other side of Avonford. Was she frantically busy? What about meeting for lunch as it was such a glorious day? In Bournemouth the gardens would be looking like spring.

'Sorry, Sally. No can do. I'm up to my eyes in decorating.' Out of the blue, she knew exactly what she would do. 'Today I'm going to get stuck in and not let myself be tempted away. Will that mess up your plans? Can you get someone else?'

'Hilda's coming. We're meeting at ten o'clock, shopping first, then lunch, then we thought perhaps a cinema. Leave the decorating and come with us, why don't you? It won't run away.'

'You know me, I have to strike while the mood takes me.'

Sally laughed good-naturedly. Claudia and her mood-driven energy were well known.

When she'd rung off, Claudia went up the stairs two at a time. That was what she'd do, she'd decorate the old nursery. Half an hour later she'd taken the measurements and was on her way to Lymington to buy wallpaper, paste and paint. The sky seemed even bluer, she turned on the radio as she drove and sang along with some pop song even though she couldn't find its tune. She'd buy a new paste brush and a two-inch paint brush – oh yes, and she'd need turps. The day had become full of promise.

By late afternoon the furniture was all in the middle of the room covered with a dust sheet, and the last obstinate piece of wallpaper was being soaked from the wall. Dressed in an old, paint-stained boiler suit, with her hair tied in a scarf, she felt dirty, stiffer than she liked to admit, but completely happy in her muddle.

103

'That's the lot,' she said aloud, 'the last pocket of resistance wiped out.' She stuffed the strips of old wallpaper into bin liners and, full of good intentions that she would clear up as she went along, tied up the tops ready to carry them downstairs to the shed. It was as she tied the last one that the silence was disturbed by a ring at the front door bell.

I'll be out, she decided. But there's a light up here and no curtains. Still I don't have to answer it, they'll get tired and go away. She stood very still, she even breathed carefully. Probably someone selling cleaning stuff, or the vicar doing his infrequent round. Curiosity was getting the better of her although she wasn't going to risk being seen peeping. As the bell rang again she sidled along the landing and into the bathroom, then climbed on to the stool so that she could see out of the open frosted glass window. The caller had decided that despite the upstairs light being on, no-one was at home, so he was going back down the path to where his car was parked.

'Wait!' she yelled. 'Wait, I'm coming down.'

She turned too quickly, the stool rocked precariously. There was nothing to grab, no way of saving herself.

She was emerging through a thick, dark mist. Why was she lying down? This wasn't *her* bed . . . yet it was familiar, it felt right to be here . . . Teddy . . . She felt his hand on her wrist and knew he was taking her pulse yet she hadn't the energy nor yet the curiosity to wonder why. Then she closed her eyes.

'Melly's room . . .?' Claudia's returning reason could only go one step at a time and, in her muddled state, her concentration focused on the fact that the bed she was lying on wasn't her own. That there was a seering pain in her temple, that Teddy was here with her, his familiar bag opened on the chair, was something she could come to only as she regained a firmer hold on herself. 'How . . . Melly's bed?'

'You slipped. This was the nearest place for Adrian to carry you.'

Adrian. Now the mists were clearing.

'Stool . . . stool tipped. Looking to see who . . .' It was hard to string a coherent sentence together when a regiment of drummers beat a tattoo on her brain.

Her paint-stained boiler suit told Teddy that she had been embarking on one of her sudden inspirational schemes. This was no time to enquire. A nasty bump on her forehead, but thank God nothing worse. Her heartbeat was regular, her pulse already getting strong. Even so he wanted to be sure she hung on to her consciousness, so he propped her up on her pillows and sat on the edge of the bed.

'Adrian had been in Southampton, he decided to drive this bit further and come and see us. Nice of him. He tells me he was just going away, thinking you were out, when you shouted from the bathroom.'

'Stool wobbled. I fell. Was letting him in. Couldn't.'

'When you didn't come to the door he thought you must have expected him to let himself in through the kitchen. So that's what he did.'

When her soul was her own again and it wasn't an effort for her to follow what he said, he would fill her in with the rest of the story, how Adrian had carried her to the nearest bedroom then phoned the surgery with an urgent message. The receptionist had bleeped him and, as luck had it, he'd been only half a mile from home, his rounds done and on his way to the Medical Centre for teatime surgery. From her fall to his arrival no more than five minutes could have elapsed.

'What's time?' She still felt that her words came from faraway, but with each second her mind was clearing. Her head hurt horribly, but it was what she thought of as a 'healthy hurt'. Pain she could handle; feeling muzzy and not quite belonging to her surroundings she couldn't. Adrian . . . Even without a muzzy head her mind was in confusion.

'Time I was at surgery,' Teddy was saying. 'Adrian will come up and stay with you. I want you to promise me you'll not try and get off the bed until I come back. I'll get through as fast as I can.'

'Adrian – here? Still here?'

'He promised to stay with you while I did surgery. So I suggested he spent the night here.'

'Dinner. Nothing done.' It was cowardly to hide her confusion behind the mundane, but it helped her hold her sudden panic at bay.

'Leave it to us,' said Teddy, whose cooking skill had never been stretched beyond the occasional bacon and egg. He packed his bag and closed it with a click. Then stooped to kiss the top of her head. She saw the way his glance travelled the length of her workmanlike garb, before he looked at her with eyebrows raised.

'The nursery.' She answered his unspoken question. 'Got all the stuff, paint, paper, everything.'

'I might have guessed.' Experience had taught him that her bursts of enthusiasm seldom ended in success, but after all these years he'd accepted he couldn't change her. Looking at her in her dirty overalls, a bump like a green golf ball already swelling on her temple, exasperation and love vied with each other. Love won.

She listened as he went down the stairs, then she heard muted voices as he and Adrian talked. Wriggling to sit up straighter she was tempted to forget her instructions and get off the bed, she even swung her legs to the ground. But such a swimmy feeling came over her that she pulled them back and gratefully rested against the piled pillows. Lying down she had believed there was nothing wrong except a headache, it was frightening to know she wasn't mistress of her own actions.

As the front door slammed behind Teddy, she heard Adrian coming up the stairs. How could she face him here at home? Panic gripped her, but there was no escape.

'I have instructions to keep you awake and talking.' He sounded just as he always had; her visit to his flat might never have happened. She was too confused to be sure whether she was relieved or humiliated.

'Was hiding,' it was an effort to marshal her thoughts into a coherent sentence, 'thought the bell was vicar on his round, selling cleaning stuff, or—' Any sort of chatter must be better than picking up where she'd last said goodbye to him.

'The vicar selling cleaning stuff?' He'd understood her perfectly well, but was determined to keep her talking and, at this juncture, as keen as she was to keep off dangerous ground.

'Silly,' she laughed, 'ouch!' She put her hand gingerly to the side of her right eye where the laughter lines pulled at the swelling on her head. 'Or even Jehovah's Witnesses, thought it might have been them. Climbed up to see.'

'If I hadn't come you wouldn't have fallen. Claudia, I'm sorry.' Sorry that she'd fallen? Sorry he'd made love to her? She kept her gaze fixed firmly on her dirty trainers still on her feet. 'I almost rang you from Southampton, but decided it would be – be best just to arrive and surprise you. Teddy has asked me to stay the night. Is that all right?'

''Course it's all right, *we've* told you before.' Purposely she emphasized that the invitation was from Teddy too. 'But dinner – Teddy said I had to wait here till he's home.'

'I'm a man of many talents, not least I can produce a passable spaghetti bolognaise, a superb curry or even a stir fry. Leave it to me, I'll find the basis of something I promise you.'

'Can't let you do that. You're guest—'

'I'm the cause of your fall. Anyway I enjoy cooking. I've looked after myself for years. All I ask is a kitchen to myself and a few "ooos" and "aahhs" of praise at the result.'

She laughed despite herself; even her sore head couldn't take away her pleasure.

106

'Lovely you've come.' And she meant it. She wasn't in a state yet to analyse her thoughts.

By eight o'clock he had produced a professional looking moussaka and salad. Under Teddy's watchful eye Claudia had replaced her workmanlike overalls with jeans and a slouchy jumper. Not very elegant, but comfortable and in keeping with her throbbing head and general feeling of weakness.

'You know what this woman of mine was doing when you arrived?' Teddy said to Adrian during the meal. 'Decorating the old nursery – your room when you were here. Was it that bad? I hadn't noticed.'

'I was fed up with the colour, that's why I did it.' Food had given her back some of her usual spirit. 'The paper was insipid and I hate mushroom paint. What I bought is much better, sort of pale green and gold, but positive, not wishy-washy. And white paint. Then I'll get new curtains made.'

'Fair enough, that's your department. But on one thing I'm adamant,' Teddy told her, 'you are not to do it yourself. In the morning I want you to phone Marshalls and get them to send someone to finish what you've started.'

'I don't want a man from Marshalls underfoot.' She must have been more upset by her fall than she was prepared to admit, she could hear an ominous croak in her voice. 'It wasn't because the room was awful, it was because I was bored.' She glowered at him, her mouth sulky. 'I needed to be doing something.'

'If you need to do something, why don't you sew the curtains? You can't break your neck doing that.'

'Hate sewing. Anyway I wasn't decorating when I fell, you know I wasn't.'

'Even so, for once I'm putting my foot down. What do other women do with themselves?'

If Claudia's expression had been on the children, Gwen Pomfrey would have told them to 'Watch out! I see you've got that black dog on your back.'

'May I make a suggestion?' Adrian put in. 'You may think it's an impertinence but I hope you won't,' he smiled disarmingly at the pair of them but he spoke to Teddy. 'It's this. Let me stay a few days, I'd love to decorate that room. A cheek, I know, but I came to think of it as mine when I was here back in the autumn. I won't let Claudia risk her neck, honestly. She can be foreman, I'll be labourer. What do you say?'

Teddy accepted his offer gratefully. He was touched by the young artist's simple admission that he had a feeling of belonging at Russets.

107

'At least I shan't have to worry what you'll be getting up to,' Teddy told Claudia as they settled for sleep in a position unfamiliar to either of them. Instead of lying on their right, she sitting in his lap, tonight she couldn't bear pressure on her bruised right temple. So they turned on the left, uncomfortably conscious of arms and shoulders and legs, not being able to relax. 'Having him here is like having one of the youngsters coming home, isn't it.'

'I wouldn't say that. But he really seemed to want to stay didn't he? You don't think he offered because it was his fault I'd fallen?'

'Hardly his fault,' Teddy laughed. 'You know what I think? He's not had parents, or not for years, that's why he likes to drop in here the way he does. Goodnight, dear. If you want me, wake me won't you.'

Her chuckle showed she was on the mend.

'I don't think I'm better enough to be wanting you. But, of course, if I make a sudden recovery—'

'Go to sleep, you wanton hussy.'

In minutes he was asleep. Claudia moved far enough away to lie on her back, wide awake. There had been no man in her life except Teddy – until that day. 'I haven't taken anything that was his' Adrian had believed. But how could that be. Suppose Teddy knew – how hurt he would be – or would he be disgusted, would he think the things about her that Mellie had hinted? Tomorrow I'll tell Adrian to go. If I have to have men from Marshalls then that will be my punishment.

Her decision made, sleep was overtaking her. Was she awake and thinking or was she asleep and dreaming? Clearly she saw herself working in the nursery with Adrian, she could hear the sound of laughter, she felt alive, bright . . .

Along the corridor, Adrian lay in the single room that, when the family had come for the birthday, had been used by Barry. If Teddy could have looked into his mind, seen the pictures conjured in his imagination, pictures with life, warmth, movement, he might not have slept with such sweet content.

The family was scattered, but not many days ever went by without phone calls.

Hearing that Adrian was again staying at Russets, Melly's immediate reaction was alarm. But she congratulated herself that she gave no sign of it in her cheerful comment.

'A new venture for him, painting skirtings! You should have told us you wanted it done, Mum. Last week was half term, we could have come down if we'd known. Trevor's a first-class paper hanger.'

'I didn't want it done. I wanted to *do* it. But your father got all pig-headed just because I fell off a stool. It's all right, though, Adrian and I are doing it between us and enjoying the novelty.' It surprised her how much pleasure she got from saying it to Melly. She was seeing a side to her nature she didn't know she had! 'When it's done, we're going to Lymington to the fabric shop. With his artist's eye I'm leaving him to chose the material for the curtains and then we shall celebrate a job well done by his taking me out to lunch.'

'That's kind of him, Mum.'

'It's totally gallant to be seen out with me at all! The green lump on my head is as bright as a "Go" signal. I must look like a battered wife.'

Between them was the memory of the pictures, never mentioned directly and yet always there.

'Poor old Mum,' her voice was solicitous, 'how rotten for you. It's a blessing you didn't break anything. There was an article in the medical page of the paper this morning about brittle bones in older women. It happens to so many women as they age and they don't even know until they have a fall. It's a good thing there's a thick carpet in the bathroom or you might have been all plastered up.' Except for telling her bluntly, Melly couldn't think of any other way of reminding her mother she was making a fool of herself.

'You're talking rubbish!' Which told them both that the message was received and understood.

On the first morning, with Teddy gone and Gwen not yet arrived, Claudia had faced Adrian.

'You shouldn't have come here. And even more, I shouldn't have – shouldn't have—'

'Pax.' His smile was disarming. 'This is Russets, the home of Claudia Carlyle, what is it I've heard you say of yourself? Mum, Gran – but most of all you are the wife of Teddy. I told you, *that* Claudia is beyond my reach. Now, let's get to work. And let's surprise them all with our talent.'

They set to work, and true to his word they seemed to have slipped back to those happy autumn days. So nothing Melly said had any power to cast a shadow. Measuring, pasting, painting, and this time Claudia had the novel satisfaction of seeing a job she had started coming to fruition. Neither of them mentioned her visit to his flat, but surely it must have been at the forefront of his mind every bit as much as it was hers. Unspoken, it must have been with them, their relationship coloured by it; it was in his glance when she turned

109

unexpectedly and found him watching her; it was in hers as she passed him a strip of pasted wallpaper.

Melly was worried and angry. Her imagination was running riot. Remembering what Adrian had produced from his original visit, whatever sort of poses would be the outcome of days spent decorating?

Dad's such an innocent; I can't tell the boys or even Trevor; it has to be up to me to find a really huge spanner to throw into the works.

She found one. It arrived on the doormat at Russets two days later in the form of a letter from Harvey. Claudia collected the mail and read it first, then passed it to Teddy when he came into the kitchen where she was preparing breakfast.

I happened to be talking to Melly who tells me that Adrian Crighton is staying with you again. That turned my thoughts to Mum's portrait and something I've been turning over in my mind for some time. Is Adrian drivingly busy, I wonder, or could he dally with you a bit longer and take on a commission to paint Erica's portrait? Sound him out for me, will you, and if he's willing to take it on perhaps he could give me a ring. You may have read in the papers that Josef Szpiegelberg has been taken ill. From out of the blue I have been asked to take his place in a series of concerts in Berlin and Prague. You can imagine, Erica is anything but keen. We've been there so recently they've hardly had a chance to change the shop windows! I thought perhaps this would be an ideal opportunity for the portrait. I know she'd much rather come down and stay with you than sit through more concerts.

Reading the last sentence, Claudia frowned. *She* knew it was true. But did the letter mean that Erica had spoken to Harvey as she had to her about the tours? She'd told no-one about Erica's outburst. When they'd arrived back in England they'd phoned, Harvey had been quiet but they'd expected nothing more, the end of a demanding tour always left him drained. Erica, on the other hand, usually arrived home full of chatter. This time there had been chatter, but Claudia had heard it as forced. She had told herself she was imagining troubles simply because she knew Erica's first euphoria had lost its gloss, if anything had been wrong Teddy would have detected it and from the sound of the natural bantering going on between him and his favourite daughter-in-law clearly he detected no undercurrent.

She expected Teddy to be overjoyed at the prospect of Erica's visit. His frown surprised her.

'What does he mean? "Erica anything but keen . . . hardly had time to change the shop windows . . ." He's the one who has the strain, it's her place to be there with him,. She's his wife, damn it.'

'And if that's what she's going to remain, he must give her the choice. He has his work, he has companionship of like-minded people; rehearsals, performances, travelling, sleeping, that's about what the tours consist of. What is there in it for her? You can't wonder if she's not overjoyed at the prospect of packing her bags again so soon. She must get thoroughly fed up.'

Teddy put the letter back in the envelope and flipped it on to the kitchen table.

'Fed up? You're telling me she needs space like the other one? God spare me from today's generation of young wives. And you back them instead of standing up for your sons. What sort of a tour will it be for Harvey, going back each night to an empty hotel room? I suppose she's persuaded him to write suggesting this. He's not happy with the idea, don't you know your own son well enough to be able to read between the lines? I've a good mind to tell them I'm not having it.'

'Then you're a bigger fool than I'd have thought. After all it's only one tour and it may well be true he'd been thinking of having her portrait painted. He could hardly have suggested Adrian should go there while he was away.'

'With today's people, I wouldn't know.'

'Oh, Teddy, you're talking about "today's people" as if they are a different breed. This is Harvey and Erica. If Adrian will take the commission, then of course she'll come here – and of course you'll love having her.'

Adrian agreed to do the portrait. Naturally he did, it was a heaven-sent opportunity for him to stay on at Russets. When he had been making his preliminary sketches of Claudia he had wanted to watch her from every angle, watch her changing expressions, understand what was behind the façade. He'd met Erica the weekend of Teddy's birthday, he knew just how lovely she was, her looks were an open book. He would ask her to sit for him each morning for an hour or so. But she wasn't arriving until the following week. In the meantime he and Claudia worked together, pasting, papering, painting, laugh-ing, cursing then laughing again, all the more aware of each other because of that hour they didn't mention. She believed she presented the image of that Claudia who was happy amongst her family, loving her husband, content with her life – the Claudia who remained un-touched by the amorous encounter of that second self. She ought to have remembered the portrait and realized that he saw beneath the surface to the fundamental spirit.

111

Each day he became more fascinated by her, more certain that her visit to his flat was just the beginning. Watching her he wanted to touch the curve of her slim, rounded bottom as she squatted to trim at the skirting, or to hold his hand under her breast as she stretched high to butt the top edges to the picture rail. But he mustn't. Not here. The disfiguring bruise on her forehead did nothing to mar her attractiveness, he saw it as a sign of courage that not once had she shown any self-pity. By next week the nursery would be finished, Erica would be here. He'd work in the mornings – in the evenings he would slot into place as a welcome guest in the house – but that still left the afternoons.

'Coming here has been a lifeline, Claudia. Honest to God, I think we should have snapped if I'd gone with Harvey.'

'Don't say that, Erica. He understands you don't find it easy, you feel out on a limb.'

'Is that what he told you? That I'm tired of it? That's not fair of him, it's not all my fault.' Claudia could hear the dangerous croak in the husky American voice.

'I'll tell you exactly what he said, in fact you can read what he wrote.' She opened the bureau and took a pile of letters from the cubbyhole, found the one she wanted and passed it to troubled-looking girl.

Erica read it, then passed it back.

'I never told him I was bored. I never told him I'm fed up with the same old round. It was different in the beginning, I suppose it was because he was fresh married to me that people were interested to meet me as well as him – not because of *me*, I could have been anything from a film star to a fish fryer, it wouldn't have made any difference, I was worth photographing because I was the new Mrs Harvey Carlyle –'

'The only Mrs Harvey Carlyle, Erica. If the newspapers made a meal of you to start with and then lost interest, that's not Harvey's fault.'

'It's no-one's fault. Except my own. I ought to have had the sense to know that falling in love is one thing, making your life around someone else's is different again.'

'Just hang on to the first part, the falling in love with someone bit.'

Erica examined her beautifully manicured deep pink nails, anything rather than meet Claudia's earnest eyes.

'It's not just me. How do you think he feels? See what he says in your letter: "they won't even have changed the shop windows". He'd never said that to me any more than I'd told him those eternal concerts drive me crazy. Only interested in shops. Is that how he sees me? People pay huge sums to listen to him playing, and I'm so fed up with that damned piano I could take an axe to it. If he were a farmer he wouldn't bring his cows into the house; if he were a accountant he wouldn't spread his work all over the dining table. Yet this is supposed to be different.'

'Maybe it's time you had a baby, Erica.'

'No!' The speed of her spontaneous answer frightened Claudia. 'A baby can't be like a plaything to keep me amused. There are too many children upset by broken marriages. If we ever have a family it must be because we plan them and are both ready for them. Not to fill a gap and give me something to occupy my mind, take the place of the resentment.'

'Does Harvey know all this?'

'Guess so. It sounds that way from what he wrote to you.' She turned her back, frightened to speak. She mustn't cry.

Claudia came to her side and put her arm around her waist.

'I'm glad you've come down to us for a while. By the time he comes home both of you will have time to miss each other, you'll both have your priorities right.'

'Me, you mean. I wish he had another woman, a whole bunch of women. I could deal with that.'

Claudia laughed.

'He probably couldn't.'

'You're dead right he couldn't. He can't bring himself to spare the time for a wife who has to be grateful for the crumbs, small chance for a mistress who'd expect a large slice of cake.'

How bitter she sounded. This was Harvey she was talking about, her voice harsh with scorn.

'Ah, I hear Adrian's car. You concentrate on enjoying having your portrait painted. I did. And when Harvey comes home you'll both see things differently.'

He'll probably phone her this evening when he arrives in Berlin, Claudia clutched at the hope. If only he'd say the right thing to her. So many fears and doubts chased each other in Claudia's mind: heartache for Harvey who had been so proud of Erica's love; anger for the lovely young American girl who had been caught up in the glamour of marrying a celebrity; pity for her too that she realized too late what life to a serious concert pianist must involve. No wonder when Adrian came into the room she turned to him in a glow of welcome.

The next morning Erica sat before him in the freshly decorated – and paint-smelling – old nursery room.

*

A week went by with no phone call from Harvey. He must have written instead, it wasn't unknown for letters from the Continent to take as long as that.

'Anything from Harvey?' It was almost Teddy's first words to Claudia when he came home on the evening of Erica's tenth day with them.

'A card for us. A letter for Erica.'

'Ah, that's good. The boy all right? Where's his card?'

'On the bureau. He says the usual things, flight good, hotel OK. Typical postcard talk.'

'Too soon to hear how the recitals are going I expect. Did Erica have any news? I suppose hers was personal.'

Claudia hesitated, then without quite looking at him, said, 'If it was personal, I don't think it was what she was wanting to hear. She's been very quiet today – and, Teddy, it looked to me as though she'd been crying.'

'Probably wishing she'd gone with him like she should have. Let's hope she's learnt a lesson. How soon is dinner?'

In the mornings Adrian worked in the nursery, sometimes Erica sat as long as two hours; they talked, he made sketches. Sometimes he dismissed her in far less time. Once she was free she invariably went out, drove to Bournemouth or Southampton, sometimes even as far as Salisbury. Her restless spirit wouldn't let her be still.

The weather was bright and mild, for the first two afternoons of that period Adrian helped Claudia in the garden. She liked that, it was restoring her confidence (in herself? in him? she didn't delve), she saw it as companionable and comfortable that they worked together, rooting out weeds, giving the lawn its first cut of the season, trimming the edges, clipping the hedges. Melly would have been reassured if she could have seen her mother's cheerful acceptance of having him there.

But soon he would be gone. The portrait was nearly finished. It did justice to Erica's clean-cut features, to the gentle slope of her pale shoulders and her swan-like neck. The mouth curved into a smile, there was a hint of light in the brown eyes. So why wasn't it a happy picture? Erica's charm, greater even than her natural good looks, had always been her excitement in living. It eluded Adrian's brush. But was that so surprising, when even those who knew her far better couldn't rekindle it?

'I thought what she needed was a break from Harvey and his music,' Claudia said to Teddy. 'Well, so she did, but what's happened to her old *joie-de-vivre*? What do you think? Is it just the music she's

114

fed up with? I can understand how hard it must be for her, it's not even her scene. She thrives on jazz, so she must find it hard to take. What worries me is, is it just that she's bored or is it more fundamental? How does Harvey feel I wonder?' Because she knew he'd always been fond of Erica she wasn't frightened to say these things. It had been so different when the trouble had come from Jenny.

The two of them were walking along a forest track on a bright Sunday afternoon, seeing the very first signs that the miracle of spring was trying to push its way through its winter covering of years of leaf mould. She was aware of the changing season, yet on this March day she couldn't rejoice in it. She was too worried, she needed Teddy's reassurance that she was letting her imagination run away with her.

'She doesn't have to share his music. But her place is with him, he deserves to have her there. It's time she had a baby, gave herself something to think about.'

Claudia remembered suggesting the same thing, yet now she felt her hackles rise in Erica's defence.

'There *are* other things in life for a woman except bedding and breeding. Times have changed, women expect more out of life than they used.'

'And you think they get more by not supporting their husbands?' There was no smile in his voice. Still side by side, yet she felt the distance between them. 'Christ! Can you wonder one marriage in three – or is it two? – ends in divorce? As you know, I never thought Jennifer any asset to James, although to give her her due she seemed to work hard in the parish. Until this recent episode.'

'I told you, when I phoned the rectory yesterday evening she was at a Sunday School meeting organizing the Easter Sunday children's procession. She always helps with costumes. I thought she'd pulled out of all that sort of thing, I said so to James—'

'What in the world for? If she's seen sense, don't you start making trouble. Much better for James – for his pride too – if he thinks we weren't aware how difficult she was being. In any case, a lot of our fears turned out to be groundless. She stayed away because she was being a dutiful do-gooder.' For a minute there was silence between them. She knew so much more than he did about the troubles at Brightley, yet invariably she heard his dislike when he talked about Jenny. Then, when she didn't answer, 'When you mentioned it to James, what did he tell you? How did he sound?'

'He sounded like the old James. That's why I knew I could ask him about her taking her jobs on again. He said she was wonderful, absolutely throwing herself into the parish work. I even got the

115

impression some of the St Luke's Ladies might get their noses put out of joint.'

'Thank God for that. It worried me to death to see him like he was. You must have seen it too, he was drawn, no longer young . . .'

She shrugged her shoulders. 'They can't stay young for ever,' she said. 'Youth doesn't necessarily make for happiness. But Teddy he sounded confident, untroubled.'

'And now we get young Erica playing the prima donna. How much longer is Harvey away? When the portrait's finished perhaps she could fly out and join him. They need to be together.'

'Just at present, I think that's about the last thing she needs. And Harvey can do without an emotional upset while he's so heavily committed.'

'Thank God for Melly.'

She remembered it wasn't so long ago that he'd thanked God for Harvey and Erica.

Reaching the end of the enclosure they came to a pile of timber, huge hewn trees.

'Let's climb to the top and look at the view for a while. It's one of those days when you can see for ever. Don't you just love this place? This pile of logs was here in the autumn, Adrian and I had a make-shift picnic – shared a can of Coke and ate a pocketful of chestnuts we'd picked up.' Just to say it brought back the carefree joy of those outings. Or was it more than carefree joy? Even then had she known deep in her inner heart where they were heading? 'Come on Teddy, up we go.'

'No, I think we should get home. We've been out a long time.'

'What does that matter? You're not on call. Anyway, the others are home.'

'Precisely.'

'Really, you've got a one-track mind! First you think Adrian will get after Melly, now you're frightened to leave him alone with Erica. What do you think he is, some sort of a sex maniac? In any case, the girls do have minds of their own you know.'

'Just at the moment Erica's mind is in a receptive state. Add to that that she is sexual dynamite, and that Adrian is a normal young man, then he can't fail to be roused by her.'

'Rubbish. You'd think he were a rampant forest stag the way you talk.'

'You don't know men.'

They strode on towards home and after a minute she started to laugh.

'I don't know men. Not even you? I'll have to make sure I don't leave *you* alone with her. Poor old Teddy, I didn't know she got you in such a tizzy.'

'Don't be ridiculous!' came his quick and pompous report.

Chapter 8

Next morning brought a thicker envelope to Erica addressed in Harvey's hand. She took it to her room where she was preparing for her final sitting.

In the utility room the washing machine was churning happily and, by the time Gwen Pomfrey propped her cycle against the side of the house, Claudia was drying the last of the breakfast dishes.

'Monday. Nothing like Monday morning for giving a person a push to be getting on. Like taking the bit between our teeth.' Gwen put on her old-fashioned wrap-around overall and went to the cupboard for the tools of her trade.

'Bedroom day. Better not touch the nursery I suppose, that young artist fellow will still be busying himself in there.'

'Yes. Perhaps you'd better start with our room, I think Erica is still using hers dressing. They say today will be her last sitting. I thought it was finished, but he wants her there one more time.'

'Likes her company I dare say.'

'We all do. And his. I suppose he'll go back to London any day now. Harvey is due home on Thursday, so before we know it it'll be just us here again.'

'Soon be Easter. Perhaps the children will be down. I like it when they come, the place feels lived in.'

'You're a glutton for work, Gwen.'

'No point in cleaning if there's no dirt to shift. I like a bit of muddle, or there's no satisfaction in leaving it spick and span at the end.' Leaving Claudia putting away the breakfast dishes she plodded up the stairs, in one hand she carried a handled wooden box containing cleaning materials, in the other the vacuum with the flex thrown across her shoulders.

At the top of the stairs she stopped, her head cocked on one side as she listened. Then, tiptoeing along the corridor, she hovered outside Erica's door. Her look of happy determination at the prospect of a morning's work gave way to a worried frown. Oh dear, oh dear, whatever the trouble was it was best to tell Mrs C.

Instinct prompted her to put her feet down quietly as she retraced her steps to the kitchen.

'Mrs C. You'd better come and have a listen. Something must have upset Erica. Hate to hear a person crying like that. Was she all right at breakfast?'

'Yes. Are you sure?'

Gwen was concerned, anxious to get Claudia upstairs quickly to comfort the poor young girl.

'Yes. You'd better go to her Mrs C.'

There was no way Claudia could escape her inexplicable fear. She was swamped by a feeling of doom. It must be something Harvey had put in his letter. But what? She answered the question almost before she asked it. But it made no sense. They had always seemed such a happy couple. Why should Harvey do this to Erica? He loved her, he couldn't want to hurt her . . .? Could he? Please make it not be what I think. I know something is wrong between them, but please make it be just a difference of opinion, something that can be sorted out with no real damage.

'I'll go up. You'd better do downstairs today instead Gwen.'

'Best I had. If she's got things to get off her chest, she won't do it with me clattering about in the next room.'

'It's me. May I come in?' Claudia spoke as she tapped on the bedroom door, opening it without waiting for an answer.

Sprawled across the bed, wearing only exquisitely dainty silk underwear, was Erica. Sexual dynamite, that's how Teddy had described her. If Harvey had the love – and loyalty, for there was nothing of a coquette about Erica – of a woman who was sexual dynamite what could have gone wrong for them? They had the most important ingredient in a married relationship. What could it matter if he was a pianist, a plasterer or a pigman, if they loved each other and were happy in bed they could sort out their differences.

'It can't be as bad as that.' She sat on the bed, her hand on the slim white shoulder as Erica lay with her face buried in the duvet. 'Can't you tell me? Was it Harvey's letter?'

A snort told her it was.

'Read it if you like,' Erica gulped, turning her swollen face in Claudia's direction. 'Nothing in it he couldn't have written to a maiden aunt.'

'But Erica, that's just Harvey isn't it? He runs from emotion, he

119

always has.' She was talking to give Erica a chance to snatch at control. 'I remember his letters used to tear me to bits when he first went to boarding school. He was miserable as sin – I knew because James told us what a hard time he was having to settle – but his letters were stark sentences telling us the things he was doing, never a hint how lost he was without us.'

'I'd suggested I met him when he finished.' The words rushed out, each short sentence was a race against the need to breathe for that's when sobs still caught in her throat. 'His last concert's on Friday . . . I'd booked my flight, didn't tell you and Teddy, not . . . not till Harvey said yes . . . But he's told me not to come . . . said he wants to get home . . . says we have to talk about things . . . Couldn't say it plainer . . .'

How she shivered. Claudia wanted to take her in her arms, but sympathy would have been her undoing just as she was fighting back the tears. That feeling of doom was darkening.

'I think he's wrong. You could both do with a holiday.'

'That's what I told him . . . no music . . . we'd have time to see each other . . . really see each other . . . But he doesn't want to.' She foraged in her pocket for a handkerchief to mop her face. 'It's no good pretending . . . we're washed up . . . here, read it, see what I mean. Dear Erica . . .' Walking to the basin she ran cold water and started to rinse her face.

Claudia looked at the pages that had been thrust into her hands, she didn't want to read the letter but words jumped up at her: 'Dear Erica', 'not the time for a holiday', 'well received', 'enthusiastic audiences', 'not fair to expect it of you', 'lack of common interests', 'review our situation'. Enough for her to get the gist of his message and enough, too, for her to know without a doubt that his own unhappiness was as deep as Erica's. What could she say? What could she do? Help me think clearly, please help me to see a way to guide them. But how can I? There's no black or white, neither of them is right and neither of them wrong. Lack of common interests could be overcome. How many couples, happy couples, shared the same interests? The same sense of humour, ah, that mattered, and tolerance and above all else love. She looked at Erica, standing by the window with her back to the room, so young and vulnerable. Her underwear had been designed to titillate, yet to Claudia she looked more like a miserable child than a glamorous woman who was sexual dynamite.

'He's unhappy too, Erica. And perhaps he's right about the holiday, at home you'll see things more clearly. Be honest with each other. You don't need to be part of his work, not many wives are that. If you love each other, none of that matters.'

120

'I know.' Erica's voice was small, it held no ring of confidence. 'I don't want to sit for Adrian this morning – look a sight. Don't want him to see me. Can you tell him, Claudia? I'll get dressed and do my face, then I'm going out. I'm going to Bournemouth.'

'Do you want to go on your own, or shall I come with you?' Claudia tried to put some enthusiasm into the suggestion, perhaps it would do both of them good to make an effort to enjoy themselves. After a day out things might not look so hopeless.

'No, I'm OK. I'll be glad if you'll think up some excuse or other for Adrian. You won't tell him that I've been crying will you? I'm OK, honest I am. Disappointed that I'm not getting a holiday. And I think Harvey's crazy. Imagine us sitting in that beastly flat in Manchester discussing our future. Enough to kill all hope!' Claudia laughed, playing along with her and thankful to see her fighting her way on top of the situation. 'You read in the letter, he says he's landing at Heathrow at 9.35 Wednesday evening. He wants me to meet him so that I can drive him straight home.'

'And that's good, Erica. He wants to come home and to have you waiting for him. Sort out your differences, then have your holiday with no clouds overhead.'

Erica nodded. But she still didn't turn round to look at Claudia.

'You'll fix Adrian?'

'I'll tell him now. I'll say you've heard that Harvey is arriving sooner than you'd expected and have things to do in Bournemouth. If he digs, I'll play it as it goes.'

Now they were on smoother ground, at least the day ahead knocked into shape, she was able to give Erica an affectionate hug without fear of the floodgates re-opening.

In the nursery Adrian was waiting, the portrait on the easel and, to Claudia's eye, finished and signed. He took the news that he'd lost his model remarkably cheerfully.

'Then Claudia, that leaves you and me fancy free. Come with me to Lymington. Harvey has left me to select a frame, we'll take the canvas with us.'

'But you said it wasn't finished?'

'I said no such thing,' he laughed. 'Another sitting meant another day here.'

His answer wasn't expected, any more than was the sudden inexplicable joy that bubbled in her. Immediately she stamped it down; how could she so easily forget Harvey and Erica and their unhappiness?

He'd noted her spontaneous delight, just as he'd noted how quickly

121

she took herself in hand. He didn't mean to give her time to find excuses.

'Let's get going, then,' he gave her his most artless smile. 'First the picture framer, then I've something to show you. No, no questions. A surprise.'

'Give me five minutes.'

He listened as she ran down the stairs, he watched from the window as Erica reversed her car out of the drive. The portrait was finished, he couldn't stay any longer. Months ago Claudia and Teddy had told him 'We love having you, you seem like part of the family.' On this visit that's how he had behaved too; those few hours at his flat had altered their relationship, he'd known he must tread carefully or, here at Russets, she might back away from him.

The material chosen for the frame, Claudia and Adrian drove out of Lymington through the familiar forest road to the Queen's Head.

'Lunch first. Surprise after,' he told her, 'then for a bonus, and if there's time, we'll go for a tramp, see if the forest shows stirrings of spring as we tread on a carpet of last autumn's leaves.'

She heard his remark as symbolic; last autumn the forest had been theirs.

'I love surprises,' was all she said. It was enough for Adrian, he couldn't know the fundamental Claudia without being able to hear what was left unsaid.

'Eat up, we don't want to waste time,' he urged.

Today they didn't bother with anything more than a bowl of soup and crusty bread, washed down by a glass of cider. Then they were back in his car. Last autumn they'd been to areas she looked on as 'home ground', places she had known for years; now, though, Adrian took the Ringwood road, then on to Fordingbridge. If they carried straight on they'd come to Salisbury, not one of her usual haunts but even so she'd driven there many times. Ah, but this must be where the surprise started, he turned off, crossed a cattle grid and they were again in the New Forest, and to prove it two ponies came to stand in the road in front of them. Both of them were in foal, neither of them was in a hurry. The delay added to Claudia's pleasure. Somewhere held at bay was a dull pain that Harvey and Erica had lost their way; there was even guilt that she didn't feel the anguish that she had when James and Jenny had floundered. Don't think about it now, think about it later. If there is trouble, real trouble, how's Teddy going to react, will he be as bitter against Erica as he was – and still is deep in his heart – against Jenny? He ought to try and understand: marriage ought to be an even partnership, but he sees Erica as a pretty toy, someone to be there waiting when Harvey has a moment. Ought to have babies, that's what he thinks. Well, that's what Jenny did, but even then she could do no right for him. Are fathers-in-law always so ready to condemn? There's nothing we can do, nothing except be there to listen if we're needed . . . Don't think about it now, if you do it will spoil all this. This afternoon isn't just moments to live now, it's got to be bright, good, this time tomorrow Adrian will be gone, memory of it has to last. Like that morning at the flat? No, don't think about that either. What sort of a woman am I? Fifty-five years old, a grandmother – but am I no better that Melly hints, making a fool of myself chasing a handsome young man who could have any woman he chose? Did I say 'could have', more likely 'does have'. Of course I'm nothing of the kind. And I've certainly never chased after him or any other man. I'm not in love with him, how could I be? I love Teddy, I always have, Teddy, our family, our home. How could I possibly be in love with anyone else? But is it wicked to want to live every second? Nothing's going to stop me enjoying this afternoon, just look at that clear sky, what a sin to bury your mind in imaginary troubles that might never happen when that canopy of blue is over you. I'm *me*, Claudia, I'm attractive because that's how he sees me, I'm desirable because I know he wants me. Wants me? How is it I'm so sure? He's been alone with me often enough at the house and he's given no sign of wanting me. But he does – if he didn't he would be avoiding me after the last time. I mustn't let that happen again. Last time I was on a slippery slope and couldn't stop myself. Slippery slope? No, no, not that! A slope takes you down to the depths. I was on a ski lift, up, up . . .

'I hope you're admiring the scenery,' his voice teased. Clearly he knew she'd been looking at it and seeing nothing. 'Here we are. This is it.' He turned into a track, and went past a bungalow which seemed to be the only house anywhere around.

'A farm?' But it couldn't be, a farm had outbuildings, cowsheds, machinery.

'A fruit farm. In three or four months the hoards will descend, there will be a board by the road inviting folk to Pick Your Own.'

'And this is where we're going? At this time of year?'

'This is indeed where we're going.'

At the end of the track was a patch of rough ground, presumably the car park for the self-pickers, and just beyond that a construction the like of which she'd never seen.

'And you can't pretend you're not surprised.' He drew up in front of it.

'A sort of shed on wheels, solid wheels. Whatever is it?'

'It started life as a gun carrier in the Great War. Imagine, Claudia, the story it could tell, Flanders Fields, trench warfare. Then I wouldn't mind betting it was lived in, maybe some itinerant craftman, or a pedlar calling around the countryside with his wares. Anyway, now it's used each summer during the fruit season, this is where they weigh the baskets of fruit.'

'Where do you come in?'

'Can't you see the potential? I know it's just an empty waggon – and damned cold too this afternoon – but I'll get a calor gas fire and I'll put enough in it to make it habitable. There are plenty of good pubs around, I shan't have to cook. I mean to paint here. I've come to love the forest.'

'But—'

'It's more than a surprise, Claudia, I want it to be a secret too. Stay at Russets, that's what you're going to say isn't it? I can't do that.' He didn't enlarge on why he couldn't do it, and she didn't try and change his mind. Instead he gave her that guileless smile and urged: 'It's going to be great! For three months I can enjoy springtime in this wonderful area, just look at it, for more than nine hundred years it has grown and fluorished.'

'It's the same New Forest at home.'

'We saw it together in autumn. The same forest. And soon it will be spring.'

His mouth sought hers. She could read everything or nothing into that light kiss.

The elderly gun carrier was cold and cheerless, there was nowhere even to sit. So, leaving the car where it was, they walked to the boundary of the fruit farm, crossed the cattle grid that separated it from the forest, and started to climb a grassy slope to an enclosure of beech and oak. This was new ground to them both. They made no plans, he had the sensitivity – or cunning – to know plans weren't Claudia's way of doing things, she liked to live by impulse.

'Will you tell a lie for me, Claudia?' he asked her as they drove home.

'What sort of a lie?'

'Now that I've shared my secret with you, I think it would be better if I left. It seems fairer. As soon as we get back I'd like to load up and get on my way. Can you make my apologies, thank Teddy, tell Erica about the frame – and this is the lie – say that I had a phone call, think of some valid reason why I had to get back to London immediately. It's better that way.' He took her hand as he said the last few words.

Willingly she agreed, surprised at her relief. As long as he was there the image of that wooden shack on wheels would be there between them, between Teddy and her, between Teddy and him.

They were the first to arrive back at Russets, Erica must have decided to make a day of it in Bournemouth. Within minutes Adrian had thrown his things into his bag, collected up his painting gear and was ready to leave.

'I'll be in touch,' he told her. Then he was in the car and away without a backward glance. What had she expected? What had she wanted? Russets claimed her. She looked at her watch then went through the kitchen to the utility room to collect up the vegetables she had to prepare for the evening meal.

The best of the day was gone, already the sun was sinking, its rays hardly bright enough to cast shadows. But she felt restless. So she collected her kneeling mat and small fork and went outside to pull out weeds. The afternoon had become no more than a golden memory, worries much nearer home were taking control. What did Harvey really feel? Was his unemotional letter to Erica simply his way of hiding his hurt? Or did he believe they'd made a mistake? Nothing in common, he'd said. But that was silly. Teddy was a doctor, but it wouldn't interest her to read his medical journals – not that she'd understand them if she did. Putting a plaster on a cut was about her limit. James seemed to expect poor Jenny to immerse her-self in parish work, but what she did – what she'd apparently gone back to doing – were her own allotted tasks. Harvey needed no back-up as far as his work went. If Erica didn't care for his sort of music that couldn't stop him loving her. And surely she must love him. The memory of the girl's crying came between her and the daffodil bed; she sat back on her heels, her face a mask of sadness. Would she and Teddy be able to share this worry any more than they had James's? She ducked answering the question.

The gnats had fooled themselves into believing it was spring al-ready, Claudia could see swarms of them circling aimlessly above the not-yet-pruned rose bushes. She began to feel itchy and decided it was time to go in, have a bath and get changed from her faithful jeans.

In the bedroom she put a tape into the player, Gregorian Chants, something calm to untangle the muddled knots in her mind. With the volume high and the door of the en-suite bathroom open she could hear the gentle, sacred plainsong. It sent her thoughts to James and that, in turn, helped her to believe that troubles were transient. His world has fallen back into place again, it'll be like that for the others. Please let it. Please. She wanted her plea to merge with the chanting of the monks, as if that way it had a better chance of being heard.

The warm water was relaxing, half listening, half letting herself sink into sublime assurance that by Wednesday night, once Harvey was home, they would see just where their priorities were. Stepping from the bath she took the warm towel, wrapped it around her and went through to her bedroom. It was only then that she realized how thoroughly her thoughts had been involved with her family. 'I don't take anything that is theirs,' she could almost hear Adrian saying it. Elbows on the dressing table she rested her chin in her hands, staring at the woman in the looking glass. She'd had her face too long to see it as anything but worn. Mellie would tell her that she was letting Adrian make a fool of her, Mellie would look at her with pitying contempt. Mum . . . Gran . . . just a stupid woman chasing youth that's gone. But it wasn't true, it had nothing to do with youth.

'*Veni, Creator Spiritus,*' the monks chanted.

She bit the corners of her trembling mouth. In that moment she longed for the anguish of tears, she watched in the mirror as her face contorted, became ugly.

Look at you, you who like to pretend you're attractive. No wonder Teddy never worries about leaving Adrian alone with *you*. What am I crying for today? I didn't cry after I'd been to bed with him. Yes but today was different, I can't say how, I just know it was different. We'd never really been alone since he'd made love to me, not till today – except here at home and that doesn't count, he told me that, he said that here I was *their* Claudia. Did I go out with him expecting it to happen again, wanting it to? No! Did I? I don't know, I don't know. Teddy, what's happened to me, am I frightened of getting old like Melly says? Perhaps I am. No, it's nothing to do with age. I don't feel old, just – just miserable – there's nothing to look forward to. I'm not going to that place of his, I'll tell him when he phones, he can't make me go. Am I crying because he's gone or am I crying because I'm ashamed? Or am I crying because I can't talk to Teddy – not about James and Jenny, not about Erica and Harvey, not about me, most of all not about me. What if he'd been to bed with some girl, would I want him to tell me? Yes, I would. I'd want to know. Then what? It would always be there between us. Teddy, I'm so miserable, I've never been so alone. Why can't we talk about the things that matter? I'm further away from you than if you'd died – no, don't say that, don't even think it. If Teddy died there would be no secrets, he would know what I'd done. Wouldn't he? When you die you're supposed to go to heaven, but how could he be in heaven if he knew I'd been to bed with Adrian – not been raped by him, but let him take off all my clothes, wanted it to happen, I can see it all.

'Gloria Patri et Filio et Spiritui Sancto.' In the purity of sound she was scarred beyond healing.

By this time her crying had worn itself out, all that remained was the occasional trembling gasp to catch in her throat. Her face red and blotching from her almost silent weeping. It was like looking at a stranger.

Wash your face in cold water. That's it. And again. Bathe your eyes. Pull yourself together. Pretend nothing is wrong. Act. Please help me to hide it from the others. I don't want to talk about it, don't let me have to talk about it. I've got to think of a reason why he had to go tonight. I've got to get dressed and do my face, 'all that rubbish on your face', that's what Teddy calls it. She snorted and rinsed in cold water again for good measure.

'Claudia, whatever's wrong?' Those were Erica's first words. So much for the care Claudia had taken to camouflage the traces!

'Nothing now. It was a silly thing to do, I got myself shut in the log shed. I forgot the latch was down and the wind caught the door and slammed it shut.'

'You were hurt?' It seemed to Erica an odd reason for such puffy eyelids. Immediately she was suspicious, her first thoughts being of Harvey. Perhaps he'd phoned while she'd been out, perhaps Claudia had been upset by things he'd told her. 'Harvey's phoned. That's it, isn't it?'

Surprise made Claudia's answer spontaneous and honest.

'Harvey? No, I've heard nothing. I behaved like a fool, I'm not proud. But Erica I hate the dark shed, I kept hammering on the door, I thought I'd never get out. There was something scurrying about – uggh! Don't let's talk about it.'

Erica's suspicions vanished.

'Couldn't you make Adrian hear?'

'In the end I did. But he was upstairs sorting up his things. He had a phone call, he decided to go back to London today instead of in the morning.'

'How funny of him. He didn't even say goodbye. But I suppose that was my fault, I just never thought he wouldn't be here when I came home. What about my final sitting?'

'I don't think he really needed one. He took the canvas to Lymington this morning and left it for framing.'

'Even so, I'm surprised he went off after you'd had an upset like that. I'd no idea you hated the woodshed so much.'

'I hate mice. It'll teach me to check I put the latch up next time so that I don't get locked in.' Then, realizing that the log basket in the

127

drawing room had been getting low last night, she had the fore-thought to add: 'The silly thing is that I got myself into such a state, I came out then without any wood!'

'I'll get it, don't worry.'

'Don't tell Teddy, will you? Most of the time I'm here on my own and he'll panic if he thinks I'm as nutty as that. I can't think what got into me.'

'It was probably my fault. It was a bad start to the day. I didn't go to Bournemouth like I said. I meant to, but I parked in Christchurch. The first time Harvey brought me to see you we went to Christchurch together. I just love that Priory church, it was the first really ancient place I went to here in England – first ancient place anywhere I guess. It was just the same today. A special sort of silence. I remember thinking that first time how it had stood for centuries, seen folk like us make mistakes, hurt each other, not try hard enough, all that sort of thing. Claudia, it's going to be all right with Harvey and me. It's no use pretending to you, we're going through a bad patch. But that's all it's going to be. Tomorrow I shall meet him, we'll start afresh. If it's *my* fault, then it won't be after today.'

Claudia took her hand.

'They say marriages are made in heaven. Not true. There has never been one that hasn't had to be worked at.'

'I'll be working, I made a sort of vow that I would. It was that old building that set me thinking. Nothing to do with it being a church, just the wonderful timelessness of it, knowing that it's seen happiness and sorrow, given sanctuary, seen people make mistakes. And it'll still be there, just the same, long after we're dead and forgotten, happiness, troubles, the lot. I went in there feeling I couldn't bear so much misery. Then I got to looking at it, its great walls, its strength. And I knew anything worth having endures through troubled times.' Claudia had never heard Erica talk so seriously. She felt touched that she had been the one to hear her confidence – for she knew it was a confidence. Immediately, though, the girl's mood lifted. Already the Priory and its influence, her afternoon at Lymington sitting on a bench in the meadow where there was little activity on the water on a Tuesday afternoon except the ferry setting out for Yarmouth, all that was behind her. Now she wanted to look forward. If there was a hurdle to get over, well, what else were hurdles for? 'First thing in the morning I'm going to get my hair done, I made the appointment on the way home.' Then, with a smile that lit her lovely face. 'Tomorrow I'm having my hair restyled, I decided while I was out. I mean to go to Heathrow looking my best. You know what? I'm going to make that son of yours fall in love like he never knew.'

'I hope he knows what a lucky chap he is. Now, what about those logs. We'll get them together, the basket is almost empty and it's going to be a cold evening.'

She knew Teddy was watching her. Despite her carefully applied eye make-up, and far more of it than usual, surely he must see that she'd been crying. Thank goodness that in her new determination Erica was more talkative than she had been lately, Claudia hoped that her own silence was going unnoticed.

'You say you didn't sit for him this morning? I understood at breakfast he needed you once more?'

'Seems he didn't. It was finished Teddy, we all knew it was. He'd even signed it. Anyway when he found I'd gone out, he took it off to decide on the frame. Isn't that right, Claudia?'

'Yes. They're going to let us know when it can be collected.'

'Humph. So this morning's session was his excuse to have two more hours of her company.' He looked across the table at Claudia with a grin, seeming to include her in his good-natured teasing of their pretty daughter-in-law, and at the same time showing that he hadn't forgotten his misgivings about Adrian staying with Melly or, for that matter, taking on the commission in Erica's own home.

Change the subject, don't talk about him. While he'd been like one of the family, he must have been arranging to rent the old gun carriage.

'Are you feeling all right, dear? And you're not eating.' Teddy's concerned voice cut across her thoughts.

'Feel a bit muzzy, maybe a cold coming. Not really hungry, I'll just have a coffee afterwards.'

'You have an early night. Erica and I can clear this lot away.'

'Surely we can,' Erica agreed. 'I'll bring your drink up to you when you've had time to get into bed.'

'No!' It took a supreme effort to force something that might pass for a laugh. 'I'll take you up on your clearing the things, but I'd rather just curl up and be lazy by the television than go to bed.'

Teddy seemed content with that. He threw another log on the open fire, saw she was comfortable and with the remote control to hand, then went to the kitchen where Erica was already stacking the dishwasher. Like a butterfly flitting from plant to plant, resting nowhere, touching and moving on, Claudia flicked aimlessly through the channels. A few seconds of an American film so old it was black and white, then to a documentary about elephant hunters. Another button to press and there was a woman in a home for battered wives, so immediately on again, this time to what must have been a play or a film, two bodies in bed and veiled by a single sheet as they acted out

129

the unbelievable contortions of a love scene. She pressed the 'off' button, it was easy to erase the pictures from the screen but the sudden stillness was no escape from her thoughts. As if to protect herself, she pressed Channel Two and turned up the sound. The ivory hunters put up a smoke screen for her to hide behind when the dining table was cleared.

From above the fireplace the portrait looked down on her, Claudia the girl seeing through the eyes of the woman she'd become, her trust and hopefulness unchanged. She turned her head into the cushion, her eyes closed.

Help me to forget. If only I could talk about it to Teddy. But You see, I can't do that. I can't talk about it to anyone, but most of all not to Teddy. If I did, each time he touched me it would be there, not just for me but for him too.

'Beautiful . . . perfect . . .' And willingly I believed. Did he think by saying things like that I'd be so flattered I'd be more willing? 'Perfect . . .' I'm nearly fifty-six, three grown-up children, grandchildren. I am what I've become. If Teddy had said it I would have known that for him it was still true. Me ages ago, or me now, I'm just *me* for Teddy. 'Beautiful . . . perfect . . .' Maybe it might still be true for him, but imagine him saying it! Perhaps that's what I craved, someone actually to notice me. It's five weeks since I went to London, yet it's really come home to me today. That's because I was all agog for it to happen again. I was, I must have been, or why would I have gone off with him so willingly. A surprise, he said. What was I expecting? Women are two a penny to him. That shows I'm old. My first time with Teddy, I remember it was like a milestone, important, wonderfully important. It's not like that these days, maybe it wasn't for a lot of brides even then. That's what Adrian's always been used to. He might even have imagined he was doing me a favour! Throwing in a bit of high-flown talk, believing that that's what our generation expect. Like proper dancing instead of jigging about as if you're in the jungle. And now he's got his forest hideaway and thinks I'll be grateful. Well, I won't. I ought to have told him – instead I let him kiss me. If he'd had a couch there—

'Erica's just bringing the coffee,' Teddy's voice cut through her thoughts where the elephants had failed. 'You have a brandy with yours.' His scrutiny was disconcerting, it told her as clearly as any words that her eye make-up had done nothing to camouflage her stiff and swollen lids. 'You'll miss Adrian.' She couldn't bear to look at him, guilt and shame must be written all over her. 'But cheer up darling, at least we seem to have been worrying for nothing . . .' He nodded his head in the direction of the kitchen.

'Yes.' Her voice was unnecessarily loud in her effort to play the role he expected.

'Are you watching this jungle thing?'

'No, it was just company. Turn it off if you like.'

With the television off, a goblet of brandy on the table he'd pulled close to her, he made a move to sit with Claudia on the sofa.

'Shift an inch.' As he spoke he raised her from the cushion, sat down and pulled her against him. It was the way they often sat in the evening, she with her legs drawn up on to the seat, his arm around her as she leant against him. Habit! That's what she was, as much habit to him as each morning's clean clothes, each evening's milk bottles on the doorstep. There was no joy in habit, no thrill of excitement. She resented being part of life's routine, always here, always to be relied on; and she hated herself for that burning resentment.

'I'll sit up, I've been lying long enough.'

'It's a pity Adrian cleared off so quickly.' Teddy was trying to let her know he understood the real cause of her wretchedness. There was sympathy in his voice. 'With Erica gone too, you'll find the house quiet. Why did you say he went?'

The question put her on her mettle, did her more good than all the sympathy.

'I don't know all the details, just that he had a phone call from some woman whose portrait he'd painted. She wanted something additional in the background, I suppose you can paint and overpaint with oil or acrylic or whatever he uses. Anyway she's going to be in London tomorrow and wanted to bring him the canvas in the morning. I don't know any more than that.' Surely no-one would doubt a yarn so complicated!

'I wonder how she knew where to phone?'

Her wits must have sharpened up, she pulled an answer out of the air straight away.

'The cleaning lady was at the flat getting sorted up ready, expecting him tomorrow or the next day, so she answered the call and gave this number.'

'I expect he'll be down again soon.'

Moving closer to Teddy, she raised her feet on to the sofa and leant against him. He put his arm around her, a natural movement, probably he wasn't conscious of what he did. She closed her eyes tight against the sting of tears, then reached for the goblet and hid behind a great gulp of brandy.

'Can't you tell me what it is? Have you heard something from James?

131

Is it trouble with Jennifer again? Or Harvey? Was there something you didn't want to tell Erica?'

Always it has to be them! Never me!

'Erica's full of determination and I've not heard anything from Brightley. So you've got nothing to worry about.'

'So what is it? Erica told me you'd been upset, some yarn about getting locked in the woodshed.'

'Sounds silly, I wasn't going to tell you. It's just I hate mice, you know I do. I didn't check the latch was up, the door slammed on me. I don't want to talk about it.'

He reached to the bedside table and she heard him switch on the tape. Some people turn to a stiff drink at the end of a busy day, some unwind before a noisy television, Teddy's balm was the unemotional chanting of the monks. Not tonight, her mind cried silently, the sound carrying her back to the misery and degradation she'd seen on the face in the mirror.

Running from the memory she clung to Teddy.

'Hold me tight, it's silly but I was so scared. Hold me, Teddy.'

He knew the lock had broken on the door of the woodshed. She was hiding the truth from him. But what? Adrian going couldn't upset her like it, and Erica had seemed bright. So what? Perhaps it was the beginning of an illness, he a doctor and he'd not seen the signs.

Lying across him her action was a cry for help, she wanted him to make love to her, to drive away the devils of memory, to cleanse her. Any other night, at the first sign he would have been with her. Habit? Contentment? Tonight nothing was further from his mind.

'Try and get to sleep, darling,' he told her, gently turning her away from him and keeping a protective arm across her.

Sleep! How could she know what dreams lay in wait to taunt her? It wasn't sleep she wanted, it was passion, so fierce and demanding that there was room in her mind and body for nothing else but themselves.

Gently he kissed the back of her head.

'Alleluia, Dies sanctifacus' came the calm and steadfast voices and, just as she had this afternoon, so he combined his own silent plea with the sound. She had never lied to him rather than share her worries. Don't let her be ill, I beg You not that.

Chapter 9

'We ought to give the picture framer a call,' Teddy said towards the end of the following week. 'I thought we should have been told Erica's portrait was ready before this.'

'There's no panic. Harvey doesn't plan to come down at the moment. It looks as though we shall be on our own for Easter if Melly and Trevor are going to the Lakes. I do hope it's bright for them; he wants to walk, and I expect she'll be painting.' The difference wasn't in what she said, but in her consciously bright manner.

'Perhaps that's what we could do with, a few days away somewhere,' Teddy suggested. 'What do you say? Geoff Knight would do locum for a while, probably be glad to. I don't think he's finding it easy to adjust to retirement.'

'If you want to. Yes, of course we could go away somewhere.'

He looked at her helplessly. He was at a loss to understand her unfathomable reserve.

'I must go. We'll talk about it this evening,' he said, his cheerfulnes on a par with her own. 'You think where you'd like to go, then I'll have a word with Geoff.'

That was how it had been with them for more than a week. Now when he collected up his things ready to go out to the car she raised her face to kiss him goodbye. He might have been a departing guest. He wasn't looking for an empassioned embrace, a friendly peck had been habit for years. But a friendly peck could hold warmth and love, its familiarity of scent and touch had been part of the start of their day.

'Nothing urgent waiting, Mary?' He checked with the receptionist when he arrived at the Medical Centre. 'Good. Don't send the first patient in till I tell you I'm ready, I need to make a phone call first.'

'Right you are, Doctor.' She nodded her head in the direction of the waiting room, her whisper held a warning. 'Mrs Carey is first, she

133

was waiting outside when I got here. Her appointment is for nine o'clock.'

Teddy got the message. A minute past nine and Mrs Carey, the senior care assistant at the local retirement home, would protest. He looked at his watch.

'That gives me four minutes,' he managed a friendly laugh.

For Melly to have a call before nine o'clock immediately set her alarm bells ringing.

'Dad, what's the matter? Has something happened?'

'Only my most cantankerous patient will be banging on my door dead on nine o'clock and I wanted to speak to you first.'

'Must be Mrs Carey,' Melly laughed. The fat and officious carer was a legend in the locality.

'True. Melly, how are you fixed to slip down to see us?'

'I knew something was the matter, I could sense it.'

'Nothing's the matter, I told you. I just thought it would be a nice surprise for your mother. The matter, you say. Well, perhaps there is. Not a sudden calamity. It's just that she seems a bit down in the dumps. The house is suddenly empty. She'd hoped the children would be down in their holidays but Barry's going off with the school to France and Patsy, would you believe, is a fairy in the Brightley Theatre Group's *A Midsummer Night's Dream* and is frightened to miss a rehearsal. Melly, I'd be really grateful if you could just slip down for a few hours, cheer your mother up. You know how she likes the hustle of a full house. Well, of course Erica and Adrian were with us till last week. Now suddenly she feels the blank.'

'I'm sure.'

'Melly?'

'When do you want me Dad? Trevor breaks up today week and we thought we'd head north straight away.'

'Ah. Now I'm coming to something else. Erica's portrait is being framed. Could you drop it off to Harvey on your way to the Lakes? It wouldn't add much to the journey. You could tell your Mother you'd driven down to pick it up. That would explain your reason for coming, she would suspect that I'd asked you to come.'

'A reason for coming home? Come on, Dad, since when do I need that?'

'Never, you know that. She's a bit – a bit – prickly. Melly, perhaps she'll talk to you. She tells me she's fine, nothing wrong with her. But she's not herself. I can't force her to a doctor – perhaps I'm imagining. You don't think she'd hide it from it if she had something wrong do you? Perhaps you might be able to get her to open up.'

'I'll come tomorrow Dad. Don't tell her. I'll just walk in on you.'

'Bless you. Melly, thank you.'

'I meant to come pretty soon anyway – there's something I want to talk to you both about. But not now. It can wait until the right moment. If you're good I'll stay the night. Off you go, Dad, and best of luck with Mrs Carey.'

A few short sentences with Melly and he was ready to face the day. From the passage outside the surgery door came Mrs Carey's rasping voice.

'Time is time! Nine o'clock was my appointment. I've not got all day to waste.'

Teddy couldn't hear the receptionist's reply, but he could read her thoughts! He pushed the button of his intercom.

'Will you send my first patient in now please Mary.' And just as he'd expected, the door opened before he'd finished the sentence.

He had never had any ambition to specialize, to him there could be no work more satisfying that that of a General Practitioner. There was scarcely a person in Avonford he didn't know, he'd brought babies into the world, helped his patients through illnesses and accidents, he'd tended the sick and dying, given practical comfort to the bereaved. He was thankful there were but few 'Mrs Careys' on his register and this morning he could easily have done without her.

'Come along in, Mrs Carey. Take a seat.' His smile was automatic, his manner courteous. Years of experience had taught him how to cross the barrier that divided the family man from the family doctor.

'Stone the crows, Mrs C! Take a look out of the window!'

She watched as Claudia did as she said. Just lately Mrs C hadn't been a bit her own self, the joy seemed to have gone right out of her. But look at her now, her face alight with pleasure. Fancy young Melly driving all this way and never telling a soul she was coming. A good thing she'd not sent a message though, there was twice the joy in a surprise like this. Gwen Pomfrey dried her hands and got ready for the hug Melly never failed to give her.

'Melly!' Claudia rushed out as the car drew up. Even the memory of those pictures didn't have a chance against the surprise and pleasure of seeing her. 'I can't believe it. Nothing wrong?'

'I decided last night. Trevor said he could manage without me, gave me a twenty-four-hour leave of absence. Is that all right with you?'

Claudia's hug was answer enough.

Gwen Pomfrey had known all the young Carlyles since they were children, but this one had always been her special favourite. When she was taken in Melly's bearlike embrace her elderly heart was full of pride.

135

'Brought your overnight case I see. Case! I can just imagine how screwed up your things will be in a silly bit of a bag like that. While you talk to your mother, you let me take that up to your room and set things to rights for you.' As if a speck of dust ever had a chance to settle in the unused bedrooms.

'Don't be long, Gwen, Mum's just going to make us some coffee. Aren't you Mum?'

Claudia laughed as naturally as she would have a fortnight ago.

'We'll all three have our coffee together, shall we?' Melly linked her arm through her mother's. 'Then I want to see Erica's portrait. That's the second reason for my coming.'

Pouring water on to the coffee Claudia had her back towards Melly. Mention of Adrian's work stirred ghosts she'd been fighting to leave sleeping.

'Second? What's the first?'

'To check on you both, of course, see that you're behaving yourselves,' came the laughing reply. She watched her mother's back as if that would give her the answer she sought. 'Do you realize, this'll be the first year we've not spent Easter here – in fact, the first one I've ever been anywhere but here. Remember the Easter egg hunts we used to have in the garden when we were kids? I wonder if Jenny and James do that sort of thing for theirs like you and Dad did for us. A shame if they don't. Those are the kind of things children build their memories on, not the services and parish functions and all the flap-doodle those two poor little beggars have to put up with.'

'That's not fair, Melly. James and Jenny are good parents. There's more to bringing up children than letting them have a good time.'

'I just bet there is too. I suppose that's why I couldn't have Easter go by and not come to see my Dad and Mum.' Whatever sort of a fool you've been, none of it can really be important to you. Us, Dad, me and the boys, that's where you belong. If only I could say exactly what I think – but I mustn't, if I did it would always be there to remember. It would stain all those happy memories. Dad's worried sick, thinks there's something wrong with you. I can't tell him I'm pretty sure what it is: Adrian's given you the brush-off and you've come face-to-face with yourself. You were asking for trouble, oh Mum, let it go. Dad, me, the boys, we're what matter. 'Is the portrait good Mum?' she plunged on, anything to fill the silence. 'Well, of course it must be. With a subject like Erica, how could it fail – and Adrian can find something beautiful in anyone. What I thought we'd do – unless Harvey is planning to get down here – is to take it up with us, make a detour and let Erica give us lunch on our way to Ambleside. Is it boxed for safe travelling, or can I see it?'

136

'It's still with the framer. He promised to ring when it was ready. I haven't heard. After coffee I'll phone and see if I can persuade him to have it ready later in the day.'

The framer promised to have it ready that afternoon and Mellie's impulse was to leave everything and make straight for Lymington there and then at eleven to'clock in the morning. But Claudia had made the coffee, Gwen had been told to hurry back downstairs so that they could have it together – and Mellie was far too fond of her to disappoint her. She gave herself the satisfaction of knowing she was piling pleasure on pleasure for Gwen; not only was there her already shiny bedroom to be 'given an extra rub up', but also patient and detailed descriptions of the work she was doing in preparation for an exhibition in the summer.

Affectionate duty done, she and Claudia were soon on the way into town. There was so much to pack into a few short hours: a visit to *Sea Urchin*, even though she wouldn't sail her with only Claudia as crew; a bar lunch in her favourite pub by the Quay; a browse around the bookshop; then on up the street to a local art exhibition at the Community Centre. She lived at high speed, that was her way, it was a trait she'd inherited from Claudia. But today as they walked briskly up the hilly High Street she kept a surreptitious watch, remembering Teddy's reason for asking her to come.

They arrived back to a spotless Russets late in the afternoon, and while Melly unboxed the portrait Claudia checked the Answerphone.

'Hello. Adrian here. I'm sorry you weren't home when I rang. I thought I'd tell you that I've started working not too many miles away from you. I hope I'll get to see you soon.'

'Didn't he tell you he'd got another commission hereabouts?' Mellie said, while she silently admitted to herself that he sounded perfectly normal and friendly.

'No, he didn't mention new commissions anywhere, let alone here. But who's to say what he means by "not too many miles"? Check if there are any other messages, will you, while I make a pot of tea.'

So he was back. This minute he'd be in that funny wooden wagon thing, probably watching for her car to come bumping up the track. A good thing she'd been out when he phoned. He wouldn't ring again this evening, or if he did it would be to talk to Teddy. Tomorrow morning? Would Mellie be gone? If not she'd let her answer the phone, she could talk to him. Let him be the one to make up his own story! But if Mellie's gone, if I'm by myself, then I'll tell him – I'll be firm, I won't quarrel, I'll tell him I'm not coming, I'll not get upset, I'll sound cool, disinterested.

She ought to have known what Teddy's reaction would be when Melly mentioned the Answerphone message.

'What a shame you were out, Claudia, but he's sure to call back or perhaps just look in, that's what he sometimes does. You could always see if he's free to have a day or two here at Easter – unless he has somewhere fixed.'

He was pleased with his suggestion. Only Melly noticed Claudia's silence.

'He's a real ladies' man is our Adrian,' she laughed. Even if the fire had been put out there was no harm in damping down the ashes! 'Do you reckon he has an eye for Erica? She's not silly though, a girl looking like that must have had enough attractive men making passes at her not to fall for his practised line of flattery.' There now, she couldn't say it clearer.

'You're as bad as your father,' Claudia snapped. 'Did you realize he commissioned my portrait so that you weren't put in temptation's way? Now here you are suggesting he's chasing after Erica.'

'Dad thought that about *me*? No fear, I've known Adrian Crighton too long. He's like a butterfly, flits from flower to flower, all of them fresh, young and lovely, but none of them holding his attention for long.' She chuckled tolerantly, somehow giving the impression that she was privy to his confidence. 'No, Adrian is a modern-day Casanova. It would have gone over your head of course, I mean he naturally wouldn't have seen you in that light. Maybe he looks on you and Dad as surrogate parents, it's nice the way he comes and goes so casually.' Perhaps I ought to have been an actress instead of a painter. That must be the last shot. I don't care if it was below the belt. Even if she hadn't actually posed for the pictures, he must have been jolly intimate with her. It's disgusting, humiliating for her, for Dad, even for me. I wonder how it is I can look at her and still love her. If Dad ever found out, if he got hurt, then I'd never, never forgive her.

It was while Claudia was fetching the after-dinner coffee that Teddy reminded Melly she'd told him there was something she wanted to discuss with them.

'Nothing bad?' He needed to be reassured.

'There's bad – and there's bad. It certainly isn't filling me with joy if that's what you mean.'

'What's that?' Claudia came back just in time to hear the last part of her sentence. 'What have I missed? Not a hitch with the exhibition?'

'No! It mustn't be!' The actress in her had bowed out. This was Melly, all her anger and fright exposed. 'I kept hoping I wouldn't

138

have to say anything, that I'd find a way and not have to drop my bombshell.'

There was nothing hidden in the look that passed between Claudia and Teddy. The last months had jolted them out of the fool's paradise where they'd taken their family's happiness for granted. It was the first honest, unguarded moment they'd shared in recent days.

'Tell us, Melly.' Whatever her trouble, Teddy was ready to help her. 'That's what we're here for.'

'No point in putting it off any longer. Maybe you can give me a magic potion to sort me out?' She laughed when she said it, but there was no doubt it was a cry for help.

'You're pregnant!' Claudia was the first to understand. 'But Melly, that's splendid. What's the problem? Are you having a bad time? You've seen your doctor?'

'Yes, I'm having a bad time, a miserable, beastly time,' she answered. 'And no, I haven't seen a doctor.'

'It'll soon pass, Melly,' Claudia tried to reassure her, but she was more sensitive to her mood than Teddy appeared to be. She sensed that Melly's beastly time had nothing to do with morning sickness. 'How far gone are you?'

'About three months. Too far for there to be any hope. I nearly came down to you Dad, to see if you could sort me out. But – well, you can't can you, not ask your father to give you an abortion! The Sunday papers would have a field day if they got hold of it!' There was a dangerous note of hysteria in her laugh.

'I don't understand,' Teddy reached to take her hand in his. 'You know I couldn't do that – your child, our grandchild. Is Trevor the problem? Isn't he pleased?'

'Trevor's like the cat who's stuffed himself full of cream.' One hand in his, the other fist clenched on the dining table, she kept her head down. She mustn't let them guess how hard it was not to give way to tears. Always she'd come to them with her hurts and they'd made her better, but this time they could do nothing. 'All very well for him, he won't have to waddle about like a prize cow.' The first tear fell on to her shirt front; it was her undoing. 'Don't want it,' she wept. 'One day – that's what I'd always thought, one day when we were ready. And I'm *not* ready. How will I manage at the exhibition, lumbering around like that? Fat and clumsy, swollen ankles, back aches. Remember how Jenny was. She didn't seem to mind. I wanted this exhibition so much, can't you see, I've worked and worked.'

He saw her as she had been as a small child, sobbing when a kitten she'd been given had been run over; coming to his surgery to blurt

139

out her misery and humiliation when she'd forgotten her lines in the school play. His little Mellie.

'There will be other times. Your work won't spoil, you can save it for later when you start work again.' Teddy rubbed his thumb tenderly along the back of her hand. 'When the time comes you may find it's not as important as you'd imagined. Once the baby arrives you'll see things differently.'

'Trust a man to say a damn fool thing like that!' she snorted. 'Oh, Dad, I'm sorry.' She clung to his hand with both of hers. 'Didn't mean it like that about you. But it was different for you and Mum, and anyway – anyway – her only career was marriage. Things are different today. You must have been pleased right from the start Mum. Later on, will I feel different, will I begin to sort of bond with it? All I know is that I don't want a baby. I'm not ready. I just want to be *me*.'

Claudia tried to be honest. 'Perhaps that's what happens, you start to feel different as your body gets used to the idea. And most people look back afterwards, I'm sure, and imagine they'd been pleased right from the start. There must be those who try for a baby for years always hoping. But for most of us it is frightening. Suddenly your body isn't your own, your life isn't your own.'

'What nonsense you talk,' Teddy laughed.

'You wouldn't know, Dad. Anymore than Trevor would. Mum understands.'

'Yes, I do. But I'd honestly forgotten. And so will you once the baby takes over – and especially when it arrives.'

'You reckon that somewhere in me there lurks a maternal streak? I wanted to see if I could get a termination – this summer is so important, I've been aiming at this exhibition for ages. Trevor couldn't understand, I hurt him badly by wanting to get rid of it. I didn't mean to hurt him. I just wanted things different. So I've tried to make amends and let him think I'm getting to accept. But I'm not. I can't. I don't tell him that I go running every day, I've almost turned myself inside out in that hateful gym – and all it does to me is get me fitter and fitter.' She snorted as she gasped for breath. 'Just been wasting time when I would rather have been working. He's so cock-a-hoop. I'm just beginning to get somewhere with my work . . . I mean it's a piece of cake for Trev, it's not going to bugger up his career one iota.'

She glowered at Teddy as if because he were male he had to shoulder part of the blame. But it was Claudia who spoke.

'If all your exercising hasn't altered anything, then Melly you must try and accept. If you don't you'll end up bitter towards Trevor because he doesn't understand and bitter towards the poor little scrap who can't help being born. It won't be a baby for long.'

Her words bounced back at her. What was she saying? That children only take your time, your love, your care, your thought, when they're tiny? James . . . Harvey . . . and now Melly. 'I just want to be *me*', had been Melly's cry. But what happens to that fundamental *me*?

'You're feeling well? No problems?' That from Teddy.

'I told you, my problem is that I'm disgustingly healthy.' She turned her tear blotched face to him defiantly. 'Go on, you can say what you feel, I shan't mind. Trevor expected an all-singing all-dancing reaction of joy too, but I can't – I just can't.'

Teddy rumpled her hair affectionately.

'Bless you Melly. You'll be a lovely mother, never you fear.'

'A few more Easters and you and Trevor will be hiding the choco-late eggs. Don't worry about being excited, let nature take care of that side of it.' Claudia felt a surge of pity for this unwanted scrap of humanity, and of anger at Trevor that he could have seen Melly's hopes dashed and expect her not to care. What chance would she have of producing good work for the exhibition?

'Somewhere at the back of the sideboard there lurks a bottle of fizzy left from New Year,' Teddy said. 'Find the glasses Claudia while I open it. It's been waiting for a special moment.'

Yes, it was a special moment. Teddy uncorked the champagne, his mind half on Melly and three quarters on Claudia.

'To us,' he raised his glass, 'and to the new one who'll soon be one of us.'

'I'm glad I've told you, not just pretended it was all planned.' She wiped the palms of her hands across her eyes. 'It has sort of helped a bit.'

Lying in bed Teddy watched Claudia massaging cream into her face, the nightly ritual in her battle to cling to the remains of youth.

'It's been a good evening, hasn't it?'

She knew his words were an understatement of what he was really saying to her. The afternoon of her self-analysis had built a wall of ice around her; she hadn't been able to break through it any more than he'd been able to scale it. Perhaps Melly's tears had helped it to thaw. For the first time for more than a week, the woman in the mirror held his gaze. Help me back, she cried silently. The real *me*? I don't know what the real me is. I envy Melly her tears and her fight-ing, she's alive, she might be frightened of not reaching her goal but at least she knows what it is, she hasn't lost her identity.

141

He held back the duvet and she got into bed. For a minute they lay still, as if neither of them were sure of the next move.

'Hello, my darling,' he whispered, turning to her and touching her face tenderly. She knew he wanted her to explain why for all these days she'd been out of his reach.

'I think we can stop worrying about them all,' she whispered back to him, 'James and Harvey have weathered their bad patches, Melly will make a lovely mother.'

Hardly words of love and yet to Teddy they lifted the cloud that had hung over them.

'We'll sort out that holiday tomorrow,' he murmured later as they drifted towards sleep, 'now that we know the children are all right. Better to be away now than later, Mellie might need us then.'

When Claudia picked up the receiver she had no doubt whose voice she'd hear.

Melly had left the previous teatime, Teddy was doing his morning surgery, Gwen was Hoovering an already clean carpet.

'Claudia?'

'Yes.'

'You got my message? You knew I was back?'

'Melly's been down, she and I were collecting Erica's picture when you called.'

'You say she's been. That means she's just gone back? I waited for you all day yesterday. You'll come today?'

'I'm not coming.' She said it quickly, almost shouted it.

'But Claudia I want to show you my little wooden nest. If I promise to be a good boy? Why do you say you won't come?'

'You know why. Adrian, I'm ashamed, I'm humiliated—'

He laughed. 'What a load of rubbish. Humiliated! Listen to me – first I'll give you the number of the call box, I haven't that much change.' Then, 'Just listen while I talk. We have been friends for months. All right, we were lovers too – yes and that's what I wanted from the moment I saw you. I want you still, and you're right, that's why I fixed up to rent this little love nest to lure you to. But that's not all we are, we are friends, we enjoy being together. Please Claudia, don't run out on me. If I promise, cubs' honour – I didn't tell you I used to be a cub did I? – promise that I won't molest you. Just drive over and see the miracle I've done here. Cubs' honour . . . Yes?'

'I can't.'

'I'll be watching for you. Nice pub down the road, we'll have lunch—'

'No—'

'Cubs' honour . . .'

His money ran out, the line was dead. She replaced the receiver. He'd be waiting in the call box, expecting her to ring him back. Well, she wasn't going to. The number he'd given her was bold and clear on the scrap of paper. Her hand still rested on the receiver. And it was at that precise moment that, through the hall window, she saw Teddy's car turn into the drive. She slipped the piece of paper into the drawer of the hall table, then opened the front door to him.

'An unusual time of morning. Nothing wrong?'

'No. I spoke to Geoff. Get your hair done or whatever you have to do, and start packing. The day after tomorrow we are foot loose, point the car wherever fancy takes us. He's taking over for two weeks, can't get back to work soon enough.'

She had been determined not to go to Adrian's wooden nest, but the certainty of a fortnight's holiday ahead of her gave her new confidence. It would be churlish to go away without telling him. She'd drive over and admire his homemaking – as if anyone could make a home out of anything so basic – she'd show him that she had faith in his cub's honour.

If her confidence was rooted in the knowledge she was about to be lifted out of reach of temptation, then it was certainly nurtured in the few hours she spent with Adrian. He never failed to make her feel attractive, yet not by a single word or act did he break his promise. There was little in the way of comfort in his temporary home, it was a workroom with a divan, nothing more. But it was warm, the glow of the Calor gas heater a gleaming and friendly eye at one end. Not that they spent long inside. A ploughman's lunch at the pub then a walk across the open forestland and, finally, as he saw her into her car, the light touch of his lips brushing against hers.

'Thank you for not running away from me, Claudia. And promise you'll come again. Tomorrow? When you get back? My regards to Teddy.'

That cast the first shadow. They both knew she wouldn't be telling Teddy she'd seen him.

Dr Geoff Knight had lived in the area for about six months, having decided that retirement would be easier in a new district than near his old practice in Surrey. As Teddy had known, he was delighted to stand in for a fortnight, he even pressed Teddy with: 'Time's my own. Just give me a ring if you find you want me a day or two extra – if the weather's good you might not want to rush home.'

So with a new freedom Teddy and Claudia left Avonford, the vague plan being that they would head for Scotland. Their more immediate idea was that in getting there they follow their noses in a northerly direction, keep away from the trunk route and stop where their fancy took them. Address unknown, free of all responsibility.

But so strong were their family ties that as, three hours and two brief stops after leaving Avonford, they took a circuitous route around Reading, crossed the Thames at Streatley, driving in the direction of Oxford, Teddy's: 'We'll just look in, shall we?' needed no explanation. It needed no answer either. As if they would come as near to Brightley and not look in!

James was a happy man. Sometimes when he was least prepared, like a physical pain he would remember what it had been like only a few months ago. Immediately the thought would be stamped on as if the memory were sent by the devil to try him, just as the whole incident had been sent by the devil for the same reason. Now Jenny was back with him, she was at his side in the parish, she was the mainstay of the Brightley Singers; and since that dreadful period there was a new radiance about her, an inner happiness. He thanked God with all his heart, he asked for forgiveness that at the time of his travail he'd failed his Master, he'd not had sufficient trust to be able to say 'Not my will, but Thine'. Even so he had been forgiven, his prayers had been answered.

He wished Jenny could find it in her heart to talk to him, tell him of her own road to at last finding fulfilment in the part she played in the parish. He couldn't question her. She'd been unhappy, she'd felt imprisoned by the demands made on her. Then something had touched her spirit. His prayers of thankfulness weren't simply that she had again taken up her role, overcome her former resentments, even spoke with a new brightness in her voice; they were that his dear Jenny had at last found contentment, had learnt to accept without bitterness.

Three afternoons a week she went to The Grange, a nursing home run by a friend of hers, someone she'd known for years and who had been acquainted with her parents. How many women would do so much voluntarily? A drive of more than fifteen miles each way, a willingness to do anything that was asked of her. She wasn't a trained nurse, but there was plenty to do caring for the elderly, the frail and the dying. No job would be beneath her, he thought proudly as he settled down to make notes on a talk he was going to give to the pupils he was preparing for Confirmation at a local boarding school. There was a down to earth understanding about Jenny, the patients would open their hearts to her.

144

Times of undisturbed solitude were necessary to James, he was ashamed to admit how much he relished the stillness of the house on Monday, Wednesday and Friday afternoons, secure in the knowledge that she was doing what she found satisfying and that in a few hours she'd be home. When he'd thought he'd lost her love he'd been distraught; yet, had he never met her, never had a family to love, the monastic life would have suited him well. His paper still blank in front of him, he put down his pen, letting his mind roam unreined.

With two healthy children, naturally they didn't intend to have more. He'd always been careful. At the word 'always' his mind baulked, 'always' implied sexual love had been important to them. It hadn't. It was after Christmas that Jenny had told him she had started to take the pill. It was tampering with nature, he ought to disapprove. But it had made a difference to their lives. They used to go weeks, often months, without sex playing any part. Did she want more than he could give her? Was that why she'd started to take the pill? There was a new freedom now. That, and the belief that it was what she wanted, were what turned his mind that way more often. He couldn't resist a feeling of self-congratuation that he'd been able to give her this new contentment. His mind leapt out of hand as memory brought another picture alive, but this time he shied from thoughts of the temptation she had put before him. Lust of the flesh, carnal pleasure, these things weren't love. He pulled the blank sheets of paper towards him, determined to work. For James sexual love followed a strict pattern, it was an expression of devotion between husband and wife.

It took all his willpower to concentrate on this evening's Confirmation class. He had no more than a dozen words written when he heard a car on the gravel drive.

There was no doubt of his pleasure, his welcome was just as Claudia had imagined.

'Jenny's out, you say? She won't be long?'

'You remember she's taken to helping at The Grange, she really is absolutely marvellous.' He beamed with pride. 'She doesn't get in till about five o'clock as a rule. Can I get you something to eat?'

'No, dear, but I'll make some tea, shall I?' Claudia hugged him for no reason except that he was James. 'So good to be here again. Last time seems a lifetime ago.'

He knew she was remembering those days just before Christmas, the uncertainty, his own sense of failure.

'A lifetime, Mum. You'll see how well Jenny looks. It's as if those days away, looking after her mother's friend, gave her a pointer to this need she must have had. She's known Margaret Cummins who runs The Grange most of her life, she knew where the nursing home was, but it had never entered her head to contact her. Then, you remember, she went to see this elderly lady who had cared for her mother. It must have made her see her own place in the pattern, it certainly gave her a purpose.'

'They always say it's the busy people who find time to take on extra,' Teddy said, 'and I know she's always been busy in the parish.'

'So she still is, Dad. She's got tremendous drive. It seems the more she does, the more she is prepared to do. Nothing is neglected here, the children must be aware of the tremendous drive in her.' And again the smile that said more than any words. 'If things clash, say a Mothers' Union meeting the same time as she's due at The Grange, then instead of being glad to slide out of it she suggests they change the meeting to the next day. No-one minds, they are a good crowd here.'

'The St Luke's Ladies?' Claudia teased gently, she'd heard plenty of Jenny's comments on the merry band of church workers in the past.

'Honestly they are, Mum. I always told her so. But she sees it for herself now. It worried me, the way things used to be.'

'What time do the youngsters get in?' Teddy changed the subject, his imagination couldn't stretch far enough to take in the wonders of his 'born again' daughter-in-law.

Their meandering holiday had no timetable. They arrived at Brightley on the Monday, expecting to stay a night if it were suggested and to take the family out to dinner. In fact they stayed two nights, the dinner outing having to be shifted until the Tuesday evening because of James's Confirmation class.

'Must you go?' Jenny said to them after the children had gone off to catch the school bus on Wednesday morning. 'We'd love you to stay on a while. I'm at the home, of course, this afternoon but that needn't drive you away. Tomorrow the children have their Sports Day, they'd be thrilled if you were there to cheer them on.'

'No, my dear. We are supposed to be on our way to Scotland. Maybe we'll look in again on the way home about the end of next week. Not to stay, just to say hello.'

So they piled their cases back in the car and set off, James and Jenny waving them on their way.

'She's brighter, isn't she,' Claudia said. 'I know you don't see her as God's gift, but I've always been fond of Jenny.' Then as if what she told him was all part and parcel of what had gone before: 'She's on the pill. She told me. And looked so pleased about it.'

146

'She told you?' There was something in Teddy that resented James's wife and mother discussing anything so personal.

'Why shouldn't she? We've always got along, have been in sympathy. I could have hugged her, Teddy. Isn't it funny how different they all are, the three girls? Erica wouldn't need to share anything so personal – I don't think even Melly would. But Jenny, she was proud as anything, I could tell she was. You know what I think? I think it's made them like bed better, and that's what's given her this abundant goodwill towards the world. Poor Jenny.'

'I dare say you're right. It might have made her more tolerant, but it's done nothing to smarten her up. The boys' wives are so different, aren't they.'

'They're both jolly nice. You know what I think? I think we ought to find the main road and get on our way, or it'll be time to start for home before we reach Scotland at all.'

There were times when she could honestly believe she had overcome the affair with Adrian, when she could look back as if it had happened to someone else. But there were other times when she'd know that other self was only slumbering in her, waiting to catch her unawares when she was slotted back deep in the rut of daily living and taunt her with that wild need to snatch at life. Adrian, such fun to be with, Adrian whose silent glance could make her heart race with excitement – then the memory of Melly, her veiled warnings, her contempt. Shame and humiliations were a physical pain; her heart would race, her arms and legs feel weak.

The holiday helped. In a different environment and her time spent together with Teddy, she could believe that everything else was a fading dream – nightmare? The days went so fast. They walked on the foothills of Ben Nevis in the sunshine of early spring, they sailed to the Isle of Skye in the mist, they took photographs on the wonderful sands of the Moray Firth, and spent the whole of their last Friday in Edinburgh.

'I've just spoken to Geoff,' Teddy came into their hotel bedroom where she was prettying herself for dinner that evening. 'I've let myself be persuaded to leave it to him for an extra day. That means we can take time with the drive, perhaps have a night or so in York. How would you like that?'

'I like it everywhere.'

So she did. And as they worked their way on southward she went on liking it – in York where they spent Saturday night and Sunday morning, and at Lincoln where they spent their final night. They would be back in Avonford by the end of Monday. They'd said they would call at the rectory on the way home, but this time it would have to be a flying visit.

'It'll only be James. Mondays, Wednesdays and Fridays are Jenny's afternoons at The Grange,' Claudia said as they came to Brightley village. But it was James they mostly wanted to see.

However, his car wasn't in and there was no answer to their ring. So they dropped a note through the letterbox and went on their way.

'We'll go back the way we came,' Teddy said when they were a few miles from Brightley. 'According to James the nursing home is only just round the corner by the crossroads where we take the Wallingford road. Instead of turning right, we go left but it's no distance. We'll just look in and have a quick word with her.'

'That would be nice.' Claudia seemed to settle more comfortably in her seat, a sign that all was well with her world. Teddy had actually suggested calling to see Jenny! It really was the finishing touch to a lovely holiday.

It was no use hiding from what you didn't want to see, but afterwards it was hard not to wish they had turned right at the crossroad and gone straight home.

They knew that Miss Cummins was an old acquaintance of Jenny's, but it was hard to imagine two women less alike. Jenny was a generation younger than the trim and pretty woman with iron grey hair and blue eyes which still held the bright innocence of a child.

'Dr and Mrs Carlyle,' she came out of her office to greet them on hearing who the callers were. 'You've come on the wrong day for Jenny. What a pity. She comes in on Wednesdays. And she's marvellous. The residents love her.'

'Never mind,' Teddy gave no sign of surprise. 'We did call at the rectory but there was no-one in. It was just a chance worth taking that we might have found her here. But she must have been shopping.'

Back in the car he started the engine without a word. Glancing at him quickly Claudia recognized the expression she'd so often seen when he'd talked of Jenny: more than tight-lipped, his face was void of expression yet his silence was harder to take than any anger would have been.

'I don't understand,' she said quietly.

Teddy didn't answer. He didn't understand either, but that didn't prevent him forming immovable opinions.

Chapter 10

'Look what I've got!' Spreading them like a fan, Erica waved two tickets in front of Harvey's face. 'They're like gold dust, but I was lucky, there had been two returns. I thought I'd have to pay over the odds and answer one of those ads in the paper.'

Harvey took the tickets to read what it was she was so excited over.

'Jazz! A whole evening of jazz!'

'Please, Harvey. You never listen to it, if you did you'd know why it gets to me like it does. But you won't try, you just get pompous as if I don't know what I'm talking about. These are the absolute best. I heard them once in New York.'

'I realize they are. And I'm not pompous. They just aren't my scene. Anyway, this concert's tomorrow evening—'

'I know. Here we are in London, three whole days of freedom before your recital. They might have been playing last week or next, but instead it's tomorrow. And then I was able to get the returns. Do you believe in fate?'

'Honestly, I hate letting you down.'

'No, you don't. You don't even try to like my sort of music. I've sat through concert after concert for you. Please, Harvey. Come with me, try it just once.'

How could he refuse her when she looked at him like that? He put his arm around her slim waist and drew her towards him.

'Darling Erica, I'd listen to an evening of jungle drums if it would please you,' then covering his brief moment of seriousness, 'although I'd probably be a right pain complaining about it. But tomorrow Lucinda Leighton is arriving in London. You'll like to meet her I know, someone from your own country. The evening is booked as far as she and I are concerned. It's ages since I've seen her and I've only played with her once on an American tour. It's all arranged, the pianos are being brought in for us. Of course there will be rehearsal

149

with the orchestra the next day, but we need time to bring our scores together. Each perfecting our own is a vastly different thing from combining them in a double concerto.' When Erica didn't answer he concluded she'd accepted the impossibility of their going to the jazz concert. Putting the suggestion behind him, and ignorant of her reaction to what he was saying, there was a laugh in his voice as he went on: 'I remember the only other time we played together, it was enormous fun. Not a serious concerto, it was a recital, music for four hands. We were a lot younger then, pretty well unknown. Now our reception is important, this has to be a serious success.'

'I see. Just forget I asked. I guess I ought to have enquired whether I might expect you to have any free time – unimportant free time for us to be in London together. Or does a wife only get the "in bed time" when there is nothing more demanding.' In her disappointment she sounded like a sulky child.

'Honestly I'm sorry. I'd not looked on these days as a holiday, I'm here to work. When the concert is over we'll stay on for a day or two if you like, see if there's a show you'd like to go to. The box office will willingly take tomorrow's tickets back if they're as hard to come by as you say.'

'Take them back? How come? I told you, I'm going to the concert.'

He tipped her chin and kissed her lightly on the mouth.

'What a crass idiot I am. Of course you must go to your concert. Darling, I'm sorry, I'm truly sorry.'

Her anger melted and her arms wrapped around him. She knew she was putty in his hands, at that moment as he held her she asked nothing more. But presently, looking at the tickets she'd been so excited to get, disappointment led to self-reproach. I'm so weak, she chided herself. I know I'm outside the things that really matter to him. Yes, but he does love me, I know that too. He loves me to be there to come home to. That's what I've got to accept. It's that or nothing. He can't stop me going to the Festival Hall tomorrow; I can't stop him spending his evening pounding the piano with Lucinda Leighton. But there's a difference: I shall be wishing he was with me, while he won't be giving me a thought!

Her anticipation had been for more than the traditional jazz she loved, more even than sharing it with Harvey (although she'd let her imagination run riot and let herself believe that it would open his eyes to what he'd been missing). So much of her eagerness stemmed from being here in London. The throbbing heart of her adopted country, it still held a thrill to the young American girl; she'd pictured them coming out into the June darkness, stopping to gaze at the lights reflected on the Thames, at the Palace of Westminster, the tower of Big Ben standing like a sentinel. She'd still go to the concert, she'd take the same pains in getting ready, she'd come back to the hotel fired with enthusiasm wanting to make Harvey regret what he'd missed. But the magic was gone.

There was an urgency behind Melly's long hours of work each day. They were already well into April and she was preparing for an exhibition in June. By that time she would be six months pregnant. Until the exhibition her work was getting a hundred per cent of her concentration; when it was over she mentally promised herself that she'd give her attention just as wholeheartedly to preparing for the baby. Later she would feel differently about it, wasn't that what her mother had told her. But would she? Her anger had given way to stoic resignation. For the first weeks, except for missing periods, there had been nothing to tell her she was pregnant. Quite suddenly all that had changed, she still felt well but her body appeared to be making up for a slow start. She looked at the veins on her breasts, the darkened and enlarged nipples, and might have been examining a stranger. When her jeans wouldn't fasten her reaction was revulsion. Her energy never flagged, it was her driving force as from morn until night she worked.

When the telephone rang, out of habit she grabbed a cleaning rag for her fingers even though the day was too young for the build-up of paint that would come later.

'Hi, Melly, it's me. We're in town, did you know?' And there was no doubt who 'me' was.

'Erica! I saw the notice that Harvey was in London for a concert tonight. I didn't know you were both staying. When did you come down?'

'Day before yesterday. He's bogged down as always. I'm rattling around on my own, so I just wondered if I could buy you lunch. Anywhere you say – either right in town or somewhere out near you.'

To Melly, time was precious. But she couldn't miss the underlying cry of loneliness. Erica would find other people to talk to, solitude wasn't in her nature, but other people were outsiders whereas *she* was family, *she* belonged to Harvey.

'I'd like that Erica. Tell you what, I'll drive in, I could park at the Marble Arch underground park.'

As they made their arrangements Melly found she was looking forward to her unexpected day out. A few more months and she wouldn't be able to take off at a moment's notice, she thought resentfully. Her body was already beginning to feel clumsy, not her own any more. She had been given an appointment to start pre-natal

151

relaxation classes. Trevor had persuaded her she should attend. A floor full of women in various stages of pregnancy, all of them wanting to compare progress, as if producing a baby was their purpose in life. She'd never gone back. The incident had alienated her even further from the prospect of motherhood.

But she meant to play fair. The exhibition must come first, then she'd buy all the bits a baby needed and go through the business of a confinement; she'd even stop painting for those first weeks of the new life. Now, though, she pulled on her first pair of maternity jeans and loose top, then concentrated on making up her face to take attention away from what she felt was beyond hope and would only get worse.

Erica had envisaged them eating in a hotel, but by common consent they went to a pub, bringing their food to an outside table amongst the noise and fumes of the London street.

'This is just great. I wish I could paint really vivid word pictures, so that I could tell them back home.'

Melly looked around her and laughed.

'Hardly a romantic pavement café!'

'No, but that's what makes it so good. Pavement cafés, crowded with tourists, they don't breathe the life of a place. This does. Students, nurses, office workers, cab drivers, artists – at least one – proper real people eat here, people who make up a city that works for its keep.'

'Where's my big brother eating? I wish he could have come.'

'I guess I've given up even wishing it, I just take it for granted now that he'll be somewhere else. And that brings me to something I was meaning to tell you. Guess who I went to the Festival Hall with last night?'

'To give real colour to your letter home it ought at least to have been the Prince of Wales! Or was it the Prime Minister?'

'You know the trouble with you English folk, you take your heritage for granted, you don't stop, look and listen. It takes us Americans to appreciate. Anyway, last night – no, the royal princes couldn't make it. But I met Adrian Crighton, just by chance. Both of us on our lonesome and me with two tickets in my purse and a husband too busy doing his practice to come. I got to know Adrian quite well of course while I was sitting for him, but even so no girl likes to say they've been stood up, even by a husband. He enjoyed it though, he's dotty on jazz too. So we had a great night out.'

'He was working somewhere near Mum and Dad. But of course with them being away he wouldn't have got to Russets to see them.'

'He seemed to know they'd been away, but he didn't say he'd seen

152

them. Maybe he's still working that way, he didn't tell me, but I got the impression he expected to get to see them soon.'

'They'll like that.' Melly was pleased with her casual comment.

'Sure they will. Of course I got along well with him too – if I hadn't I wouldn't have wanted him to come to the concert last night – but he and Claudia were real friends, spent a lot of time together. Everyone looked on him as family.'

'They might have looked on him as family, Erica, but there is no family man lurking inside Adrian Crighton waiting for a chance to get out, believe me. He's a law unto himself, uses everyone to his best advantage. I love him dearly, but then I have no illusions. Any woman – any person – who looks on him as more than a passing ship putting into harbour to replenish the ship's victuals is asking for trouble. Now, what about pud? Are you treating me to a pud too?'

It was later, as they walked in Hyde Park, that Erica went back to what she'd been saying about wanting to share all this with the folk at home.

'Letters can't be the same, I'm full to the brim with things I want to tell them.'

'Can't you persuade Harvey to take you back on holiday? He can't be hard up. It's not as though he's an impecunious teacher!'

'Sure he's got the money. It's time he's short of. If you could look at his diary you'd see, he's got no real break for months. Oh there are plenty of free days – except that he'll fill them with hours of practice – but no time when he could fly home with me for a proper holiday. The merry-go-round just goes right on, there's never a chance to get off it.'

'He must need a holiday.'

'Guess so, or so you would expect. But it's a sort of drug to him. Even when he's home it's practice, practice, practice. And when he's had a good session he's on a real high.' She shrugged. 'A high in a one-man balloon, one I can never share with him.'

'Not many wives share a husband's career. Or husbands a wife's. You know what you should do? You should give yourself a challenge, not say anything to anyone, not even Harvey. Write a book, or take up photography, or fashion designing. Something that's really your own. Surprise him.'

'Do something without telling him ... and maybe I'll do just that.'

Already the plan was forming in her mind. In two days' time they'd go north, she wait until they were home – and then she knew exactly what she'd do.

*

153

The congregation had been sparse by any standard. The week following Easter – like the first Sunday after Christmas – the pews were mostly empty for morning service.

James had offered prayers for those in troubled Rwanda and pointed out the collection plate he had left at the back of the church. After the congregation had filed out Jenny collected it and and took it to the vestry, counting the contents as she went.

'Twenty-seven in the congregation, three pounds sixty-seven on the plate.'

'There are so many ways of giving, every bank is a collecting point,' James made excuses for his flock.

'And how much do you think people voluntarily give?'

'Oh, come, Jenny, people are enormously generous. Think of the millions they collect for Save the Children with their television appeal, and Comic Relief.'

Appeals for relief aid for the refugees and starving in Rwanda were plastered up in towns and villages up and down the country. But recounting the three pounds and sixty-seven pence Jenny knew there had to be a better way of collecting than an easy-to-ignore plate.

'I've got half an idea, I'll work on it,' she said. 'People might put their odd change into a bowl, but that's no good. Leave it to me.'

She didn't tell him that she had spent most of the service getting her plans in place. Once she'd checked that everything was ready for the Sunday School and both teachers were going to be there, she had taken her usual place between Barry and Patsy and let her mind take wing, just as it did each Sunday morning. These days there was plenty in her thoughts that gave her pleasure, the hour slipped by.

Brightley would not only give, it would enjoy giving. Village participation, that's what would open the purse strings.

'You think we should have a house-to-house collection?' James proffered. 'You'll need a licence of course. Then I'm sure the St Luke's La—'

'No! This mustn't be a church thing, this must concern everyone. James, we want money from the village not just from the congregation. Tomorrow I'll go to the Clerk to the Justice's office, see how soon I can get a drinks licence. Then I'll have to arrange to use the Village Green. We'll want a band, we'll need a barbecue. I've only got the morning tomorrow, but I'll make an early start.'

There she stood, solid and determined, her four-year-old winter coat belted around her thick waist, her brogues bright from years of polishing, her skirt an unfortunate two inches longer than her coat. James looked at her and marvelled.

By the next evening the wheels were in motion. The last Saturday in April was to be known as Brightley's Aid Day: the scoutmaster had promised to produce a bar tent and be responsible for getting the drinks, a chorister from St Lukes played a trumpet in a brass band and had promised to 'have a word with the lads, but I'm sure they'll want to do their bit'. That was the general response, people wanted to 'do their bit', even those very same people who had glanced the other way as they walked past the plate in church.

Claudia had been home more than a week and in that time she'd not once gone out to the fruit farm. Had there been a message on the Answerphone she would have forced herself to erase it from the machine and from her mind too; but there was no message to ignore.

Having tempted everyone into believing it was spring, late April played at being January. Known as 'the bug', there was a spate of 'flu which, in a rural area, meant that Claudia could never be sure when Teddy would get through his house visits. The carefree holiday seemed like another life and they two other people. There had been epidemics through the years, weeks when he had worked long hours, to say nothing of all the time that the house could never be left unattended because someone had to be on hand to take telephone messages.

Maybe we've got soft. Me, particularly. Claudia knelt on the windowseat watching the cold rain roll down the glass. Yes, but in those days we both pulled the same way. And now? We don't pull opposite ways – I know Jenny's a problem but by and large we don't. Even over Jenny, although we don't talk about it, can't talk about it, yet what we want is for James to be happy. But he is, he's happier than he's ever been. That's what hurts, that's what makes it so impossible to talk about it.

The shrill bell of the telephone brought her back to the moment.

'Hello?'

'Claudia, it's me.' No question who 'me' was.

'Lovely surprise, Erica. You enjoyed your days in London?'

'I love London – and I saw Melly, that was nice. Oh, and Adrian. Bumped into him and we went to a jazz session together.'

'So you had a good time.' Adrian in London, not at his 'wooden nest'. She ought not to mind, she ought to be glad if he'd given up the idea . . .

'Listen, I've just come back from the booking agent. Claudia, I'm going home.'

'Oh no!' Everything else was pushed from Claudia's mind.

'Not that sort of going home! I'm going back on a holiday, going to see Mom and the uncles and aunts. And Sara's having a hard time,

I want to see Sara. When the divorce is through maybe I'll bring her back on a visit.' Claudia knew that Erica's elder sister, Sara, was divorcing her much married husband.

'Harvey can manage to fit a holiday in? That's marvellous.'

'No, only me. I guess I'm the useless one with time heavy on my hands. I wish he could come, more than anything I wish it. But I'm not too sure that he does, he'd be fretting for the ivories.'

'All the same, he ought to have a holiday.'

'I never know whether to be glad no-one expects anything of me, or envy him his obsession with his work. Anyway, he's happy for me to go, he knows I miss Mom and the others. I fly out of Manchester the day after tomorrow and I aim to be back by June. About six weeks. Sara's case should be through by then.'

Teddy was late home that evening. With a dinner reheated in the micro, the nine o'clock news loaded with doom and gloom, knowing that Erica was holidaying without Harvey did nothing to brighten the atmosphere.

'It's not a sin, Teddy. Think of the times I took the children away without you. You didn't think the bottom was falling out of our marriage.'

'Not the same thing at all, you know it isn't.'

Yes, she knew it wasn't.

'I used to love these trips when the children were tiny,' Claudia said as they joined the M3 and Teddy pulled across into the fast lane. 'Remember Teddy how Barry used to sit on his tiny three-wheeler watching for us. They seemed such a happy little bunch . . .' Her voice trailed to silence, she wished she hadn't said it.

Jenny's name had hardly been mentioned since the day of their visit to The Grange. If only they could have talked about it, shared their anxiety; was James being deceived? Was he building his happiness on a lie? They couldn't voice their fear. If James had suspected that he was being lied to, if he'd been angry, distraught, then they could have shared his fears with him and with each other.

After talking to Miss Cummins, they'd driven away from The Grange in a silence that became increasingly difficult to break. When at last Teddy spoke it had been more to himself than to Claudia.

'Good husband, home, family – what's the matter with the silly bitch? Creeping back to her girlfriend I suppose.'

'We don't know that. Anyway if she and Paula Stonehouse are still friends, it doesn't have to be the sort of affair you're always trying to imply. Jenny's happier than I've ever seen her – James is too.'

'What in hell is she playing at? The boy was so proud when he told

156

us – three afternoons a week. So where is she? Tell me that, if you've got such confidence in her.'

'You're not fair to her. You never have been. I don't know what she does any more than you do. Perhaps she's got a part-time job and doesn't tell him because she knows he would rather she spent her time on parish work. Teddy, it's a happy house again. We could feel it when we were there. Can't we try just to be grateful? And don't forget she told me about the pill. You say how proud James was when he told us how hard she works; that's true, so he was. But if we're talking of pride, I'll never forget her face, sort of glowing she was, when she said she was on the pill. As if after all these years they'd found each other.'

'So why can't she be honest with him? Would he treat her like it? You know perfectly well he wouldn't.'

She'd hated to see him like this, cold and uncompromising.

'I don't understand either.' Tentatively she'd put her hand out to touch him, but either he hadn't noticed or hadn't wanted to notice. 'Somewhere there's an explanation. Perhaps Miss Cummins doesn't know how often she goes in, after all she's not on the pay roll. I'm sure we're worrying for nothing. Maybe she's on a course of some sort, something she wants to keep as a surprise until she's finished.'

'And what sort of a marriage is that? How many weeks has she been cheating James, deceiving him? Just think how he looked when he told us about her: proud, confident. She's never been the right woman for him. I've always told you so. You're the boy's mother, I don't understand how you can look for loopholes, excuses to make it right that she is playing false with him?'

'Don't let's talk about it. Please Teddy, it's no use you and me arguing.'

'Push it under the carpet. Pretend she's giving the sort of service James believes.'

'Teddy, we mustn't pre-judge, there will be a perfectly good explanation. We must just hang on to that – for James's sake we must. I'm not going to let us discuss him like we are. He loves her. We have no right to condemn her when we don't know anything about it, nor to talk about his marriage behind his back. He loves her.'

She'd turned away from him, partly to shut out the sight of his cold anger and partly so that he wouldn't know how near she was to tears. Darling James, what is she doing to you? Any other woman and we'd be wondering if there was another man. But not Jenny, not down-to-earth, solid, plodding Jenny. Whatever she's doing it's not taking anything from the family, I've never known the rectory such a happy place.

157

They'd driven the rest of the way home without talking any more about it, in fact without talking at all.

Now they were on their way to share in Brightley's Aid Day.

'Teddy,' Claudia took her courage in her hands as they turned off the Oxford road and followed the sign to 'Brightley 1 mile', 'when we were with them last time – James and the others I mean – everything was fine. We all had a lovely time.'

'Well?'

'Well, none of them know we called at The Grange, they'll expect everything to be just like it was then. We can't arrive looking dour and critical. Please, Teddy, let's make it a happy weekend. If you can't look agreeable for *my* sake, at least you might try for *James's*.'

'So it's my fault?'

'Don't be so damned childish.' I mustn't cry. He wouldn't understand, he'd think they were temper tears.

Teddy took his eyes off the road long enough to look at her and suspect tears were near the surface.

'Do you think I'd upset James? I'll behave.' He rested a hand on her knee. 'We mustn't quarrel over it, Claudia, not you and me.'

His sudden gentleness was almost her undoing.

In the kitchen Jenny was ladling cream into individual dishes, a heaped tablespoonful for each table of four. Next, the same for strawberry jam.

'Have you unfolded all the tables from the hall, Barry?' she asked without turning when she heard a movement from the open doorway behind her.

'Mrs Carlyle I believe?'

Hearing his voice, Jenny spun round, excited and confused at seeing him here in the familiar background of home.

'Ken, how nice and early you are. Come in. I'll take you to meet James, I think he's putting out the rows of chairs in the Hall ready for the competitions. Tea will be after that, but I want to get all this stuff taken across to the kitchen ready. Bar and burgers on the green; tea, cakes, cream teas for the less adventurous in the Village Hall after you've given out the winners' certificates.' She was talking too much.

So sure of himself, she knew he was aware of her confusion. She felt as gauche as she had the day she'd met him unexpectedly on Streatley Hill. Yet why should she? Why should being here in her own kitchen strip her of the joy and freedom that was part of being with him.

'Let me help you.' He came to her side at the table. 'I know just

158

what you do, I was watching you from the doorway. A dollop of jam in each glass dish. I can do that.'

'Do you think we shall get enough people for all these? I usually only do thirty jams and thirty creams for the bazaar – and we don't have a bar and bergers to compete with there either. But then we've never had a celebrity before.'

'I believe you exaggerate my pulling power.' Again she saw the way his eyes were laughing. Had it been a mistake asking him here?

'If you're not careful you can get sticky when you get near the bottom of the jars. It's one good heaped tablespoonful on each little dish, or two flat ones if that's easier. I'll start putting the scones out, eight on each serving dish.'

How can he step so easily from one compartment of life to another? I shouldn't have suggested we ask him here. 'We' that's James and me. But I'm not just that. There's the other half of me: 'we' . . . Ken and me. What a crazy thing to do, to bring James and Ken together, and worse still for me to be with them both.

'You've only put seven on that one.' Still spooning jam, Ken was watching her.

'So I have. I made all these, 240 of them. Then there are masses of cakes made by the church helpers.'

'You have many talents. But then you know that.'

'Don't Ken. Please don't.'

She dragged a wooden chair to the cupboard and, in her usual inelegant way, clambered on to it to reach another pile of serving plates. Just at that moment James came into the room.

'I'll take those,' he said. Then, having put them on the bench, put out his hands to help her down. She'd heaved herself up, but getting down was more difficult. If only she could have leant forward and let him lift her, or simply taken a light and dainty leap to the ground. 'Careful,' he admonished, 'lean on my shoulders.'

She felt both of them watching her. How must they see her, standing there like a beached whale?

'I got up, I can get down,' she answered gruffly. 'James, this is Ken. He's been helping.'

For a moment, from her high perch, she looked at the pair of them. And in that moment she was frightened by a truth there was no running away from.

The situation was saved by a commotion outside. Barry had seen Teddy's car coming up the drive.

Brightley buzzed with activity. Ken Sheldrake did the honours, pronouncing it open with a short speech, its serious content laced with easy humour. He watched the sports and cheered as loudly as anyone, then pinned rosettes on event winners; with the local respresentative on the council and the headmistress of the school he judged the talent competition (and, being the only entrant in the stringed instrument section, Patsy was awarded a Winner's Certificate, printed without charge by the local printer). On the Green the beer tent was well patronized, while people queued for beefburgers despite it being mid-afternoon and all this as a background to, first, the children's races and, next, the Morris Men. In the Village Hall the music contest and the talent show were followed by teas, by which time strains of the brass band on the Green filled the chilly air.

'May I have the pleasure?' Teddy solemnly held his crooked arm towards Patsy. With head high and feet firmly planted she let him lead her to the centre of the grass where to the strains of the Blue Danube they opened the dancing, Patsy's count of 'one, two, three' clearly audible to Claudia as she waltzed past with James.

'It seems an odd way to help the hungry and homeless, Mum.' James was unable to throw himself into the fun with the abandon shown by many of the locals.

'It's a wonderful way to help them, Jamie. Doesn't it show that the world is good, people enjoy being together. Isn't that the message you preach, that in loving and sharing there's joy? I've never been more conscious of Brightley loving its neighbour. And at the end of it you'll find that the people you want to help will feel a tangible benefit. Sort of like Brightley's love reaching out to a far-away neighbour.'

James held her a little closer.

'I ought to have you preach my sermons for me, Mum, you get to the point much more easily than I can. Look at Jenny over there, she thought up this entire thing. I wonder if it wasn't more than sheer luck that sent Ken Sheldrake to visit a patient at The Grange the very day she had the idea. He's the son of that friend of her mother's she looked after back in the winter, so he could hardly refuse her.'

'Divine intervention?' This time he knew she was teasing.

'You may laugh, but some of these people have come from as far away as Oxford – again, thanks to the item Jen put in all the local papers – you can't tell me they would have bothered without a celebrity. Just look at her, Mum, she's been mingling with the people, shaking that bucket for cash all the afternoon.'

Claudia looked. Today Jenny was in her favourite and unbecoming jeans with an anorak, the rattle of her bucket of coins making itself heard right across the Green.

On the stroke of six the band struck up the National Anthem and Brightley got the message. Time to go home. 'Just over £900.' The count over, James came over to join Teddy on the Green where he was picking up any remaining odd scraps of paper, lollipop sticks, plastic cups and paper napkins sticky with tomato ketchup and putting them into a dustbin liner. In the tent the scoutmaster was stacking away his empties while his troop were boxing up the plastic 'glasses' to take them back to the Scout Hall to wash. 'Nine hundred pounds and no expenses, everyone gave their services voluntarily. A local bank manager lives in the village and he agreed to act as Treasurer, he's been bagging up the money almost as it came in. Jenny was right, people want to get involved – and she was right too that the more they enjoy themselves the more generous they are.'

'She's worked hard.' Teddy congratulated himself on the warmth he infused into his tone.

'She's marvellous, I just can't tell you Dad. The more she does, the more she seems prepared to do. By the way, I forgot to mention when you looked in on the way to Scotland – that woman, Paula Stonehouse, the one Jenny got entangled with last year, she's left the district. They put their house on the market and it sold within a week or two. I'm told they've gone off to the Mediterannean somewhere. A tax haven for him, I imagine. I'm glad they've gone. The girls seemed to have fallen out, but bad feelings cast a shadow. Nice people have moved into their house, very willing to be involved with the church too.'

'So, life's good, James?'

'Never been better. Great afternoon wasn't it, Dad. The children did well. Patsy's already talking about wanting to have her Winner's Certificate framed!' he laughed.

'I booked our table at the The Pheasant for eight, that should give us time. I thought we'd better not be too late, and by eight the youngsters ought to have worked up an appetite despite the burgers.'

'Thanks Dad. It puts the final touch on the day, you taking us out to eat.' He glanced at his watch, making a quick calculation. 'I'll go over to the church and say Evensong, it's almost six-thirty. They both knew that it would be a solitary affair, but one that James never missed.

Claudia came over to join them. It was a natural action to slip her arm through Teddy's, just as it was for him to acknowledge the action by a scarcely perceptible tightening of his grip. Only then did she realize what she'd done and how he'd responded. Together they watched James walk across to the gate that led into the churchyard, it was one of those moments that would stay with her always.

'Do me up, Dad,' Patsy turned her back to James so that he could

161

pull up her zip. 'Wasn't it a super afternoon. Did I do my fiddle all right Dad?'

'Splendidly. I was very proud of you Patsy.'

Her round face flushed with joy that was almost too much.

'Silly,' she said gruffly.

Neither of them had noticed Jenny watching them from just outside Patsy's bedroom door.

'You two seem to be ready. I'll just make sure Barry is getting on all right.'

'You see to yourself, Jen, you've not even started to get changed and it's a quarter to seven.'

'There were things I wanted to do. I used the tablecloths from the Parish Room for teas, I wanted to get them washed. They're in the dryer now. That's how I've got a bit late. I'll just have a quick check on Barry.'

'Barry can dress himself. The sheets could have waited, you don't usually rush like that. You get ready.'

She didn't argue, but she went into Barry's room just the same.

'You look nice,' she told him.

'I'm starving hungry. Are you ready Mum?'

'Do I look ready?' she laughed.

'You look OK to me. But this is a smarten-up job I suppose. I put a clean shirt on.'

'Good lad.' Her eyes seemed to devour him. She wanted to hug him to her. There were a thousand things she wanted to say to him, but she could say none of them. He was too young to understand. And even if he'd been older, nothing could mitigate the selfishness of what she was doing. 'Barry . . .'

'What's up, Mum?'

'Nothing. Just "oh, Barry".'

'You know what Gran's Gwen Pomfrey would call you? She'd say "She's a funny ossity, that one."'

'And I expect she'd be right. It's about what I look too. I must go and change my dress.'

But first she called down the stairs to where the others were all assembled:

'I'll bring my own car and meet you there. I'm all behind. You don't want them to think you're not coming or they may not keep the table on a Saturday night.'

It was so easy. From her bedroom window she watched them go. Only then did the enormity of what she was doing hit her. They'd gone. Without a backward glance they'd piled into Teddy's car and gone. She looked round the bedroom she and James had shared for

162

twelve years, let her wide, strong hand move on the counterpane on the side that had always been hers. Then she walked around to his side. Frightened, looking for strength, she lowered herself heavily to her knees where she had seen James kneel how many hundreds of times through their years. James . . . he had never rebuked her that she didn't share his silent vespers. But neither had he let her come between him and moments that were as necessary to him as food and drink.

Tonight he would kneel here on this very spot. Would he find the comfort he sought? Jenny wanted to pray, but her mind rushed ahead of her, a jumble of prayer and self analysis.

I never meant it to end like this, You know I didn't. Perhaps You don't want to listen to me, I'm just making excuses. I vowed to be faithful, I've broken my vows. I am a sinner. And I can't repent. I can't. The first time Ken and I were together – I don't mean all those years ago, I mean last winter – that first time, in my heart I was faithful to James. I suppose letting it happen at all was a sin. But it's not a body that really counts, it's a soul. And that first time I just used Ken, I pretended, imagined, that it was happening to me with James. I knew something was missing with James and me, I'm not sure if I understood what it was I wanted. I must have, or I wouldn't have let it happen with Ken. Would I? That was the day I realized how it could have been for us, for James and me. I wanted to encourage James, guide him, tempt him – but tempt makes it sound wicked. And there's nothing wicked. I loved James. Do I still love him? Of course I do. But not that way, not any more. I'm not blaming him, You know that. Or am I? You must know, even if I don't. One thing I swear is the truth, when Ken made love to me it was like a miracle, and all I wanted was that it could be like that for James and me. It's hard to look back, to be honest. But I must. And You know how hard I tried, I ached, yearned to make it wonderful like that for James and me, to make it bring us together. He would never have told me, he's far too kind to hurt anyone, but I felt he was shocked, I knew he shied away. These last months, it's being with Ken that has made me able to cope with my life here. He gives me all my vitality. Now though he's going away. With him gone, back to the old order – I can't, I just can't. In the beginning I told You I went to bed with Ken while I loved just James. But it's not like that any more. There, now I've told You, and telling You matters, there's no going back on it. Damn James, damn all the do-gooding he expects of me, damn his calm and his kindness, damn the effort it takes for him to make love to me, damn him. None of this need have happened.

She sat back on her heels, her face a mask of misery.

Barry . . . Patsy . . . How can I bear to leave them? How can I do this to my children? Will it scar them? Please, this above all I beg you, don't let them be hurt. They love James dearly. I don't want them to forget me, I don't want them to hate me for what I'm going to do. But please, please, more important than anything else, don't let them be miserable, help them to accept.

Downstairs the telephone rang. Don't answer it, she told herself. That'll be James to see why you haven't come. Let it ring. In a minute he'll think you've already left home . . . nine . . . ten . . . She struggled heavily to her feet . . . eleven . . . twelve. Silence, a silence that filled the house and put distance between her and all that had gone before.

By half past eight Claudia suggested that they ought to order. By quarter past nine, his meal half eaten, James left the others discussing what to chose for pudding and, borrowing Teddy's car, drove home, expecting at every bend in the road to come upon the scene of an accident.

When he reached the rectory there was Jenny's car tight against the wall of the house outside the window of the Parish Room where she'd put it this morning when they'd been making all the space they could for visitors' parking.

164

Chapter 11

'Dr Carlyle, excuse me. There is a telephone call for you – just through the bar.'

At the waiter's words a quick glance flashed between Teddy and Claudia, but it was Barry who spoke their fears.

'It must be Dad. Something's happened to Mum. That's why she's late.'

'He's probably found her trying to change a tyre or something,' Teddy passed the children the menu. 'I'll see what he wants while you choose yourselves something disgustingly rich and fanciful.'

It wasn't the choice put before them so much as his confident manner that restored their evening. Claudia managed to play her part, setting her face into a look of anticipation as she too picked up a menu.

'Dad, it's James.'

'What is it? Shall I come? Is it an accident?'

'No.' The one word was flat, expressionless.

'Tell me, son. What's happened to Jenny? What's kept her?'

'Later. I'll tell you later.' Could this be the same man who only hours before had assured his father that life was good, had never been better? 'Can you make some excuse to Mum and the children, tell them Jenny's been fetched away, tell them – tell them – she's had to go – Dad, I can't take it in.'

The truth was there in his floundering words.

'You mean she's gone off? Christ! What's the matter with that bloody woman?'

'Please, Dad, don't. I can't believe it. Please, for the children's sake, tell them she was sent for – no, fetched – say they wanted her at The Grange.'

'The children aren't half-wits. You expect them to believe a voluntary worker would be sent for, let alone fetched, even in a crisis?' Teddy spoke quietly, all around him was the noise of the bar.

165

'They won't suspect. She's told us before that they've asked her to go in outside her usual time. They never doubted – I never doubted.' His voice was dangerously near to breaking, Teddy had to save him from the final humiliation.

'Right. Leave it to me. I'll tell them the line was engaged here so she'd left you a scribbled note.' Then, conscious that a customer from the bar had come to use the second phone by his side, his voice changed, he assumed what sounded to his own ears a false heartiness. 'Who was it you said fetched her?' He dug for any plausible story and what he came up with couldn't have been less fortunate. 'That chap Sheldrake? Well, naturally he'd remember how she'd helped his mother. His aunt you say? Right I'll explain to the others.'

'I can't think straight – can't take it in – she was fine Dad, you saw for yourself. Today was all her doing. And all the time did she know? I can't think, I can't believe it . . .'

'You know the best thing you can do?'

'I don't think I know anything.'

'Come back here and finish your meal. I'll tell the others Jenny has been fetched away for a day or two. What do you say?'

Silence.

'James?'

'I can't come back. Could you, if it were Mum?'

Teddy scowled. Claudia and Jennifer! What a ridiculous comparison!

'Right you are. I'll see they understand. We shan't be long. I'll explain – and the rest is up to you when the youngsters get home. They're the ones who matter.'

'I know. That's what frightens me. Can't be happening . . . Jenny leaving the children . . . I can't understand . . . can't take it in.'

'Go and have a stiff drink. We'll bring them home when they've finished whatever exotic desserts they've decided on.'

On the way back to the restaurant he caught sight of himself in the mirror above the bar, his face like a thundercloud. That wouldn't do. If *he* couldn't act *his* part, how in the devil could poor young James manage?

'Was it James? Nothing's wrong is it?' He saw the fear in Claudia's eyes and knew her imagination had Jenny's car a write-off somewhere between Brightley and The Pheasant.

'Not in the way you're meaning. He found a scribbled note from Jennifer. She'd tried to ring here but the line was engaged. That chap Sheldrake had come back for her. Some elderly aunt ill. I suppose he remembered how good she'd been to his mother and fell back on her.

166

James isn't coming back, he's had quite a day and we've more or less finished. I told him I'd ring for a taxi to take us home.'

The wool was pulled safely over the children's eyes, but Claudia wasn't so easily fooled. Teddy's over-cheerful voice didn't match up with the story he told – and suddenly it was 'Jennifer' again. An inexplicable fear gripped her. She was back in the kitchen at Russets, James's face crumpling in despair. But only this evening Teddy had told her that Paula and her husband had moved away. It made no sense.

'Poor Jenny! And she'd had quite a day too.' She played her part. It must be a part, she had no doubt. 'That's the trouble with doing a kindness, people impose on you. After the way Kenneth Sheldrake had helped Brightley today she could hardly refuse him.'

'It's always like that for Mum,' Barry championed her, 'but what a rotten shame when we were coming out for a special dinner. She ought to have said no.'

'She's not made that way, Barry. Are you having a dessert, Teddy, or the cheeseboard?'

'I won't bother. It's pretty late, time we got these young people home.'

'When's Mum getting back?' Barry wanted to know. 'Will she be very late?'

'I got the impression she would have to stay over the weekend at least, until some sort of arrangements could be made.'

'Poor James.' Claudia was aware of Teddy's quick frown, a reminder to be careful what she said in front of the children, but it was for their benefit that she went on, 'And poor Jenny too. They've were on such a high after the day being such a success. Why ever couldn't the Sheldrake aunt have waited until morning to get ill. Jenny mightn't have minded a break from arranging Sunday School, but she was looking forward to our all coming out together this evening.'

There was no sign of James waiting at the rectory, just a note on the hall table.

Mum, can you chase the children to bed. There are things I need to see to in the vestry. J.

Going upstairs to run their bath water, and deciding that it would hurt no-one and speed their departure to let them jump in together, she looked out of the window at the end of the first-floor landing. The vestry was in darkness; the glow of the stained-glass eastern window told her that James was in the chancel just as she'd known he would be. Teddy followed her up and came to stand by her side.

167

'They're attacking their nightly hot chocolate. I don't know where they put it!'

'Tell me, Teddy.'

'All I know is that she's cleared off. God knows where to. She left him a note. Christ, I could strangle that bitch.' She gripped his fingers, but there was no response. 'You see where he's gone to.' He nodded his head towards the dimly lit chancel.

'I knew that's where he'd be. It takes him out of our reach. I feel inadequate.'

'Any solace he might find on his knees there isn't going to feed the children, iron their shirts, remember their dinner money on Monday mornings.'

A scurry of feet told them the hot chocolate was finished.

'Come on, you two,' she yelled over the banisters in what the family had always teasingly referred to as her 'jolly hockeysticks' voice, knowing that it meant she was rallying them to enjoy something they weren't in the least keen about. 'You can bath together, I'm running the water. Gather up your jimjams and get stripped off. If I haven't chased you into bed before your father comes home I shall get the sack!' Then to Teddy: 'We go home tomorrow. Can we do that?'

'I have to, you know that. Don't let's start talking – not till James has told us everything he knows. She's probably acting up again like she did before – attention-seeking.'

Much later James locked the church and came home. Pale and drawn, he looked as though he'd got little comfort from his hours on his knees.

'They went to bed happily enough,' Claudia greeted him. Her banal statement rang out too loudly in the silent room. She moved towards him, held out her hand then, when he made no movement, let it drop to her side.

'We have to talk, James. It's no use hiding from what has to be faced. There are the children to be considered.'

'You think I don't know? I won't fail the children. I might be a useless husband, but I'll never let Barry and Patsy down.'

Fine words, but darling James, who is going to get their meals ready for when they come home from school? Who is going to see the buttons are sewn on their shirts? Who is going to check them on their learning homework? Who is going to be there for them when you are tending your flock? Claudia knew what the answer must be; there was no-one else. She turned away from James and from Teddy too, frightened that they would read her thoughts, know her sudden panic. There's no-one but me. James can't always be at home for them.

Imagine them coming back to this great empty house after school. Teddy's right – she's a selfish bitch.

'Did she tell you where she's going, James?' While Claudia's thoughts had raced away with her, Teddy was trying to hang on to some sort of constructive reasoning. 'Has she got a job? But damn it, why now? Why today?'

For answer James took a letter from his inside pocket and passed it to his father.

'This is all I know. You'd better read it.'

I'm sorry to do it this way, James. I wish we could have talked. But I know we couldn't. What I am doing is beyond your forgiveness. I know that too. For months Ken has been my lover. Lover, James. For the comfort of one another . . . wasn't that what we said in our marriage vows. So you did your Christian duty. I'm not criticizing you, we are all made differently. But I can't live any longer as a work horse; that's what I am, with an occasional ration to keep me sweet.

'You shouldn't give me this, James, this is between you and Jennifer.' Teddy reached to pass it back.

'No. Read it, Dad. Read all of it. You see, she's right. Some of it has been my fault. How can a man tell? We have two children . . . I never imagined . . . Go on, read it all.'

These last months I've been happier than at any time in my life. As a form of gratitude for joy I never expected, I have worked willingly in the parish. It would have gone on like that, but after what I learnt this afternoon I know it can't. Ken is moving away. Immediately. I can't go back to how it used to be. It's too late for that.

Don't try and forgive me, I don't deserve forgiveness. I am doing the lowest thing a woman can do. I am walking away from my children. I can't believe what I'm doing, but I shall do it. I must. I'm no loss to you, I'm not even honest. I've lied to you for months. When you've been proud that I've been helping the aged and sick I've been with Ken. I'm not fit to be their mother. But I love them. If there is one good thing about me it's that I truly love them. Yet I *must* do this.

But it's not all my fault. I wanted the love I found with Ken to come from you. I humiliated myself trying to give what you found repugnant. We can't live together James. I want happiness for you, but I'm not a saint. I can't give the rest of my life to doing the things you expect of me. You serve your God, you're lucky that in doing that you find your own salvation; you expect

169

me to serve your parishioners, subordinate all that I am into coercing them to be active supporters of your church. I've told you all this before – before I realized that life could hold joy as well as service.

Judge me as you will. When I first let – let? welcomed – Ken show me how to enjoy love, I gave him my body but my heart was yours. Now it's too late.

I'm sorry James. Please, don't let the children stop loving me. No, I shouldn't ask it, I don't deserve it. Most of all, don't let them be unhappy. If it were you who were going – but you wouldn't, you're too good, you love duty next to God – their lives would be shattered. We have had so much that was good. I must be mad. I must be possessed of devils, isn't that what you'd say? Perhaps I am. Oh, James, I am so desperately sorry.

Jen.

P. S. I've washed the parish tablecloths. They need ironing. You'll have to draw lots amongst your Ladies as to who does them. Don't let Patsy, she's not old enough to use a hot iron.

Without passing it to Claudia Teddy folded it and handed it back to James.

'How will you manage?' The question looked to a future at Brightley without Jenny. There was no: 'Perhaps she'll change her mind,' or 'Give her time to think. She'll come back,' the sort of comments James had wanted.

It was strange that for the first time in all the years he'd known her, Teddy felt a sense of sadness for his unbecoming daughter-in-law and, although he tried not to see it, of disappointment in James. Damn it, was he a man or a boy? Jenny had needed a man's passion, and what had James had to offer? Duty, an occasional ration to keep her sweet. How little we any of us know each other. Unemotional, hardworking Jenny; and inside her was a woman crying out for love. How much did she really mean to James? Less than his God, less than his duty, less than his children, less than the St Luke's Ladies probably for, in his eyes, they were part of his church, with him they served his God. And his poor workhorse of a wife . . .?

'Manage?' James looked from Teddy to Claudia, then back again. 'You think she really means it? For myself, somehow I shall find the will. But the children. How can she leave the children? I'm out so much.'

'Then James, you'll have to be out less until you can find a house-keeper. How many evenings do you have services – except for going across to say Evensong? Only Sunday unless it's something special.'

Claudia heard the authoritative tone and moved to sit on the arm of James's chair.

'It's not services. It doesn't even matter if I don't go to choir practice. But I do a lot of evening visiting, the church can't neglect people because they work during the day.'

'If your children don't come before uninvited visiting, then the sooner you hire a housekeeper the better.'

Claudia looked at him in horror. How could he speak to James like it? At any time it was unkind, but to be so brusque tonight was cruel. She rested her hand on James's shoulder and was rewarded by a look of such trust that it tore at her heart.

'Don't take any notice, Jamie, Teddy's upset, we're all upset. You both know what's happened. I don't know anything.'

Teddy answered, telling her the bare facts.

'What's happened is that Jenny has gone off with Ken Sheldrake. He told her this afternoon he was getting out – and she's gone too.'

'But how well does she know him? I mean . . .?'

'Extremely well. He's been her lover for months.'

The pill! It was falling into place.

'I thought everything was so good.' At James's words, her arm tightened around his shoulders. 'She was part of all I did here, the parish side of things seemed to absorb her. Except for The Grange. But she wasn't there, Mum. In the letter, she told me she'd been with him while I thought she was there.' His mouth was working, he had reached the point of no return – and he didn't care. These were his parents, like a child he wanted to cry and for them to comfort him. 'How could she do it. And why? What could she find with him when she had a home and family here?'

'Hush, Jamie love, hush.' Claudia rocked him against her, looking appealingly over his head towards Teddy.

'When do the children break for half term?'

'I can't remember. It must be soon. Jenny would know.'

'I have to go home tomorrow,' Teddy told him. 'Are you listening to me James?'

'Sorry Dad. How could she do it? No warning. No hint. Nothing.'

'I shall leave your mother here and at half term you drive them down to Russets. By the time we bring them back at the end of the week you'll need to have a housekeeper to look after things.'

'Everything was so good. How was I to guess . . . A housekeeper . . . can't believe . . .'

'If it makes it easier, stick to the story that she's been called away. Even let the busybodies in the parish think it until we have the children out of the way.'

'I can't live a lie.'

'James, you have been living a lie for a long time, one that has done more harm than whether or not to involve every village gossip in your marital affairs.'

The quick look Claudia threw at him was full of meaning. James needed sympathy and love, he didn't need Teddy's bracing manner that seemed to tell him to pull his socks up.

There were last-minute things to do at the rectory. The dog to put out and get back in again; the cat to put out to come back at her leisure through the cat flap; the milk bottles to be washed and put in the crate by the side door – and that was a job and a half after the delivery they'd had this morning for the village teas, milk that had been donated by the dairy thanks to Jenny's efforts.

Teddy and Claudia were the last to go up. When she put the landing light off she looked for a glimmer showing under James's door. But there was nothing to relieve the darkness. She crept silently to listen. No sound. Imagine how he must be feeling lying there alone. Please, James of all people, surely You'll help him, make him strong, make him able to cope. Tomorrow morning he'll have to face the children, he'll have to face his flock too. Teddy and I intended to be on our way home by church time. Now we'll be here. But not at church; we'll keep the children at home too. He'll manage much better without having us watching him, worrying for him. How can she do it to him? To them? Yes and to us too?

Later, lying in the spare room, speaking in a whisper, Teddy told her what Jenny had written.

'Poor Jamie. And most of all Barry and Patsy.'

'Can sex mean nothing to him? Even tonight he didn't comprehend.' Teddy was at a loss to understand, she could hear that even in words that were no more than a whisper. 'How can a couple not know? If you went to bed with another man, can you imagine me not knowing?'

She stared up into the darkness. How dared she criticize Jenny, Jenny who'd been hungry for the fulfilment of love?

'He must find a housekeeper. You'll have to see he gets on with advertising, there's no time to hang about hoping she'll have a change of heart. Christ, what a mess that damn woman has made of all our lives. If the housekeeper isn't already here by the end of half term you'll have to come back again. As if a housekeeper can give the children the affection they need. We'll have to be prepared to have them for their long summer holiday if that's what they want.'

In the darkness they lay still, looking ahead, imagining.

'They'll miss their friends,' Claudia's whisper held no expression, her voice was dangerously tight, 'they'll miss their parents, they'll resent the fact that we're too old for them.'

'What's this,' he teased, '*you* talking about losing your youth?'

'I'm serious, Teddy. Of course we're not old. I never feel older than – oh, no special age, just not old. But with them, first and foremost we're Gran and Grandad. They see us as old as time, you know they do. Damn her. How can she mess up everyone's lives like it just because she had more fun in bed with someone else. It's hideous.'

'It's selfish. But she's not the first.'

Silence, for Claudia a silence full of shame and despair. 'I'm selfish too.' If only I could tell you, cleanse myself like a believer taking Confession. I'm stupid, unseeing, greedy, unfaithful, unthinking. At that moment the carefree abandon she'd known with Adrian meant less than nothing, she saw herself as all those things.

'You? How?'

Even if I could tell you, how could I make you understand when I can't even understand myself? Jenny went to bed with Ken because she hadn't known the joy of loving with darling Jamie. But me? I was flattered, chasing rainbows . . .

'I'm selfish because I don't want our lives to be taken over. I love them all, honestly I love them, but imagine how our home will be changed. I want us to stay as we were.'

And she did. More than anything she wanted to be able to put the clock back, look at the life she'd taken for granted, look at it and appreciate it.

'I know,' Teddy was saying. 'If we have to make them see our home as theirs too for a while it's not going to easy, there'll be noise, there'll be mud tramped in the house, there'll be arguments about television programmes—'

'And we say we're not old! Doesn't caring about things like that prove we're old?'

'Darling, you're crying. Please don't cry.' Teddy gathered her gently to him.

'I ought to be crying just for them. I'm so ashamed. I'm crying for us too, it's all such a mess. What does it matter if we're jogged out of our rut? But a housekeeper can't give them a proper home. Nothing will ever be like it used to be again. Suppose she never comes back, what sort of a life for any of them then?'

'She won't come back, Claudia. How can she? If ever a marriage was built on sandy soil it was that one. But darling, James's life will go on, and the children's too. While they're with us for half term he

173

must tell the hierarchy of his parish that she's left him, let the gossip run riot and die down. It'll be a nine-day wonder.'

She dug in his pyjama pocket and found his handkerchief, mopping her face as she answered.

'To the parish it might be, but not to him and not to the children. Not to us.'

James hated lies. But for the children's sake he went along with the story of Ken Sheldrake's aunt. He came home from the eight o'clock service to hear Claudia explaining to them that their mother had telephoned late last night to say the elderly lady had been taken into hospital for an emergency operation. She was to be allowed home within the next day or so on the understanding that someone would be there to care for her. So it seemed likely Jenny would be away for quite a while.

'I shall stay here until you break up for half term and if she hasn't got home by then you two can come back with me to Russets.'

'That'll be great! We'd like that wouldn't we Patsy? Mum won't have to be worrying.'

Momentarily Patsy's face beamed with pleasure, but it soon clouded.

'What about you Dad? I mean, with Mum away, at half term we could all do our jobs like we did before. Remember?'

'I think it would be best if you went home with Gran for those days. You always have a good time there. I really am grateful, Mum, I don't know how I would have got through—'

'I'll cook for mid-day,' her voice cut across his, 'Teddy won't want to wait too late before getting home. So this morning you two can have time off from church and help me. How's that?'

'Sounds like a good plan to me,' Barry beamed, while Patsy looked at James for his approval.

It was the same when, nearing the end Claudia's second week with them they talked of the holiday at Russets.

'You'll be all by yourself, Dad.' So like her mother, Patsy's round face was full of concern.

'I shall be fine. In fact next week I am out so much that if you didn't go home with your Gran I'd have to ask her to stay on here.' Claudia set her face in what she imagined was a pleasant expression, fighting not to show her resentment that James could take her for granted so casually. Of course he could, poor darling James, hadn't he been used badly enough already without her adding to his hurt. 'There's just one more thing I'm going to ask, Mum. I can cope with

174

looking after the cat, all she needs is a plate of food and a saucer of milk. But I really haven't time to spare walking Henry. It's never been my job to exercise him. He'd be much better off going with you if you'll take him?'

'Can we Gran? Can we take Henry?'

Hearing his name the dog started to beat an eager tattoo with his tail on the floor as he sat watching them. The word 'walking' hadn't escaped him either. He seemed to know that whatever outing was under discussion, the decision rested on Claudia; he cocked his head on one side as he looked at her, waiting expectantly.

She agreed to take him, there was no other way.

'And my rabbits, too?' Barry reminded her. 'We always take them when we go to the cottage. They're really no trouble. And they're mine, I'm responsible, I can't go off and just leave them.' An unfortunate choice of words, but he wasn't to know that.

'OK Barry,' she agreed, 'rabbits too. You'll have to keep the hutch in the utility room, we've had foxes in the garden recently.'

With the plans made and James's assurance that he would be happier knowing they were at Russets, even Patsy began to look forward to their holiday. In a burst of sympathy for them Claudia told them to bring a few things to do, to put out anything they wanted her to pack for them. The pile turned into a mountain. Football, cricket set, a pile of books, fishing tackle, a water pistol, a bugle, two spaceman story videotapes which he'd bought with tokens on his birthday – all that from Barry's room alone. Sneaked in amongst the cricket things she saw Egbert, the teddy bear Jenny had given him when she was hardly any bigger than his new furry friend. Everywhere Barry went, Egbert had been sure to go, the bald patches were evidence of the loving he'd had. Now Barry was too old for a teddy bear, he knew he was, why else would he have tried to tuck him in where he wouldn't be noticed. Taking it in her hands she sat on the edge of the child's bed. Jenny, Jenny, how can you do this to them? Or to yourself? How can you be so stupid? And James, why couldn't you have come down to earth long enough to know there is more to a marriage than ironing the shirts and chatting to the old ladies in the village? Carefully, so that Barry wouldn't see it had been shifted, she hid the teddy bear back amongst the bat and wickets.

Patsy's pile of treasures took up less space but promised to be the more disruptive to the quiet running of Russets. She had set aside her tape-recorder, various tapes ranging from community hymn singing, to country music, to solo violin to pop music; Patsy's taste was comprehensive. There was a neat pile of books, none of which looked as though they'd ever been read, no doubt presents that had been

175

deemed good for her. Then, the most threatening – her violin, a recorder and a pile of music. Patsy spurned cuddly toys, there was nothing remotely childlike in the one and only doll, a well developed and glamorous young lady about nine inches tall dressed in a bikini. Her wardrobe of clothes was standing at her side, attire more suitable to a minature call-girl than a doll. As a toy, she appeared completly out of character for Patsy. Again Claudia's mind turned to Jenny. Who, looking at Jenny, would have dreamed of her frustrations and her longings. As Gwen Pomfrey so rightly says: 'You can't judge a sausage by its overcoat.'

Mentally Claudia had planned that she and James would collect the children as they came out of school at the start of the half term break on Friday, and he would drive them straight to Avonford. It would mean he'd have to make an early start back to be in time for the nine-thirty Saturday Eucharist, but that shouldn't be a problem.

'Friday, Mum? I'm afraid I can't manage that. I've a PCC meeting Friday evening. If necessary I'll drive straight back, just drop you off. But, see for yourself, that weekend is completely booked.' He passed his diary across his desk for her to see the proof of his words.

Friday: afternoon visiting St Jude parish; 7 p.m. PCC Meeting. Saturday 9.30 Eucharist; morn. visits to Alf Digby, Eva Holbrook; afternoon hospital visit; 6.30 evensong. Sunday Services 8 a.m., 10.30 a.m. and 6.30 St Jude.

'You see Mum, there's not a chance until Monday. I could slip down Monday morning as long as I'm back in time for the Diocesan Meeting at three o'clock.'

'James, I'm not staying here until Monday. That's more than a fortnight.'

'I do appreciate it, I don't know how I would have managed.'

'Never mind that. You'll just have to tell your parishioners that for once your family is being put first.' She wished she could recall her words, or at least say them differently. 'James, love, if I had my car here – or if we weren't to be like a travelling circus and could go by rail to Brockenhurst – I wouldn't ask you to cancel anything. But I want to get home and it's better for the children to be at Russets when they're not at school, they'll miss Jenny less there. Anyway, it's not much fun for Teddy, stuck down there on his own.'

'Mum this isn't like an ordinary job. These people I've got down for visiting, they are expecting me. They are sick people, they know the day and the time I call each week to give them the Sacrament.' He chewed his lip, looking at her so earnestly and yet not knowing how to make her realize the impossibility of what she was asking of him. 'It wouldn't be me – *me*, the children's father, your son – who would be failing them. I am only a go-between. I *cannot*, cannot and will not, send a message that's it's not convenient. You must see, surely you can understand.'

'Oh James, what can we do with you? Don't try and turn yourself into a saint. Haven't you learnt your lesson?'

'I'll hire a car for you. Of course you want to get back to Dad, I can understand that. And if I get any replies to my advertisement for a housekeeper, I'll arrange to see her – them? – next week while the children are away. I suppose Mum if I fix something you couldn't drive up just long enough to meet her, help me decide? You've got more idea than I have. Someone elderly, I thought. I wish I could steal your Gwen.'

'Dream on, lad. Anyway, the children need someone younger, someone who would be interested in what they do at school, someone who can put a bit of cheer into the house.'

His mouth tightened.

'I'm looking for a housekeeper, not a companion, not a surrogate mother for my children.'

Claudia turned to the door, leaving him to get on with whatever it was had brought him to his study.

'You're looking for someone who will give them time and security. If you really want me, I'll come up. Gwen will come in a few hours extra while I'm out.' Gran . . . Mum . . . What a moment to remember the freedom of golden autumn days. 'Don't do anything about booking a car right away. Maybe I'll think of something.'

She repeated some of this to Teddy when he phoned that evening. Nine o'clock was his time for ringing, knowing the children would be out of earshot. On this particular evening she had the place to herself, James was out casting his net at the village youth club discussion group.

'I was a bit snappy. I told him he shouldn't be putting every Tom, Dick and Harry before his family.'

'Quite right. But he is as he is. How's he coping?'

'On the surface absolutely normally. His feet hardly touch the ground. You can't tell me every parish priest carries on like he does, a sort of messenger from on high. It's – it's – over the top. It's not healthy.'

At her sudden outburst, Teddy laughed.

'Healthy or not, it's James. We wouldn't have him less of a person than he is.'

'Next week I expect he'll be interviewing for the job. I said I'd drive up.'

'Watch it, Claudia, we mustn't let him think we're interfering.

'It was his idea. I'd rather he wanted to make his own choice, but I don't think he's much interested, I think he sees it as incidental to the things that really matter. As for interfering, I just wish – wish – wish none of it had happened.'

'Umph. I'll give Geoffrey a ring, see if he can do a stint for me on Friday. I'll put him in the picture. He'll be glad to if he's free.'

So it was arranged. Teddy would get to Brightley by lunch time Friday. They'd load the car, collect the children from school and head straight for Russets. It was only after she'd rung off that Claudia remembered she hadn't warned him about Henry and the rabbits, nor the tapes, the videos, the violin, the recorder . . .

The rabbits might have been blissfully unaware that they'd moved residence; Gwen was anything but blissfully unaware of their presence in 'her' utility room.

'Before we know it we shall be getting vermin in the house! One thing I can't abide it's chewed up animal food. Look at the silly creatures, nibbling away there.'

'You like them really, Gwen.' Barry wasn't a bit put off by her sharp tongue. He might look like his handsome father, Gwen thought, but this one's going to go through life like a charm. Can't say he gets it from that mother of his either.

'I suppose if you're born a rabbit, then there's nought to be done but put up with it and hope you don't get put in the cooking pot before you've had your bit of fun,' she conceded grudgingly.

'You know what they really like, Gwen? Dandelions, that's their favourite. I'm going out on a dandelion hunt. At home I can find them easy as anything, we've got a sort of wild bit, it would be a paddock except that we haven't got a pony or a donkey or anything. Masses of dandelions though.'

'You won't find many of them allowed to flourish in this garden, boy. Now then, out of my way, I'm going to give this floor a going over before I start upstairs. And before you go out hunting for your dandelions, just you scarper up to your room and see it's tidy ready for cleaning. Leave your bits about and you know where they go – into the bin bag.'

Barry knew her bark was worse than her bite. He and Gwen had a good understanding of each other.

From the hall, where she'd been arranging a trug of flowers she'd just brought in, Claudia listened to them. Gwen had jumped to the

178

suggestion she should come in for five mornings a week instead of three, glad to see herself as part of the family crisis. Like the children, she'd been told no more than that Jenny had been called away to care for a sick friend.

On his way to the stairs, Barry saw Claudia in the hall, he raised his eyebrows and nodded his head in the direction of the utility room. Claudia gave him a conspiratorial wink, but there was no unkindness to Gwen, it stamped their approval on their acknowledgement that she was 'a bit of a tartar', something that would have pleased her no end.

'And tell young Patsy what I say. When I've done yours, hers is the next,' she called after him. 'Bin bag is the place for muddle.'

'Patsy's room is always tidy, Gwen.'

'Good job someone's is,' came the parting volley. The shrill ring of the telephone bell almost drowned her words. It was a sound that had the power to fill her with dread. James . . . Jenny . . . Harvey . . . Melly . . .? It was a relief to recognize it was Adrian.

'I've been away,' he told her.

'So have I.'

'But now you're back and I'm back. The sun's shining, the sap's rising—'

'Adrian. I don't want to hear. I don't want to talk about any of it. I ought not to have gone out to see that silly hut thing, there's no point. I'm not coming again, I—'

'Hey, hey, hey,' he laughed. 'Slowly, I can't keep up with you. What are you frightened of, Claudia?'

'Nothing. Of course I'm not.'

'Maybe we don't see things from the same angle. Are you saying there is no friendship between us – it's sex or nothing?'

Her face was hot, she was thankful he couldn't see her.

'What nonsense! You know Teddy and I have always looked on you only one stage removed from our own family.' She congratulated herself that he would never guess how hard her heart was thumping.

'Then may I invite myself to supper? Take you up on that open invitation.'

'We have the children here – we're a bit tied up—'

'To show we are still friends . . . please Claudia.'

She drew herself to her full height, an instinctive movement as she snatched at cool, casual indifference.

'Teddy will be delighted to know that you phoned. We'll expect you this evening at, say, a quarter to eight. We shall like to hear about what you are working on down here.'

'That's my girl!' he chuckled delightedly, knocking her hard-fought-for dignity from its perch.

'Don't—' Then she swallowed her impulsive reaction and told him 'Don't be late.'

The call over she started up the stairs, her pace slackening with each tread until, before she reached the top, she stopped. What had been her overriding feeling at hearing his voice? Humiliation? No, not quite that. Shame? Perhaps. Temptation? No! No! she silently screamed. But the thought couldn't be pushed aside with such ease. Not temptation for Adrian, but what about the freedom of being with him, the sheer pleasure of knowing he enjoyed her company, of being free and unfettered, of not being moulded into the role expected of her. If only that could have been enough . . . Hearing him talk just now it would have been easy to believe that's all they'd been to each other; perhaps it hadn't mattered to him that he had taken her to bed, that just as if some other spirit had taken possession of her she'd gloried in passion and lust. And she condemned Jenny! She'd fled from his flat only to weaken again when he took her to his 'wooden nest'; reason had rescued her again and she'd escaped. So was she less sure of herself than she professed? Was she frightened that he still had some power over her?

She sat on the stair, her mind alive with conflicting emotions.

'Whatever are you doing sitting there, Gran,' Barry's voice broke into her reverie.

'I was thinking. I've invited Adrian to supper – you remember Adrian, he was at Grandad's birthday party – now I'm wondering about food.' There spoke the voice of Gran. It seemed to satisfy Barry who stepped past her and clattered on down the stairs to report that he'd tidied his room.

Pulling her mind into order she hurried up the last few stairs and along to Patsy's room. If she expected to find the same chaos as she knew there was in Barry's, she was wrong. Books were in a tidy pile on the bedside table, violin case propped in the corner, Suzette the doll had been changed from her bikini into a sequined gown and given a place of honour on the mantelpiece.

'Gracious, you've soon got your things tidy!' Her over enthusiastic greeting was her answer to the sight of Patsy, her straight hair tied back off her fat little face, sitting in front of the dressing table carefully penning a letter. How vulnerable she looked.

'I haven't done anything to my room, Gran. Do you want me to tidy it?' So unnaturally polite. Always a solemn child, now any sparkle she might have had was gone. Claudia suspected the little girl was more receptive to atmosphere than they'd believed; her love for her father bordered on worship, it was likely she had been able to sense his unhappiness even though she couldn't understand the reason.

'No, it's fine. Gwen will be coming to vacuum and so forth later, I just wanted to make sure it was straight for her. What a tidy person you are. What are you doing?' She made herself ask it casually. Clearly what she was doing was writing a letter. If she said it was for her mother it would have to be posted to the rectory, they'd tell her her father would re-address it.

'Writing to Dad. Do you think he'll manage all the week by himself if Mum doesn't get back? When she was away before, we all did jobs. But now he's all by himself and it must be ever so miserable for him. It really does worry me, Gran. That other time, Barry did the animals – but they're here so that's all right. But I did the tidying. Now there's no-one. He'd like me to be there with him till Mum gets home. I ought to have stayed.'

'Your Dad's fine, love. And you know what the Ladies are, I bet they're all vying with each other to see who can feed him up best.'

'It's not the same though, is it. You didn't like it when Grandad was by himself.'

Patsy believed what she felt was worry for her father; Claudia knew it was homesickness for him.

'Why don't you go downstairs and phone the rectory, see if he's at home. Surprise him. He'd like that.' Except for emergencies, there was a household rule that long-distance calls should be timed for the evening when the charge rates were lower. But looking at Patsy, Claudia knew this was an emergency.

'Can I? I won't tell him I'm worrying about him. I'll say we are having a lovely time.'

Claudia was forgotten as the little girl rushed down the stairs with all the grace of a baby elephant, then into the drawing room closing the door firmly behind her.

Adrian arrived on time, Teddy greeted him with genuine pleasure. As for Claudia, on the surface she was pleasantly friendly, below the surface she was a seething tumult of conflicting emotions. It was the children who kept her feet on the ground; away from home 'Gran' was their anchor.

Chapter 12

It was late evening on the Thursday of that same week when Claudia arrived home from Brightley. Teddy had left the garage door open ready for her and, as she parked her car next to his, she noticed that Gwen's bike was still propped against the side of the house.

'How did it go?' Teddy had heard her drive in and wanted to see her genuine reaction without prying eyes and flapping ears.

'He took some persuading, but I got my way. Jean Machin is her name. About forty-five, no beauty, no man-eater – and no experience as a paid housekeeper. But plenty of experience of family life. Oh, she's Miss not Mrs. She's lived on the family farm, with elderly parents, a widowed brother and his children. He's remarrying and she sees it as the time to move on. A nice woman, solid, kind.' She kissed him abstractedly. 'Quite a day. Are the children still up?' A cowardly streak in her hoped he'd say 'No.' It had been enough of a day already.

'It's cold supper, we were waiting to have it with you. Now James has engaged a housekeeper we can't pretend to them any longer, they've got to be told Claudia. Tonight we can do it together.'

'Isn't morning better? Nothing looks as bleak in the morning.'

'Morning or evening, this will hit them hard. Neither you nor I can protect them.' Then, because it was easier to ask than to think ahead to the next few hours: 'How's James getting on?'

'Surprisingly well. A fruit cake in the tin, a homemade quiche in the fridge, fresh cut flowers in his study, flowers that didn't come from the rectory garden. Have you noticed how even the most laced up of women feel they can shower a man of the cloth with bounty and attention without running the risk of scandal. Age doesn't come into it, married or single it makes no difference. Perhaps they think that by looking after his welfare they are scoring points for themselves from on high.'

Teddy locked the garage, turning her words over in his mind.

'He must hate it. James of all men needs his privacy.'

'I got the impression their solicitude doesn't penetrate his privacy. He accepts what they do with gratitude, but I don't think he sees it as personal to *him*. In his innocence, bless his heart, he sees it as their chance to serve the church, he sees it as a sort of sign that his seeds haven't been sown on rocky soil.'

'Hello Gran,' Barry, followed by a sneezing and bouncing Henry, rushed at her through the door from the utility room. 'Did you have a super day out?'

'I'll tell you all about it later. Super? No. But it was something that had to be done. And you? Have you behaved yourselves for Gwen?'

Words, just empty words that glossed over the surface of what there was no escaping. Gwen had been there since before nine in the morning, she must have been more than ready to go home.

'I've been thinking,' she said when Claudia went through to the kitchen to collect the tray of cold supper, 'why don't you let the poor mites get a supper inside them first? Sure enough you can't duck from telling them, but it'll give them a good lining for it to settle on. Bet your life they won't want to eat after.' Yesterday Claudia had told her the real reason for the children's visit and the reason for her journey back to Brightley. Poor little souls, well she'd given them as good a time as she could today, tramped miles with them and let Henry have a real treat of a run; they'd even managed to get a good bag of dandelions for those silly rabbits they put such store in. 'I'll hang on, just to see to the dishwasher and clear up, you don't want that waiting for you after you've dealt with whatever upsets there's sure to be.'

'Bless you Gwen. It can't be put off any longer. James told one or two people in the parish at the weekend. So by now I expect the whole of Brightley knows.'

'Silly, stupid woman. Never did have any time for her myself. You know that's the truth. James would never hurt a fly, a kinder little boy there never was. And he gets used like this! You know what I'd like, Mrs C? I'd like to meet that madam face-to-face, give her a piece of my mind. There's going to be tears tonight, and no mistake.'

It was past their normal bedtime, that gave Claudia an excuse to run a deep bath for them to share. She had a theory that being immersed in warm water would be some sort of physical comfort. It wouldn't be *her* arms they'd need, nor yet Teddy's; but the enveloping warmth, the physical movement of the water, might hold off some of their isolation.

'I'll give you five minutes to scrub the remains of your afternoon hike off you, then I'm coming to check you over.' Again she hid behind her 'jolly hockeystick' voice, putting off the moment.

But when she went into the steam-filled room Teddy was already there, perched on the stool. He'd told them! She could see it in their faces.

'She's not written us any letters. Dad would have told us if she had. Not written us at all.' Barry was filling the sponge with water then squeezing it, concentrating all his attention on watching the water cascade on to his chest. 'We don't know where she is.' He frowned, putting extra effort into the next squeeze, scowling at it as if it were responsible for his mother's action.

'She will. I think everyone needs a bit of time, son.' Teddy didn't talk down to them.

'Did Dad know? When he sent us to stay with you and Gran, did he know?'

'Yes. It was the evening of the Aid Day. You remember? He thought you'd be happier down here with us during your holidays.'

'Us and Henry. You remember that don't you, Gran? Dad said he didn't mind keeping Tabitha, it was us and Henry . . .'

Claudia stepped into the breach.

'Did Grandad tell you where I've really been today?'

'Was that more fibs? Didn't you go out with your friend?'

'No Barry. I went to Brightley.'

So far Patsy had sat there, solid and unmoved, just listening. From her face it was impossible to know what was going on in her mind. When she heard where Claudia had been she seemed to spring to life.

'You've seen Dad? Why couldn't we come with you? 'Course Dad would have wanted to see us, Barry's just being silly. It's not fair trying to be cross with Dad. What did he say when you went all that way and didn't take us with you?'

'He knew I was leaving you here, Patsy. He had some ladies to interview, he wanted me to help him choose the right one to come and live at the rectory, look after you all.'

'You mean he wants somebody else, he doesn't want it to be like we sorted out before? We can manage, Gran. Don't let him choose anyone else. We shouldn't have come here,' she started to cry, 'we should have stayed at home and helped Dad. Then he would have seen that we can manage. Why couldn't he just want *us*?' She stood up ready to clamber out of the bath. 'I want to go home. Let me go home.'

Claudia caught her and enveloped her in a towel, hugging her tight.

184

'Let me go. I want Dad. Let go of me.' She really wasn't respons-ible for her actions, but her teeth in Claudia's neck hurt none the less for that.

'That's enough. Stop that noise.' Teddy hauled her off Claudia and gave her a sharp tap on her flushed and tear-wet cheek.

She caught her breath, her shudder turning into a long trembling sob, then she threw herself against him and let him hold her.

'Want Dad. Want to go home.' Gulping for air, her sobs seemed to come from the depths of her fat wet little body. A loud belch warned them. The lavatory was next to the bathroom and carrying her wrapped in her towel, crying, retching, shaking as if she had the ague, Teddy got her there just in time. So much for Gwen's 'good lining' for the news to settle on.

'Barry?' Claudia sat on the edge of the bath. 'You don't mean those things. Your Daddy wanted you both to be here because he thought just for the moment it would be difficult at home. Perhaps it's wrong of him to be out so much, but I think he's running away from being at home. You know what he is, he spends hours in the church, or visiting people who need him.'

'Patsy needs him.' Another mammoth squeeze of the sponge.

'Of course she does, you both do. And he needs you too. But because all of you are unhappy you might try and take it out on each other – like Patsy did to me just now. I know it wasn't *me* she was angry with, it was life. But all of you should try to get all the cross-ness out of your system, hit out at Grandad and me if you want to, so that when you go home together there's nothing left but gladness to be with each other.'

He pouted.

'Mum won't be there. Dad's mostly out anyway. Don't see why we have to have some other lady, we don't even know her.'

Taking a leaf out of Teddy's book she answered him seriously.

'I liked her Barry. She has lived on a farm, she's been used to looking after her brother's children after their mother died. Now he's getting married again. That's why she's looking for a housekeeper's job. I don't expect she's very happy either, but be nice to her Barry. She'll see the everyday things run smoothly – because it's when things go wrong that you would start to get cross with each other. And they would go wrong, you know. Listen – let's picture how it might so easily be. You get up one cold morning, your Dad puts on a shirt then finds the button has come off the cuff; you can't find a clean pair of socks; Patsy's shoes are muddy from yesterday and there is a knot in the lace. As if all that isn't bad enough, while Patsy's getting the breakfast table ready and you're making the toast, the phone rings.

Your Dad is still puffing and fuming about his shirt so you answer the phone – the toast burns – the postman bangs on the door because a book your Dad has sent away for is too fat to go through the letter-box, the school bus is almost due and Patsy can't find her recorder, Tabitha comes in through the cat flap wet from the rain and jumps on to the dresser, her muddy pawmarks all over your homework—'

By this time Barry had started to giggle, but it was a laugh that held no humour, a 'cry laugh'.

'Out you get.' She put out her arms to raise him up and was ready for him when, wet and miserable, he forgot to be brave and wrapped his arms and legs around her sobbing miserably.

'Was she fed up with us, Gran? She couldn't have been. Why didn't she tell us? She didn't even say goodbye . . .'

He was so much easier than Patsy. She was back a quarter of a century holding James in her arms. From along the corridor she could hear Teddy's soft voice in Patsy's bedroom.

A beautiful May dusk, full of the scent of springtime. What would she and Teddy have been doing? Probably if he'd had a short surgery they would have had an hour or two on *Sea Urchin*, or perhaps gone to Milford beach, or walked in the open forest and ended up having a long drink outside a pub while the forest ponies watched them with benign tolerance and daylight faded. That's how it used to be. But nothing could be the same again. Even when the children had gone home, their own peace of mind had been stripped from them. Happiness wasn't personal pleasure, it was heart's ease. She was tired, her shoulders were stiff from her long drive. This evening she felt old, as old as she probably was in the eyes of the children.

'Barry love, things will sort out.'

'You mean she'll come home again?' How it hurt to hear that sudden hope.

'Don't bank on that, Barry. But when the dust settles, your Mum and Dad will have to sort things out, it will all be made neat and tidy. And you'll see your Mum, you'll go and stay with her. This is the worst bit.'

'Not just us, Gran. It's Mum too. How can we know that she's got somewhere nice to live? She can't just not have a place to be? But we don't know where. Don't you know, Gran? You'd tell me if you knew wouldn't you?'

'I promise you I would. I'm sure you needn't worry that she hasn't a proper home to live in. She loves you, I think she loves your father—'

'I don't love him! If he made her want to go away, I don't want to love him any more.'

186

'It wasn't that. He was dreadfully sad about it. Sometimes people want different things from their lives.' How much could she expect him to understand?

'He just wants silly old St Luke,' he hiccoughed.

If there was an answer, she couldn't think of it.

That night was the worst, if unhappiness can be measured in tears. Next day the only change was that the children argued more than usual. Claudia suspected that they avoided talking about what had happened, yet instinctively they were on different sides, their defences up.

Two days later once more the car was packed. Half term was over. With no period of notice to work out at another post, Jean Machin had moved in the day after James had offered her the job. That had given her two days to familiarize herself with her new surroundings.

She'd never been so nervous as she was as she watched the estate car draw up at the side of the house. Mrs Carlyle, the rector's mother, had been a kindly woman, the rector himself would be no trouble at all. But what about the children? Little Tessa and Robin, her brother's twins, had been too young to resent her when she'd had to take their mother's place. Just thinking about the two of them made her ache with love. But she had no right to love them like that, they weren't hers, and now they'd learn to look on Harry's new wife, Susan, as a mother. And they would, they *must*, that was the way for them to be a happy family. But what about these? They'd probably hate her, resent her. Poor little souls. Fancy a woman with a fine husband and two dear children walking out.

She wasn't a churchgoing woman, never had time for it working a seven-day week on the farm; but she sent a silent bargain to wing on its way towards the pale teatime sky. 'Poor little souls. I'll do my best to see they're looked after – and if they could come to like me a bit too, well that would make it better for all of us. No logic in it, but it's a feeling I've got that if I can make them happy, then things will be alright for my little Tessa and Robin too.'

One of the reasons behind Erica's sudden decision to go home to the States had been that her sister Sara's divorce was going through the Court. Not that she went straight to California where the case was being heard; New England was where their roots were, where her mother, Clare Farley, still lived surrounded by various Farley aunts and uncles.

The two girls had always been close, only nineteen months separated them, a gap that had counted for nothing. The other gap, from

187

California to England, couldn't be ignored and when Mark L. Hyman made it clear that he intended to fight Sara's suit sparing no expense, Erica knew she had to be there to support her. Mark was Sara's first husband, handsome, rich, he had swept her off her inexperienced feet and lifted her from a small-town background to something that in the beginning she'd seen as glamorous and exciting. She was his fourth wife, he'd soon palled of her youth and freshness, in fact he'd soon tarnished both. But money and looks gave him an attraction that outweighed his fickle nature, already a beautiful and talented dancer was waiting in the wings, willing and stupid enough to put her head in the noose that Sara sought to escape.

The divorce should have been a rubber stamp affair, but battle had raged between Sara's advocate and Mark's over her settlement. Only son of a weathy industrialist, he had inherited a vast steel works; in his own right he had made a fortune from a chain of casinos, everything he touched turned to gold. But with this divorce Sara would become his fourth ex-wife, each more expensive than the last. That's why rather than pay without a fight he contested her divorce suit, digging into every shadowy corner in his desire to blacken her character; by the time a figure was reached and blazoned across the front pages on a day when there was no startling world news to report, even though his attempts to expose Sara as a gold-digger and an adultress had failed, her name was besmirshed. For that one day her picture was in the press and on the television, it caught passing interest and earned her much sympathy – as well as the comfortable settlement. Before long the details would be forgotten, any mention that she'd been married to Mark L. Hyman would conjure up vague memories of his accusations, the rights and wrongs of the case would be less important than that there had been a court battle, truth and lies would merge.

That's why Erica's visit that had started in her hometown in New England took her on to California, and what led to her being away longer than she'd intended.

A phone call to Brightley told them very little. James assured them that Miss Machin looked after everything very well; Patsy came to the phone and sounded her normal self; Barry answered their questions, when asked how he got on with Miss Machin he told them 'She is very kind'. His voice was quiet and flat. He sounded crushed, lost.

Claudia and Teddy worried about him in silence. Anxiety has many facets, this time it didn't drive a wedge between them as their uneasy suspicions about Jenny had. Even so, neither of them wanted to voice their pity for him. To imagine his misery and to know they were

188

powerless hurt too much to talk about, even though they found no respite from their thoughts. How could they enjoy a few weekend hours on *Sea Urchin*, or a walk through the forest to the pub that was their summertime favourite for an *al fresco* lunch? Just as they began to relax into pleasure at being where they were, the thought of him would be there. His withdrawn voice haunted them, it took the joy out of their days. In the sudden early June heatwave, even lovemaking couldn't be the spontaneous sensual frolic of other years. Instead it was no more than stolen moments, the joy of abandon quickly over.

When Adrian arrived unexpectedly, Adrian at his most charming and persuasive wanting to take Claudia to his retreat, she knew she was free of him, she was liberated. She could look him in the eye, even her shame and guilt buried too deep to touch her. She was free. Barry had something to do with her feelings, but she didn't delve.

'Yes,' she told him, 'I'll come. I'd like to see your work. You'll soon be packing up to go back to London. We plan to come up to Melly's exhibition.'

'You'll come to the shack with me?' His meaning was clear.

'What do you want me to say? No, I won't come, I couldn't trust myself? But I do trust myself, Adrian. You did me good, made me sort the dross from the gold.'

He looked at her speculatively.

'I could give you an afternoon to remember when you're ninety,' his smile was that of a mischievous boy and, in that moment, she liked him more than she ever had. 'But if you have memories enough without my adding to them, then I'll stay and help you cut the grass.'

That's what he did, not going back to his shack – or 'the place where I'm working' as later he referred to it to Teddy – until it was almost dark and they'd eaten supper.

'I shan't see you again before I go back to London,' he told them, 'but perhaps at Melly's exhibition at the end of the month.'

He shook hands with Teddy, then kissed Claudia. At that same second the phone rang and Teddy went to answer it.

'You're wrong, Claudia,' he told her. 'You won't forget me. If a flame isn't fanned it flickers and dies. You're bowed down with family, don't let it snuff out the flame.'

'It kept burning a good many years before you burnt your fingers on it.'

She prided herself the point scored was hers. They heard Teddy put the receiver back and Adrian turned to leave.

It was the next morning when Gwen got off her bike outside Russets just as the postman arrived in his van.

189

'I'll take any letters for here.' She held out her hand.

''Gainst the rules, post is supposed to be delivered right to the house.' He was new to the job and still worked to the book.

'Stuff and nonsense!' Her hand still waited. So he gave in and passed her an airmail from America. 'Is this all there is? Just the one?'

'That's the lot. Addressed to Carlyle.'

'Not so surprising, that's their name.' Stupid man! Then she forgot him and stomped up the drive. 'Morning Mrs C. I met the post fellow – bit of a dunderhead if you ask me. Just the one letter for you, from Erica. Not one of her nice long ones.'

'I expect it's just to tell us when she's planning to come home.' Claudia slit around the side of the airmail letter and opened the sheet to read. 'Oh . . .'

'Trouble, Mrs C? Don't say there's another load of trouble?'

'No Gwen, not trouble. Just disappointment – especially for Harvey.' She told Gwen the bare facts, told them in a cheerful voice that didn't hint at the unexplained foreboding she felt.

During her marriage Sara had lived in California, her world had been removed both physically and socially from their New England background. By the time the divorce case closed and a settlement was agreed she found herself wealthy, free and friendless. She couldn't return to the bosom of her family any more than she could remain amongst the people belonging to that part of her life she wanted to forget.

'Come back to England with me,' Erica persuaded, 'stay with us. Harvey would be glad.' And that was true, she added silently, he'd be glad; with Sara there he wouldn't have to worry that I don't fit in with his friends and his interests, He'd be free to work. Work? If she thought he looked on it as work, she could accept. But it wasn't work, it was like a drug to him.

'Sure, I'll come to England with you – if you'll do some travelling with me first. I've earned every dime I've been allowed, now I'm going to spend some of it. Come on Erica, we'll do every capital of Europe. Let's go globe-trotting! We can afford it, I've got lots and lots of money. Phone Harvey and tell him I really do need you, make sure he can live without you for – how much longer? Three months? We'll go to Rome, Venice, we'll go to Egypt and get our photos taken in front of the pyramids, we'll go to India and see the Taj Mahal—'

'Hey, hang on, you said Europe.'

'What the heck. The world will be our oyster. Just for three months. Do you realize we lived in a little hick town, saw nothing,

190

knew nothing. Honestly, I was way out of my depth when Mark swept me off my feet. I guess he liked that, it made me some sort of a novelty. But not for long. And you, where had you ever been till you met Harvey and he fell for you? Nowhere. We didn't know any more about the big, big world than all our aunts and uncles, God bless them. We'll take three months with money to spend, free to do as we please, go where we please. There's nothing like travel to give a girl confidence. If you won't come . . .' she shrugged, 'don't know what. I want to get right away, forget all the – the shame – disgrace—' Then, talking through a giggle that couldn't be repressed, 'Just enjoy the money! Please Erica, please.'

That 'Please Erica, please' had never failed. And it didn't fail now. Erica phoned Harvey but after two attempts and no answer decided it would be better to write. Next she wrote that airmail letter to Claudia. She and Sara would be on the move, they'd have no fixed address. It was as if she was cutting herself off from her past and her future. She was doing it for Sara – and yet they were alike enough that she couldn't suppress a bubble of excitement. 'Do something of your own,' had been Melly's advice. Well, this beat all the pottery classes!

To a background of the monotonous hum of the engines Erica let herself imagine that she was on her way to Manchester instead of Cairo, that as she came through the familiar customs barrier she would see Harvey waiting for her. How easy it was to put the expression she longed for on his face.

'Don't go to sleep,' Sara's elbow dug her in the ribs, 'don't waste any of it sleeping. I wonder where that is we're flying over. Can you see out? Next time it can be your turn to have the window seat.'

Erica watched her affectionately. Nothing ever changed Sara, when she was eighty she'd still be a child at heart. Marriage hadn't touched her. That was sad. To fall in love, to marry, to be full of hope, at least in the beginning to be happy, then all the hurts, knowing your husband was unfaithful, tired of you – what if it were Harvey? I couldn't bear it, I don't think I could live if he stopped wanting me. Oh, I know sometimes I get miserable and jealous, but jealous of his piano not of another woman. But nothing's left any mark on Sara, not the happiness, not the misery, not the sordidness of the alimony case. I could understand it if she were bitter, if she were warped with hate, but she is just as if none of it had ever happened except that she's rich.

'Isn't this fun!' Sara gave a shudder of excitement just like she used to when she was tiny and something good happened. 'Remember how we used to be so sure that when we grew up we would get a sort of automatic freedom. This is it, Erica.'

'Grew up?' Erica teased, 'Who told you you'd grown up?'

Sara pouted. 'Oh yes I have, and that's why I appreciate all this. I thought marriage was about being grown up and free. But I was wrong.' Again that giggle. 'More like a job with a thumping good pension at the end of it. I've learnt my lesson, from now on it'll be just me, Sara Farley.' Her maiden name, spoken with a ring of pride. Already, before they'd even crossed the Atlantic she was finding some of the confidence she'd lacked.

Every few days a postcard arrived at Russets, brief and to the point it would say 'Here for two days, saw pyramids yesterday, leaving for Budapest this evening,' 'What would we do without crease-proof clothes? Budapest is beautiful, next stop Prague,' 'Enjoying introducing Sara to Prague,' 'Gibraltar, an outpost of your empire! It's like being in England, seeing "Bobbys" again.' 'Vienna city of my dreams, and I can see why,' 'Rome. Crowds. We saw the Pope. I felt cheap, making it a side show. I envied the nun next to me and wished we'd gone someplace else.' In the beginning there had been nothing but delight, gradually the tone was changing. 'We're too late for Paris in April, but it's great in June too. Tomorrow on to Amsterdam. We seem so near home. I miss having letters. My love to you all,' 'I'm not cut out to be a hobo. Have phoned Harvey four times but he's never there.' Cards that told them nothing and yet told them everything. Erica had been away too long.

Barry made his decision. It was partly because of Patsy that he felt so badly; if she'd not appeared so satisfied with the new arrangements, if she'd been as miserable as he was, then it might have been possible to wait longer, always hoping for the letter that never came. But his mind was made up.

By the second Saturday in June he decided he could wait no longer, it was time to put his plan into action.

'Can I take sandwiches and go out on my bike, Dad? I'll be back about teatime, but just a morning ride doesn't give me time to get any real practice.'

'We can't let a child of his age go off alone!' Jean Machin came into the room just in time to hear what he asked. 'Such dreadful things one reads.'

Barry hated her. No-one was going to stop him, he'd got his plan laid. He had chosen his moment to ask permission when he could tell from his father's face he was thinking of something else, he had expected a grunt of approval. And then, just at that very second, in had bustled Miss Machin with the dish of breakfast and interfered as if she had the right. He hated her. It was *her* fault he had to lie.

'I won't be on my own Miss Machin, you needn't worry,' he spoke solemnly, there was never any insolence in Barry's manner. 'There are four of us. I said I'd meet the others at the end of Brightley Lane at half past nine.' His mind worked fast, he knew half past nine was the time for the Saturday morning Eucharist service. 'Really you don't need to be worried, Mum always let me go out for rides with the others.'

'Well, if your father agrees and you promise to be back by teatime. And you ought to tell us where you mean to go. Isn't that so, Rector?'

'Yes. Yes, Barry, you must do as Miss Machin says. It's going to be a nice day, but even so you see you're back here by whatever time she tells you.'

'Half past four,' Jean Machin gave her word. 'And mind you're careful Barry, take money for the telephone in case you run into trouble, a puncture or anything.'

'Yes, I'll do that. And if I could have a few sandwiches, Miss Machin? I can make them if you won't have time.' He took sadistic pleasure in making himself over-polite to the woman who was in his mother's place.

Patsy was attacking a breakfast of sausage, tomato and scrambled egg, munching just the same as she always had. Barry glared across the table at her, in his misery he wanted to hate her too. He'd heard her chattering to Miss Machin, sounding just the same as she used to when she'd been talking to Mum. He knew why she did it, she did it because it made the house sound a cheerful place and that would please Dad. Just like the St Luke's Lot, as he thought of the Ladies, they fawn round Patsy trying to please Dad by being nice to her. They'd do it to me too if I'd let them, but I won't. Not likely. The silly kid laps it up; I expect she does that to please Dad too. All anyone cares about is pleasing Dad, being sorry for Dad. No-one ever says they wonder about Mum, no-one cares about her. Well, I do. I'll show them!

Just after nine o'clock, while Miss Machin was parcelling him up a man-sized lunch, he went up to his room. From his window he watched his father going across the lawn towards the gate into the churchyard. He had to bite the corners of his mouth hard to stop it twitching. It wasn't that he wanted to cry, how could he cry today of all days, Action Day? The butterflies in his tummy were excitement – but it was terribly hard watching Dad and not being able to tell him.

193

Once James had gone from view the action started. In a cocoa tin on his wardrobe shelf Barry kept his much counted hoard of wealth, he'd not spent a single penny since his birthday the week after he came home from Avonford. And he'd never had so many presents as this year – they must have been trying to be kind to him to cheer Dad up. The churchwarden and his jolly wife had given him a book token for five pounds, but Dad had been surprisingly understanding about it when he'd explained that he was saving for a two-man tent and had bought it off him. Apart from that he'd had a ten-pound note from Harvey and Erica (although Erica hadn't really had anything to do with it as she was goodness knows where, seeing the world), and he hadn't spent any of his weekly seventy-five pence pocket money since he came back from Russets and the plan had started to take shape. Altogether he had £20.13p which he zipped carefully into his inside pocket. He couldn't take much in his saddlebag, a pair of clean socks, his toothbrush and his nearly new pullover (folded carefully) that Gran had bought him in Lymington during half term. Egbert was lying disconsolately on the floor where he'd fallen out of bed and, after a moment's hesitation, Barry added him to the pile. He'd have to be careful no-one saw the bulging saddlebag or it would alert suspicion. As it was he hid his bundle under his anorak as he went down the stairs and out to the shed. Once the bag was packed he made a show of feeding Twitch and Frisk. Today he'd give them extra and hope they didn't scoff it in one go.

The church bell began to toll, a reminder to the four or five regular Saturday morning communicants. Only on Sundays was there a full peal, Mondays to Fridays the ringers were mostly at work and Saturday was their day off. So only old Mr Cripps called the faithful with one mournful bell. It was the last thing Barry heard as he cycled away from the village down Brightley Lane. At the main road he just kept pedalling, his imaginary companions, invented to satisfy Miss Machin, forgotten.

In the car it never seemed very far to Oxford. On a bike it was a long slog. By the time he reached the railway station already the morning was almost gone. He had to wait nearly an hour before the slow train pulled up at the platform and he pushed his bike to the luggage van. It was the first time he'd ever travelled alone, the first time he'd ever taken his bike on a train too, but he was determined not to let it show. He gave every appearance of being interested in nothing beyond the pile of sandwiches he was ploughing through as they careered through the Oxfordshire countryside. When the train jolted to a standstill at each station he checked he was still on the right track. Then he saw it: Goring and Streatley. His heart was pounding. Perhaps only minutes now before it happened. He was frightened to let himself look at the pictures thrown at him by his imagination. To hold back excitement that was almost too fearful to bear, he kept telling himself he couldn't be certain. There might be a snag. Supposing he couldn't find her . . .? Supposing they were out . . .? Supposing no-one could tell him where the house was . . .? He'd written down the address from the telephone directory, but the house might be a long way out of the village. He'd ask at the post office or the paper shop, someone would know where Kenneth Sheldrake lived.

'Wakeley Cottage? You won't find anyone there. Kenneth Sheldrake, that's who you'll be after. We don't deliver to him any more. His cottage is on the market for sale, so I'm told.'

Barry's mouth felt dry, he swallowed.

'Do you know where they went?'

'They? There was no "they", Ken Sheldrake lived by himself. I bet it's his autograph you're after. You watch his Inspector Durrant, is that it?'

'Yes. Yes that's right. I was told he lived here, I thought he lived with his mother.'

'Never to my knowledge. She used to live nearby, till she died two years or more back. Her old house is a retirement home these days, big house it is. Not like Wakeley Cottage. Be hard pushed to get more than one living in there.'

Died more than two years ago! But Mum had told them . . . Barry shied away from following that train of thought.

It was already well after two o'clock. What could he do? If he went home that would be the end of everything. Nobody cared that he was miserable, they didn't even notice. In his most polite and adult voice he thanked the newsagent for his help and went outside to collect his bicycle.

He'd burnt his boats. Just like Mum had, he'd burnt his boats. Until now he'd felt it was asking for bad luck to consider his Contingency Plan, but it had been there at the back of his mind. Cycling back to the station, his confidence began to revive. There may be trouble waiting for him, but what he was going to do now would show Dad and that Miss Machin – and Patsy too – that even if they could carry on as if it didn't matter that Mum had gone away, he couldn't. And he wasn't going to try!

Chapter 13

While Barry had been pedalling towards Oxford on that Saturday morning, the removal van had already been on the M3 Motorway heading south and loaded with two pianos. The piano tuner was due at Croughton Hall, a sixteenth-century manor near Avonford, at eleven o'clock. This evening was to be an important one in Avonford's calendar. Local papers for miles around had carried details of it.

> After much local support, negotiations have been completed for the purchase of an acre of land on the outskirts of Avonford village, the site for a proposed hospice. For two years sponsored events fêtes, dances and donations have helped to make this possible.
>
> Now that planning permission has been obtained and the land purchased efforts will be redoubled in the hope that building will commence early next year.
>
> The next major event will be at beautiful Croughton Hall by kind permission of Sir Francis and Lady Arlington. After a sherry reception, there will follow an evening of music for two pianos in the Grand Hall where the artistes will be Harvey Carlisle and Lucinda Leighton. Harvey Carlyle, a pianist of international repute, will need no introduction and, indeed this is not the first time he has given his support to the cause. With him on the evening of Saturday 20th June will be Lucinda Leighton, recently come to this country from her native America since when she has shared the concert platform with Harvey Carlyle on various occasions.
>
> 'An Evening for Two Keyboards' promises to be an event not to be missed. Limited tickets are available at a price of £15 each.
> For details see Forthcoming Events.

Harvey brought Lucinda down to Russets on the Saturday morning, they passed the removal van bearing their instruments when they were not far out of London. He imagined the welcome awaiting them: his father would have made sure this wasn't his Saturday for morning surgery; his mother would glance up hopefully at the sound of every car; and he would stake his last penny that Gwen had persuaded them they needed her today! Yes, he was looking forward to the moment of arrival. But there was something else. He enjoyed enormously showing Lucinda his country, she was a very satisfactory companion. There was nothing of the glamour girl about her, her straight hair was cut in a fringe and hung either just above or just below her shoulders depending on when the last cut had been – the emphasis being on 'cut', not 'style' – her freckled face was devoid of cosmetics, her clothes just something to cover her body. Neither fat nor slim, more at home in jeans and all enveloping shirts than in the evening dresses she had to wear when she played, she had no claim to beauty. Yet when she smiled, as she so often did, she seemed to radiate an inner warmth. Harvey had become very fond of her over the last few months, they had so many interests in common, and for pure fun there was nothing to compare with the hours they'd spent improvising on two keyboards, making musical conversations, laughing together. He looked forward to introducing her to his parents, letting her feel herself to be part of an English home.

They'd left London early for two reasons: one so that he could leave the motorway and take the Stockbridge route, making time for coffee and a walk along the wide straight street, one of his favourite places, before going on for another stop in Romsey where he meant to take her into the cool peace of the old Abbey; the second simply that even allowing time to enjoy the journey, he was keen to arrive.

In fact they drove in soon after midday. Unable to contain her patience any longer Claudia had found herself a job in the front garden, dead-heading the first flush of roses. It was a perfect summer day, as if even the elements were in her favour. Just below the surface of her consciousness were a thousand worries, none of them of her own making and none of them in her control. But today she was determined to push them to the back of her mind and concentrate of enjoying having Harvey home. She was ready to revel in the praise and glory that would be showered on him this evening. Then there was Teddy, as the senior doctor from whom the original proposal for the hospice had come, it fell to him to speak to the assembly during the interval. Today Claudia was entitled to be proud. Anxieties for Melly who was pushing herself relentlessly towards her exhibition, anxieties for James and the children, yes and even for Jenny from whom she'd heard nothing, anxieties for Erica who had been away too long, all these were being put 'on hold'.

All the morning she'd looked out at the sound of each approaching car (just as Harvey had known she would), yet when the moment came she was so lost in imagining how splendid the evening was going to be that the car was through the open gateway before she heard it coming.

'How's my Mum?' And she was taken in his bear like hug, Harvey's greeting never varied. Then, without waiting to hear how she was, he went to open the car door for Lucinda. 'Come and meet my Mum, Lucinda.'

'Gladly I will. He's always talking about you, Mrs Carlyle, about everything here at his home. I'm glad to be here.'

'It's lovely to have you. And very good of you to give your weekend to helping our fund-raising efforts. Every single ticket is sold for tonight and at £15 a head that's going to mean real money for the cause.'

'From our point of view I promise you it's no hardship. We love playing together. Isn't that true, Harvey?'

'Absolutely.' Then looking seriously at Claudia, 'Absolutely true, Mum, playing together is a totally new experience. Later on, when the time is right to talk, I'll elaborate. Right now though we'd better get tonight's glad rags upstairs. Which room is Luce having?'

'The front spare.'

'Where's Dad? Why hasn't he come out to say how-do? Not working, surely?'

'He shouldn't be. But you know what he is. Mrs Parsons phoned him, here at home. You remember old Mr and Mrs Parsons, he used to be the cobbler.'

'Nice old boy. When I was a kid, Lucinda, he used to be the shoe mender, worked in a sort of lean-to on the side of his bungalow. He must be as old as the hills.'

'He's certainly not young,' Claudia agreed. 'The Parsons were some of Teddy's first patients here.' Her smile included Lucinda as she explained, 'These days there's a Medical Centre. Don't get me wrong, it's a good system, a doctor always on call. But the older patients, well some of them wouldn't dream of seeing anyone but Teddy. In a village like Avonford he got a lot of satisfaction out of looking after everyone's health.'

'You mean they phone him up here, at his own home? And doesn't he mind?'

'Until a few years ago everyone phoned here for him, until the four practitioners joined forces and the Centre for the whole area was opened. There was a sort of family feeling about village doctoring. No, of course he doesn't mind. Old dears like the Parsons have been his preserve for too long to mind. Come on, let's go in. Gwen's come in specially because you're coming home, Harvey.'

A hold-all in each hand and his dinner suit zipped into a cover and slung on his arm, he leaped ahead of the others, making for the back door and Gwen. Claudia waited while Lucinda collected her own evening dress from the back of the car. They looked at each other in tolerant amusement as they heard the high-pitched squeals of Gwen's delight.

'He's told me about your Gwen, too,' Lucinda smiled. 'I always feel Harvey is a home bird at heart. Am I right?'

'He's pleased to come home, but how long he'd stay pleased I don't know. He's been on the concert treadmill a long time. He and Erica spend most of their lives on the move.' Purposely she spoke about Erica. There was something in the easy intimacy between Harvey and Lucinda that made her wary. And she remembered his words: 'Later on I'll elaborate.'

'I've met Erica just once,' Lucinda was saying. 'She isn't musical is she, she told me so herself. She seemed proud to say it.'

Claudia was on the defensive, yet she hardly knew why. After all, what Lucinda said was nothing more than the truth.

'It's good for him to leave it all behind sometimes. His happiness with Erica is something apart. And they *are* happy – very.' She was interfering, if Harvey, Erica and Lucinda were three sides of a triangle then it wasn't up to *her* to straighten it out. But they weren't, they mustn't be. That way couldn't lead to happiness for any of them.

'I think it's a shame though. There'll always be part of him Erica can't reach.'

'Oh, nonsense,' Claudia laughed, 'you'll be telling me next that there's part of Teddy I can't reach because I don't know anything about medicine.'

'No, I wouldn't say that. That's quite different. I'm sure Dr Carlyle loves his work, and I'm sure he's a good doctor, but when he relaxes he doesn't want to discuss anatomy. That's the difference. Harvey's music is his pleasure as well as his work.'

'Then he's a lucky man. And I still think it's good for him to escape from it sometimes, to escape to Erica where it can't intrude.'

'Hey, just hark at us, won't you! We sound like a pair of agony aunts. Harvey and Erica are fine, you don't need to tell me. And he's missing her like crazy. I only brought this one gown with me, I hope it'll do. What do you think?'

The pink chiffon dress with its layered skirt looked entirely out of character for the plain but smiling girl. Perhaps it would transform her; by this evening she might look as attractive as Claudia was sure she was well meaning.

'It'll do splendidly, it's very pretty. Let's go in, Harvey will take you to show you where to hang it.'

She was determined not to listen to the niggling voice that attempted to pull one of her worries out of its 'on hold' position: Erica and Harvey, on the surface completely incompatible and yet, sometimes, clearly so happy with each other. 'At least we never have to worry about Erica and Harvey,' more than once she and Teddy had said it. She tried to push from her mind the sight of Erica's tears.

But it didn't matter how much you cared, there was nothing anyone could do. In her imagination she saw what this Saturday morning must be like for James and the children; even Jenny, there could be no heart's ease for Jenny no matter what other wonders she'd discovered with Ken Sheldrake. She told herself she did no-one any good by worrying, yet how could she not worry? James knew she gave love, and so must Barry and Patsy know it, they must be pleased when the post brought the occasional unexpected little presents that caught her eye for them; but the sleepless nights, the empty helplessness, they were her own secret. She was sure it was the same for Teddy, yet to talk would be an admission of the misery and sense of uselessness.

Ushering Lucinda indoors she squared her shoulders and put a rein on her imaginings. Today nothing was going to cast a shadow. Worries would still be there tomorrow – well, let them wait until then. Today she was Teddy's wife – Dr Carlyle, who had been the instigator of all the plans for the hospice; and she was Harvey's mother – Harvey Carlyle the celebrated pianist whose presence was bringing people to Croughton Hall from a distance of twenty miles or more.

The evening was everything she had expected or, more accurately, it was more than she'd expected, for she hadn't foreseen the accord between the two pianists. She felt that they weren't so much sharing their music with the audience as with each other. Surely everyone listening must have been aware of the way Lucinda looked at him, waiting for the sign for the first note; surely they must have seen the sudden warmth in her smile as she turned to him at the last chord; and no-one could have missed how he held his hand to draw her forward to acknowledge the applause. Probably the only person not to be conscious of it was Harvey himself, the action was spontaneous and natural.

Claudia was aware of Teddy's reaction. He applauded as heartily as everyone else but his mind was moving the same way as hers. If only Erica would come home.

With the ending of the concert, for them the evening wasn't over. Sir Francis and his wife had invited them for an informal dinner. It was quite two hours past Claudia and Teddy's usual meal time, so what better than pleasant company, good food and the gracious surroundings of the small family dining room to put the finishing touch to what – with that one exception that by the time they took their places around the oval table, Claudia could almost believe she'd imagined – had been an evening to treasure in memory.

This was almost the longest day of the year, but heavy cloud had rolled in during the evening, only a storm would clear the heavy air. When there was a lull in the conversation they could hear distant thunder, and by the time they set out to drive home the wind had whipped up and the first splashes of rain were falling. Teddy knew every bend in the road, but ponies, and even cattle belonging to foresters with grazing rights, were no respecters of traffic, especially when they were upset by the noise of the fast approaching storm. One pony stood in the middle of the road seemingly hypnotized by the headlights until a vivid flash of lightning terrified her into action. Rearing on to her hind legs her neigh had an unearthly sound, followed by a crash of thunder that sent her to charge across the heath like a devil out of hell. Half a mile on, a cow, less disturbed by the storm and torrential downpour, decided not to give them passage and Harvey, with an old mac over his head and an umbrella for prodding, persuaded her back to the verge. Then the rumble of the tyres on the cattle grid, they were out of the forest and almost home.

'It's been a lovely evening, even the storm can't spoil it.' Claudia wriggled down in her seat, stretching her legs out in front of her. Had she had the talents of a cat she would have purred.

'I'm grateful,' Teddy turned his head just for a second towards the two on the back seat. 'Sir Francis made a gift of the sherry and you two, well you gave us all a wonderful evening. There were 150 tickets sold.'

'All profit, Teddy? That's . . .' a pause while Claudia worked it out, 'that's £2,250. In one evening! A coffee morning makes about £150 – if we're lucky! No wonder he's grateful.'

'We enjoyed every moment, didn't we Harvey? When we play like that I always look on it as pleasure playing. We've practised together a lot, sometimes four hands on one keyboard. It's a really fun thing to do.'

'That's right,' Harvey agreed. 'It's what I meant this morning, Mum. The piano is my instrument, I've never had any regrets, and

201

playing with an orchestra is a tremendous thrill but, of necessity, it's orderly, correct to the last note. What Luce and I do – I don't mean on an occasion like this evening, we behaved ourselves very well this evening – but when we have spare time and it's for pure pleasure, well we just – just – well, that's it, it's pure pleasure.'

Again that feeling of panic. Be careful, Harvey, don't tempt trouble. That's what it would be, trouble for you, trouble for Erica, trouble for Lucinda. She glanced in the driving mirror and saw the tight set of Teddy's mouth. Trouble for us too. Not again, please not again.

'I'll open the garage door, Dad.' Harvey opened the back door as the car was brought to a standstill. Of the three of them he was the only one unaware of any undercurrent. And what about Lucinda? Surely she didn't look at Harvey as she had this evening for nothing?

Then the problem was swept aside as Claudia saw a movement near the front door of the house.

'Harvey! Don't get out. Wait. See, there's someone over there in the shadows.'

The figure was moving towards them, no more than a shadowy shape in the fog.

Barry had started his day with such hope, he'd not been able to stop himself believing that by bedtime he would have been with his mother. He'd always expected she must have gone to Streatley. Now he didn't know where she was. Most of his birthday money had been spent on his train tickets and without money it was no use trying to think up another plan.

'Have you got far to go, son?' The ticket collector at Brockenhurst saw Barry push his lampless bike out to the road. 'Talk about coming up to the longest day, you'll not get far without a light on that bike this evening. This storm's going to be a real cracker when it does roll in on us. It's been around an hour or more. Good job when the rain comes, the air'll start to clear then.' With the exception of Barry the few passengers who'd got off the train had been driven away.

'Not far. I had my light pinched,' he lied, surprised at how easy it was to sound convincing. 'But it's all right they're driving out to meet me, we'll fix my bike to the roof rack to get home.'

'That's the way. No night to be cycling. Hear it? It's getting closer if you ask me.'

Barry wished the ticket collector goodnight and set off in the direction of Avonford. Once out of Brockenhurst and into the forest roads the storm was threatening. Once or twice he saw flashes of fork lightning, the thunder didn't rumble so much as crack. He pedalled hard.

Ponies, upset by the atmosphere thudded across the sun hardened ground, going nowhere in particular. He didn't really mind storms, yet tonight he was frightened, there was something eerie, the animals' fear transmitted itself to him. He was hungry and, try as he would to put the image out of his mind, he couldn't stop thinking about what must be happening at home. He ought to have been back hours ago. Would Dad have gone to the police? Perhaps they'd guess this was where he'd be, any minute a policeman might step out in front of him . . .

Only one thing helped to keep his courage up and that was the thought that soon he'd be at Russets. Even if Grandad had been called out somewhere, Gran was always at home. She'd talk to his father, she'd make things right. Perhaps she'd let him stay until they could trace his mother. Yes, he decided, that's what he would ask her; she would explain to Dad, make it so that no-one was hurt by what he'd done. He couldn't bear to go back to the rectory, he'd have to explain, actually say aloud, why he had left. It wasn't Miss Machin's fault, she'd tried hard to be kind. But he couldn't bear it, he just couldn't bear it. The thick dark clouds had robbed the summer day of the last of its light, he could hear the pounding rain dancing all around him as he crossed the open forest; then through the trees, but this was even more scaring, the branches moaned and swayed and he recalled dreadful tales he'd heard of what happened to people who sheltered under trees in a thunder storm. Then into a clearing and, his eyes accustomed to the glooming, he was able to read the sign: 'Avonford 1 mile'. Buoyed up with hope he pedalled on.

There were no lights on in the house. Perhaps they were in the drawing room at the back, but usually the hall was lit. There was a car in the drive, parked right to one side so that the way to the garage was clear. A visitor? For one frightening moment he imagined his father must have guessed what he'd done and come to take him home. In the light of a passing car he recognized with a surge of relief that the one parked was Harvey's.

He rang the door bell. No answering movement, no sudden beam of light. Every minute or two he rang again. He knew it was silly, but he couldn't stop himself. The sound of the bell was comforting. His surroundings were illuminated by brilliant lightning and in the same second thunder so loud he buried his face in the crook of his arm against the front door. He waited, counted to a hundred . . . the rain didn't seem quite so heavy . . . but took all his courage to come out of the shelter of the porch and grope around to the side of the house where he'd propped his bike. He'd get his saddle bag. The feeling of it

203

was comforting and familiar, if he slipped his hand in at the side he could feel Egbert. Back to the porch and another buzz on the bell. It must be dreadfully late, he felt he'd been here hours and hours. The only place to sit was on the doormat, so that's what he did, leaning back against the front door. His tummy rumbled, a loud reminder of his emptiness.

His hand stole through to touch Egbert again. Mum, I can't think where you are. If I just knew, even if I promised I wouldn't come and find you, if I just knew where you were. I think about you, nearly all the time I'm thinking about you. Don't you think about us? And if you do, can't you see – oh, Mum, where are you? He wiped the tears away with the palms of his hands, but what was the good of that when he couldn't stop them coming?

Time lost all meaning, he was shaking with cold, wet and misery. In the beginning if he heard a car he would listen hopefully, but as he got more and more miserable he lost all hope. He'd thought that after that noisy clap of thunder the storm had been moving away, but suddenly the wind picked up again. More lightning, more crashing thunder.

His imagination ran riot: Harvey must have left his car here, probably all of them had gone to Moorleigh to the cottage. Or perhaps they'd already gone to London to stay with Aunt Melly for the exhibition. What would he do if no-one came back. He hadn't enough money to get home. Anyway he couldn't go back there, not without Mum . . .

Then between him and the gate the raindrops became a million shining jewels in the beam of headlights as the car turned into the drive. They were home. He blundered out from the porch . . .

No words had ever sounded so wonderful as his grandfather's: 'Good God! Barry! Where's your father? I don't see his car.' In a flood of relief he stumbled towards the familiar voice. 'It's all right old chap, we're home now.'

He ought not to be crying, he ought to be able to stop shaking.

'I went to find Mum,' he sobbed. 'But she wasn't there. So I came here.'

'Of course you did. Let's get you into the warm.'

Barry let himself be led, he was like a wind-up toy whose spring had broken.

'First things first,' Claudia had forgotten that this was to have been her worry-free day, 'a hot bath Barry, you can manage without food just while you get warm.'

'Gran, is it all right Gran? You're not cross?'

'Of course we aren't cross, darling. Let's go and run a bath, you can tell me all about it while you warm up. And I must take off my good dress before it gets splashed.'

He took her hand, his grip was like a vice.

'What's Dad going to say? Couldn't even say goodbye,' he gulped, 'he'd have told me I couldn't—' another gulp, 'couldn't look for Mum. Where's she gone, Gran? Perhaps she's – she's—' Only in his mind the word 'dead' shrieked at him. He couldn't say it, to say it would be like making it come true.

'Upstairs, love. We'll talk once you're in the warm water.'

And they did, while she sat on the stool wrapped in a dressing gown over her underwear. Not the end to the evening she'd envisaged, but none of that mattered to her as she listened to his outpourings. It hurt to see him so desperately unhappy, yet she felt a surge of thankfulness that he'd come to them.

At first his words were no more than blubbering and disjointed pieces of his day for her to knit together. Then gradually as he grew quieter he confessed how he knew he was wicked to hate Miss Machin, she tried so hard to be kind. But he couldn't help it. He hated her being kind, he hated to see her there where it ought to have been Mum. Patsy didn't seem to mind, she wouldn't care about anything just as long as she pleased Dad, that's all any of the St Luke's Lot cared about too. Everybody was worrying about Dad, no-one worried a bit about Mum. Only him. Barry glared at his toes, frightened to hear her answer and yet wanting it to hurt him. It was easier to feel that people were angry with him than that they made allowances.

Claudia listened, trying to see things through his eyes, or at any rate feel them through his heart.

'We do worry about her, Barry. I know your father does. More than anything he wants her to come home.'

'Home? You think she might come home, Gran?' How easy it was to plant a seed of hope.

'I don't know, Barry. It's no good dreaming dreams. If she'd been happy she wouldn't have been tempted away by Ken Sheldrake.'

'She seemed to really like us.'

He fought down a trembling sob as he fixed his concentration on the waterfall from the sponge. She was reminded of that other night when the children had been told Jenny had gone. Had James been right in not telling them that through his solicitor he had been given an address to contact Jenny? He'd told nobody where she was. He'd said that it was up to her, if she wanted to write to them then she knew where they were. Had he been frightened that Barry would do the very thing he'd done today, go to find her?

'She loves you Barry. She loves Patsy. I honestly believe she loves your father too. But – oh, we've got to be grown up about it, it's no use pretending: she doesn't love the life she's expected to lead, a sort of unpaid back-up to your father, an example of good Christian living.'

'You mean Mum isn't good? That's a beastly mean thing to say. Mum's jolly good.'

'The sort of rector's wife the parish expects hasn't got much to do with being truly good, it's a sort of social worker's role, listening first to one, then to another, saying the tactful thing, keeping everyone happy so that they think coming to church turns them into a merry bunch of pilgrims.' She'd been speaking her thoughts aloud, only when she saw Barry's puzzled expression did she realize he would hear her words as a betrayal of James.

'But doesn't it, Gran? All Dad's Lot, they jolly about the place, they really are ever so happy.' The warm water had healing power, already his voice was getting strong and normal. 'D'you know, Gran, the other day I heard Dad ask Mrs Chedzey if she'd mind washing all the choir surplices. I knew just what she was thinking, she was blaming Mum for going away and not doing them. I expect she could feel me hating her, I hoped she could. Mum always did all the washing you see. Dad's Lot knew that. But Mrs Chedzey was pleased as anything – glad Mum had gone most likely so she could have a chance to do something for him. Merry bunch of pilgrims,' he repeated Claudia's phrase, swirling the water round him as he spoke, 'that's what they are. And they're merrier than ever now Mum isn't there. I hate them.'

'Your Dad will have been very worried, Barry.'

'Don't let's talk about it Gran. I'm terrifically hungry. Is there anything I can eat?'

'I shouldn't wonder. I'll go down and heat something up for you, soup or something, while you get dried.'

As she came out of the bathroom she heard the ting of the telephone receiver being replaced. James would have been told that Barry was safe.

'Gran! Gran! I brought my toothbrush, but I forgot to put in my pyjamas.'

'You'll have to swim about in a pair of mine tonight. I'll see what I can find.'

'Not with flowers on or sissy things like that, Gran.'

Barry was recovering. Claudia felt like Cinderella at five past midnight, her lovely evening was over, she was Gran again. A glance in her dressing table mirror as she found a pair of plain white silk pyjamas showed her a face that had parted company with youth. This morning she'd liked to think the lines came from laughter; tonight she knew they didn't. There was no smile creasing her face as she surveyed the woman in the looking glass, a woman whose lines around her eyes had all the permanency of the furrows of a ploughed field.

'You spoke to poor Jamie?' It was a statement as much as a question as she joined the others and waited for Barry to come down.

'I'll tell you about it later. See the child fed and into bed first.'

She knew that by 'later' he meant when they were alone. Lucinda was a guest, to them she was almost a stranger.

A minute or two later, with the legs and sleeves of Claudia's silk pyjamas rolled up and holding the trousers tight around his skinny waist, Barry hovered shyly in the doorway of the drawing room. Lucinda's presence was having its effect on him too.

His day had taken its toll. He ate a bowl of warm soup and a roll of bread and was soon in bed.

'Don't worry about your father,' Claudia bent to kiss him. 'Grandad phoned him and explained. Just cuddle down and go to sleep.' She pretended she hadn't seen the lump hidden under the covers, he'd hate her to notice that he'd brought Egbert.

She hadn't heard the phone ring, but Teddy was talking on the kitchen extension when she came downstairs. She went to stand by his side, hoping to hear what was being said. At this time of night it could only be James – or Trevor! Was something wrong with Melly?

'I'm glad I called you. Have you notified his wife? Then leave it to me. No, I'll do it straight away. It would be easier for her coming from me.' Then putting the phone down he rested his arm on Claudia's shoulder. 'Old Mr Parsons. He died about ten minutes ago. I must go and talk to her.'

She leant against him.

'In the midst of life we are in death,' she whispered the familiar words. 'This morning their day started like any other and it ends like this.'

'It's the hardest part of doctoring. Never gets any easier.' He crushed her to him. 'Don't wait up for me. I'm going to phone her first, say I'm coming round to talk to her.'

'She'll be in bed. She'll guess what it is.'

'I'll be there in minutes. I can't risk her ringing the hospital and asking the night staff.'

She listened as he spoke to the old lady, explaining that he wanted to talk to her about her husband. He said no more and Mrs Parsons didn't ask. But Claudia was sure she must know that nothing else would make him call on her at this time of night. Then taking his bag with him he went out into the wet night.

Claudia stared unseeingly out of the kitchen window. Upstairs slept her grandson, a runaway from a broken home; in the drawing room was her younger son, frighteningly compatible with a young woman who wasn't his wife; in London her daughter was expecting a baby that seemed to interest her not a jot. And her? For months she'd shied from remembering Adrian, she'd wrapped herself in shame that she had let him rekindle in her the timeless joy of living. He didn't rape me, he didn't lure me to bed. No, I wanted it as much as he did. As if that would prove to me that marriage, family, all the trappings of daily living hadn't put out that flame he talked about. What a fool, what a weak, senseless fool I must have been. I wanted to tell Teddy, I thought that was the way to take away the guilt. But I know now – there's nothing to tell, nothing that has any power. Do I wish it had never happened? Instinctively her answer was 'Yes, of course I do'. But was that true? It's not as simple as that, there was a half under- stood truth she wanted to grasp. The person we are when we're young – even young like Barry and Patsy – is always there. Adrian calls it the 'fundamental you', it's like a natural stone waiting to be cut. Each meaningful experience, love, sadness, joy, tenderness, laughter, tears, ambition, appreciation, each of them shapes the stone, the more we experience the brighter the prisms of the jewel. So do I regret that time with Adrian? Am I a lesser person because of the shame I felt for wanting it to happen? Think deeper, beyond the thrill of knowing he wanted me, beyond the abasement that I'd broken faith with Teddy – then what? No, I have no regret, I'm glad, grateful. It pulled me out of my rut of routine, showed me what was precious. Like a diamond that had been cleaned, to shine brighter than it ever could before, it's colours clear and brilliant.

Her heart and mind travelled with Teddy as he drove through the village to the bungalow that had been the Parsons' home for the fifty- two years of their marriage. But what of Mrs Parsons? Could grief like hers add a new facet, give her a deeper awareness?

Claudia shivered, despite the sultry night. How could the old lady bear the pain, the emptiness?

Chapter 14

It was nearly two o'clock by the time Teddy came to bed. He had gone far beyond the bounds of duty with Mrs Parsons, to her he was both doctor and friend.

'How is she?' Claudia whispered, just when he thought he'd managed to get into bed without waking her.

'Gallant. She isn't the sort to make a parade of her troubles. We talked a long time – I'm awash with tea. She was still up when I got there and you know how late it was. I think she'd been dreading going up to the empty room. I didn't realize it until much later, I was just about to leave and she asked me to stay while she got herself into bed.'

'What an awful night for her.' Her hand reached for his and she felt his fingers grip.

'She'll sleep. Without her seeing, I managed to slip a pill into her final cup of tea. She won't know anything helped nature, she won't suppose she needed it.'

'Teddy, you spoke to Jamie. He must feel so dreadful that Barry actually ran away and couldn't talk to him.'

'By now he probably does, but not then. Then it was just relief. His evening had been a nightmare. He'd phoned all Barry's friends. He'd believed there was a party of boys cycling together for the day, but none of the usual crowd knew anything. He'd contacted the police—'

'How awful for him! And all the time we were out enjoying ourselves. He must have been trying to get us all the evening.'

'No, he didn't call us, he said he'd wanted to, but so far away he felt it wasn't fair to worry us, there was nothing we could do. He didn't want to involve us in his troubles.'

'He really thinks we're not?'

'Anyway, when he heard Barry was safe he was so relieved, so

209

thankful, that if I hadn't reminded him I honestly believe he would have forgotten he had to report back to the police.'

'Sunday tomorrow – today – he won't be able to come down for him until after the weekend.'

'Claudia, we had a long talk, James and I. That's what he expected, he'd drive down on Monday and take Barry back, Tuesday he'd be off to school with a note of explanation for Monday's absence and that would be the end of it.'

'James mustn't tell them the truth at school! I don't care how he abhors lies, he mustn't tell them that Barry was so miserable he'd run away. Think how he'd hate all his friends to know.'

'It's all taken care of, darling. I told you we talked, I made him see things weren't as simple as he appeared to imagine. In the morning I'll phone Philip Huntley, ask him to spare me half an hour. I know I can trust him to keep a confidenee, so I'll go over and see him, tell him the whole thing.'

'Whatever has Philip Huntley got to do with it?' He was Principal of Chawley where both their own boys had attended until they went away to school.

'Put yourself in Barry's place, imagine how he must have been saving his money, looking forward, planning; imagine how he must have felt when Jennifer wasn't at Streatley; he must have known his choices, to go home and accept the new order or to trust us and come here. He trusted us. We have to help him.'

'But we can't! We can't encourage him away from James.'

'I told you, James and I had a long talk. He says this housekeeper he's got is extremely kind—'

'Barry said that too. He isn't blaming her, he's just blaming life.'

'A pity he isn't putting the blame where it belongs – with Jennifer. But it's the boy who matters. My guess is that before he's been down here long he'll be wanting to get back to the rectory. Living with grandparents is no substitute for his own home. Bad enough he's lost his mother, now he's to be parted from James and Patsy too. But it has to be. Until he's been lonely for them he isn't ready to go home. James is coming down on Monday, he'll talk to Barry, he'll give him the choice. Perhaps that'll be all it needs, just his father's undivided attention. I doubt if any of them often have that.'

'Live with us? Permanently? Actually live?'

She didn't seem able to take in what he was suggesting. Her quietly spoken words hung in the silence of the dark room. He didn't answer immediately, instead he gave her time to find her own answer.

After a while he said, 'He must have an alternative to what his home has become. We can't fail him. Can we?'

210

Another silence. But she knew Teddy was right.

'Just now I said James mustn't tell them at school that Barry had run off. But if he stays here and goes to Chawley they'll have to be told. They can't pretend it's a family move, everyone knows James.' In a roundabout way she answered his question.

His soft laugh was like a caress, then raising her hand and kissing it, he turned her on to her side in their usual sleeping position.

'You under estimate your menfolk, my love. Everything is organized. Tomorrow, Philip Huntley; Monday James will talk things over with Barry; then either they both go back to Brightley, or James goes back alone and writes to the school explaining that due to domestic problems for the present Barry is making his home with us and giving them details of the school he will be attending. How's that for efficiency?'

'You make it sound simple. Poor Jamie, spurned by his wife and it becomes a domestic problem. It's seventeen years since Harvey left Chawley, I never thought I'd be doing that journey every morning again.' Then she imagined old Mrs Parsons alone in her large bed, lost in the depth of a drug induced sleep. Her own trouble were nothing, she had people to love, people to care for. 'Poor little chap. Thank goodness he knew he could come to us.'

'Are you coming down to the boat this morning, Dad?' Harvey asked at breakfast.

'Unfortunately, no. I have one or two things to see to and I want to look in on Mrs Parsons. Do you sail, Lucinda?'

'I grew up with the sea. You've no idea how I've missed sailing since I flit the home nest. Would you mind if we took your boat out without you?'

'Of course not. I just wish I were coming with you. The storm's cleared the air, it's going to be a perfect morning for it.'

'What about you, Barry?' Harvey's invitation catapulted Barry's spirits upward.

'You mean I can come too? Can I, Grandad? Would it be all right?'

'See you obey skipper's instructions – and be sure to wear a life jacket – then it sounds to me a very good plan.'

'Great!' Lucinda smiled at Barry across the table, 'this looks like being a fun morning.'

Harvey hadn't invited him as if they were taking pity on him, and from the way Lucinda beamed he felt they wanted him there because it would be better with him than without. His misery was almost wiped out. He'd show them that he had the makings of a sailor!

During the morning, misery and uncertainty would sweep over him

211

unexpectedly. But Harvey kept him too busy to let his mind wander for long. He felt useful, he carried out instructions promptly, he was one of the team.

When they arrived back at Russets he was bursting with self importance.

'Barry, come into the dining room will you.'

'Right you are, Grandad.' He heard the bravado in his tone, he felt sure everyone must have heard it. His newly acquired skills were pushed into the background by ghosts of yesterday.

'Sit down, chap.' A friendly enough greeting, but Barry didn't feel quite up to a man-to-man approach. Gingerly he perched on the edge of the chair. 'We didn't talk about anything last night.' (So it *was* about yesterday! Barry tried to swallow, his mouth suddenly dry. He'd thought it was all over, he'd thought . . . he'd thought . . . he didn't know what he'd thought. Neither did he know the fright that Teddy could see in his blue eyes.) 'Naturally I phoned your father last night, told him you were here. We had a long talk.'

'Was Dad very cross?' A dry mouth makes for a small voice.

'Cross? He'd been too worried to be cross I should think. He'd contacted all your friends, no-one knew anything about you. In the end he had to tell the police you hadn't come home.'

'Oh crumbs . . .' Barry's thumb was gripped hard between his teeth. It hurt, but still he bit on it, needing a pain that he could understand.

'I suggested that you stay down here, but naturally he wants you to go home.'

'It's awful there. You don't know, you've never seen it. Miss Machin is ever so kind, she makes nice food, she never gets cross, she does all the things so that it's comfy, she even takes Henry out when we're at school. And it's awful Grandad. Those are Mum's things she's doing.' Biting his thumb couldn't save him, couldn't even hold his jaw steady. He felt his face crumpling just as if he were some silly blubbering baby. He was ashamed. Grandad had treated him like a proper grown-up person and here he was with his beastly tears falling all down the front of his shirt. 'I won't go back,' he yelled believing that a loud voice made him sound strong. At the same time he clutched at what had been no more than a shadowy idea at the back of his mind. 'I've got a plan. I know how I can find Mum. He can't stop me.'

'Barry,' Teddy passed him a large clean handkerchief, 'no-one is going to make you do anything. That's why I want us to have a quiet talk together. I want to explain to you how your Dad feels, you're quite old enough to understand. But first I'll tell you what I have proposed. You may have heard of Chawley, your father's old school

212

and Harvey's too until he went off to study music. I have talked to Mr Huntley, the Principal, and told him that we are anticipating you'll be living here. There's a place for you at Chawley, it's a very happy school, and a successful one too – all boys.'

'Dad took Mum and Patsy and me there once when they had a fête. Right on the cliff.'

'That's right. Lovely position. Anyway, that's where you'll go if you live here. But tomorrow your father is coming to talk to you—'

'Oh no! No, Grandad, no! If I see him I'll never be able to say I won't go back there. If I tell him I don't want to he'll think it's because of *him*. I won't be able to say it. Can you stay with us while he talks. Please. Help me not to go back.'

'You have to face up to things, Barry. He realizes how you feel about Miss Machin. I said just now you are old enough to understand something of how he feels. So imagine what it must be like for him to see a stranger in your mother's place. There must be times when he'd like to drive away from it all.'

Barry sniffed, frowned, then sniffed again.

'He wouldn't do that, he'd not leave the church.'

Teddy knew he was ill equipped to give the right answer, but he had to try.

'The church is only a building. What the church stands for is what matters to your father and, wherever he went, that would always go with him.' He thought he hadn't done too badly and watched Barry's face to see the effect of his words.

'Don't say that to Dad – that it's only a building. Honestly Grandad he'd be ever so upset.'

'Then I won't. All I'm saying to you is that he is unhappy too. Your mother has hurt him more than you realize.'

'I know whose fault it is.'

Teddy supposed Jennifer's disgraceful affair with Ken Sheldrake had been talked about at school, these days there was nothing that went over children's heads. He waited, trying to muster up some suitable reply.

'It's St Luke's fault,' Barry explained, 'and the St Luke's Lot who make such a fuss of Dad. Don't expect he even notices Mum isn't there. I hate them; bet Mum hates them too. All those silly women making excuses to do things for him. They come to the door with little presents, chocolates for Patsy and me, invitations for us to be taken to Oxford to the theatre or to the skating rink with their children, all that sort of thing. They think they can make up to us for Mum not being there. Well, I won't eat the chocolate and I pretend I've got got homework and things so that I can't go on the outings.

213

Dad never makes me go, but I think he gets cross. Patsy likes the chocolate but I don't know if she really likes the outings, she just goes because most of all she wants to please Dad.'

'Barry, when your father comes tomorrow say the things to him that you have to me. You'll find he understands far better than you think.'

Barry frowned, glaring at a point somewhere in the middle of the dining table.

'You mean you think I should go back with him. You don't want me to be here with Gran and you.'

It was too much for Teddy. He pulled the boy off the edge of the seat where he was perched, it was a natural action just as it was natural for Barry to forget he was no longer the age to be nursed. He buried his face against his grandfather's neck.

'You know we want you here,' Teddy told him. 'Not just you, Barry, any of you who come. This is home, we are all one family, we belong to each other.'

'And Mum. If Mum would come back she'd belong too.'

'Of course.' For Barry's sake Tedd made himself say it, sure his words would never be put to the test.

That afternoon, at Philip Huntley's suggestion, he took the boy with him to see Chawley. Barry's future began to have a shape. He came back to Russets talking about the things he's seen, the boys he'd met.

Late that evening, after Harvey and Lucinda had set off back to London and Barry was in bed and asleep, it was Claudia who spoke to James. How hard it was to tell a man that his son needed time away from home. She did her best. And went to bed physically exhausted while her mind still raced. Were they doing the right thing in offering Barry a temporary escape? Why was the boy could let Teddy or her see his tears, recognize his misery, yet he hid it from James? Too young to understand, yet did he hold James responsible, blame the hold the church and its entourage had on him? That could only be a fraction of the reason, she knew that, Teddy knew it – and James? she wasn't sure what James knew – but if the church had been all that was wrong between them, in an otherwise good relationship Jenny could have accepted.

And in the dark of her bedroom, feigning sleep, Claudia added a rider: Jenny could have accepted sharing him with the church, just as Erica accepted sharing Harvey with his music.

Harvey and Erica lived on the outskirts of Manchester. Tonight though he was delivering Lucinda to the Thameside apartment she

214

rented near Maidenhead before going on to the club he used when he stayed in London on his own.

'We made the journey in good time,' she said as she reached over to the back seat to collect her dress. 'It's not even ten yet. Come and have coffee before you go on.'

'Good idea,' he agreed.

It had been strange taking another woman home to Russets. Even with the shadow of James's troubles hanging over the house, he couldn't remember when he'd had such a carefree weekend. The sudden surge of longing that took hold of him could have nothing to do with the weekend – except that at Russets his room had held so many traces of Erica: a jar of her hand lotion and a phial of her perfume left on the dressing table, the lingering scent from her clothes in the wardrobe. He gripped the steering wheel, suddenly overcome by a surge of longing. In another hour or so he'd be unpacking at the club, he imagined the faceless adequacy of the room – the club, a hotel room, even back in the emptiness of their own apartment . . . Most of the time he kept busy, too busy to let the loneliness catch up with him. Yet thirty-six hours at Russets and he was thrown off course. To feel like he did was natural and healthy, he told himself. She'd been away for weeks, months. Soon she'd be home . . . Then his imagination took a sideways leap, he was at Croughton Hall, sharing the joy of making music, or this afternoon in the forest scuffing through the leaves, pouncing on the nuts they uncovered with as much triumph as young Barry. Think of Erica, just think of her. It's Erica you want . . .

'Wakey-wakey, you were miles away.'

'Not so many miles. Thank you for coming down to Avonford with me, Luce. I suppose I was remembering the weekend and comparing it with what's ahead at journey's end in London.'

'I'm glad it wasn't the thought of my coffee that put that look on your face,' Lucinda laughed.

'Your coffee is just what I need. I'll get your case from the boot, you take your dress.'

By the time they were inside her apartment he had overcome his momentary desires, his feet were on the ground and a friendly smile back on his face. While she made the coffee he looked through a pile of music she had on top of the piano.

'Hey, Luce, this looks interesting. Will it drive the neighbours mad if we run through it?'

'We're sound proof, or so they say. What's that you've got?' She put the tray down and came to his side to look at the music.

By now he didn't have to stamp on his yearning, it was put aside in

215

their shared interest as they read through the score then went to the piano each with one hand tinkering with the notes.

'Coffee first, then we'll do it properly.'

She was frightened to look at him, surely he must be able to read her thoughts. She must hang on to the image of Erica, in their one brief meeting she'd seen her as everything any man could want, lovely to look at, feminine, seductive. Lucinda knew by comparison she had no allure; so she played 'the girl next door' role to the full, never giving a hint to Harvey that all her fantasies were of him. He was happily married, he loved his wife, she was just the girl he enjoyed making music with.

And make music they did. Sitting close together on the long piano stool she played the treble and he the bass. First, following the score, they played the duet for four hands he'd found on the piano. Then they improvised, enjoying themselves; trained and gifted musicians, their ear was instinctive, their fingers practised. This was relaxation, this was fun. She wished it might never end.

He wished it too, with an intensity that was frightening. This was a meeting of minds, but it was more; he was frightened by the intensity of his feelings, feelings he had no right to. The moment came when she closed the lid of the piano, lightly her hand brushed against his and in an unguarded moment they turned to each other.

There was no running away from where they were heading, neither of them wanted to run from it. There was no tomorrow, there was only now.

After the last twenty-four hours Claudia was ready for anything fate threw at her. Even so it was Teddy whose immediate reaction was to reach for the receiver at the first shrill ring of the telephone. His years of being the only GP in Avonford died hard.

'Teddy Carlyle,' he said instinctively, before he came to enough to realise that the call must be personal.

Like a shot, Claudia sat up at his side.

'It's me. Erica.'

'Is everything all right? Have you got home? You should have let us know. Harvey's in London—'

'No, I'm back with my Mom. We got a fax waiting for us in Copenhagen. Mom had been taken into hospital, it all happened with no warning. Of course we came straight back here.'

'My dear, I'm sorry.'

'No, it's all right Teddy. It was only her appendix. By the time we got to the hospital this afternoon she was sitting up looking pretty as a picture, all her troubles gone. I rang because I wanted to tell

216

Harvey. Our grand tour is through, I shall be here now until Mom's really fit again, then Sara will come back for a spell in England.'

'Good. Harvey's been missing you. Time you were back.'

'He is OK. Teddy? I never get to talk with him.'

'He's fine, my dear. He was down here for the weekend.' Now, what stopped him saying more?

'Pretty soon, so shall I be. I'll bring Sara. I've been missing you both, looking forward to catching up on all the family when I get back. Give Melly my love, I hope she's doing fine. I guess Mom will be a few weeks, but we're just glad to be able to be here for her. You say Harvey's gone to London – is he at that club where he stays?'

'That's right.'

'I'll call him right away. Have you got the number?' She seemed to have no idea that it was three o'clock in the morning, world time changes never entered her head. He got out of bed and fetched his diary from the top of the tallboy, then read out the telephone number to her.

'But Erica, you can't ring at this time of night.'

He didn't think she even listened.

When she'd rung off and he'd told Claudia the gist of the conversation they were drifting back towards sleep when the bell rang again.

'Teddy, it's me again. I rang that number. Teddy, he hasn't checked in. They said he'd booked a room, but he hadn't come. I tried our home number and he's not there either. What can have happened?'

'He was giving someone a lift, I'm not sure how far, Maidenhead or Windsor I think. I expect he's stayed the night there, probably had a drink or two and thought better of driving. I'll see he gets your message as soon as he surfaces. Don't worry, I'm sure there's no need.' How calm he sounded, she would never guess at the twin fears that fought in his mind. Suppose there had been an accident! Or suppose it were true that he'd stayed with this person he'd been giving a lift to!

They abandoned all thought of sleep.

Next morning as soon as he thought someone would be in the office Teddy rang Harvey's agent with an urgent message: please ask him to contact his parents. At least he had the excuse of Erica's message.

Claudia's talk with James on that Sunday evening must have taught him either diplomacy or cunning. In bringing Frisk and Twitch with him he made an outward sign of acceptance. A clever ploy or an act of kindness?

'Dad's come.' If the reason for James's action wasn't clear, neither

217

were Barry's feelings as he saw the car turn in at the gate. 'What's he going to say, Gran? If he wasn't wild at what I did, he must have been miserable. That's worse . . .'

This morning even James's and Barry's troubles faded into insignificance. Where was Harvey? It was impossible to put out of her mind the way Lucinda had looked at him, or the elusive something in his manner that had reminded her time and again of the Harvey of old. She remembered his letter to Erica, she remembered Erica's tears.

She took control of her thoughts and smiled at Barry encouragingly.

'Go out and say hello to him,' she urged. 'That's what he'll be hoping.'

It was what Barry wanted, but he didn't trust himself. He wanted to hurl himself at his father, know that nothing had been changed by what he'd done; but he was frightened that if he did that it would send the wrong message. Gran and Grandad said he could live here, he couldn't go home to Brightley as if he didn't care that Mum wasn't there. If she'd died – even thinking it made him feel wicked – but if he and Dad and Patsy could all have cried together and everyone would have known that they were still loving her, then he would have even faced having to accept Miss Machin. But in Brightley no-one loved Mum any more, he could feel it.

'Go on. He's getting out of the car.' Claudia urged him.

He did as she said, going through the kitchen where Gwen was preparing vegetables, then across the utility room to the back door. He stopped in his tracks, his attention taken by the bench where he'd kept the rabbit hutch at half-term. Why had Gwen done that? It had been cleared, it was quite empty.

He didn't rush out as Claudia had hoped, gingerly he came out of the back door and along the path to where James was already out of the car with the hatch-back open. Then he saw! At that moment, had James's arms been empty, in his relief Barry would have run to him as he wanted. But you can't hug a man carrying a rabbit hutch.

'You've brought Frisk and Twitch! I never expected – crumbs, thanks Dad.'

'As long as you stay here, I thought you'd rather look after them yourself.'

'That's great. Poor old Gwen. She'll do her nut! Did she know, Dad? Had you told Gran you were bringing them?'

'I didn't think of it until I was getting in the car this morning.'

Barry thought of the bench, its space cleared in readiness. He felt a rush of affection towards Gwen of the caustic tongue.

218

Slipping into her expected role she raised her eyes to the ceiling in horror as the utility room residents were carried in.

'Ach! Not those silly useless creatures back in my way again! You know what it'll be? Straw on my nice clean floor, bits of carrot pushed through the wire.'

'You don't mean it Gwen. Look at Frisk, he's recognized you, I'm sure he has.'

'Mean it, that I do! Only place they'd be any use would be under a nice crust of pastry, and as for being ornamental, can you honestly say they do anything for this room?'

'Yes, Gwen, I honestly can. Cor . . .' Two small furry animals, twitching their whiskers, waiting for him to look after them, already they were returning him to normality. He must find them some food. Gwen wouldn't mind, he'd take something from the vegetable rack.

Behind him, still in the utility room, Claudia had come to join in the greetings. Gwen glowed with pleasure at James's kiss. Listening to them some of Barry's dread returned. Nothing ever changed at Russets, every time they'd come even for a day there had been the same excitement. Those had been visits that had always ended in their driving back to Brightley. This was different, don't listen to it being just like every other time, this time Dad had come to visit *him* too. They said he could stay here, they said they wanted him . . . He looked at his father with uncertainty, fear, but most of all with misery.

Chapter 15

The man-to-man talk took place as James and Barry walked in the forest, just the two of them. At home Claudia and Gwen watched anxiously for their return; out on his rounds Teddy had them always waiting their opportunity to break into his thoughts.

None of them were to know exactly what passed between father and son, only that the outcome was that Barry should take his place at Chawley for the time being and that James had been told about Action Day. How deeply they'd dug, whether Barry had trusted himself to open his heart or whether he'd been been too frightened of disgracing himself with tears remained their own secret.

It was about midday when Harvey rang.

'I had a message to phone you. What's wrong, Mum?'

'We wanted to tell you – there was a call from Erica last night. She'd been trying to ring you.'

'Where from?'

'She's with her mother.' She explained about the sisters' return to the States. 'We gave her the number of the club, she wanted to talk to you herself.' She paused. Perhaps now he'd say something, tell her why he hadn't been there. When he didn't, she went on, 'Half an hour later she rang back and said she'd got through to the club, they'd told her you had a room reserved but hadn't arrived.'

Silence.

'Harvey – it was nearly three o'clock in the morning.'

Silence.

'Hello. Are you still there?'

'Yes, Mum, I'm here.' It would have been so easy to tell her, but he overcame the impulse.

'She's been away a long time, Harvey. As soon as her mother is over the operation she wants to come home. You've been missing her—'

'Yes. No. It's not that.'

'Do what's right, Harvey. Right for everyone.'

'You mean you know?'

'I'm putting two and two together, I can add to four quite nicely.'

'It was a wonderful weekend. Mum, I don't regret a moment of it. You understand what I'm saying? I don't regret anything. Perhaps you think I ought to, but I can't. You did like Luce didn't you, you and Dad?'

'What do you want me to say? Of course I liked her, and I could see you did, I could see how she felt about you too. But Harvey, Erica loves you. Do what's right, it's the only way to deserve happiness.'

'I wasn't going to say anything.'

'You didn't need to. I told you, I'm not blind. As soon as she told us you weren't at the club it fell into place. Normally I would have panicked that you'd been in an accident, but last night I just knew.'

'Has James come?' He changed the subject.

'He's brought Barry his rabbits.'

'Poor old Mum.'

But was she? The last thing she and Teddy had looked for was a child permanently in the house, a four-mile drive to school each morning and teatime, no freedom to enjoy their own friends in the evenings, no summertime leisurely garden suppers and when winter came no fireside evenings by themselves. And yet she was grateful that this was where they were able to come, she and Teddy were their roots; Harvey knew it, even Barry had known it.

Melly's pictures were hung, invitations sent out, posters displayed, even the added expense of an announcement in the 'What's On in London' notices in two of the broadsheet papers. She lived on a high during these final days of preparation, physically she was more tired than she would admit, yet mentally she found it impossible to relax. In bed she ached with fatigue while still her mind raced.

The evening before the opening, art critics were invited for a private viewing. It was all she had ever dreamed – except that at nearly seven months pregnant she looked and felt like a baby elephant. At the start she'd resented pregnancy as an intrusion on her liberty, but through the last weeks although she had hated her lumbering movements, her clumsiness, yet as a person she'd not thought of the baby at all. Her mind and her energy were geared to one thing, the exhibition.

'Melly, I'd meant to come up and stay a day or two, I'd looked forward to it so much,' Claudia told her, speaking freely as Barry was at school. 'We could come on the Sunday, there and back in a day and bring Barry with us, but it's not the same as being there for all the excitement.'

'It's not worth it, Mum. You can see the pictures any time without pushing around with a crowd – says she hopefully. I'd rather have you come to see me later, I'll need you much more when everything has gone flat. Everything but my girth! Anyway Mum, Barry's had a rotten time, you've got to be there for him.'

Claudia sensed that Melly's reaction was relief that she wouldn't have to stretch her attention to include parents; this exhibition was her final fling before her career had to be put on hold. The disappointment was all Claudia's, hers and Teddy's.

They ordered flowers to be delivered on the morning of the 29th, the Big Day. They bought all the daily papers and scanned them for even a few short lines. In fact on Wednesday, two days after the exhibition opened, the Arts Page gave two whole columns to it.

'An international concert pianist for a son, and international artist for a daughter . . .' Teddy exaggerated with pride.

Claudia didn't answer. She was thinking of James, rejected by this wife, his home run by a housekeeper, his son miles away. People went to Harvey's concerts wanting to listen; people crowded the gallery to see Melly's pictures wanting to look; but what of the parishioners of a country village? James gave all that he was to bringing sight to the inwardly blind. If he caught a lost soul in his net he was grateful that he'd been guided; if the soul eluded him he saw himself as unworthy. Dear, gentle Jamie, there would be no fanfare of success for him.

Melly had dreamed of this and worked for it, promising that after it was over and the pictures taken down she would concentrate on the coming baby. True to her word she spent her first morning writing a list of what she had to buy, and the same afternoon started her shopping: babygrows, vests, cot sheets, cotton wool . . . the items were ticked as she went down the list. Only love couldn't be bought.

It was stolen time, six days away from the world or as far away as a rented cottage in deepest Dorset. In the sitting room was a tinny toned, untuned piano, with four broken strings; the radio was elderly and had been no more than 'good enough for a letting cottage' even in its infancy. Music had bound them, but for six days Harvey and Lucinda would live without it.

He didn't want to compare those days with the rare occasions he and Erica had been on holiday. But how could he help it? Then he'd been conscious that he must make an effort, make sure she could see he was enjoying himself. There could be no hint that he was missing his piano – 'his mistress' as she called it. Now he made no effort, there wasn't the need. It was mid-July, the heatwave of early summer had been replaced by dull, grey days. In the sunshine the wide, undulating landscape would have been a scene of serenity; under a leaden sky and lost in damp that was not quite rain it was bleak and cheerless. If it was isolation Harvey and Lucinda were seeking the elements were on their side. Together each morning they walked the mile to the nearest village, where they bought the daily food and the daily paper.

'There's chill in the air more like January than July,' they heard the butcher saying to one of the villagers as they went in to buy their lunch.

'First thing when I get home, I tell you Harry I'm going to put a match to my fire. Not so much for the warmth as the comfort.'

Harvey and Lucinda smiled at each other knowingly. At the newsagents they remembered to buy a box of matches. A fire in the little grate in July was unreal as every thing else. There was a feeling of make-believe about living in this primitive place, it reminded Harvey of when they'd been children and Melly would coerce him into playing 'mothers and fathers'. He told himself make-believe was all this could ever be to either of them, so soon their meaningful lives would swallow them up.

There was a sense that they were suspended in a timeless vacuum, neither of them had ever lived in such a ramshackle place before. They'd seen the advertisement on a card in the newsagent's window when Lucinda had gone to pay her paper bill. 'To Let: Idyllic country cottage in deepest Dorset available for holiday let.' They'd phoned immediately, then driven straight to the owner's house not a mile away to pay a week's rent and collect the key. The image they'd carried with them as they motored down had been a far cry from the reality of Tucker's Cottage; but then, had it been the idyllic hideaway the card in the window had promised, surely it wouldn't have been vacant in July! The general standard of the furnishings was much the same as that of the piano and the radio. On one end of the sofa a spring was poking through the worn upholstery, the table had to be balanced with a wedge of cardboard under one leg. But none of these things mattered, in fact Harvey and Lucinda needed the laughter of each new discovery. Like the lump in their mattress, a lump so tall that they christened it Ben Nevis.

'Luce,' he said as they lay in bed on their last night, 'our time's nearly over.'

'Not yet. Don't let's even think of it yet. We've all night, we've tomorrow. I'm not looking beyond, don't spoil tonight, Harvey. This has been time out of time.'

'No. There has been more reality in these days than I've ever known. And for you? It's been the same for you, I know it has.' He pushed her fringe from her forehead, raising himself on his elbow to look at her. 'What a bloody mess I've let things get into. I've messed up Erica's life, I'm messing up yours—'

'No! No, you're not Harvey. Everything means more to me since we've been together, even music – I can't explain. *Everything* is clearer, the funny smell of the damp earth, the sound of that dog barking across the valley. Jokes are funnier—'

'Luce, I love you.'

Next morning she took the car to the village, filled the tank with petrol and checked the tyre pressures. Today there was no need to shop, even the paper would be at home and waiting. Her trip was no more than an excuse to go out, to leave Harvey by himself. He'd said there was something he needed to think about.

When she got back to the cottage she saw the letter lying on the table, addressed and ready to post.

'I'm sorry it has to be a Saturday, but you *will* come won't you Claudia. I'm useless at choosing clothes. And this time I really want something special.'

Tricia and Bert Caldcott had known Claudia and Teddy for years. It was a comfortable unpressurized friendship, every few months either one couple or the other would suggest a meeting. But this was no ordinary meeting, Tricia wanted Claudia to go with her to Bournemouth to buy an outfit for her daughter's wedding. Saturdays were precious, especially Saturdays when Teddy hadn't a morning surgery. Had Tricia had even a normal interest in fashion she might not have developed such faith in what she'd heard about Esther Hymann who imported exclusive models from the Continent and sold them in semi-private shows throughout the country. Her base was Bournemouth and she had promised to be there to see Tricia on that Saturday morning. To anyone else Claudia could have said, 'If you've got Esther's opinion, what do you want with mine?' But to Tricia she couldn't say it.

'You know the sort of thing I'm comfortable in,' Tricia persuaded. 'No, not comfortable, I shan't be that. But at least you can see what would look utterly stupid on me. I'm just not the dressy sort.' Which was true as Tricia passion in life was breeding and showing Cairn terriers.

'Well, we're not having you going to Cynny's wedding in jeans and smelling of dog,' Claudia laughed good-humouredly. 'Yes, I'll come, of course I will. Teddy and Barry will probably be glad to get rid of me.'

224

So, not much after nine o'clock, about the time Harvey and Lucinda were saying a regretful farewell to their hideaway home, Claudia and Tricia were hunting for a space in the car park in crowded holiday-packed Bournemouth.

'You mean you're going to tell them where we've been?' Lucinda wasn't sure that she was ready to face his family. She thought of the photographs on the occasional table in the drawing room at Russets: James with his wife and children, Harvey and Erica together on the back lawn, Melly at about sixteen on her pony, Melly and Trevor at their wedding. And where would she fit in? Harvey and his mistress!

'Of course I'm going to tell them. I want to tell the world.'

He had posted his letter, the sound of it dropping into the letterbox giving him a thrill of liberation. He ought to be ridden with guilt, he knew he ought, but guilt couldn't dent the relief that a great load had been lifted from his mind. He had written to Erica with complete honesty and, in the cottage alone, he had read the words aloud. Reason had told him nothing had changed, he was married to Erica, he didn't want to hurt her, what he was doing inevitably *would* hurt her. But it was like lancing a boil, until it was done there could be no healthy way forward. Until Luce, his wonderful Luce, there had been no other woman, but he and Erica must have both known that it took more to make a good marriage than they had found once the first excitement paled. If either of them had been bored, then it must have been her. He had been absorbed by his career, for him there'd been no space in his mind for boredom.

In the past, whenever his thoughts had taken that track he had bolstered his spirit by remembering the good moments; to think of making love to her had always been the panacea to clear his mind of minor irritations. Now though he shied from the memory, he only wanted to think of Lucinda. Reason told him that Erica would be better off without him, free to make a life with someone who shared her interests. And with his letter not yet collected from the post box, he made himself believe that she would see things the same way. It wouldn't come as a bolt from the blue to her, he remembered that other letter – and chose not to remember that her answer to it had been to become ever more willing to feed on the crumbs he spared her.

Today he wouldn't question her response, he'd let himself assume that her months of travelling had shown her there was more to life than wasting her hours and resenting the time he spent away from her.

'Avonford is hardly out of our way. Luce, they're going to hear very soon, I'd rather we talked to them. Anyway, they won't be surprised. I think they could see it even before it happened.'

'It? You mean sleeping together? But there's more than that, Harvey.'

He took her hand as he drove.

'There's one heck of a lot more. That's what's so good, what makes it inevitable. Sleeping together, as you so delicately put it, is unbelievably wonderful. Put me to the test and right this minute I could prove to you just how wonderful.'

'Don't tempt a girl,' she laughed. Then seriously, 'Harvey I can't think of being with you as a sin. But that's what folk would call it. They'd see me as a marriage breaker. To me it's more like a miracle.'

'Me too. That's why I'm not going to allow us live a lie. What we have is too good.'

Even so, for her some of the glory was dimmed as they approached Avonford. Their six days had been perfect – broken springs on the sofa, Ben Nevis in the bed, a radio that had to be thumped to get any sound from it, an open fire that sent clouds of smoke back down the chimney, things that because they were so removed from   mal day-to-day existence set the brief spell apart. Time   She wasn't ready to have something which belonge   .nd to Harvey discussed even by his family, see⁻   ₁   .iew of his marriage.

When the reached Russets only Gw   ₃ there.

'Harvey! Mrs C wasn't exp⌐⌐⌐   ₔ, was she? Did she rush off and forget to tell me?'   .r'

'Rush off? How long's sl   be? Is she just in the village or has she swanned off to Bournemouth or somewhere?'

'Bournemouth. Don't know about swanning off, she's promised to help Mrs Caldecott choose her outfit for the wedding.'

'Of course, Cynny's wedding. When's Mum due back? And, now I come to think of it, how come you're here on Saturday?'

'I told Mrs C I'd just give an eye to things, see the dinner was forward ready for when she gets back. From what she's been told to expect, it looks like being an all-day job.'

'Isn't Dad here?'

'He and Barry – well, I give you one guess where you'll find them. Why don't you go and see if you're in time to catch up with them. I doubt he'd go far with only your Barry on board with him.'

'Have we got time, Harvey? You've promised to be at Queen Mary's at half six, don't forget.'

'As if I would,' he laughed. 'And this evening they have an extra treat, you'll be there with me.'

Gwen looked from one to the other. She reckoned it took a good deal to fool her, and you'd have to be blind not to see those two were sweet on each other. This love business, if you asked her she'd had a lucky escape missing out on it, no matter what the stories in the magazines tried to make out. There was Harvey with a wife the other side of the world . . . there was James all alone . . . and as for Barry, if love could make a woman do what that mother of his had – well, like she said, she was better off to have given it a miss and stuck to her independence.

The noise started quite suddenly as they drove into Lymington, a loud knocking – more of a clank – somewhere under the bonnet of the car. They looked at each other helplessly. Harvey's knowledge of car maintenance went as far as changing a wheel, but as for engines, they were a strange world to him. Trained at a school with an emphasis on music, always aware that his hands were vital to his career, messing about with cars had never come within his sphere.

He knew there was a garage nearby and hoped that there would be a man on hand who could right the fault despite it being more than halfway through a Saturday morning. He was unlucky. There was a man but the fault would need major surgery!

'Have to have the head off the engine, strip her right down,' he told Harvey.

'Will that take long. I have to be in London this evening.'

'Not in this car, you won't.' The mechanic gave him a pitying look, surprised any man could be so ignorant. 'I can make a start on, let me see now, let's say Tuesday, give us a ring on Thursday and see how it's going.'

'We've got cases in the back. I'll come back and collect them a bit later on.'

'Make it before one o'clock. Half day today you see. But I'll be here till one.' It was then a quarter to twelve.

Ten minutes' brisk walk brought them to the quay where, fortunately, Teddy and Barry had been amusing themselves on board but still moored.

'You've been playing together somewhere? What a splendid surprise. You're here for the weekend?'

'No, Dad, I have to be at St Mary's House at six-thirty. You remember St Mary's, a residential home for the elderly. I always fix up to go in for an evening when I'm staying in town, got a soft spot for some of my old dears, I couldn't possibly let them down. We've been in Dorset—' This wasn't the moment. 'We thought we'd look in, it wasn't much out of the way, then Gwen said you were here. But Dad my car's just packed up on me. I'll have to try and get a hire one to get me back. I've left it at the garage.'

'I doubt you'll get a car locally, not at such short notice at this time of year. Go over to the Clubhouse and ring around while Barry and I close up here. If you can't get one, I'll drive you up to town. Your mother isn't expected home till the shops close, you know what women are when they get out on the loose.'

It didn't surprise Teddy that the phone calls brought no success; but it did surprise him that when they called at the repair garage on the way home, a week's luggage for two people was transferred into the back of his car. He passed no comment but he wasn't looking forward to what he thought he would hear during the course of the drive to London.

'Can I come too? Please Grandad. I haven't been to London for simply ages. And I'd be company for you coming home.' A sign that he liked them being together or that he didn't want to be at Russets on his own? Either way, Teddy was glad to take him. If Harvey was getting too fond of Lucinda Leighton he didn't want to know about it. Erica had been away too long, it was time she was home. Once Harvey was with her – well, all this would fade into perspective. The boy must have been lonely and he and Lucinda naturally had dangerously close interests. Like an ostrich he kept his head in the sand.

By afternoon even Bournemouth was shrouded in drizzle that couldn't decide whether it was rain or mist, the rumble of distant thunder was a sign that a storm threatened yet it didn't actually break.

On the M3 visability was bad, and here the earlier drizzle had made its decision and come down on the side of rain, large heavy spots that hit the windscreen with force. There must have been thunder although it couldn't be heard above the noise of tyres on the wet road, the only evidence of the storm was the brilliant flashes of sheet lightning. Some drivers slackened their speed in accordance with the restrictions shown on the hazard warnings; some didn't. Teddy drove, Harvey sat by his side while Barry and Lucinda were in the back. Harvey had come home for the special purpose of telling his parents: he and Luce were together, they'd been together for a week, they were to be together for the rest of their lives. But now he couldn't say it, not with his father having to concentrate on the road conditions and especially not with Barry listening. First Jenny and now him, that's how it would seem. But as if you could compare!

The other two sat silently in the back of the car. Barry was susceptible to atmosphere, he felt that something wasn't quite right, he could sense it in the silence. As for Lucinda, she was happily lost in her own thoughts.

They were in the centre lane travelling at a steady fifty miles an hour, a metallic silver sports car overtook them in the slow lane then overtook the lorry that was travelling in front of them. Beyond that it was out of their sight as it crossed in front of the lorry to get into the third lane where another car was already coming up fast and ignoring the hazard signs. The sports car swerved, braked, skidded and somehow came to a standstill on the hard shoulder.

'Christ! Watch out!' Was it Teddy or Harvey who shouted? Too late Teddy jammed his foot on the brake. The sports car was unhurt, the speeding culprit in the fast lane was already out of way of the trouble, probably not even aware there was any. As the sports car crossed in front of the lorry, first one way and then back again, its trailer jack-knifed, while at the same instant Teddy took immediate avoiding action, yanking the steering wheel towards the slow lane where more circumspect drivers had foreseen trouble and slowed down. But nothing could prevent it happening. The screech of brakes, the sound of tearing metal, the screams – whose? It had happened in seconds, the screech of tyres on the wet road, the whip of safety belts forcing them back into their seats, the noise of metal on metal – then, in contrast, utter stillness.

The silence lasted only seconds, but to Lucinda it held the stillness of the grave. Barry was the first to move, screaming hysterically, hardly knowing he did it.

'Harvey, say something. Harvey!' Lucinda cried in panic.

He was slumped to the left, his head against the door frame. He'd stretched his arms out in front of him, a natural protective action, now his left arm was trapped in the crushed metal and broken glass of the windscreen. But he was mercifully unconscious. On the driver's side the metal of the front of the car was concertinaed, crushing and trapping Teddy's unconscious body. Unconscious? Lucinda shuddered, then she knew no more. Within minutes the blue flashing lights could be seen through the curtain of rain – except that the only one to see them was Barry.

'All right, son, we'll soon have you all out of there.' The paramedic sounded more confident that he felt. Any second the fire service would be here, they'd need their cutting equipment in the front. Meanwhile Barry was lifted out and on to a stretcher, then Lucinda, both carried into the waiting ambulance.

'The others?' Barry screamed. Couldn't they understand? The others were still in the car. 'Can't leave the others. Get them!' Frantically he punched the paramedic. 'Don't leave them.' Why didn't they do as he said? 'No, no, no.' He was beside himself. 'Grandad . . .'

'It's all right, son, they're bringing the others in the second ambulance. We'll get you along to the hospital while they're loading them up.'

The driver was already in his seat, the high-pitched siren clearing their way. They'd soon be at the hospital with these two. The front passenger would be following pretty soon, but it was going to be a longer job to get the lad's grandad out.

Gwen answered the ring at the front-door bell and came face to face with Constable Percy Clegg. Never a chatty woman, but she'd been on nodding terms with Percy for a good many years as she drank her nightly single glass of stout in the The Bell.

'What brings you, Constable? No good asking for the doctor, he's had to go off to London.' She liked to let it be known she knew what was going on at Russets.

'It's Mrs Carlyle I want to see, Miss Pomfrey. Would she be in?'

'That she wouldn't. Having the day in Bournemouth. Unless this weather drives her home early I'm not expecting her for a while yet. No-one here but me.' Then, her imagination taking an uncharacteristic leap into action. 'What's the trouble? Not bad news you've brought us? No, of course it wouldn't be.' She wasn't even going to start imagining.

'A report's come through to the station. The doctor' car has been involved in a motoring incident. When's Mrs Carlyle due home? Can you contact her? It's pretty urgent, Gwen.' A kindly man, he sensed this was a moment to use her christian name.

'Oh my dear Lord, what's happened to the doctor?'

'All I know is there's been a motorway incident. There were four people in the car –'

'I know all that! Was the doctor, our young Harvey, Barry, that's the doctor's grandson, and an American girl. Don't remember her name.'

'Mrs Carlyle mustn't drive herself. It wouldn't be right, after getting news like that. If there's no-one here to take her, a car from the station will see her to the hospital. Bad business, Gwen. It's the doctor whose caught it worst, so I'm told.'

'Best you come in. Have a word on the phone with James. James will tell you what's best to do. He's their eldest –'

'Ah, I remember him. But he's miles away.'

'They're all miles away, that's the truth of it. But Barry, the boy in the car, he's James's son. Best you have a word with James. But as for Mrs C, how to get her home quick I just can't think.'

*

230

A white police car was parked outside as she turned into the drive.

'Mrs Carlyle?'

'Yes? You want me? What's happened?' Teddy and Barry had been going to the boat. But Teddy never took risks with the sea . . .

She heard what he said, but there was no reason in it. He said Teddy had been on the M3 going towards London, that there had been three passengers, one of them a young boy. Barry! But who? Why?

Ignoring the rain Gwen came hurrying out.

'It's true what they're telling you, Mrs C. Harvey and that Lucinda girl called here, then his car broke down and he had to leave it for repairs. So the doctor was driving them up, Harvey was due somewhere this evening. Oh dear, oh Lord, how bad any of it is – so far away – They've phoned James, he'll be there ahead of you.'

Like a sleepwalker Claudia opened the door to get back in her car.

'Oh no, they're here to take you. All by yourself like that, if only Melly or one of them could be going with you.' For Gwen shock had given way to panic. 'Mrs C, you'll ring me won't you. I'm not going home. I'm waiting here till I get news.'

Claudia promised. But whether she'd even taken in what was said Gwen didn't know.

James didn't say Evensong at St Luke's that evening. He told Miss Machin that his father and brother had been involved in an accident, for Patsy's sake he didn't mention Barry. But it was Barry who was at the front of his mind as he took the road south. How he and Jenny had failed the child. Patsy didn't worry him so much, it was Barry who was so scarred by what had happened. In the drawer of his desk James had the letter from her solicitor, telling him her whereabouts so that he could set the wheels in motion for a divorce. As if he would! He would never divorce her, it would be a betrayal of his faith. What if he contacted her, told her what her going had done to Barry? Was there a chance she might come home? She doesn't love me, that I could learn to accept, I have no choice but to accept; all the years when I thought we were happy did she have no idea how much I needed her, how much I loved her? There's more to marriage than sex. All right, I let her down. Me with my counselling! Young couples I've talked to, couples where unfaithfulness had meant sex, how superior I always felt, so sure that our union was deeper, finer than that. She sees me as nothing of a man – but that's not true. Lust, a gratification of man's lust. I abhorred it, I saw it – I do see it – as a denegration of love. All through the years, was that what she wanted of me? No. No. We had companionship, common interests; sex brought two children into the world, surely that was proof of our love? I can't believe she doesn't care more for her son than for – for the sensual thrill she gets from Kenneth Sheldrake. That won't last for ever. True union must be deeper than that. Can't she see that Barry will never change – and for me there could never be anyone but her. I'd do anything, I'd live any way she wanted . . . duty, what was it she called it, an occasional treat to keep her working? . . . is that how she saw it? For me it was good. That time when she'd been away, remember how it was the night she came home. I believed her when she said she'd been with Mrs Sheldrake. Was that the first lie? That night, my thankfulness, it was like a miracle, she'd come back to me. Duty? She must have known I wanted her, not to please her but because I was thankful, thankful with all my soul. Remember the things she wrote. I failed her. I even failed her that night, yet I didn't know. To me it was an expression of sheer joy, she was home, she wanted to be with me. So did I take her for granted? I thought we were beyond all that, taking each other for granted must be what marriage is about. Isn't it? What about Mum and Dad? They've never had any bad patches – have they?

The rain was heavier, the windscreen wipers could scarcely keep up with it, it rolled down the windscreen like tears, his tears. Pulling into a lay-by he leant forward, his head against the hard steering wheel.

'Forgive me,' he spoke aloud, 'Even tonight I'm full of self pity. Make me strong, make me able to help Mum. She must be somewhere on her way, how must she be feeling? Dad, Harvey, even Barry though they say he's not hurt. But Mum, help Mum, I beg not just for my sake but for hers.'

He'd been in the lay-by no more than a minute but, suddenly relieved of the concentration of driving, the short break had been like an oasis. He switched on the engine and pulled out into the roadway, and this time he didn't stop until he drew into the Accident and Emergency car park at the hospital.

It was one of those wards favoured by those who think small is beautiful. Four beds, set into an overlarge alcove open on to the corridor. It might have made for easy nursing, but sitting by Barry's bedside James felt it was like being in some sort of reception bay. A single room would have had privacy (and loneliness probably); the old-fashioned ward with twenty or thirty beds was impersonal but it had the advantage of bringing home that the patients were all brothers (or sisters) under the skin, there was a camaraderie between them. Of course this was a short stay place, people brought in from

232

accidents, put to bed until they were either allowed home or transferred to a ward. Barry was going to be amongst the first kind.

There was a constant movement in the corridor, trolleys of dressings, trolleys of drugs, women in striped blouses and navy blue skirts rushing about their mysterious business. Each time James heard approaching steps he looked up hopefully, expecting it would be Claudia. Only two of the four beds were occupied, one by Barry and one by an elderly woman with her wrist in plaster and her teeth in a dish on the bedside cabinet. Both patients were fast asleep.

A senior nurse had said that it was anticipated Barry would be well enough to go home tomorrow. Home! Would he accept the rectory any better now than he had a few weeks ago? But he would have no choice, Mum couldn't take him back to Russets, probably she'd not even go back there herself. James had been called to roadside accidents on the Oxford road, he remembered watching as a victim was cut free. This time the victim had been Dad, crushed metal cut so that he could be lifted to the stretcher. The staff had told James nothing except that his father was in the operating theatre and that the police were bringing Mrs Carlyle. Police bringing Mrs Carlyle – Mum this very minute in a police car. James closed his eyes, in the silence of the hospital room he tried to pray. Thy will be done ... that's what he should beg. Where was his faith that he couldn't lay his burden on his God, and then trust. Fear ought to have no place. I can't do it, I can't let go. It's not just for myself, this is Dad I'm pleading for, and for Mum. Surely it can't be Your will to shatter their lives. How can I preach to other people about faith and trust yet when I'm tested always I fail. Help me. I beg, don't punish my weakness by hurting them. Nor Harvey. If this is Your way to bring Barry home, then help us to come close. Even now I can't say it – Thy will not mine ...

He hadn't heard her come in, but he felt an arm around his shoulder.

'Mum!'

'He looks peaceful, asleep there. They say he wasn't hurt, only frightened, shocked.'

'You mean Dad?' For one mindless moment joy swept over him.

Claudia shook her head.

'He's in the operating theatre still. His right leg is badly hurt, I don't know more than that. Harvey's left hand is a mess, the small bones – not his fingers, the bones in his hand – were broken, he was very cut. He's plastered and they're giving him blood. We can see him later. But Teddy—' She'd given her bulletin in an even voice, but now James heard her fright, '–they didn't tell me much. Have to wait till he comes out of the theatre.'

233

'We'll talk to the surgeon, Mum.'

'James, he's going to be well. I'm imagining things are worse than they are because I had to come in a police car . . .' She gripped his hand. 'James, keep praying. The medical people will do their part, but we've got to do ours. He's going to be well, I know he is. We've got to believe.'

James was humbled by her trust. Only Claudia knew that knitted into that trust was superstition, if she let herself harbour the thought of lasting damage or – no, don't give it space to get into your mind – then that would be tempting fate.

'Have this chair, Mum, I'll get another. We'll wait together until they tell us you can see Dad.'

'First I must go and see Lucinda.'

'Lucinda? Who's Lucinda?'

'Lucinda Leighton, the American pianist. She and Harvey make music together. Teddy was bringing them back to London – something about Harvey's car breaking down.' She looked at him help-lessly. Always so full of energy, this evening she looked older than her years, vulnerable. 'How long will Teddy be I wonder?'

She went off to search in the other square four-bedders. Lucinda was in an identical space off the far end of the corridor, but she wasn't alone, she was talking to a young woman who was writing in a notebook. The police? Surely they weren't pressing for details of the accident already?

'Mrs Carlyle, have you heard anything? Have you heard if Harvey is badly hurt?'

'He's out of the theatre, but it's too soon to see him.'

The girl with the notebook looked from one to the other, then rose to the occasion with aplomb.

'Until he's properly come round we shan't know Harvey Carlyle's injuries I imagine? I suppose you were coming back together from a recital?'

'No, actually, we weren't.'

'Who's your friend, Lucinda?' From the notebook and the alert manner Claudia had already decided if not *who* she was, at least what she wanted. Perhaps Lucinda welcomed publicity, but her own in-stinct was to shield Harvey from it.

'She's from the press. But there's really nothing more I can say. The weather was atrocious, cars were going much too fast, not taking a bit of notice of those warnings. The lorry in front braked to avoid some fool in a sports car who overtook on the wrong side then shot out in front of it, then it jack-knifed. There was no way of avoiding it. From what I could see Harvey was thrown against the door, he went out cold, it was a hell of a whack. But a nurse just told me that it's his arm that's hurt, somehow he got it entangled in the windscreen. I think that's what happened, I half remember him sort of reaching his arms forward like you do, but I cracked my head too and I'm hazy. I keep asking about him, but none of them in here seem to know any details. If you can find out anything, promise you'll come back and tell his Mom and me won't you.'

The reporter promised and departed. She didn't come back, perhaps there was nothing more to tell than Lucinda already knew. But she wasted no time in phoning in her news flash. The evening bulletins on radio and television carried the story and by next morning there wasn't a national paper that didn't spare it at least a single column. The newspapers put in more padding than time had allowed on television, they told of how Harvey Carlyle had been travelling back to London with Lucinda Leighton, a fellow pianist, and his father and nephew. Some went further and carried Harvey's picture. He was a young man at the height of an international career, but it was a career to be blighted by the extensive and probably permanent damage sustained to his left hand and wrist. A brief mention that Lucinda Leighton had been concussed. 'All four were taken to hospital but it is anticipated Lucinda Leighton will be fit to return home within twenty-four hours.'

No word of injuries to Barry, which wasn't surprising as after a night of drugged sleep he woke none the worse for the incident; no mention either that Teddy – the unnamed father – had suffered a double fracture to his femur, crushed and splintered patella and compound fracture of the tibia.

At the rectory Jean Machin turned off the nine o'clock news, crept to the foot of the stairs and waited. The rules were that Patsy didn't listen to her radio in bed, but with earphones there was no way of telling what she got up to. And she was an odd child, her tastes were wide, there was no guessing what programme she might be tuned into. Supposing she heard about the accident on the news. The rector hadn't said anything about Barry being in the car.

If Patsy had heard anything she would have come down. Even so, Jean wasn't taking any chances, she crept up stairs and quietly peeped into the bedroom. The room was unnaturally tidy, even her slippers side by side under the chair. Her transistor radio had been put away for the night, the flex for the headphones perfectly coiled around it. With her mouth open, snoring softly, Patsy slept. It was a wonder she didn't wake up though, for in the short time the door was open came the shrill bell of the telephone. Jean shut the door as quietly as speed would allow and hurried down to answer it.

'Brightley Rectory. I'm sorry the rector isn't at home at the moment, may I give him a message when he gets back?'

'Where is he? Is he at the hospital? It's Barry I want to know about.'

'Who am I talking to?' Jean asked, but she was sure what the answer would be.

'This is his wife. I want to know about Barry.'

'I know nothing about Barry. I didn't even know he was in the car with the rector's brother until I heard the news at nine o'clock. But then, how would I know? Barry doesn't live here now.' Jean felt buoyed up, ready to stand her ground against this woman who'd run off and left her children. What right had she to know anything?

'I don't understand. What do you mean, Barry doesn't live there?' Standing in the phone box, seeing the torn directory, the wall covered with graffiti and phone numbers much the same as youthful enthusiasts plastered on the walls of public lavatories, Jenny imagined the familiar rooms of the rectory. Blindfold she could walk around the house, each curve of the banisters, each door handle or window latch recognized. Barry didn't live there! Because of her? Because of what she'd done?

'What hospital have they been taken to? If you don't tell me I shall ask the police, they'll find out for me. I have a right to know.'

'And the boy had a right to a mother. I'm just a paid housekeeper, I've no right to so much as an opinion. But that doesn't stop me having one, nor will it stop me telling you what I think of a woman who breaks a child's life like you have his. It's no use your asking me whether he was hurt in the accident, if I hadn't just heard it on the news I'd not have known he was in the car. I suppose the rector didn't want to frighten Patsy. The children have had suffering enough.'

'Just tell me the hospital, I'll find out from them.'

'When I'm ready I'll tell you, but . . .' a pause while Jenny fed another coin into the meter, '. . . but first you put yourself in that child's place. Always as polite and good as gold to me, yet all the time he must have been saving his money to get away. He went down to the New Forest, the rector didn't force him to come back, but it fair broke him up that the poor lad wouldn't stay here. My guess would be that Patsy would have been much the same if her dad had run out on them. As if he would!'

'Where is he? That's all I need from you, just an address.'

'I've said what had to be said. Said more than I would face to face I expect, but that's a treat I can do without! One more thing, it's not

236

from the rector I've heard about you and your fancy man, it's from the parish. They think the world of the rector in the village, you don't need me to tell you that, those who go to church and those who don't as well. There's no forgiveness in their hearts for anyone who could treat him like you did.'

'Where's Barry?'

This time Jean told her. Another second and they'd rung off.

Jean backed away from the phone, suddenly weak and trembling, glad to sit on the foot of the stairs. Where had she found the courage to speak to the children's mother like that? She'd never thought she'd had it in her! She'd heard her own voice, shrill and commanding, she'd been intoxicated by the sound. Now, in the silence, she seemed to have turned to cotton-wool. She didn't want to take back a single word of it – but if the phone were to ring now, she couldn't do it again.

'Come on Henry, you have your run while I put the bottles out.' She forced herself to her feet. There was no better pick-me-up than routine.

Henry's tail twitched, just enough to let her know he'd heard her. There was a vast difference between the word 'run' and the word 'walk'. 'Walk' would have brought forth sneezes of glee and he would have gone straight to his lead. 'Run' meant a quick sniff and any urgent call of nature down in the long grass by the paddock. Henry was a dog of habit.

Opposite the dreary telephone kiosk was a taxi rank and behind it the drivers' base which would be open until the early hours. Crossing the cheerless street Jenny approached a driver to enquire how much it would cost her to be driven to the hospital where Barry was.

'Now? Tonight?'

'Yes. I know it's a bad night, but it can't be much more than twenty miles.'

'Twenty miles on a Saturday night's going to cost you somewhere around £30, maybe nearer £35. No good guessing how far it is, depends what comes up on the meter, lady.'

'Look, I've not got that much on me. Let me see—' Under the light of a street lamp she counted her money. 'Twenty-two, twenty-three, a bit of loose change. It's urgent. Won't you trust me to pay you later?'

''Tisn't that I wouldn't help, lady. But I got a living to get the same as everyone else. Any road, rules are rules, I have to be paid on the dot.' Then turning in relief to a young man with an ring hanging on his ear and a girl hanging on his arm. 'Taxi, sir?'

'Thanks, mate.'

237

Jenny was left alone on the damp pavement. There was nothing for it but to go back into the phone box and ask directory enquiries for the hospital number.

The switchboard operator told her with an air of authority that she needed Accident and Casualty. The line was engaged, he'd connect her as soon as it was free. Seconds seemed liked minutes, she had her pile of change in front of her, ready to keep the meter fed. Come on . . . come on . . .

At last a brisk female voice told her she was through to the Accident and Emergency Department.

'I want to know how Barry Carlyle is. He was brought in after a road accident.'

'Who is it enquiring?' The voice held no encouragement, she heard it as aimed at making her an outsider.

'Jennifer Carlyle, Barry's mother.'

'He's being kept in overnight, but once the doctor has seen him in the morning he'll probably be allowed home.'

'But how is he?'

'He was only detained for shock.'

'Is he frightened? Is anyone with him?'

'His father is there – and his grandmother I think the lady is. But he's sound asleep and quite comfortable.'

'When he wakes can you tell him I phoned. You will, won't you? Say I send him my love.'

'Certainly. But I think he's more likely to sleep soundly all through the night.'

Another minute and, her hands thrust deep into the pockets of her shapeless gabardene raincoat, Jenny was back in the night air. Perhaps the nurse would remember, but more likely she would have gone off duty when Barry woke and he'd never know.

When first she'd talked to the housekeeper she'd had only one thing on her mind: she must get to Barry. Now though she remembered the woman's words, her accusation that everything was *her* fault, *she* had taken away the children's natural right to security. Now he was lying in a hospital bed, her darling Barry, she could picture him so clearly, asleep and looking as she'd seen him thousands of times. But that had been his own bed, that had been his secure world. Now on one side of his bed was Claudia and on the other James. James . . . she stopped walking . . . in that moment she believed she wished she could have stopped living.

Chapter 16

James had phone calls to make too. The first, irrespective of the fact that it was nearly ten at night, an hour he knew would be considered indecently late, was to long-retired Canon Metcalf, kindly, doddering, hampered by arthritis but with a hale and hearty, quick-witted wife. Fortunately it was his wife, Dorothea, who answered the call. In fact the canon's nightly timetable never varied: watch the nine o'clock news, followed by the weather forecast, then switch off the set and take the small measure of neat malt whisky Dorothea poured for him. The ritual took until nine-fifty, when unfailingly he kissed her goodnight and started slowly up the stairs. It was then that she settled down for an hour's read with a gin and tonic certain that after nine o'clock none of their friends would disturb them.

This evening the news had been most upsetting. They knew that Harvey Carlyle, the one who'd been involved in this motorway accident, was brother of the rector of Brightley, some eight miles from where they'd settled in retirement. Poor man, as if he hadn't had troubles enough with that wife of his, without a tragedy like this hitting the family. They heard, of course, that there had been a nephew in the car, but since the incident had occurred miles from Brightley they assumed it must be some other member of the family.

A quick frown was her reaction to the telephone bell.

'Hello, Dorothea Metcalf here,' were her first words, only the manner she spoke them conveying the message 'What in the world do you want at this time of night!'

'Mrs Metcalf, forgive me for disturbing you at this hour,' James understood the words and the unspoken message, 'this is James Carlyle speaking.'

'Reverend Carlyle, we heard the dreadful news. My dear, I am so sorry. Is it about that that you want to speak to my husband?'

'I fear it is.'

'Will I do? The canon's already retired for the night. If I must, I'll fetch him down. We have no phone in the bedroom and the stairs are such a trial to him. Try me, why don't you. I can always carry a message.'

So James tried her. He explained that Barry was being detained overnight in hospital, he told her there would be communicants at St Lukes's for the nine-thirty service the next morning. And just as he had hoped, she promised that she would drive the canon to Brightley, James could leave it in her hands. Then she enquired after his brother and his father.

'What a dreadful shock, and for the poor child too. You may rest assured that they will be remembered in your church tomorrow. Now you get back to your son – and I'll go up to tell Cuthbert that he's on parade in the morning.'

For Teddy and Harvey there was a gap in their understanding, memories of the day had as many holes as a colander. Harvey had regained consciousness before he reached the hospital; after that, sedation had held him distant from pain and treatment alike, not even the horror of the accident got through the protective clouds he floated in. As for Teddy, he had arrived at the hospital unconscious, had wavered near enough to the brink of reason to know he was in unfamiliar surroundings, that he was the centre of action and of such seering agony that he had pulled back into the realms of shadowland (in truth a position induced by injection). Then had come the x-rays, and a brief spell when he'd known he was lying on a trolley gazing up at the high white ceiling of a long corridor. He accepted just as he would have accepted a ghastly and impossible dream. He'd known he was being moved, going through swing doors. In a brief moment of clarity he'd wanted to say 'Tell Claudia', he'd believed he'd opened his mouth to speak but he couldn't form the words, there had been no sound. Must tell them, Claudia, must tell Claudia ... his mouth wouldn't move ... a man in a dark green coat, wearing a mask across his mouth and with his hair covered with a tight green hat was bending over him, talking to him. What was he saying? ... what was he ...? wha ...? Everything was lost on him as they pushed the trolley into the theatre and lifted him on to the operating table.

A hospital never sleeps, but in the four-bedded oversized cubicles that prevailed in every department the lights were dimmed, in the corridors the daytime bustle of staff was replaced by only the occasional muffled tramp of rubber-soled shoes.

Both Harvey and Teddy were orthopaedic cases and, probably

more by luck than design, they were put in two of the four beds in one of the Orthopaedic Surgical cubicles. Once Claudia was told that Teddy had been brought out of the recovery room she left Barry sleeping soundly, James at his side trying valiantly to keep awake.

In the Orthopaedic Ward the night nurse told her, 'He'll sleep for hours. Of course you can see him – and your son, he's the bed opposite – but both of them will sleep. In a minute I'll take you along to a room where you can rest. I'll see you're woken if there's any change.'

'Can't I stay here? Please. I couldn't possible rest.'

'You really ought to.'

'Please. I'll rest in the chair. Let me stay. I'll be quiet.'

They let her stay. How much of the night she was awake and how much she slept she would never know. The hours became one long vigil, a nightmare of fears that pushed their way into her imagination no matter how hard she fought them.

She moved her chair close to Teddy's bed, holding his hand in hers; she forced her eyes to stay open, each time her vision blurred and she felt herself slipping away she blinked hard and opened her lids wide. She had no power over her rambling mind.

Teddy . . . often enough she'd seen him asleep, but tonight he looked different. They told her he had come out of the anaesthetic, but this wasn't a natural sleep. His face was like parchment, his breathing shallow. Teddy . . . come back to me Teddy . . . if only you'd move, turn over, sigh, snore, just to show you're sleeping. I'm so frightened . . . no, I mustn't say that, I've got to trust, please, please, help me to trust, bring him back to me . . . all the things we've worried and pulled different ways about . . . Teddy, they've told me about Harvey, Harvey who loves music more than he even loves Erica, every bone in the back of his hand was broken, and his wrist . . . perhaps he'll play again but it can never be the same. Imagine if Harvey can't play . . . there's nothing we can do to ease it for him, he has to carry his own cross. All of them do. Jenny and James . . . Harvey and Erica – and now there's his Luce, how will you feel when you realize what's happened? All our worrying can't smooth their paths, all we can do is be there for them. James and Jenny, Harvey and Erica, Melly not wanting her baby, Trevor, doting, dull Trevor – but that can't be how Melly sees him. They all have to shape their own lives – we gave them the rough diamond, we can't cut it for them, joy, sorrow, love, pain, they have to bear all those things for themselves just like we have. But you and me . . . I couldn't be wholly *me* if you weren't here . . . same as you, you're not properly *you* without me. If only you'd wake up, if only I could say all these things to you. Tonight I can understand so clearly.

241

Teddy, Teddy, if only you'd open your eyes, just for a second, just to see I'm here. The surgeon wouldn't commit himself – perhaps they never do. Saved the leg . . . too early to predict extent of recovery . . . words, just words. Darling, I'll help you, if you can't walk any more I'll push you. Nothing's ever going to be like it was, but even if they can't ever make your leg right, what's one leg? You're still *you*.

Her thoughts raced away with her. Reaction to shock, perhaps that's what it was, combined with relief that even though Teddy looked so unnaturally still and pale yet each time the nurse came to check him she was satisfied. Tonight Claudia had caught a fleeting glimpse of truth, she wanted to share it with Teddy. She leant forward, drooped forward, rested her head next to his on the pillow. She rubbed her cheek against his. And as if he knew, he grunted softly. In relief and thankfulness she gave up the fight to keep her eyes open.

That's how they were when the nurse did her round.

'I'm sorry, son. But there's nothing else for it.' James looked earnestly at Barry. It was the following morning. All night the boy had slept, some of it so too had James, sitting in the far-from-easy chair by the side of the bed. The nurse had brought him the message that Jenny had phoned. Looking at the boy who'd run away from living without his mother, imagining Jenny whose night must be being spent in the arms of Ken Sheldrake, reliving the past, shying away from the future, so the hours had ticked slowly by.

'You're *sorry*? You mean you liked it better when I was with Gran and Grandad?'

James got stiffly up and moved to sit on the edge of the bed, then took Barry's hand.

'I hated it, Barry. I want you at home.' He was desperately tired. Ashamed of his weakness, he could feel his face working, he couldn't hold it steady. 'I want you at home – I want your mother at home.' With a superhuman effort he controlled his voice, kept it low so that what he said belonged just to the two of them in this semi-public place.

'Mum?' Just to hear his father talking about her sparked new hope. 'Have you heard something about Mum?'

'It's my fault. My fault she went, my fault she doesn't try to see you. Barry, she heard about the accident—'

'How could she? You mean you knew where she was? You told her?'

'She heard it on the news I expect. The nurse said it was on at nine o'clock. Harvey is news. And he was quite badly hurt.'

'I remember. Harvey and Grandad. I remember. What's happened to Grandad. The car was squashed, Grandad was—'

'They were hurt, but they are going to be all right. Your mother must have heard about the accident on the news. She phoned the hospital, the nurse told me. She sent you her love.'

'But she didn't come.' The spark had died. 'Just want her to come home, Dad.'

There was no hope in his voice, there was no hope in James's face. Their action was so natural, did James raise him from the pillow and pull him into his arms, or did Barry sit up and drag his father towards him? Neither of them knew, and what did it matter?

Morning found Teddy awake, propped up and determined that he had nothing to do now but get better. By his side Claudia looked at him with something akin to worship in her relief.

This time yesterday she had been in Bournemouth with Tricia Caldecott, it seemed a lifetime ago instead of twenty-four hours. After her night of vigilance, coupled with finally sleeping in such an unnatural position, she ached in every joint, and yet she felt more alive than she had for years, scales had fallen from her vision. Was it the same for Teddy? In a moment of pure joy, she was sure it was. As their years had gone on how much had Teddy come into her awareness? Or she into his? Hardly at all. There had been times, many many times when they had been conscious of happiness in their unity, but that had only cemented their acceptance of each other. He'd become so much part of her life, her cares had been his cares, his loves and loyalties hers. 'Teddy and Claudia', 'Mum and Dad', 'Grandad and Gran', two halves that made one whole. Wasn't it that that had driven her to Adrian?

Sitting by Teddy's bedside, watching his still form, she had been shaken by paralysing fear. In a moment the accident had happened, in a moment their lives had been altered. Nothing should ever be taken for granted. If Teddy weren't here there would be no purpose in anything. They both cared about the family, they both worried about them, loved them. But the family weren't their purpose for living, they were the background to it.

By morning he was awake, drugged with pain-killers, his suntan giving his unnaturally parchment complexion an unhealthy, yellowish hue. But his spirit was untouched. Her solemn introspection gave way to joy that some might see as ill placed. But she knew he understood. She smiled to herself. She'd never had to spell things out to Teddy. He was watching her now, his eyes shining with determination. It was crazy, she told herself, a woman of her age having the bubbly feeling

243

of a teenager in love for the first time! She smiled at him, that smile that crinkled around her eyes before it reached her mouth. In answer he half closed his eyes, pursed his lips so slightly that she could almost believe she'd imagined it. Yet she knew she hadn't. Without speaking, both of them laughed. This was *their* world. Around them were their family, their dear family. But what she and Teddy had was safe and firm, as certain as the sunshine on a clear day bringing life and growth to the earth. Supposing the outcome of the accident had been different, supposing – no, don't think about it. Be grateful, be thankful, but don't imagine the 'might have been'. She slipped her hand into his and felt his fingers tighten.

Harvey was only yards away, his plastered arm and hand lying outside the bed covers. He too had slept all night, a sleep induced by some magic tablet she was sure, for how else could he escape his fears for the future? Later he would have to face the probability that in those few seconds, the accident had changed the course of his life. Lucinda was with him, sitting on the edge of his bed wearing a hospital wrap over a hospital nightgown. She must know, but Claudia was sure her uppermost emotion was thankfulness as she talked to him about physiotherapy, talked in a positive voice.

Before setting off for Brightley, James and Barry came to say good-bye. James had already been in earlier, while Barry was having a final check before being discharged. He'd told them that last night he'd spoken to Melly, persuaded her not to visit until today. He'd phoned Russets too, sure that Gwen wouldn't have gone home until she'd heard. Claudia was ashamed. How could she have forgotten dear, faithful Gwen waiting by the telephone. But last night her mind had been on another plane.

Now James's eyes went to Harvey and Lucinda, while in his mind he saw a third – Erica, whose love for Harvey had in it an element of hero-worship. Harvey couldn't do this to her . . . could he? At one time James would have been so sure he couldn't; now, he was sure of nothing.

'Twitch and Frisk are at Grandad's,' Barry reminded his father as the car sped northward. The previous day's heavy rain had gone, re-turning them to the dull, dreary weather Harvey and Lucinda had 'enjoyed' in Dorset.

'Gwen will see to them.'

They drove in silence for some miles. This was what Barry had dreaded, that his father would collect him and make him go home. Yet, suddenly he wasn't frightened of what it would be like there. He knew it would be beastly, he'd still hate kind Miss Machin. But he

244

would bear it because he knew now that his father hated it too. He'd believed that no-one cared about his mother, but that wasn't true. His father was miserable without her, just like he was.

They'd been travelling about twenty minutes when James drew into a lay-by and took his diary from his pocket to check something.

'It won't take us a minute,' he said, 'it's only a bit out of our way. There's somewhere I have to call on the way home.'

Barry felt resentful. Even today, when they were sharing being sad about Mum, Dad has to have things to do. It must be something for church, he'd only go out of his way for silly old St Luke. Where were they going? The sign said 'Reading'. That was miles from Brightley. Probably he was going to collect something for the church, new books, or a new altar cloth, or – goodness knows, something his Lot had asked him to pick up.

They came to the edge of town and turned into a road that looked as though it had fallen on hard times, the once trim semi-detached Victorian houses wearing an air of neglect. Some had brightly coloured paintwork; most had lost their railings so that cars could be parked in the small front gardens. Two women were gossiping, one out in her slippers, the other with her hair in rollers, while further along a dog finished off what was left of someone's discarded takeaway supper. There were lots of cars parked by the kerb, one was jacked up with jean-clad legs sticking out from underneath. Barry couldn't see what anyone here could have to do with St Luke.

James just about managed to park between two cars, one of them with its radio blaring.

'Wait in the car. I don't expect I shall be many minutes,' he said as he got out, then crossed the road and walked to a house a bit further along without waiting for a reply. Barry watched. Like the others, it was a scruffy house, even from this distance Barry could see that and the man who opened the door a few inches to James's knock was in keeping with everything else, a bent figure of indeterminable age with a cigarette dangling from his bottom lip. They said something, then – what was Dad doing, he'd pushed the door open and stepped right past the old man even though he hadn't been invited inside? A long few seconds, then the front door closed. The programme on the nearby car radio changed.

Barry began to feel uneasy, gripped by a new fear. A place like this couldn't have anything to do with the church or with Brightley. Over the last few months so much had changed that he was prepared for anything, even that his father had some lady here. Was that the sort of thing grown up people did? It happened all the time on television . . . yes, but Dad . . .? He got more and more uneasy as the minutes went by.

245

At last the front door opened and James appeared carrying a large, zip holdall, a familiar looking holdall. And then he saw her!

Fortunately no cars were coming, for Barry looked neither to right nor left, he didn't even stop to shut the door as he dashed across the road and along the pavement to hurl himself into Jenny's arms.

A crushed hand and a broken wrist, once plastered, didn't merit a hospital bed. The only reason Harvey was kept in was his consistently high temperature. Teddy's temperature was stable, even in the first few hours it was clear he meant to overcome what he called 'a few broken bones'. Even so, he had had a serious operation on his knee and there was no chance of his being discharged until he had learnt to manage stairs on his crutches. Claudia found accommodation in a nearby guest house.

On the Sunday afternoon Melly and Trevor came. Her night had been little better than Claudia's and the sleepless hours had left their mark. Trevor fussed over her like a mother hen. In the past his attitude had irritated Claudia, she had wondered how Melly could stand it. But the lesson of her hours of vigil were still clear, she viewed the couple from a little further back. And she found she liked what she saw.

On Monday morning Harvey was alone in the day room. When the doctor did his round he anticipated being told he could go home. Home? Lucinda would be here soon, she'd wait for him to get his discharge and then they'd go to her flat. Erica's letter had been posted on Friday, three days ago. It might even reach her this morning. His arm ached, the plaster was heavy even though he rested it in a sling. What was he going to do? What sort of a future was he loading on to Luce? If he were half a man he'd tell her he'd changed his mind. The thought had been niggling at him, a series of pictures chasing across his imagination: Luce with all the promise of her career ahead of her, Luce who'd loved him for his music before she'd even known him as a man. Could he do it to her? But what if he didn't, what if he put on a show of realizing he'd made a mistake, said that if they couldn't share their music they hadn't enough to hold them in a lasting relationship?

I can't do it, yet I should. That was one voice in him, only to be answered by another even more certain: if I said that to her she'd not believe me, she wouldn't listen, she'd know it couldn't be true. If we had nothing better than that cottage to live in it wouldn't matter to her or to me either. I never knew there could be such happiness as we had – six days in a ramshackle cottage, yet it encompassed everything. We had no music. Ah, but we did. We made no music, but it was there in our minds, it was there in our heads, it was there in our conversation.

Sitting in one of the wooden-armed upright chairs that were set around the walls of the day room he closed his eyes. He wished he were a child again, he could have cried and been comforted. What was he going to do? The rug had been pulled from under his feet, the future had had a known shape, a tall mountain for him to climb. He could still see the mountain but he'd been spun around and set facing another direction – towards what?

'I don't know what to do . . .' He whispered to the empty room.

Footsteps. Someone was coming, the clip-clop of high heels didn't belong to staff. Expectantly he looked towards the door, his mind cleared of everything but hope that Luce had arrived.

'Harvey, darling Harvey, I came right away just as soon as I read about it.' Erica! Slim, lithe, she was across the room in a few quick steps and on her knees by his side. 'Say you're pleased. Were you waiting for me? You must have known I'd get the first plane out.'

'How did you know? When did you leave home?'

'I knew from the papers. Saturday evening there was a picture of us, both of us, on the front page. You're famous, darling, I guess I got slipped into American papers because I'm one of their own. What happened to you must have been reported all over. Your poor hand!' Kneeling by his side she touched her lips gently against the fingers that protruded from his plaster.

'Don't Erica.'

'Honey, did I hurt you?'

'No. It's not that.' Then in a feeble effort at joking: 'You don't need to kneel before me, you're allowed on your feet.'

'Let me kneel. I'm sort of full to overflowing with loving you, with anger that this could have happened to you. I read an article on the plane coming over, written by some high-up orthopaedic specialist. Oh Harvey, I know I used to get fed up, tell you that the piano was worse than a mistress, but I'd give anything for this not to have happened. Why couldn't it have been me instead?'

'You mustn't say that, Erica.' No, you mustn't. It's hard enough to hurt you without that. 'We have to take what's dished out. Anyway, if I had half the guts that Dad's got I'd not let myself be defeated, I wouldn't even consider that I may never be the same as I was.'

'Teddy? I thought you were coming back from a concert with the American girl, Lucinda someone. That's what the paper said. Teddy was hurt?'

'Yes. Much worse than I was. One leg in a hell of a mess, they had to cut him out of the car. But he's already learning to use crutches, you can't keep Dad down.'

'But you can't compare his leg with your hand. As long as his bone knits up or gets pinned or whatever they do, and as long as it isn't too painful, he can live with a limp if he has to. But what will you do if – if—? Harvey, say you're glad to have me home. I'll look after you darling,' she smiled her lovely smile, her eyes just as adoring as they had been in the early days, then she rested her head on his knee, her arms round his waste.

A movement in the open doorway – and there was Lucinda. She must have heard what Erica was saying, she took in the scene at a glance.

'Tell me you're glad, Harvey,' Erica repeated, 'I've been missing you so much. But all that's over. Things will be different now.'

'Erica, I want to talk to you.' His eyes sought Lucinda's.

Silently she held up her hand, gave him a warning shake of her head.

'Hi!' Her greeting included them both. 'Am I barging in where I'm not needed? I didn't know Harvey was expecting you back in time to take him home.'

The smile Erica turned on Lucinda was aimed to draw them together as fellow Americans, as two young women caught up in a hospital environment that was unfamiliar to them, and most as two people both wanting to help Harvey. There was no hint of jealousy, why should there be, Erica's only rival had been his piano.

'Luce, I'm glad you've come. I must talk to Erica, we must all talk. She left before my letter came—'

From one to the other Erica looked. Something was wrong, she'd known that from the first moment but she'd thought it was because Harvey was frightened to look ahead. She'd thought that she could make it easier for him. Now, suddenly the fear was all hers.

'What letter?'

If anything was designed to raise Harvey's temperature it must be this! As he started to explain, Lucinda backed quietly out of the room. Almost word for word he repeated to Erica what he'd written. Still she knelt, he couldn't bear to see the stricken look on her face.

'I'm sorry, I'm desperately sorry. I'm not right for you any more than you are for me. We can't build our lives on anything but honesty, Erica. You'll find someone else, someone who cares about the same things as you—'

'You can't cast me off like an old shirt! What have I ever done but trail around fitting my life around yours? I shouldn't have gone off with Sara,' she was crying now, her voice getting louder, 'if I'd been here for you you wouldn't have wanted some other woman in your bed. You'd have played the piano with her – and I wouldn't have minded – but the rest was mine. Harvey, I'm home now. If you want to share your music with her – if you get well enough to be able to – then I'll not mind, honestly I'll accept. The rest was always mine, and so it will be again. You never chased after other women, I knew you didn't, and I knew why. What we had was too good.' Kneeling up straight she shook his shoulders, only realizing what she did when he cried out in pain.

'I'm sorry. Honestly Erica I never meant it to happen. However badly you think of me, it can't be bad enough. But I can't help myself, If you won't agree to a divorce, then Luce and I will live together. I don't care one way or the other.'

'Go to hell with her for all I care,' she gulped. Her mascara was smeared on her cheek, her silky blonde hair was ruffled. He was moved with pity and affection for her. 'And what about when you can't play any more? You and your precious Lucinda fancy you have this great love because you share your music. Take that away and what have you? If she goes on with her career you'll grow resentful.'

'Hush, Erica. That's not true.'

'Of course it's true, bloody, bloody, true.' She needed to scream it at him. 'And if she gives it up because of you, she'll end up hating you for it. But it wouldn't be like that with me. I wouldn't care if you never touched a piano again. I'll always love you. I'll take care of you.'

Neither of them had heard the whispering between Lucinda and a nurse in the corridor. Up to that point the nurse had been persuaded not to put an end to an interview that Harvey was in no state for. Now, though, she came into the room with professional calm.

'Come along now, Mrs Carlyle, he's doing very nicely. The doctor is starting his round Mr Carlyle, if your wife likes to wait in here we'll see what he says about letting you out today. You go back to the ward and be ready for him.'

For the waiting patients the morning round seemed interminably long. But at last Harvey's turn came, the curtains were drawn around his bed. Until an hour ago his mind had been focused on the moment of release, driving back to Maidenhead with Luce, driving towards a new life. But now he didn't look beyond the moment. He had no intention of living with Erica, but was there truth in what she said about Lucinda? Would he impede her career? Would she grow resentful? Would it sour their love?

Despite the emotional scene – or perhaps the nurse had told the doctor and he had made allowances – Harvey was given his

249

discharge. Then on to Teddy where the doctor's visit was brief this morning, no more than a short friendly chat between two men of the same fraternity.

'I'm off Dad.' With a nurse's help and the sleeve cut out of his shirt Harvey had been made ready for the outside world. 'I'll be in to see you in a day or so, keep the good work going with the crutches.' He couldn't bring himself to say Erica had come, that she was waiting for him in the day room. But he wouldn't go home with her, he wouldn't.

In the day room Lucinda was waiting alone.

James's letter was brief, he didn't elaborate on the bare fact:

> I hope you'll be as happy and as thankful as I am when you hear that Jenny is home with us. On the way from the hospital I called at the address I'd been given. If you had any doubts, then one look at Barry's face when he saw would have dispelled them. And me? The deeper the troughs, the higher the peaks. Over these past months you will never know how deep the troughs have been.

'I just hope he's done the right thing in bringing her home,' Teddy said.

'Of course he has. She must have found the wonderful lover had feet of clay. That could be it – he was better in bed than standing on them!' She chuckled, so pleased with the news that she could have found a silver lining in the blackest of clouds.

Teddy was less certain.

'You can laugh, but you didn't read what she wrote to James. You don't change your mind about something so fundamental. He's too trusting, too keen to believe in her.'

Could he be right? By the end of the day, Claudia's initial relief was wavering. She decided that the next day, instead of spending most of it with Teddy as she had, she'd go to Brightley, walk in on them unexpectedly. With no car the trip needed organizing: a train to Reading, then another to Oxford, then a taxi. She wanted to beg 'Please make Teddy be wrong, please make her have discovered it's always been just James she wants.' But something held her back. Perhaps it was that she felt she was pushing their luck, she was frightened to ask it and not have her petition heard. So, giving a loophole and yet still leading to ultimate good, as the taxi turned into Brightley Lane, she reworded her request. 'James has been so miserable, they've all been miserable. Please make all that be over now, don't take his new happiness away from him.' And then, slipping it in

250

for good measure, 'She can't be all bad, she really did love James, for ages and ages she wanted only James. I really can't understand how he could have been so sexually disinterested, it isn't as if Teddy and I brought him up any differently from the others. There's nothing You can't do if You think it's right, perhaps knowing she was with another man might have woken Jamie up. Or if it hadn't, perhaps you'll make him look back at these months she's been with Ken Sheldrake and believe he's been riven with desire for what he's lost. That might be all it takes to stir him up. Please help him, if he thinks what he's doing is good in Your sight, then he might settle into enjoying himself.'

Jenny saw her get out of the taxi and went out to meet her. Claudia's first thought – stamped on almost as it formed – was that three months with a lover had done nothing for her appearance. In her unbecomingly shapeless skirt and sloppy jumper she looked the same at the end of her romantic adventure as she had at the beginning.

'Jenny, Teddy heard from James yesterday. Letters only tell one half, I wanted to see for myself that you were home and happy.' As Claudia spoke she kissed her errant daughter-in-law as warmly as she always had.

'I think so, Mum. I hope so. What did James tell you?'

'That you were back, that the despair of the last months was over. I don't remember the words, but there was no doubt about his joy and thankfulness. He said he went to the address the solicitor had given him. And you chose him, Jenny. You left Kenneth Sheldrake to come home with James and Barry.'

'Is that what he said?'

Claudia tried to remember so that she could answer honestly, but the truth was that that's what she'd believed him to mean.

'It wasn't like that,' Jenny told her. 'Whether I would have come back if it had been like you think, I've no idea. For the sake of the children, particularly when James told me about Barry running away, I think I probably would. But in truth Ken and I were only together a week or two. With Ken I certainly wouldn't have been living in the sort of dump where James found me. For a while I couldn't get a proper job, I worked two hours each morning preparing vegetables at a hotel.'

'You did! But Jenny that's not the sort of work for *you*. With your degree whatever were you doing preparing vegetables?'

'Earning enough money to pay for my tatty room and feed myself. But I'd just got a proper job, I was to have started next Monday, a job that would have given me some sort of independence, a promising

251

future, a chance to get somewhere better to live so that I could have had the children sometimes. But even if I'd been stuck with the vegetables and that foul place to live, I wouldn't have come back because living here is a meal ticket. Leaving the children was the hardest thing I ever did, but I couldn't help myself.'

'Jenny, you don't have to explain yourself to me, dear. You realized your mistake, and thank goodness the whole thing is over. Barry must be in seventh heaven. Poor little love, if you could have seen him you would have sunk your pride and come back long ago.'

'I'm sure you're right. When I went I was seething with pent-up emotion. I contacted a solicitor so that James could start divorce proceedings. Purposely I told him where I was and every day I looked for a letter from the children.'

'Only the children?'

'Let's talk about something else. Tell me about Dad.'

Claudia knew she'd been shown the 'Keep Out' sign.

When, a few minutes later, James came home, any uneasiness she might have harboured vanished. It was as if the last months hadn't happened, he was walking on air as he had been on the afternoon of Brightley's Aid Day, just hours before his world crashed.

The school had accepted Barry's stay with his grandparents was to be temporary, so he'd slipped back into his former place without any problem. It was left for Claudia and Teddy to sort things out at their end.

Before the school bus was due back to Brightley, Claudia was on her way to report to Teddy on what she had found. She wouldn't paint a rosier picture than the truth, after all there was so much to be thankful about.

'It's all over with Ken Sheldrake, it lasted hardly any time at all.'

'Did he walk out on her?' Teddy wanted to know.

'I've no idea. It might have been she wanted independence. She told me this afternoon that he'd gone abroad, he has a place in Cyprus.'

'And what when he comes back? How will James stand then?'

'She won't leave the family, I'd stake everything on that. But James? He told me quite happily that they'd agreed she should have her own room. Her idea or his, I've no idea, but he doesn't seem in the least put out by it. And Jean Machin is staying, she told me herself that she'd suggested she should find another place, but Jenny had asked her to stay. It seems she is determined to get a job, a proper job, something to work for, something with a future.'

'Humph!' was Teddy's reply and in it Claudia heard criticism and disappointment. 'Ah well, never mind. It's time we stopped imagining we can shoulder all their problems for them, time we thought of ourselves.'

She brushed his lips in a teasing kiss.

'Tomorrow you shall put up with me all day. How's that?'

Ten days later the ambulance took them back down the M3, passed the scene of the accident. They were going home.

Waiting for them was a letter from Mrs Freeman. Like everyone else she had either read about the accident or heard it on the news. Time and again she'd tried to phone Russets but, as luck would have it, always at times when Gwen wasn't there.

They were touched by her concern, so that same evening they spoke to her, Claudia on the kitchen extension and Teddy with the drawing-room telephone on a table pulled near the settee. That way they had a three-way conversation.

It was after she'd been reassured that he was on the mend, and they had every hope Harvey would soon be playing again – something they both knew wasn't going to happen, but they couldn't bring themselves to say so – that they turned to more general chatter.

'As soon as you're feeling up to it, what you need is a nice break down here in the cottage. It'd do you both good. And it'll be some little while before you can be doctoring again I expect?'

'So I'm told, yes.'

'One bit of news, whether good or bad, who can say. Numbers one and two, always been let for holidays for more years than I could say, it seems Mr Drummond, he's the owner you remember, well he's put them up for sale. As I say, it could be good or it could be just the other thing, all depending on the sorts I get for neighbours. I've been the only one living here for so long, except for the summer weekly lets – and except for you folk but you're different, I never did think of you as just holiday folk.'

'Once Teddy's a bit more mobile I'm sure we'll be there. Too late for summer, but autumn can be lovely.' Autumn . . . it wasn't the sights and smells of Moorleigh that sprang into her mind, not even Dartmoor where they'd tramped so many miles, but the New Forest ablaze with the colours of autumn. This year Teddy wouldn't be walking along the familiar tracks, any more than he'd be climbing aboard *Sea Urchin*. She held the smile firmly in place in her voice. 'I've been down in the winter holidays even, when the children were young. Moorleigh is special at any time.'

That might have sown the first seeds in Teddy's mind. But there was something else, something he hadn't even talked to Claudia about yet. The consultant had left them in no doubt that it would be many months before he could hope to return to any sort of work in the practice, even carrying out clinics or in-house surgeries. The work of a country general practitioner was very different from that, he and Teddy both knew it and realized that's why he wouldn't be drawn further. In the first few hours of his being home, buoyed up with the relief that his injuries were nothing compared with what might so easily have been, Teddy could talk about his limitations without having to face up to the full reality. He and Claudia both knew they were playing the ostrich game, but they wanted no shadows to fall on his homecoming.

If it hadn't been that Mrs Freeman had already told them about the end two cottages, the letter he received the following morning would have seemed like an act of Fate. A business letter with the postmark Deremouth.

As you may be aware, I have been asked to handle the sale of Nos. 1 and 2 Victoria Terrace, Moorleigh. My reason for writing to you is to enquire whether you may be interested in allowing me also to negotiate for the sale of No. 3 (Applegarth), which I believe is still in your possession although seldom used. The three properties could convert to make an excellent single dwelling, and with the inclusion of No. 3 I am confident I could find a suitable purchaser with very little difficulty . . .

Teddy read it through, then passed it to Claudia.

'Could we be at a crossroad?'

She too read it. For the last few years they'd half-heartedly talked about selling it now that the family had all gone.

'Devon's much further away from the others,' she pointed out, knowing without being told what he had in his mind. Yet even as she said it she felt an inexplicable flutter of excitement. A new challenge. A crossroad, Teddy had called it. It might have been so different if that lorry had been just a few feet nearer . . . she was frightened even to imagine how it might have been.

'Devon's near enough for them to come when they want to. Time for change, darling, time for a new beginning. What do you say?'

Epilogue

Everything was organized. Douglas Meredith, High Class Baker and Confectioner, Moorleigh, as the writing on the side of his van proclaimed, had been commissioned to make a birthday cake worthy of the occasion. Indoors at Applegath, which now encompassed numbers 1, 2 and 3 Victoria Terrace, was a glory of summer flowers, many of them from the garden which had been transformed from the patches of weedy grass of holiday cottages.

It was 14 July, Claudia's sixtieth birthday. Today the family were all expected.

In the kitchen, a kitchen that had been created as part of the conversion, a kitchen which Jenny had described as 'enough to make your eyes water with envy', Mr Meredith's daughter Tamsin was already busy preparing the feast. A young woman with dreams, ambitions and talent to match, she had opened a catering business in Deremouth and was already building a reputation.

'Still arranging flowers?' Teddy watched Claudia with amused affection. 'Where in the world are you going to find room for this lot?'

'They're for Harvey and Lucinda. Then that's the last. Is my hair all right?'

'As it's your birthday I'll pay you all the compliments you need. You look lovely.'

'You're a fat lot of help,' she laughed. 'I mean, do you like it done this way?'

'Is it different? It always looks pretty, always has.'

Their eyes were drawn to the portrait, still hanging in the place of honour in the drawing room. In the beginning she had hated to see it there, it had seemed to lay bare her very soul, expose to the world the flame Adrian had stirred – it was her Dorian Gray. Now, though, it has lost its power to disturb her. It belonged to her, to her and to Teddy.

'Hark, there's a car. Is it one of them? Yes, look Teddy, it's Melly.' From the back of the car an excited face peered out. Then, seeing Claudia, Edwina started to wave, a wave full of pent-up excitement.

Claudia ran out to meet them, Teddy following, every bit as eager as she was but impeded by a stiff leg that wouldn't move as quickly as he wanted. Everyone talked at once, but loudest of all was Edwina.

'We've come!' She shrieked as she unstrapped herself and jumped out of the car. 'Happy birthday. We've come. We've come for your party.' A few more months and she'd be five, they saw her two or three times a year, yet anyone watching her would think they were part of her daily life. 'We've got a present for you Gran. Mum paint—'

'Hush, Ed, it's a surprise.' Trevor reached for her hand, somehow taking any sting out of his quick warning.

'It's jolly nice.' Edwina jumped up and down, not knowing how to express how nice when she wasn't allowed to say what it was. 'You're going to like it Gran. Can I give it to her Mum?'

Only three of them had arrived, but already the house was alive with excited noise.

'Not so busy now the Exhibition's over, I suppose?' Teddy asked Melly above the clamour.

'Busier Dad. That's what it's all about. I say, do you remember Adrian Crighton? Yes, of course you do, you can hardly forget with Mum looking so gorgeous from the wall. He came to the opening and guess what? He's a dark horse, didn't tell anyone beforehand. He's married. Brought his wife with him. She's a singing teacher, not a bit what I'd have expected for him, she looks old enough to be his mother.'

'That's not kind, Melly,' Trevor corrected her, 'she's certainly older than he is, but she's a charming woman.'

'I reckon it's because he never had a proper family. You know what, Mum, I used to think he had a crush on you!'

'Nonsense! He was like one of the family – just for a while.'

'Nother car come, Gran!' Edwina shouted from her vantage point by the open front door.

This time it was James. The years had left no visible mark on him, he was as handsome, as gentle in his manner. Barry was growing up fast, living up to the promise of being as good-looking as his father; in Edwina's inexperienced opinion he was already a young man and a hero above all others. Patsy was as she had been but more so, just as solid, just as plodding, but five years taller and broader, in fact getting ever more like her mother. Then there was Jenny. Nothing would ever change her build, but of them all it was Jenny who was most altered. Her first job application had been as assistant bursar of a girls' school about twenty minutes' drive from Brightley. Despite her appearance being against her she had been given the job and had taken the first step towards becoming the woman she'd grown into. Already smarter, more sure of herself, when the bursar had retired a year or so on she had filled his post. Mrs Jennifer Carlyle had become an authority to be reckoned with and, in keeping with her status and backed by a good salary, she had given way to a secret longing that had lurked unacknowledged: she had become the epitome of tailored grooming. There could never be anything glamorous about her, but these days her short, straight hair was well shaped and she indulged in foundation garments that supported her where nature failed, making of her a figure of controlled efficiency. Even Teddy had a sneaking respect for the transformation even though he could never be easy about the marriage.

Last to arrive was Harvey, he whose life had changed more than any. He could still play the piano, but nothing would ever overcome the frustration he felt for his limitations. Whether Lucinda would have gone further had she never fallen in love with him no-one would know, it was something she never thought about. She still played independently of him, and sometimes he was asked to join the panel of judges at music competitions. Occasionally they gave a recital together, a programme they would arrange themselves for three hands. Just such a one had been organized for the previous evening at Croughton Hall, a fund-raiser for the hospice which had been operating now for three years and had an endless need for support. But most of their time was taken up with teaching, their students all intending to make careers in the profession. The Carlyle Leighton School was housed in an old mansion in Buckinghamshire and it was their ambition to make it one of the country's leading music schools. If Harvey had believed he had a mountain to climb, if he'd fondly thought he was well on his way to the summit, then he knew now that his road had turned in another direction. Another mountain, the success of it would be judged not by his own triumphs but by those of their students.

Harvey had taken his happiness at Erica's expense. Six months after the divorce it had eased his conscience to hear that she had married a wealthy American industrialist. That part of his life had become remote, it had no connection with the present and the future.

Seeing his car draw up behind the other two at the side of the house everyone crowded outside to greet them.

'I don't believe it! Teddy! Look! I don't believe it!'

Even Harvey was forgotten in that moment. Claudia had thought

257

the day already perfect, all the family were coming home. But no-one had prepared her for this.

'Gwen!' Even before she spoke to Harvey or Lucinda, Claudia hugged her old friend.

'Is it all right, me being here, Mrs C? Harvey, he said he'd got it fixed. But I can see you didn't even know.'

'Oh Gwen, not knowing makes it extra marvellous.' And it was true. Except that every bedroom was going to be in use and already her mind was working on whether she could put a makeshift bed in Patsy's room for Edwina. Even James and Jenny were sharing, although she had put them in the room with two single beds. Perhaps it might have been kinder to give them a double bed and let nature do the rest. But she had a sad feeling that nature had given up on them. For a second her mind drifted down that avenue, wondering how they could be such good friends, share so many interests, clearly have affection for each other, and yet reject the ultimate expression of that love.

'Tis all right, Claudia my dear, Harvey and me got it all arranged as a secret.' She realized Mrs Freeman had come out to join the party. 'Your Miss Pomfrey is to have a bed in my place. Truth to tell, I'll be glad of her company. Leastways I will be if we hit it off. Don't see why we shouldn't, everything I've heard about her seems she's a nice enough person.'

'She is, Mrs Freeman. You both are.'

Mrs Freeman and Miss Pomfrey – for it would be some time before they were to become Gwen and Bertha to each other – took stock of each other. Time would tell, but the tidings looked promising. Later in the evening Bertha Freeman told Claudia that Miss Pomfrey was going to stay with her for a week or two. It was a lovely party, from the pride in hanging Melly's surprise present – a painting of Russets, the precision taken from photographs, the warmth of the light from fond memory – to the final reluctant goodnights that ended the day.

The weekend was ahead of them. On Saturday, except for Teddy and Claudia, they all put on their walking shoes and headed for Dartmoor. Even Edwina was one of the party, with the choice of strong, male shoulders to hoist her when she flagged.

If Teddy couldn't walk the rough paths of Dartmoor as he used to, there were compensations. Life brought changes to everyone, the important thing was to know what to grieve about and what to appreciate. That's what Claudia thought as, sixty years plus one day, she helped him prepare the barbecue in the garden ready for the walkers' return.

Seemingly from out of nowhere there was a roar of planes, the Red Arrows were giving an air display. Moorleigh was miles from the airfield where crowds watched and waited for the team to swoop and turn in perfect symmetry, but her eyes following the tightly grouped formation Claudia saw them as symbolizing the family. The front plane was Teddy and her, the marker, the one who held them on course. Then the others fanning out like an inverted 'V', turning in different directions, rolling, coming together again, each playing its own part.

'Marvellous, aren't they,' Teddy said, watching them.

She nodded. 'Perfect, every one of them.'

Tomorrow the family would be gone, three cars each heading for a different destination. But they'd come again. Like the display team of flyers, they never lost sight of the front plane.

You have been reading a novel published by Piatkus Books. We hope you have enjoyed it and that you would like to read more of our titles. Please ask for them in your local library or bookshop.

If you would like to be put on our mailing list to receive details of new publications, please send a large stamped addressed envelope (UK only) to:

Piatkus Books: 5 Windmill Street
London W1P 1HF

PIATKUS

The sign of a good book

M

WK - HOUSEBOUND READERS	
Hoult	